PRAISE FOR
THE INVISIBLE COLLEGE

"Jeff Wheeler weaves a deep and unique world filled with magic, danger, and hope. Readers will fall in love with the characters and root for their triumphs. (And I may have a crush on Robinson now.)"
—*Wall Street Journal* bestselling author Charlie N. Holmberg

"What a ride! Jeff Wheeler really brings out the big guns—literally, there are cannons—with this amazing introduction into the world of *The Invisible College*. From the prologue, I was absolutely hooked! With a world of inventive magic, a doomsday war on the horizon, and a romance you can't help but want to cheer for, this story showcases some of Jeff Wheeler's best work. Old and new fans of his masterful storytelling are going to gobble this right up and come back begging for more."
—Allison Anderson, author of the Cartographer's War series

"Jeff has written an engaging story full of ancient magic, secret handshakes, devious antagonists, and a charming hero just discovering his power."
—Luanne G. Smith, author of *The Vine Witch*

THE
VIOLENCE
OF
SOUND

ALSO BY JEFF WHEELER

Your First Million Words

Tales from Kingfountain, Muirwood, and
Beyond: The Worlds of Jeff Wheeler

The Invisible College

The Invisible College

The Violence of Sound

The Dresden Codex

Doomsday Match

Jaguar Prophecies

Final Strike

The Dawning of Muirwood Series

The Druid

The Hunted

The Betrayed

The First Argentines Series

Knight's Ransom

Warrior's Ransom

Lady's Ransom

Fate's Ransom

The Grave Kingdom Series

The Killing Fog

The Buried World

The Immortal Words

The Harbinger Series

Storm Glass

Mirror Gate

Iron Garland

Prism Cloud

Broken Veil

The Kingfountain Series

The Queen's Poisoner

The Thief's Daughter

The King's Traitor

The Hollow Crown

The Silent Shield

The Forsaken Throne

The Poisoner of Kingfountain Series

The Poisoner's Enemy

The Widow's Fate

The Maid's War

The Duke's Treason

The Poisoner's Revenge

The Legends of Muirwood Trilogy

The Wretched of Muirwood

The Blight of Muirwood

The Scourge of Muirwood

THE VIOLENCE OF SOUND

JEFF WHEELER

47NORTH

Text copyright © 2025 by Jeff Wheeler
All rights reserved.

No part of this book may be reproduced, or stored in a retrieval system, or transmitted in any form or by any means, electronic, mechanical, photocopying, recording, or otherwise, without express written permission of the publisher.

Published by 47North, Seattle

www.apub.com

Amazon, the Amazon logo, and 47North are trademarks of Amazon.com, Inc., or its affiliates.

EU product safety contact:
Amazon Media EU S. à r.l.
38, avenue John F. Kennedy, L-1855 Luxembourg
amazonpublishing-gpsr@amazon.com

ISBN-13: 9781662528606 (hardcover)
ISBN-13: 9781662521898 (paperback)
ISBN-13: 9781662521881 (digital)

Cover design and illustration by David Curtis

Printed in the United States of America

First edition

To Granny

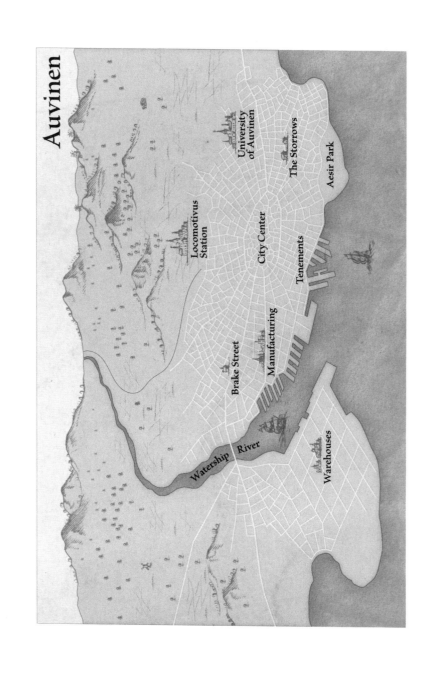

A man may imagine things that are false, but he can only understand things that are true. The Aesir are more powerful than us because they understand more truths. Truth reveals itself in many ways. In the symmetry of calculations. In unprovoked insights. Be not too hasty to cast out a seed of truth because it does not match the current order of thought or align with what is commonly believed or accepted. Some of the greatest truths began as a heresy.

—Isaac Berrow,
Master of the Royal Secret,
the Invisible College

General Colsterworth

PROLOGUE

THE SUMMER PALACE

Getting to the summer palace was a notorious waste of time. A nuisance in every conceivable way. The locomotivus station only went as high into the mountains as the town of Calcatrix, requiring the rest of the circuitous journey be made by coach. General Samuel Colsterworth had brought enough work to do on the trip, but the bumping and jostling up the pothole-ridden road into the mountains made it intolerably difficult to concentrate, and soon he abandoned the effort and cast his steely gaze out the window.

The royal court escaped the misery of hot summers by retreating to a palace that was at such an altitude that the climate was more moderate. It was only accessible by dog sleds in the winter, it being the remnant of an ancient Aesir fortress in the heart of the Assiniboine and Piran Mountains. The fortress had been built on the shore of a vast mountain lake that had the most startling turquoise color imaginable, a consequence of the rock powder carried by glacial melt.

The ruins had been discovered by accident centuries before, and the location had been adapted as part of the royal demesne. However, it was only used in the summer, when there was no chance that the occupants would be surrounded by the snow and ice that might make an attack from the Aesir possible. General Colsterworth had received many invitations to spend more time there luxuriating in the food, music, and wine, but with his overwhelming responsibilities at Gresham College in Bishopsgate, he didn't have the time to mix with the vapid and simpering fools who congregated there.

This time, refusing the invitation had been impossible. It had come from the Master of the Royal Secret himself. Inwardly, he was seething that the Brotherhood of Shadows had been a subject of such notoriety of late—it was still unthinkable that Joseph Crossthwait, one of their own, had turned out to be one of the very beings they were hunting. And, worse, he had made a scene involving some very prominent individuals in Auvinen before taking his own life. Typically the brotherhood's operations were more circumspect and didn't warrant . . . a private rebuke? Or would this be a public one?

After hours traveling the winding mountain roads, the coach finally reached the borders of the palace. The general momentarily forgot to brood about his summons as he gazed at the awe-inspiring scene. The adjoining mountain ranges met in the distance in a V that centered on the edge of the placid turquoise waters. Even at the beginning of summer, snow clung to the glacial peaks. Massive fir trees colored the slopes with variegated hues of green mixed with cobalt. It was rumored the Aesir could actually walk on water, and the splendid mountain lake had purportedly been one of their particularly favorite haunts. Although he wished for no common ground with the enemy, he could understand why—the beauty of the scene was absolutely breathtaking.

The coach slowed, joining a queue of others arriving at the summer palace. Servants in breeches, silk jackets, sashes, and tricorne hats hastily assembled to assist the passengers in disembarking. The old-fashioned uniforms hearkened back to an older time, and it seemed to the general that the royal court was as frozen in its fashions as the ice clinging to the glacial slopes.

At last it was his turn, so he returned the papers to his leather satchel and slung it over his shoulder. He was wearing his most elaborate dress uniform, his jacket practically sagging from the array of medals pinned there. He'd had his hair barbered after arriving in Calcatrix and even waxed the ends of his mustache. He'd brought no adjutant with him on the journey. Time was too precious to be wasted. He'd endure this interrogation, hopefully retain his rank, and then the storm of discontent would blow over.

At least he hoped it would.

"General Colsterworth, welcome to the summer palace," greeted an officious man with a powdered wig and jeweled collar. They grasped hands, exchanging signs that they were both members of the Invisible College. "My name is Herbert Patterson Small. We've been expecting you."

"Thank you, Mr. Small. I'm here, as you can plainly see."

"Master Drusselmehr will see you in his private suite. There is a ball this evening. An invitation is waiting in your room."

Another nuisance. The general sighed. "I was hoping to be on my way after the meeting."

"Navigating the mountain at night is too dangerous, sir. I'm sure you understand."

He did understand. And once word of his arrival spread, he knew several members of the court would consider it a grave insult if he did not call on them or allow visitors. The stay could wind up being extended indefinitely. "Lead the way, please," he said with a sigh.

The breeze had an edge to it, even after midday, which meant the night would be very cold. But like all officers who were sorcerers, he had magical buttons on his uniform that could be activated to produce heat. Besides, he'd been on the front, and the chill here had nothing on the eternal cold of warfare on a glacier. The palace itself seemed insignificant compared to the majesty of the mountains, but it was still an impressive series of structures added onto the original built by the Aesir. Soon they were inside, where the noise of the courtiers was loud enough to be disturbing. A few officers noticed his arrival and snapped to attention with crisp salutes, which he returned as he continued to follow his guide to the Genowen Flying Chair, a magical contraption that hoisted the occupants to the upper floors of the palace. A sorcerer in attendance controlled it. The general felt a pinch in his gut as the chair rose rapidly to the upper floors.

Upon arrival at the suite of the Master of the Royal Secret, Mr. Small bid the general farewell while implying he would await the outcome and then bring the general to his own suite.

A servant opened the door and greeted them, and there he was, the titular head of the Invisible College—Gilgamesh Drusselmehr. An impressive man, older than salt, with flowing silver hair and a pugnacious face full of wrinkles and crags. He had a glass eye, having lost one during an explosion in his personal alchemy as a younger man. A fearless inventor, he was beloved by children all over the world for his intricate toys, each spellbound to be alive for a fixed amount of time. The patent for that invention was still paying fat dividends, which had made Drusselmehr impossibly wealthy, and the shrewd and capable businessman had grown his fortune further. The commonly accepted wisdom was that his popularity as a giver of magical gifts had won him the necessary votes to become Master of the Royal Secret. But the general believed, cynically, that he'd achieved that title because of his calculating penchant for making friends in high places.

"General," said the thick-chested old man with his heavy Iskandir accent. "What a pleasure. This of all days."

"How could I refuse such an invitation?" the general answered blandly. He examined an Aesir artifact on a decorative display table and picked it up, giving it an admiring glance. It was a chalice holder, imbued with an intelligence to keep drinks cold. He'd seen one before, but they weren't common. Since nobles fancied them so much, they were exceedingly expensive. Aesir inventions did not suffer from entropy. The relic could be five thousand years old, and it would still look as fresh as when it had been forged. He saw another item, a more modern invention, beneath the table and recognized it as a foot massager powered by some sort of primate intelligence. It could be customized to the delicacy or pain-inflicting preference of its owner. The plentitude of such magical comforts was a sign of Drusselmehr's wealth and importance.

"Ha! Indeed you could not, sir!" He waved his hands and the servants melted away, the doors softly clicking shut. "But do you not deserve some rest after such massive endeavors, General? Ah? The mind must rest each night, and so should the body, no?"

"Shall we get this over with, sir? I have pressing matters to attend to back in Bishopsgate."

"More murders to plot, you mean?" The man's stare was icy.

General Colsterworth did not look away. "You do your part in the Invisible College. I do mine."

"People are talking, General. They are beginning to notice."

"And your role, sir, is to distract them. Do you have any idea how many civilians have been killed during the Awakening so far? Not just from the bombardments but from the malignant croup. If the people knew, there would be riots. And you summoned me here to scold me over a single death?"

"You misunderstand me, General. You are not here to be scolded. You are not a child."

"Then why am I here? You handle the politics. I handle the war."

"War *is* political, General. Surely, this is not a surprise to you. What happened in Auvinen is being whispered about here. A *doppelgänger*. In your own command."

Colsterworth bristled. That was the Tanhauser word for a Semblance.

"And he murdered that relation of Mr. Foster, a man who has now made something of a nuisance of himself. He is asking questions. He is petitioning the courts for answers." He held up his hands, then intertwined his fingers. "Your problems are becoming my problems. Men like him use laws to pry into our secrets. Secrecy is strength, General."

He folded his arms and walked to the large window that provided a dazzling view of the lake and mountains.

"I have a suspicion that may help us address the situation," Colsterworth said.

"What is this . . . suspicion?" The Master of the Royal Secret kept his gaze trained on the view, as if to signify the general was of too little importance to warrant his full attention.

"I suspect Foster's daughter may be a Semblance."

The crown of silver hair turned, and the bushy eyebrows lifted. A pleased smile lifted his wrinkled face. "Oh?"

"When I went to the Fosters' home in Auvinen, to deliver my apology, I noticed her behavior. This is the daughter who was stricken by fever as a young child and lost her hearing. Because of that plight, the Fosters helped found a school for the deaf in Auvinen."

"Go on." The man was disinterested in that part of the story. His smile had faded.

"Semblances reveal themselves in subtle ways. Especially when in the presence of a member of the Brotherhood of Shadows. The host may be unconscious of the danger we represent, but the Semblance often reacts viscerally. I noticed the dilation of her pupils, her rapid breathing. How she clutched her fiancé's arm. It was a curious reaction, one I wouldn't have expected from a woman as young as she is and about to be married."

"She may have been fearful because Crossthwait attempted to execute her fiancé?"

"As I said, it's just a suspicion. One of the reasons we suspected Hawksley was because of his own brush with death. The girl seemed above suspicion because Semblances usually have access to magic, and the deaf cannot use magic at all. I've never heard of a Semblance choosing such a host."

A wizened look crossed the old man's face as he nodded in affirmation. "You are correct, General. That would be very rare. What are your findings so far?"

"We are still investigating her past. Presently, the couple is honeymooning in Tanhauser, but I have them under surveillance."

"Be careful, General. Tread carefully. If we murder Mr. Foster's daughter, that would be very . . . indiscreet. We also need Hawksley's invention to fight this war. It wouldn't do to upset him."

"I will be certain before I authorize her death, sir. But if she *is* a Semblance, she cannot be allowed to live. The risk is too great, especially given her proximity to Hawksley. And there might be a dispute with the Hawksley patent anyway. My contact in the patent office claims there is another application that is very similar, put in by another inventor."

"Who?"

"Elizabeth Cowing. If the timings of the patents are disputed, it could take years to resolve. That is time we do not have. But Miss Cowing is a known quantity to the military. Hawksley isn't. We'd be better off working with her, particularly considering the situation with Hawksley's wife."

"We are in agreement there. What of this . . . this *strannik*? The one you captured."

The general's mind conjured the young man they'd arrested in Tanhauser for fomenting a philosophy of appeasement. He was an intense fellow who'd won over supporters who wanted to surrender to the Aesir instead of fight to protect themselves. There were fools everywhere, and the war had brought out a vast assortment of them.

"He's becoming quite popular among a distinguished set here at court," the other man continued. "I can hardly account for it. He is stern, ill-dressed, and disagreeable, yet they love him all the more for it. He is a harmless distraction at the moment, but that could change if his popularity increases. What have you discovered of his background? Where does he come from?"

"We don't know. He insults everyone who tries to speak to him. Perhaps it is time he will grow despondent in jail and . . . ?" The general lifted his eyebrows, leaving the thought unfinished. If this man already thought him a murderer, he wouldn't be the one to utter the suggestion.

The Master of the Royal Secret thought it over. "We risk making a martyr of him."

"At least martyrs are *dead*."

"You are right, of course. Maybe something more innocuous? Food poisoning?"

"I think that could be arranged."

"Good. See it is done. Some of the popular set have been asking if he'll be brought to the summer palace. They want to see his reaction to the decadence here. They *want* to be scolded, it seems, General." He chuckled softly.

Colsterworth shrugged. "Summer is tedious. They are bored."

They also wanted to be a little afraid. It was the reason Drusselmehr's toys were so popular, so expensive. He often incorporated elements of fear into the designs. A whisper when the lights were out and parents were gone. A chuckle in the dark. Children relished a hint of fear. Imagination was a powerful stimulant.

"Not *this* summer," countered the wily sorcerer. "We have the Great Exposition in Bishopsgate to look forward to! This is exactly the distraction we need. The magic. The inventions. It will draw all eyes. By the end of the summer, who will notice if a radical gets food poisoning? Or a barrister's daughter dies in a fire?"

"I get your meaning. I will be certain first."

"As certain as you can. I claim your time for the next two days. There are people I would have you meet. Those you can assuage. Then you go to your corner and I . . . to mine. All too soon winter will come, and the Aesir will strike us again. We must be prepared."

General Colsterworth nodded. "We will be."

The Aesir are an immortal race. Not that they cannot die—they can—but their bodies are immune to disease, and they do not succumb to natural causes. And yet, they are not adaptive to warm climates. They enter a dreamlike state called the Skrýmir, which can last, in mortal terms, decades or even centuries. Leaving this state is called the Awakening. And when they rise from their icy beds, they pursue their aim of exterminating mortals. There was a time, forgotten in the past, when we coexisted peacefully. When mortals were chosen to attend them in their frozen courts. They even shared their magic with us, which is what fuels our efforts to this day. But something ended that sympathy between our kinds. We lack sufficient means to conjure such memories. But they have not forgotten. And their revenge is implacable.

—Isaac Berrow,
Master of the Royal Secret,
the Invisible College

Robinson Foster Hawksley

CHAPTER ONE

The Volksoper

The screech of the metal wheels on rails sent a shiver down Robinson's spine as the street tram halted. He stepped down first and then turned and took McKenna by the hand as the bulk of the passengers exited onto the crowded street. They were in the heart of Tanhauser. The language of the people baffled him, but it was a thrill to be there. McKenna gave him a winsome smile and clenched his hand.

"Which way?" he asked her, confused by the crush of people. He stood close enough that she could read his lips. Thankfully she was fluent in the language after having spent time with her parents there in the past.

She tugged on his hand, leading the way, and they followed a visible flow of passersby. The smells of the city were heady, but there was a metallic tang in the air—iron maybe. Above the noise, he could hear the strains of violins, the blatting noise of tubas. It was a city dedicated to the arts, with rival symphonies and opera houses spreading protective webs of magic over the city night and day. Even the hotel they were staying at had a little chamber orchestra playing just inside the lobby, songs from the great composers of the last two centuries, with rhythms and melodies familiar to him. But not to McKenna. She'd lost her hearing as a young child, stricken by one of the Aesir plagues that had robbed so many in their generation of hearing and, consequently, the ability to use magic. Aided by her parents' resources and determination and her uncommonly quick mind, she had become amazingly adept at reading lips. She'd told him that she missed words from every conversation but had managed to train her brain to fill in the gaps. She also spoke exceptionally well, and with his guidance and tutoring methods, her speech was indistinguishable from someone who could hear. He knew how rare her gifts were, how exceptional she was in every way. And they, as a couple, were determined to find a way past the barrier to her use of magic too. He felt confident they would surmount it. He felt confident his wife could do anything she set her mind to.

"There, do you see it?" she declared, pointing.

He did. The Volksoper opera house was a dazzling sight to behold. It was a shrine to music, multistory, with arches, pillars, and a gilded roof that stretched over the top. It was also a geometric wonder, its angles and lines illuminated by a network of glowing quicksilver bulbs. Some statuary on the front showed ancient warriors astride majestic horses, hearkening back to an earlier era in the never-ending conflict with the Aesir.

"Do you like it?" she asked, looking at his face eagerly.

"It's breathtaking," Robinson answered. They'd only been married a short time, having left for the locomotivus station immediately after their small wedding ceremony so that they could get to Tanhauser for the performance of Shopenhauer's famous opera. It was one of McKenna's marriage gifts to him, one that she could not enjoy herself, but she'd arranged for it nonetheless because she knew he loved the opera and had never seen this particular one. His young wife was a wealthy heiress—having inherited her aunt's estate following the woman's untimely death. He wished to contribute more toward their living, and if his invention proved as useful as Mr. Foster believed it would, then he'd be in a position to do so.

Glass tubes that glowed from the combination of quicksilver gas ignited by intelligences were a common sight in every major city of the empire. But Robinson's tubes glowed when Aesir magic was used near them. A sound too subtle to be detected by most human ears revealed the binding of an intelligence to an inanimate object. The tubes homed in on that resonance. This made the tubes invaluable. He'd already signed over all his ownership shares to his wife as his wedding present. So far, they weren't worth anything, but if the demonstration at the Great Exhibition proved favorable, the value could be dear indeed.

Hand in hand, they followed other patrons to the opera house and entered. At the will-call booth, McKenna addressed the attendant in Tanhauser and received the two tickets she had ordered for them. They'd stopped at their hotel before continuing to the opera, and she had changed from her traveling dress to a more formal gown and taken the time to dress up her hair in one of the fashions of the city. Robinson only owned one suit, given to him by his father, and he wore that and a bowler hat over his tangled hair. Most of the male patrons wore black frock coats and top hats, signifying a different fashion sense in this part of the empire. But he cared for none of it.

With their tickets in hand, they followed the crush of people through a maze of arches until they were led to the upper balconies and, eventually, a small private booth on the side. He would have been happy sitting with the crowds below, but he was grateful for the intimacy of the booth and the heady feeling it gave him to look out over the huge curtain and gold-foil decorative trim of the historic opera house. The orchestra was tuning, down in the pit, and he could hear the subtle errors in their notes.

Reaching into his vest pocket, he pulled out the device his father had given him. Some might mistake it for a pocket watch, but it did not tell the time. Only recently had he discovered the secrets to its design— if the proper code was entered, the ring nestled inside the device could be removed. When worn, it permitted him to transmit his thoughts to other people and also to overhear thoughts the Aesir transmitted to each other—if one understood their ancient tongue, which, fortunately, Robinson's friend Wickins did and had been teaching him. Although some mysteries had been solved, there were more yet, including the crystal set in the top that had Aesir numbering runes. For a generation or two it had shown nine, nine, eight, and only on their trip to Tanhauser had they noticed it had changed to nine, nine, nine. They could not account for what might have caused the change. He'd also discovered the precise alloy of gold the ring was composed of, which had assisted him in creating his invention.

Robinson had originally believed the device to be of Aesir make, but now he was convinced a great sorcerer had invented it. For there was little chance the Aesir would have made a device that could be so easily used against them. Still, he had no notion of who that sorcerer had been, let alone how they had created it. His own father couldn't tell him when it had come to the Hawksley family or from whom.

Sighing, he clicked the lid shut and put it back in his pocket.

The strains of music fell quiet, and the low rumble of the audience murmuring quickly came to a stop. He squeezed McKenna's hand as the lamps began to dim.

Deep vibrations of string basses sounded, along with the battering noise of timpani drums. His heart tingled with excitement as the familiar and amazing sounds filled the air. The conductor was gesticulating wildly as additional instruments joined the melody.

The curtain opened, and Robinson leaned forward. He felt McKenna's hand on his leg. This, she could enjoy, the elaborate and gaze-wrenching sets. The costumes of mortals playing immortals with silver-colored hair. The chorus erupted from the stage. They sang in Tanhauser, of course, the language of the composer. But Robinson knew the lyrics and the story about the fabled Erlking, master of the Aesir race, who had banished his daughter for a single act of disobedience.

There was an enormous, fabricated tree in the middle of the stage with an Aesir sword sticking through it. The rear curtains depicted a snowscape of mountains, fir trees, and glaciers. Giant statues mimicked the colossal works the Aesir had carved into mountainsides.

There was so much to take in, and the sounds, the sights, the blending of voices and instruments wove a special kind of magic in Robinson's heart. He felt tears sting his eyes.

Glancing at his wife, who was staring at his face more than the scene unfolding on the stage, he felt an incredible surge of love.

"Thank you," he mouthed to her. *"This is incredible."* He hoped there was enough ambient light for her to read his lips.

"I knew you'd love it," she mouthed back to him. *"I love you so much."*

But as they sat there, taking in the glorious spectacle, it struck him that there was something familiar about the moment. It was almost as if he had been there before. Had been there with *her.* The deep baritone of the Erlking's voice trumpeted across the expansive hall. The singer they'd chosen for the role looked majestic and frightening. Powerful. He was setting the stage for the opera. Singing about his vast domain of ice and magic, of the purity of the songs sung at his court . . . and how it would all be ruined because of the rebellion of his only child.

Robinson shivered. He'd known this story for years—his whole life, it seemed—and yet it felt strangely personal tonight.

He swallowed, unsure of what he was feeling or why, but he told himself he was simply reacting the way he was supposed to. Music was intended to invoke feeling—joy, hate, pain, love, even indifference, depending on the composer's intent and goal—and the story of the Erlking's daughter was a story of forbidden love. Perhaps the tragedy felt personal because his love for McKenna had so nearly ended in tragedy.

The musical spell swept him away. Time lost meaning. And he was the first on his feet to join the standing ovation at the end.

The night air was cool against Robinson's cheeks after they left the bustling lobby and joined the crowds outside. He guided McKenna over to a glowing streetlamp so they could talk for a moment. The opera had left him emotionally winded and spent, but it had been worth every moment. Carriages were crowding the streets in both directions, so Robinson gripped McKenna's hand and maneuvered the two of them away from the commotion. People were talking in excited voices. McKenna had drifted off to sleep during part of the performance, but now she was all excitement. He knew it was because *he* was excited and loved her all the more for it.

"What was your favorite part?" she asked.

"The aria of the Erlking's daughter, of course," he answered. "The famous one. The singer was so accomplished."

"I'm glad it wasn't a disappointment."

"None of this was a disappointment! I will never forget this night. It was . . . I'm at a loss for words. It was magnificent. *Resplendent.*"

"*Oooh*, I like that word," she said with a grin, squeezing his hand. She had a prodigious gift for vocabulary and loved it when he exercised his own gift. The Hawksleys were elocutionists by training and career. Robinson's grandfather had been a professor in Covesea who had trained stage actors, politicians, and sorcerers alike.

"And you, my love, made this possible. I wish we could spend a week here instead of going back to Auvinen tomorrow."

"But you have your classes to teach. I understand. This was just a little getaway. We'll have a proper honeymoon later on."

Which reminded him that they needed to find a street tram to return to the hotel. He kissed her hand and then eased her back into the flow of the crowd. Even now, he could hardly believe they were husband and wife. That she had *wanted* to marry her older teacher. She who was so vivacious, so capable, so—

He'd turned to gaze adoringly at her and didn't see the other man until it was too late. Their shoulders collided and Robinson found himself on the street. It happened so fast. He promptly got up and offered an apology, but the larger man was already moving along, uncaring that they'd bumped into each other. Robinson turned around in a circle, worried that McKenna had been flung down too, but she wasn't on the street. He turned in a circle again, jostled once more by another person.

"Pass auf!" the man grumbled at him.

Where was she? His heart began to race. The crowd was thick and going every which way. People were dressed both well and poorly. Shouts rose up as people called for carriages.

Fear struck him. Where was she? She wasn't nearby, and he couldn't hear her voice calling for him.

Danger. He sensed danger.

"Hoxta-namorem," he sang, invoking a magical will-o'-the-wisp of light. *Go after her,* he commanded. *Find McKenna.*

The earliest historical references to Semblances are ambiguous. We lack the context of the era in which they were written. The oldest text that I have personally found was one of the ancient sagas of the Iskandir. A song poem— in their tongue fornaldarsǫgur. These song poems were passed on from generation to generation and eventually transcribed. Here is the stanza that first mentions them: "So on the tide it befell as Sigridur sat in her bower, there came to her a witch-wife exceedingly cunning, and Sigridur spoke with her on this wise. 'Fain am I,' says she, 'that we should change semblances together.' The witch-wife says, 'Even as thou wilt.' So by her wiles she brought it about that they changed semblances, and now the witch-wife sits in Sigridur's place and goes to bed by the king at night, and he knows not that he has other than Sigridur beside him."

"Witch-wife" is an Iskandir term for a female Aesir. And this is the first reference I have found that they have the power to take on a mortal body by some means of magic known only to them. And that in such a form they can deceive even a husband or a lover.

—Isaac Berrow,
Master of the Royal Secret,
the Invisible College

MaKenna Aurora
Hawksley

CHAPTER TWO

To What Purpose

The glow of the quicksilver lamps was nothing compared to the strange fire burning in McKenna's heart.

Walking hand in hand with her husband on the busy streets of Tanhauser following the opera had been such a magical moment. She'd caught a glimpse of the big man just an instant before he'd sent Rob sprawling to the street, yanking their hands apart. Concerned he was injured, McKenna had immediately started to bend down to help him when two men had gripped her arms and hoisted her away from him.

Her first confused thought had been that they were trying to protect her. But no, the men had plunged through the crowd, dragging her away from Rob.

"That's my husband," she shouted to them now in fluent Tanhauser. "Let me go!"

The men were facing the other way, each gripping one of her arms tightly. They were young men, probably in their early twenties, and wore plain clothes—long wool jackets with large collars and fur caps on their heads, which seemed very odd for the time of year. One had a pipe in the crook of his mouth, and he was chewing on the end as he and his companion hauled her away.

"Let me go!" she snarled, trying to wrest her arms free, but they easily overpowered her. "Help! Help!" she called. "Rob! Rob!" When she dragged her legs, they hoisted her a little higher and kept maneuvering through the crowd.

Strangely enough, none of the people around them paid any attention to them whatsoever. She tried to get passersby to notice her, even calling out to several well-dressed gentlemen, but they didn't act as if they heard her. There was no sign of her husband, and she feared he might have been knocked unconscious in the street. Then they were off the boulevard and heading down an alley several blocks from the opera house. There were no quicksilver lamps and the night became oppressive, filling her heart with terror. She'd been abducted. In a crowded street! How was that possible? Who were these people?

"Unhand me!" she commanded, but the men didn't heed her. At the end of the alley, they turned, and she sensed a glow coming from ahead. Craning her neck, she saw a hulk of a man striding toward them in the alley. As soon as he reached them, the two men carrying her stopped.

She tried to flee, but they kept a painful grip on her arms. She saw the newcomer's lips move, couldn't make out the words, and then magical light flooded the alley. The newest intruder was tall, very thick, and had a grizzled beard and a lopsided cap on his head. Instead of a jacket, he wore a wool pullover with a folded collar. The kind a sailor wore. He smelled of sardines.

"Who are you?" she shouted at him. She knew the words of the spell he'd cast to summon the light. But knowing the words would not help her summon magic. She'd failed every time she'd tried. It was commonly accepted that the deaf could not work magic, although she'd never been one to accept what others told her she could and could not do.

The man's eyes scrutinized her in the glow from the magical, floating light. "This the one?" he asked one of the fellows, speaking Tanhauser. Reading his lips was difficult in the dim light, but she'd made a study of it all her life, and her ability was widely considered exceptional.

"Who are you?" she repeated firmly.

None of them answered, but one of her captors nodded to the newcomer. She gathered that they believed her to be someone important. Someone worth capturing. Was it because she'd inherited her aunt's wealth? Did they want a ransom? It had never crossed her mind that such unscrupulous people would accost her. And at least one of them was from the Invisible College! Surely abducting people was against the principles of the order.

Then the newcomer looked her in the eye. "All is well, my lady. We've found you at last."

His words were incomprehensible. "Let me go this instant," she said. Why had he called her "my lady"? That was a designation for nobility, and McKenna was the daughter of a barrister. Something niggled in the back of her mind. Something she'd forgotten. Something from a dream, perhaps . . .

"The *strannik* wishes to meet you," the man said. "We bring you to him."

She was really good at intuiting meaning from subtle context clues, but the word he'd used did not match any she'd ever encountered before. "Staw-nn-k"?

"Bring me where?"

"You will see. You will be set free. I promise."

She tried to jerk her arm away, but her captors were vigilant. She feared she'd have bruises on her arms because of the ordeal.

"You must let me go," she said. "Please. I don't belong here."

A bemused smile wrinkled his mouth. "Indeed so, my lady. Indeed so. You will be set free. But we must take you to the *strannik*. He will know what to . . ." His eyes lifted from her face to look at something behind her.

McKenna turned her head and saw another will-o'-the-wisp of light coming down the alley from the way they'd come. It was a whorl of blue and violet strands, fluttering through the air like a butterfly.

She saw Rob following the strands of light, and her heart leaped with relief and then wilted with dread. Three men. Three strong men. One of them was a sorcerer too. Maybe they all were, judging on how they'd penetrated the crowd without being noticed.

"Rob, be careful!"

He was still approaching confidently, the light from his magical ball showing his face and throat clearly as he mouthed words to her across the distance, ". . . *release you. Or they will suffer.*"

McKenna turned to face the brute of a man. She hadn't caught all the words but surmised the meaning. "Release me now, or you will suffer for it."

The man didn't look impressed by the threat. He nodded to the two others, and they began dragging her away, toward the far end of the alley.

"Rob! Rob!"

The brute was walking toward her husband. She struggled harder now, wishing she could do something to free herself. And suddenly, the two men restraining her let go. She watched them crumple to the street, their faces expressions of agony, their hands clamped against their ears.

Whirling in shock, she saw the big man was also splayed on the ground. Rob's light reached her first and then he was there, squeezing her to his chest. He held her face in his hands, examining her for harm, and then grabbed her hand and tugged her away from the alley and the fallen men, all of whom were writhing. As soon as they reached the mouth of the alley, the will-o'-the-wisp of light winked out. Rob looked both ways and then escorted her into a less crowded street.

She saw a small two-horse coach dropping off two passengers in front of a small hotel and pointed to it. "I think they're getting off!"

Rob pulled her that way. The driver had a bushy mustache, a small black bowler hat, and a long riding crop for the horses.

McKenna called out to the driver in his language, and he turned to look at them before waving them over to the open-air carriage with two horses that looked worn out. The main street was lit with glass tubes, which meant she was able to communicate with Rob as they hurried toward the conveyance.

"Should we go back to the hotel?" she asked.

Rob shook his head. "No, the locomotivus station. If they knew we were at the opera tonight, they probably also know where we're staying."

"That's true," she admitted. She was relieved but still felt agitated. She wanted to get away from the area as soon as possible. "I can ask Father to contact the concierge and see if our things can be shipped to Brake Street."

Rob nodded as they closed the gap to the carriage. He helped her on and then climbed up after her. McKenna told the driver to take them to the locomotivus station quickly. He confirmed the request, snapped the whip, and the carriage began to rattle down the street. It jostled her bones.

She snuggled against Rob, gripping his arm tightly. There was enough light coming from the streetlamps for her to see his face, but he summoned the will-o'-the-wisp anyway, with the incantation he'd taught her.

"What did you do . . . to those men?"

He was gazing ahead, his expression tight with concern and worry. "I think I exploded their eardrums."

"My goodness!"

He nodded confidently. "I don't exactly remember where I learned the spell. But I used it in Auvinen when that military fellow, Mr. Crossthwait, tried to kill me the first time in the tenements. I needed to get you back to safety quickly, and I put a shield around you first. I didn't know what it might do to your eardrums and didn't want to risk harming you as well."

She shook her head. "I didn't hear a thing. Or feel any vibrations."

He smiled at her little joke and patted her arm. "That's because I blocked it. The effects as you can see are rather painful, which is why I wanted you to at least warn them. They should be out of commission for a while, but I don't feel safe. I don't think I'll feel safe until we're on a southbound locomotivus."

"They were all sorcerers, weren't they?" McKenna asked.

"I believe so," he said with a grim nod. "After that big fellow knocked me down, he cast a glamour."

"He cast what kind of spell? I . . . I may have misunderstood the word you used." She knew the word "glamor," but it did not mean anything magical, to her knowledge.

"A glamour is a powerful spell, one that can alter the perception of reality for other people. He used it to hide you in plain sight, making everyone think everything was fine. Only the higher ranks of sorcerers can learn it. The temptation to be dishonest with it would be quite alluring. Which is all the more concerning after what happened here tonight."

McKenna studied his face, seeing his concern for her mirrored there. "That *is* powerful magic. I hadn't heard the word used that way before."

"Ah, it's a matter of spelling." He was an elocutionist and couldn't help being anything but a thoughtful teacher. "The magical term has a *u* in it. G-l-a-m-o-u-r. The other meaning is one I'd ascribe to *you*," he added with a smile.

"I wasn't fishing for a compliment, Husband."

He leaned down and kissed her mouth. Pulling back so she could see his face, he said, "I hope you never have to. Did the men try to talk to you?"

She'd rather enjoyed the kiss and the compliment. Her racing heart was beginning to calm. "Not the ones holding me. But the burly fellow said something about taking me to *strannik*. Or at least that was what it looked like he said. I don't know that word."

Rob pursed his lips. "Neither do I. It could be someone's name."

"It sounded more like a title. Also he didn't call me by name but . . . he called me 'my lady.'"

Rob looked as confused as she felt, not that she blamed him—it was an abnormal way to address someone you'd just abducted.

"I know. Maybe they were mistaken? He said they were going to set me free. But then you came." She snuggled against him again. On the trip to Tanhauser, she'd had a mild panic attack, fearing she would lose him. She had a preternatural feeling that their fate was jinxed somehow. Or had it been more of a premonition? She certainly hoped not.

Rob stroked her hair, part of which had come loose in the ruckus. Then he kissed the crown of her head. Being with him made her feel safe. She'd anticipated being alone together in the hotel that night. But after what had just happened, she felt leaving the beautiful city was the wisest option. Could the military have been involved with her intended abduction? When General Colsterworth had arrived at her parents' house to interview them, following the attack by Joseph Crossthwait several days before, she'd nearly fainted in fear merely from being in his presence. He was a dangerous man. He knew things he wasn't sharing.

The coach arrived at the locomotivus station, which was thankfully open both day and night, although there were fewer departures after dark. They went to the ticket booth and were informed the next southbound locomotivus would leave in three hours. That would be midnight. She bought two tickets for a private compartment, like the one they'd had on the trip up.

Rob escorted her to a wooden bench at the designated platform, and they both sat down. She hooked her arm with his and leaned against him, staring down into the darkness of the rails. There were a few people nearby, but it was not as crowded as it had been upon their arrival.

"What if they come for me again?" she asked, looking up at Rob's face.

He was staring into the distance. "I won't let anyone hurt you, McKenna. Maybe this was a misunderstanding. A mistake."

They were comforting words. But she could tell he didn't believe them any more than she did.

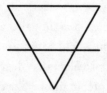

CHAPTER THREE

THE HOUSE ON BRAKE STREET

Splotches of trampled cherries discolored the sidewalk in front of Brake Street. It was Closure, the day when all the factories shut down for an entire day and the citizens of Auvinen took leisurely walks along the promenades and boulevards.

The early heat swells that year had brought some of the trees to bearing fruit earlier than usual, and the cherry trees were already dropping theirs. McKenna walked hand in hand with Rob toward her childhood home. Right after the southbound journey from Tanhauser, they'd come to convey their situation to McKenna's parents, who were grateful they were safe and had pledged to investigate the matter and bring the culprits to justice. But a month had passed, and the tension had ebbed because no further threats had materialized.

When McKenna glimpsed her former home through the gaps in the trees ahead, a sweet pang of homesickness caught her by surprise. She hadn't thought she'd experience such a sensation after merely a month of absence. Rob captured her attention with a gentle squeeze of her hand, and she glanced at his face to see his question.

"Do you . . . miss it?"

"Of course I do," she answered, then butted her shoulder against his arm. "Don't you miss your childhood home sometimes?"

He nodded. Then, with a wistful smile, he said, "And I shall take you to Covesea someday."

"You shall, Husband. But first we must finish the term." She said that part deliberately, to put his mind at ease, but she was still scheming on how to get him to attend the Great Exhibition in Bishopsgate. He'd refused to miss the classes he had already committed to teaching, to present his invention. Father was upset at Rob's recalcitrance. Oh, and he *was* recalcitrant. Some pride had undoubtedly alloyed with her husband's steely resolve to fulfill his commitment to Dean George. The more anyone pushed on the idea, the more stubborn he became.

What Rob didn't seem to understand was that it would benefit *everyone*, including Dean George, if he attended the exhibition. New investors might be found. Contracts with the military advanced. Besides which, final exams were being given that week, and it would be an easy matter for someone to proctor Rob's exams. Still. He wouldn't hear of it. And she felt certain that pushing him would only drive his obstinacy more.

As they approached the small gate barring their way, Rob paused. She saw his mouth move but didn't recognize the words. Her nose wrinkled in confusion, but she waited patiently for his explanation.

"I was asking the intelligences in charge of the defenses if any intruders had come since we left. Nothing strange has happened. And . . . Wickins beat us here. In fact, he's come twice this week."

Wickins was a lieutenant working for the Signals Intelligences of the military in Auvinen, but he was also helping Rob with his new business venture. Signals Intelligences was part of the magic that enabled long-distance communication. All living things had a spark of intelligence, and the sorcerers of the Invisible College had mastered the means of attaching such sparks to devices—whether the iron horses that pulled the street trams or the quicksilver lamps that brightened the city at night or the many massive machines, now dormant, that produced garments with intricate, unique designs. Auvinen was one of the manufacturing powerhouses in the empire, a city with bold innovations and a great many wealthy citizens.

"I hope his injury is healing," McKenna said.

"We'll see shortly." He opened the gate for her, and they walked up to the door.

He hesitated at the threshold, hand poised to knock, but McKenna grasped the handle. "It's our home too, Rob. We don't have to knock."

He gave her a sheepish grin and followed her in. Mouthwatering aromas from the kitchen wafted tantalizingly to them. It smelled like a seafood bake with saffron rice, clams, shrimp, and mussels—a delicacy that took half the day cooking at lower heat, common in seaside cities like Auvinen. It was one of McKenna's favorites, and she credited her mother's choice as the first welcoming meal at Closure with the entire Foster family following their marriage.

She was about to walk to the parlor where the family was usually gathered, but Rob put his hand on her shoulder to forestall her. His expression was troubled.

"Is something wrong?" she asked him.

"We came in the middle of an argument," he mouthed to her.

"Who?" she whispered.

"Clara and your father. It's about the exhibition."

A knot formed in her stomach.

They walked down the hall together and entered the parlor. There was the Broadwood grand, her mother's favorite instrument. Father was in his usual chair, but he didn't look relaxed. He was leaning forward, fingertips steepled together, his pince-nez glasses perched atop his nose, his graying whiskers prominently displayed. He was usually cool-headed, but she could see the fire in his eyes. Wickins looked abashed and uncomfortable. Clara, younger than McKenna by less than a year, was in a full tempest, her cheeks flushed with emotion, her countenance full of determination to get her way. Trudie, the youngest, was cowering by the window, out of which the greenhouse could be seen glimmering in the sunlight. Memories of their wedding, held in that very place, kissed her mind, but she could tell that had been a more peaceful time than what they'd entered into.

Noticing her arrival, Clara shifted so her words could be seen by McKenna. It was such a habit the entire family did it by rote whenever she was present so that she'd never have to feel excluded. "I don't understand why you're treating me like a child, Father! Help is needed and we have the space at our home in Bishopsgate. Why won't you let me do this?"

"This isn't the time to discuss it, Clara," Father said sternly.

"When *is* the proper time, Father? The exhibition is in two weeks! If Professor Hawksley won't go, and help is needed, then I should be allowed to attend. It is as simple as that."

Wickins said something, but he wasn't facing her as clearly, so she didn't catch more than, ". . . it was not my intent—"

But Clara's glare immediately silenced him.

Trudie exclaimed Rob's and McKenna's names and rushed to give both of them very enthusiastic hugs.

Mr. Foster stroked the bridge of his nose with his fingernail. "It seems you arrived in the midst of opening arguments for the prosecution," he said with a slight shake of his head. "And yet, the judge in the case is unmoved."

"That's unfair," Clara protested. She glared at McKenna. "You let *her* flaunt Society's norms. I know it's unusual, but it's our *home* in Bishopsgate. There shouldn't be anything improper about me staying at my own home."

"But you recall, Daughter, that there are no servants there, the home is closed. You'd be quite alone with Lieutenant Wickins, especially in the evenings. I have business meetings that will go late into the night and are quite unpredictable. I cannot reliably chaperone you both."

"You made no objections when Rob was teaching McKenna," Clara protested again. "Besides, he's just a friend."

McKenna saw Wickins recoil at the term. Tension continued to engulf the room.

Mr. Foster's brows almost met at the bridge of his nose. The anger in his gaze was palpable. "This is too fast, too soon. I know you've been chafing for more freedom, but it will happen in its due time."

Then Mother entered the salon, wiping her hands on a towel. "Dearest! I thought I'd heard someone come in." She gave McKenna a fierce hug and kiss and then offered some doting attention to Rob as well.

Mr. Foster rose from his comfortable chair. "Court is adjourned. The answer is still no."

"What have we decided?" Mrs. Foster asked brightly.

"Clara will not be going to Bishopsgate with Lieutenant Wickins for the exhibition. She will come when you visit so all is proper. Trudie, can you open the windows, please? This room is hotter than the greenhouse at the moment."

"Is that my fault too?" Clara said spitefully. But she didn't back down or flee the room. McKenna felt sorry for her, but she agreed with Father. Clara and Wickins were both adults, so sharing a home without a chaperone would be considered highly scandalous.

"Perhaps some music would alter the mood?" Mrs. Foster suggested, nodding to Rob.

"Actually," Rob demurred, "I was hoping you might have more information about what happened to us? Did you speak to your contact in the military?"

"I did," Mr. Foster said. Clara sulked and walked over to one of the couches, then sat down on the edge, hands resting on her knees.

She was a picture, with a smart hat pinned to her lovely, coiled hair, her pose very proper and dignified, but she maintained a pouty expression. McKenna looked at her father inquisitively.

"What did you learn?" Rob pressed.

"Colonel Harrup tells me that General Colsterworth is still at a mountain retreat presently. He's not even in Bishopsgate. The military had no knowledge of the attack, but word came back from the local police that followers of a certain man have become more . . . shall I say it . . . bold in their defiance of the government. The colonel thought it strange that your accosters wanted to take you to this man, this *strannik*, because he's currently under arrest and awaiting trial. His followers may be unaware of his incarceration."

"Thank you for the information," Rob said. "And I apologize for the discord when we arrived. It's my fault. I suppose it wouldn't be an issue if I were intending to attend the exhibition."

McKenna saw Clara cut a glare at Rob, but she was beyond his peripheral vision, and he wouldn't have noticed it.

"Are you sure you won't change your mind?" Father asked sincerely. "It's not because of Clara's headstrong intemperance that I'd urge you to do so. You are the inventor of this ingenious device, deserve the credit of the discovery, and your presence would increase the likelihood of future success for the company."

She shifted her gaze to Rob, whose jaw muscles poked out amidst his scruff. She noticed the fixing of his eyes on Father's face. She could almost see the gears of stubbornness cranking inside him faster and faster. Wickins approached and stood by Rob.

"Mr. Foster, you know I respect you and your feelings. For the reasons I've previously stated, it's quite impossible for me to attend. I have the fullest confidence in Wickins. He's your man."

"Thanks, old chap," Wickins said. "I won't let you down." He kept his gaze averted from Clara's.

Father's features creased with a sigh. "Well, I *am* disappointed in your decision, Robinson. I cannot be otherwise. I've asked the foundry to provide some assistance in the setup of the bulbs. It is not uncommon for prominent individuals from court to inspect the displays, and I believe many of them will contain artifacts of Aesir magic that shall cause the bulbs to reveal their presence. I'll be meeting with several bankers that week to try and persuade them to attend the demonstration. We shall do our best to capitalize on your invention."

"Thank you, Mr. Foster."

There was still tension in the air. McKenna could sense it and wished her father would be more sensitive to Rob's feelings. She hooked arms with her husband. "Can you play the aria of the Erlking's daughter?"

He willingly complied. McKenna sat on the other side of the Broadwood grand so she could get a good view of the room. Rob seated himself on the bench and stretched out his arms. His untidy hair dangled over his brows as he stared with fixed concentration on the keys. His lithe fingers began to play the melody, which always started gently—judging by the deliberate movements of his hands. But soon, very soon, his hands would be racing across the keys. She loved to watch him play—loved the passion of it, the way he communed with the piano.

Glancing over at her parents, McKenna noticed the looks they were exchanging. They spoke with their eyes sometimes. With glances. McKenna wished she knew what they said to one another. Things were still so new with Rob and her, but they loved talking to each other, sharing ideas, explaining their thoughts. She hoped that someday they would be able to communicate with glances too. Trudie approached the Broadwood grand and stroked the polished wood, gazing at the instrument, or was she just enjoying the sounds it was making?

McKenna noticed Wickins sitting by Clara, speaking to her surreptitiously. No matter how loud Rob played, McKenna had the advantage of eavesdropping. They were close enough that she could get a clear look at their faces and throats.

"I'm sorry, Clara, but I wasn't going to go against your father!"

"You should have," Clara replied with a look of disdain. "You know how much I want to attend the Great Exhibition. You should have stood up for me."

"Against a barrister?"

"The professor did," Clara said, her eyes shifting to McKenna's husband. There was a look in her eyes. Was it jealousy? "He defied my father. And you never will."

McKenna winced at the look of pain on Wickins's face. It clearly hurt to be compared to another man and found lacking.

It was jealousy, then. In a way. Clara didn't want Rob. She just wanted someone who would fight for her. Champion her.

The way Rob had for McKenna.

She looked back at her husband again, feeling things for him in that moment she didn't even have words for. For her, a woman who had words for everything, it was a novelty.

Robinson Foster Hawksley

CHAPTER FOUR

A Professor's Alchemy

Robinson was concentrating very hard, using a little set of pliers while staring at a white gold wire through a magnifying glass. He added a little bend to the end for a dramatic flourish, handling the delicate web of golden strands with caution and care. A little prickle went down his spine, the feeling of being watched.

He turned his neck and saw McKenna standing in the doorway of the alchemy, wearing the white nightdress he fancied. She was stroking her arms, gazing at him, her cheeks a little pink.

"I didn't even hear you," he apologized, setting down the delicate wreath-crown he was working on. He tried to make out the expression on her face and failed. Was she disappointed he was still working so late at night? It didn't look like that, but it *did* look serious. He set down the pliers and rose from the wooden chair. The alchemy smells were familiar and comforting to him—the burnt tang of solder, the incongruous odors of chymicals in their little glass bottles, the antiseptic smells of the cleaner he used to scrub the workbench.

"I didn't want to interrupt you," she said.

"I'm not even sure what time it is," he confessed. He'd had a long day working at the university, they'd enjoyed dinner together and a robust discussion, and then he'd gone to the alchemy to work. "But if I've been neglecting you, I apologize."

"No, it's not that," she said, gazing down. Was it shyness? They hadn't been married that long and were still getting used to being around each other every day. Although he was fond of Wickins, she was a far cry more pleasant a roommate than his friend had been. Rising from his chair, he closed the distance between them.

He tilted her chin up to meet her eyes. "Tell me."

"You'll laugh at me."

"Why? Is it humorous?"

Her cheeks were flaming even more. It was embarrassment. That intrigued him.

"Please," he coaxed gently, gazing at the column of buttons on the nightgown and feeling he'd rather enjoy wrapping up his work for the night.

She bit her lip and then met his gaze. "I'd just changed into my nightgown, the one you like so much, and I was going to let down my hair, but then I . . . I thought you might like to do that part."

He blinked in surprise and nodded enthusiastically.

She stroked his arm where his shirt sleeves had been rolled up to the elbow. "I came to see if you might want to do it, and then I saw you, working so hard. I don't know what you're working on, but it was so pretty. What is it?"

"It's a . . . 'wreath-crown'? I think that's the translation. Wickins said the Aesir word is *'wrea-ith.'* I think our word's etymology comes from it."

"Wrea-ith," she said, smiling at the word. He liked the way his wife's lips looked whenever she tasted a new word. She was voracious for them. After Wickins had moved to the barracks, taking his Aesir dictionary with him, she'd purchased one so she could study the language and help him with translations.

"I'm making it for you," he said. "Let's try it on. I'll need to adjust it, of course, but it should fit."

"Why do I need a wreath-crown?" she asked, her nose wrinkling.

"I believe the Aesir use them to communicate thought to thought. Now that we know the proper alloy they use—from the device I have— and since I can't afford to *buy* one, I thought I'd make it myself just to test it out. Let's see if it fits."

He took her by the hand and escorted her to the worktable. She sat across from him, her nightdress glowing in the lamplight. She gave him a fascinated look as she put her elbow on the table and examined the little web of wires he'd assembled.

"It won't fit with your hair like that, so let's take care of that business first," he said. He did enjoy letting her hair down. He pulled the pin holding the configuration in place, and the coiled bundle fell down her shoulders and back. His throat became very dry, and his cheeks were starting to burn.

Most of the wreath-crowns he had seen in display windows were worn across the forehead and fixed to the sides of the head. The prettier ones had little designs in the metal, which he hadn't done with his makeshift one, but he had added some V-shaped bending and scalloped edges. He gently lifted it from the table and set it over her head. It was a little tight, so he bent the edges outward slightly to keep it from pressing against her very hard. The silvery white gold and her nightdress gave her an otherworldly look, reminding him of the actors playing the Aesir in the opera, except their wigs had been the color of frost. The effect was uncanny.

"How does it work?" McKenna asked, giving him a look. Her finger stroked the edge of his arm.

"I have no idea. Let me try putting on the thumb ring first." He reached into his vest pocket and withdrew the device. He quickly worked the combination in the inner circles, which unlocked the innermost ring. He slid it onto the thumb of his left hand. An immediate stab of pain followed, making him wince and earning a sympathetic look from his wife.

"It still hurts," she acknowledged, patting his other hand.

He nodded. "Now think something. A command, a suggestion. Let me see if I can discern it." Taking both of her hands, he gazed at her from across the table. In his tests with Wickins, he had found the range of thought to be several miles. Actually, anywhere in Auvinen had worked. They were planning to do further experiments when Wickins went to Bishopsgate for the exhibition. It would be truly extraordinary if thoughts could be transmitted that great a distance and be heard and recorded accurately.

He stared into McKenna's eyes, waiting . . . hoping to hear her thoughts in his mind. Their previous attempts had failed, which had led him to the idea of creating the *wrea-ith*. He knew how badly she wished to use magic and really wanted to see if he could find a way to bridge the gap between her deafness and the magic of intelligences. Such a device might also make it possible for him to connect directly with her mind without spoken word. He hoped the *wrea-ith* might help channel or amplify the power of thought.

"It's not working, is it?" McKenna said.

He bit his lip. His thoughts had been distracted. "Try again." This time, he would focus. He stared at her face, her eyes, willing himself to hear her thoughts. But nothing came through. Her thoughts were veiled.

"I'm not getting anything," he admitted.

"I can tell," she said, smiling wryly.

"I know we'll figure it out, McKenna. I believe that. According to what I've read, some *wrea-iths* have gemstones embedded in the front. Apparently different types of stone have different properties. We'll try each one if we have to."

She sighed. "What if none of them work?"

"Then we'll try something else," he said, reaching over and stroking her cheek. She leaned into his hand.

"It means so much to me that you haven't given up," she said. "You are so determined."

"It's part of my nature, I think," he said. "Stubborn as an ox."

She shook her head no. "Not an ox, I think. You're persistent. That's how you made the discovery you did."

"I can't take all the credit," he deflected. "You inspire me, McKenna. You don't give up either. It must be very frustrating not being able to do the easiest spell. But you haven't quailed."

She shook her head. "It's part of *my* nature too, I suppose."

"I wish I could explain why it isn't working. There is a principle governing this that we don't fully comprehend. Several centuries ago, people thought that the weight of an object determined how fast it fell. That an apple would fall faster than a grape. It wasn't until Johann Kepler that the nature of gravity was discovered."

"I thought Isaac Berrow, the founder of the Invisible College, did that?"

"No, Berrow was born, I believe, the year Kepler died. They never met. But he took the knowledge farther than his predecessor had. Now we know about the motion of planets and large celestial bodies. One person's insight helped springboard another's. I'll keep doing research. I think no one has discovered the answer yet because they haven't been asking the right questions."

She squeezed his hand and gave him a fierce smile that made him feel tender things.

He raised her hand to his lips and kissed her knuckles. "We'll keep trying. I just need to find another key to the magic."

"I feel like I'm the one who is broken. *Everyone* was moved at the opera that night. Although I could feel the vibrations in my chest, it didn't mean as much to me. I can't *pretend* otherwise."

He nodded vigorously. "Music is one of the things capable of reaching inside each of us and unlocking the unutterable. But there are others."

Her look brightened. "I've never heard that word before. I *love* it. Unutterable."

Robinson grinned. "When that singer hit certain notes, with emotional resonance, it was . . . it was . . . profound. It's like a song to the Mind of the Sovereignty that gets answered in kind. A connection."

"And that's also why you climbed up on rooftops to play your violin during the winter," she said, gazing steadfastly at him. "I was going to get you another in Tanhauser. We'll have to get you one from a local shop instead. I want you to keep playing music. Maybe playing music will help you figure out the answer. For me, reading creates that sort of connection."

Her words struck him sharply. He felt the same agitation, the same excitement, that came from being on the verge of a discovery.

"I hope so, McKenna. I truly do. And I haven't given up hope that we'll find another way to reach magic for you."

She extracted her hand from his and then reached up and lifted the delicate wreath-crown from her head and set it on the table between them. He took off the thumb ring and set it back into the device and locked it in again. He wouldn't quit. Not for all the Aesir gold in the world.

"Since you couldn't read my mind, can I tell you what I was thinking?" She had a sly smile now. An inviting look. She fingered the collar of her nightdress.

He swallowed. "I always want to know your thoughts, Miss Fos—" He caught himself, blushed, realizing he'd been about to call her Miss Foster by accident.

"When I was standing in the doorway to your alchemy, watching you work so hard, seeing your shirt untucked, your suspenders hanging down, your hair in a delicious state of dishevelment . . ." She let the thought dangle in the air.

"Yes?"

"You looked so handsome to me in that moment. It reminded me of when we first met, and Miss Trewitt and I woke you up. Remember that day?"

"I'm *still* mortified about it," he chuckled.

She straightened her spine and gave him a rather imperial look. "Some proper meals have done you some good, Professor Hawksley. The suit your father gave you is fitting you better. You're quite handsome, you know."

Those words shocked him. "I've never been considered *that*. By anyone."

Her cheeks were starting to turn pink again. "I don't really care what anyone else thinks. When I was standing there, I was wishing we might go to our room. That's the thought I was trying to send you with the *wrea-ith*."

Her words had ignited a fire inside him. They'd also soothed some of his deepest insecurities. "I don't deserve you, McKenna," he gasped.

"Maybe you'll start believing otherwise tonight," she answered, rising from the chair and coming over to sit on his lap before he could stand up.

Her kiss stole his breath away.

CHAPTER FIVE

Rights and Duties

The commotion at the locomotivus station was indicative of an imminent departure. People thronged the platform, hugging and bidding farewell, some waving handkerchiefs and stifling tears. Porters were loading chests and luggage onto magic-powered carts. Robinson watched as McKenna leaned up and kissed Mr. Foster on the cheek.

"Goodbye, Father! I'll miss seeing you at Closure!" she said, her voice barely audible on the noisy platform.

Mrs. Foster had already offered her goodbye and was standing farther back, gripping Trudie's and Clara's hands. Trudie was nonchalant about the whole trip to Bishopsgate to set up for the exhibition in a week. Clara, on the other hand, looked upset and slightly miserable. She really wanted to go as well, and her father was refusing to accede to her wishes or even compromise. Lieutenant Wickins offered her a forlorn smile. She was disappointed in him for not standing up to her father, and it showed.

Robinson stepped forward to block the line of sight between the two silent combatants. Wickins was standing on the lowest step, gripping an onboarding rail with one hand. He noticed his friend's approach, so he came down and stepped out of the way so others could board.

"Thanks for seeing us off, Dickemore," he said, using the nickname he'd given Robinson soon after their first meeting. He gripped Robinson's hand and shook it firmly.

"You inspected the boxes after they were loaded?" Robinson asked.

"I did. They're strapped in and secure. It'll take half a dozen porters on the other side to get them going, but I'll make sure each one arrives safely." Boxing up crates of quicksilver lamps threaded with precious strands of Aesir gold had made for a delicate and expensive operation. The company Mr. Foster had partnered with was providing the materials for the demonstration, but there was still a lot of work to be done in setup and tuning. And reports of a heat wave in Bishopsgate meant the work would be unpleasant at best. Many courtiers from the imperial court had absconded to the mountains where it was cooler. Or so Robinson had heard. He'd never been one to care for gossip or social class.

"You have the designs I drew up for the display?" Robinson pressed. "You didn't leave them at the barracks?"

"In my pocket, old chap. In my pocket." He slapped his military jacket. Then he glanced over Robinson's shoulder again, and his good-humored smile faded. "Blast, she'll never let me live this down. I wish you were coming, Dickemore."

"So do I," said Mr. Foster, arriving at the step to board the locomotivus. He gave Robinson an impassive look, one that signaled he was still rather displeased with his son-in-law, but he didn't speak further on the matter as he climbed up the boarding steps. He paused at the top to wave goodbye to his family.

"Northbound! Northbound locomotivus ready to depart!" shouted one of the yard attendants.

Wickins stepped back up, quick as can be, and looked back once.

Robinson offered him a conciliatory wave. "I have faith in you, Wickins."

"It's not misplaced, Dickemore. I'll let you know how it all goes," he said from his position on the step below Mr. Foster.

A plume of frosty fog spouted from the head of the locomotivus, and the machine quivered and then levitated off the tracks. Robinson waved again as he backed up to join the family. One glance at Clara, and he got the intuition that she was battling within herself to rush forward and give Wickins, who still stood on the steps, a kiss goodbye. Or . . . wishing he gave one to her. McKenna was no longer standing with her sisters, and he felt a brief, startled sensation, but then he noticed her farther along the tracks, engulfed in the plume of chilled fog that was necessary for the magic to work properly. There was nothing wrong or unsafe about her enjoying the fog on her face. But he'd never seen her do it before, and her expression denoted she was almost relieved by the cold burst of air. Why? It discomfited him without him registering why it should do so.

The locomotivus began to move forward, propelled by the magic that activated its various interconnected parts. Another jet of fog spurted from the machine. And then it was soaring down the tracks and out of the station, quickly gone from sight.

"I'll miss Papa," Trudie said simply. They all would. He was an austere man at times, but his conversation was interesting, the house on Brake Street a sanctuary, and his absence—along with Wickins's— would be felt on Closure.

"I wish *I* were going with them," Clara said tonelessly.

Mrs. Foster sighed. But she was wise enough not to comment on her daughter's words.

Robinson observed a curious look on McKenna's face as she stood there, eyes closed, as if still enjoying the sensation of having been engulfed by the mist. He walked up to her, studying her closed eyes and the half smile on her lips. Then, as if awaking from a reverie, she opened her eyes and startled a little at finding him next to her.

"Are you all right?" he asked.

"I like the chilled air," she said, shrugging. "It reminds me of . . . something. I've been dreading summer. At least Auvinen is on the coast. There are blessings in that."

"What does it remind you of?" he asked with genuine curiosity.

She pursed her lips, shrugged, then snaked her hand into his. "Can we walk back? I want some sugared peanuts. We could pass by the legislature where the carts are."

He bowed in agreement. They bid farewell to the other family members, who were taking the carriage back to Brake Street. The boulevard outside the station was still crowded with people busy loading their crates and parcels and securing transportation. It reminded Robinson of the day he'd arrived in Auvinen from Covesea, when those men had tried to steal his chest of instruments and chymicals. That thought triggered an immediate protective feeling toward McKenna, because nefarious individuals were seeking her out, and neither of them understood why. It was an unsettled state, and a constant pressure on both of them.

After they were clear of the ruckus, they slowed their pace, enjoying the shade of the cherry trees as they walked. The midafternoon sun was beating down on the streets, causing a shimmer of heat from the iron rails embedded in the pavement. After a leisurely walk and lighthearted conversation, they arrived at one of the bubbling kettles and a seller who gladly took McKenna's coin for a bag of roasted, spiced peanuts, which they shared on the remainder of the walk back to his dingy apartment. But it was a temporary state. After his teaching obligation was over, they'd be moving.

As they went up the broken street, which still bore evidence of the ferocity of the Aesir bombardment the previous winter, he thought wistfully about what McKenna had gained before choosing to marry him. She was a wealthy heiress, owner of her aunt Margaret's home on the island of Siaconset. Mowbray House. Robinson had only been to the front door of that place, never inside. Her aunt hadn't liked him or thought him a good enough partner for her niece, so when he had gone to reveal his heart to her, he'd been turned away. He'd been allowed to leave a letter, though, and that letter had changed life for both of them.

He squeezed her hand to alert her to his query. She gazed up at him. "How often did you visit your family home in Bishopsgate? Do you have fond memories of it?"

She nodded. "Father visited it the most frequently because of his responsibilities as a barrister. The streets are more crowded. Very few trees. So many people. I prefer Auvinen."

"Are you nervous about moving to Mowbray House?" he asked.

"Why should I be? I spent many summers there. And I know the perfect room for your alchemy."

"Oh? Describe it to me."

"Clara would have put you down in the basement, I'm sure. But no, in the back of the house, there's an attic with a cupola, and rounded steps lead up to it. I think you'd like it up there because there's a view of the sea. Maybe it would remind you of Covesea."

He was touched by her thoughtfulness. Memories surfaced in his brain—a stray dog, nosing at him; his brother, laughing; a coffin, being lowered into the ground. His memories of that place were bittersweet, to be sure, as he'd lost both of his brothers, but there'd been happier times too. He noticed sweat trickling down the side of her face. For him, the shade had been quite cool.

"Are you too warm?"

She nodded. "I wish we were in Siaconset already. For some reason, the season is so stifling. Don't you feel it?"

"It feels pleasant to me." That was another oddity. She had become more sensitive to the rising temperature. She hadn't done that last year.

She shook her head. "The soldiers up north have to live in yurts by the ice trenches. Honestly, that sounds lovely right now."

"There is a canal on Jarom Street," Robinson suggested. "We could accidentally fall in?"

"But that would ruin our peanuts, I'm afraid."

"Too true. Is that why you wanted to stand by the jettison vents near the tracks?"

"It was a lovely feeling. There was no smell. Just . . . white fog. Do you know why that is?"

"I'm not an expert on locomotivus alchemy, but I believe the cold has something to do with the magnetism and levitation as well as cooling down the moving parts within the engine, and the intelligences provide the inertia to start and stop it."

She wrapped one arm around his waist to get closer to him and patted his chest. "If my handsome and *brilliant* husband says so . . ."

As they approached the final leg of the journey, Robinson noticed from a hundred paces away the sentient lights shining outside of their apartment. It was still midafternoon, which meant they had been activated by the presence of Aesir magic. After Robinson had almost been executed by Colsterworth's deputy, he'd had these lights installed at their home as an early warning measure. He slowed his stride, and McKenna glanced at his face before following his gaze to the glowing lights. Her hand clenched his shirt. Her nostrils flared, as if she were an animal reacting to a threat.

Robinson reached into his pocket and withdrew his device. He unlocked the combination and slipped on the thumb ring, experiencing a jolt in his skull. A protective feeling surged inside of him. He would let nothing happen to her. The memory of a gunshot replayed in his mind—on a dark street, on a dark winter night. The night his violin had broken.

"*Ex calibris duo,*" he murmured, summoning a protective shield. He knew his device would protect them, but he couldn't be too cautious.

The exterior lamps began to glow brighter, and suddenly a figure materialized out of nothingness, having removed the Aesir cloak that had been masking his presence. He was a stocky figure, with a balding head and a close-trimmed beard.

"Good afternoon, Professor," the man said by way of introduction. Robinson recognized him as General Colsterworth's adjutant.

"Remind me of your name?" Robinson said, coming closer. McKenna's arm, the one behind his back, was trembling. She was so close to him, pressing hard as if he would shield her.

"Peabody Stoker," replied the soldier. "I come with news from the general."

"Oh?" He didn't feel inclined to invite the man inside. Something felt off. Wrong.

"May we go inside?"

He felt McKenna's hands clench harder.

"I'd prefer it if we didn't," Robinson said. "Can't you relay your message here?"

The officer shrugged. "I was dispatched to tell you that the men who attacked your wife . . . we still haven't found them. There is this faction, you see, that wants to appease the Aesir, to become their slaves. The general believes the men who attacked Mrs. Hawksley were part of that faction. We have the ringleader in custody. It's only a matter of time before the inner circle is caught and disbanded. Rest assured that it had nothing to do with us."

"How comforting," Robinson said flatly. "Is that all?" It wasn't really news. Mr. Foster had told him as much.

"I have another assignment here in Auvinen. I came by to deliver the message as a courtesy. Good day." He nodded to them and then walked toward them. McKenna was trembling with fear.

After the soldier passed them, he lifted his cowl and disappeared. The lights from the lamps slowly dimmed and then winked out.

Robinson put his arm around McKenna's shoulders. "He's gone."

"Thank you for not letting him inside our home," she said, glancing back down the street in the direction he'd gone.

Robinson led her to the front door, activating the magic there. The dog intelligences he'd set to guard the apartment were loyal and true. They'd come to him by summons of the friendly doglike intelligence that had followed him from Covesea and had become a sort of invisible friend to both him and McKenna. They'd even considered giving it a name. Dogs tended to roam in packs, so getting the additional intelligences had been easy, for they'd all been very willing. They reported news to him in simple yet clear terms that made him frown.

"We came back too late. He was already inside," he declared.

The greatest risk will always be that the Invisible College will be conquered from an internal enemy. The war within us rages relentlessly, just as our conflict with the Aesir rages without.

I foresee that great wealth and success will come with the application of the true principles of the Unseen Powers. A true sorcerer will not hesitate to discard antiquated conceptions and practices in favor of new and better ones. They will spend relentless energy correcting, discarding, improving, and refining, with the objective of achieving the best results—and profits. Yet the Mind of the Sovereignty desires not a handy trinket. It demands the improvement of character.

A sorcerer works with inanimate objects and cooperative intelligences; the Mind works with responsive beings—ourselves—who are capable of both helping or hampering such work. The mechanism of the Unseen Powers, if I may presume to call it a "mechanism," is so delicate, so susceptible, that even our thoughts can interfere with our ability to harness their power. Ambition, Pride, Jealousy, Envy—these are traits a sorcerer must abhor. They are inimical to the Unseen Powers. Yet they are innate within each of us. Thus the future of the Invisible College will *be determined on how well these negative traits are restrained by individuals and the hierarchy and how well the positive ones are promulgated.*

—Isaac Berrow,
Master of the Royal Secret,
the Invisible College

General Colsterworth

CHAPTER SIX

GRESHAM COLLEGE

The wretched misery of the heat wave made General Colsterworth miss the crisp alpine air he'd left behind at the summer court. He'd had to resort to using hand towels to mop the sweat dripping from his brow. Perhaps an inspection of the front lines was in order, a retreat to the glacial trenches where magical buckles were sewn into all the uniforms as a matter of course. He saw the suffering in his adjutants and higher-ranking officers gathered in the war room. By the Mind, if *he* could endure the heat, so could they!

A man coughed to get his attention. "General, Colonel Harrup's report arrived. He believes that a rival of the Hawksley lamp is in the works from another sorcerer in Auvinen—Miss Cowing. We don't know if there was any collaboration between Professor Hawksley and her, but the ideas are so similar it is possible. We've found one manufacturer who's willing to overlook how the design of our tubes was obtained. But if we allow Hawksley to achieve notoriety for it at the exhibition, it will cause trouble for us later on."

The general frowned at the skulduggery. "I don't care about the blasted exhibition. Find out who invented it first. I'd rather work with

Cowing than Hawksley for multiple reasons. See if the manufacturer can produce two hundred thousand lamps in six weeks and get them shipped to the front lines. I think Miss Cowing would be more amenable to overlooking that production was started on this before an agreement was secured, which is one more reason I'd prefer for her to get the patent."

"Two hundred thousand?" declared the adjutant.

"We are sweating like pigs *now*," Colsterworth growled, "but winter will be upon us shortly, and so will the stormbreakers, the Aesir, and the accursed bog creatures they fly on! We need to be warned where they're attacking from."

"But, sir, no manufacturer can produce that many that quickly!"

"Then we'll have several of them work on it to get the job done! I want those quicksilver tubes so we can begin installing them at the farthest edges of our lines. Our lives depend upon it!"

He wasn't entirely sure if Hawksley had invented it or if his wife had played some role. For that reason alone, he did not want to work with Hawksley. Then there was the fact that the man had given over his shares in the invention to his wife . . .

No, working with the pair would be much more perilous than not working with them, even if it put the military in legal jeopardy. He'd simply have to outsmart the professor. And this news about Miss Cowing's invention was a boon. Whether she and Hawksley had consulted with each other or not, the very appearance of having done so could delegitimize Hawksley's patent application.

"I understand, sir. But getting one company to cooperate in such an . . . underhanded way is fraught with risk. Inviting more to join in the conspiracy will—"

"Save lives, Mack. It will save lives. Let the courts fight this out later. Make sure Miss Cowing sees Hawksley's tubes. If he's done something underhanded and stolen ideas from her, she'd be our greatest advocate and partner. She's become very wealthy because of military contracts. We know her and are used to doing business with her. I'm willing to wager that she'd prevail in a lawsuit between the two, especially if she's convinced she was the first with the idea. Now, we're all hot and irritable but don't forget why we're here and who we're fighting against. Get it done and don't bother me with obstacles." He noticed another underling gaping at him, looking too fearful to speak. "Out with it, Pemberton."

"S-Sir, Peabody Stoker j-just arrived. He's in your office."

These summer uniforms were awful bothersome things. He wiped sweat from his neck with the towel and nodded to the adjutant. "I've been expecting his return. I hope he brings good news." He tossed the towel down on the map desk and stormed out of the war room.

The halls of Gresham College were old and ill-fitting. It had once been a university but had been donated to the Invisible College by the founder's family. The sorcerers who belonged to this particular quorum were exclusively military. It was the hive of the imperial army, from which orders were dispensed like a queen bee commanding her drones. The building itself was rather unassuming, but there was an underground network of tunnels. The citizenry had no idea how the strange-shaped building was used. Most assumed the military was run by generals positioned nearer the palace, who held military parades and engaged in pageantry. Such efforts were for the benefit of the nobility, however—the children of the wealthy, whom he wouldn't have relied on to polish the axle spokes of his carriage let alone stand against an Aesir onslaught.

The interior corridor of the command was tight and required underlings to stand aside as he passed, but he reached his private office and found his man standing by the window.

"Is it this hot in Auvinen, Stoker? Insufferable."

"They enjoy some reprieve by the sea. Their climate is milder than here."

Colsterworth chuffed. "Then why aren't we holding the blasted exhibition there this year?"

"I don't know, sir. That's outside my purview."

"Don't be cheeky, boy. Tell me what you've learned of Foster's daughter. You better have brought me *something*."

"Sir, I believe she *is* a Semblance."

"On what evidence?"

"I found a letter written from Mrs. Foster to Hawksley describing an incident on a beach in Siaconset. The girl nearly drowned."

Colsterworth frowned. "But she's deaf. Why would the Aesir choose a host who lacks the ability to do magic?"

"I don't know, sir. Perhaps to make her less of a suspect. I encountered the Hawksleys following their return from the locomotivus station. Her reaction was immediate and showed great agitation. She practically recoiled from me. I've seen enough evidence to suggest she's a threat. If not for your orders, I would have felt justified in executing her on the spot."

"Ah, Stoker. That's what I like about you. Efficiency. Let's keep an eye on her but from a distance. I understand the couple will be relocating to the island before winter. We should send someone to spy on them. An accident at the house may solve the problem Well, a *second* accident. Watch out for Hawksley, though. He's no average sorcerer. He knows a spell that causes a violence of sound. He used it on both Crossthwait and the traitors in Tanhauser."

"Speaking of the traitors, did you catch them?"

"Yes. And executed them. In front of their *strannik*, no less. Their bodies are lying in a mass grave, attracting flies."

Stoker's eyebrows lifted. "What did he do?"

"Nothing. He was impassive as an oyster. Didn't seem to care what happened to them. He's above it all, it seems. I thought witnessing their deaths might break him and get him to reveal who his other lieutenants are."

"Shall I put a bullet in his skull, sir?"

Colsterworth shook his head. "No. Drusselmehr suggested food poisoning, but I still think it would be better if the *strannik* should hang himself in his cell."

Stoker nodded. "At least he'll be disposed of. When should we arrange for a similar *accident* to befall Foster's daughter?"

"I'll give it some thought. I'm going to the dungeon to speak to the *strannik* right now. Arrange for two officers to strangle him and plant a rope. When the guard rotation changes, they'll notice he's dead at dinnertime."

"Of course," Stoker said. He nodded and left.

Colsterworth had so many demands on his time, so many responsibilities. The one that motivated him most was preserving the lives of the people.

The *strannik* wanted a truce with the Aesir. No, not a truce. An unconditional surrender. Ideas could be as infectious as the other viruses spread by the enemy, and this one could jeopardize more lives than any other.

He felt droplets of sweat trickling down his neck again. His undershirt was soaked. He looked around for a towel and remembered he'd left it in the war room. Pity.

The general sighed and then walked down to the cellar. Thankfully it was cooler there and he began to feel some relief. There were enough kegs of saltpetr stored there to fight off the entire Aesir army. Crates filled with weapons and uniforms, winter gear. And yet, it was only one of many depots throughout the city. Bishopsgate, in the past, before the world had warmed more and more with each successive year, had once hosted humanity's last stand against the Aesir invaders. Centuries had passed, and the story had been lost to memory for most people. But the quorum at Gresham College had access to records inaccessible to other parts of the Invisible College. That was not knowledge for the common man.

The guards on duty at the prisoners' ward snapped to attention, saluted, and then opened the iron door. Colsterworth walked down the grim-smelling corridor, alert to the sounds of the suffering men. But at least it was cooler.

He thought about McKenna Hawksley as he approached the *strannik's* cell. Such a pretty young thing. A shame she had to die. But this was war, and she was a Semblance. Whatever had brought her to that lonely beach in Siaconset that day, she had not come out of the water the same person.

Did Semblances always choose their next hosts? Or were they transferred to anyone nearby who was capable of being used? No one knew. There was precious little knowledge about their dangerous enemies, even less so about their ability to infiltrate human hosts. In his mind, he could picture a little seaside cottage burning. A pyrophoric would do the trick, make the flames hot and spread quickly. Undousable by water. Quite the opposite actually. Then a little funeral service where people shuffled and sniffled and whispered the archaic words—*Ashes to ashes. Dust to dust. Justice claimeth its own.* Robinson was a clever man. Inventors could be very useful. Especially if unattached to a Semblance. The general had no idea why Hawksley had granted all his shares of his invention to his wife as a wedding gift, but if she were out of the way, it would create an opportunity to include Hawksley in the military's magical needs.

The porter unlocked the door to the *strannik's* cell. The creepy fellow was sitting on the floor, his back to the far wall, looking bored and unimpressed by his visitor. There was no anger in his eyes, no thirst for revenge after the execution of his followers.

"Ah, the general himself. When am I to receive my trial?"

"I'm afraid it's impossible to say," Colsterworth said. "At least not before winter."

"When winter comes, it will be too late."

"Perhaps."

"It will be too late for *you*, General."

"Oh? Why do you think so?"

"Because the Aesir are more powerful than you can imagine. Our only hope for survival is to kneel before them."

"So you've said. I disagree. Is there anyone you wish to see? A family member, perhaps? Or are you estranged from every person who knows you?"

The bearded fellow smirked. "All mortals are my family."

Colsterworth didn't believe he would get more information from the madman. But he felt he owed it to his position to try once more. "How many people have you twisted with your beliefs?"

"I persuade, convince, and inspire."

"How many people have you 'persuaded, convinced, and inspired'?"

"More than you know, General. More than you know."

Beheading a snake was the best way to prevent it from spreading its venom. He saw a little smile flash on the *strannik*'s face. His wrists were bound with shackles that nullified spells. It would not be difficult for two men to do away with him.

"Well, enjoy your dinner," Colsterworth said. The *strannik* was lucky they'd decided on hanging and not poison. Food poisoning would be a painful way to die. The thought of shrimp made his stomach turn and his throat itch from past memories.

"You as well," replied the enigmatic man.

General Colsterworth returned to the war room, and the heat abovestairs quickly distracted him from thoughts of the crazed man. In fact, he'd forgotten all about the *strannik* by the time he sat down to his dinner, an aromatic split pea soup with fresh bread and slices of apples and cool water to drink. Nothing fancy, nothing like the exorbitant meals he'd endured at the summer palace. The banquets were nauseating to remember. Except for the saffron salmon. That was a new favorite.

Stoker barged through the door into the war room, his face pale with dread. It was an ominous greeting.

"What happened?" the general said, his senses immediately on alert.

"He's gone."

"Who?"

"The *strannik*! He's gone!"

Colsterworth blinked in surprise. "What do you mean he's *gone*?"

"The guard went to bring supper, and he found the two officers I sent to take care of the matter. They were hanging from the rope they'd brought, one from each end. Dead. The shackles were on the ground. No sign of struggle. Their hands weren't even bound. Sir . . . I think they hung *themselves*!"

"We need to find him," Colsterworth declared, rising from his seat. "How did he get past the guards?"

"An Aesir cloak?"

"How did he get one?"

A memory stirred. The self-satisfied look on the *strannik*'s face as he bid the general enjoy his dinner.

You as well.

There is an inexorable law in the universe. For every faculty there is a function. An apple fallen from a tree bears seeds within that can replace not only one tree but many. Those seeds are encased inside, but the flesh is naturally sweet, encouraging animals and mortals alike to transport the apple from where it fell. Faculty and function. When we discover a faculty in nature, we must try to discern its function. It was just such an observation, in an orchard at my mother's manor, of watching an apple fall, that led to the idea that there are Unseen Powers pulling all things to the ground.

—Isaac Berrow,
Master of the Royal Secret,
the Invisible College

MaKenna Aurora
Hawksley

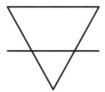

CHAPTER SEVEN

Derailed

McKenna was tidying up the alchemy when the will-o'-the-wisp of light entered the room and floated toward her. It was a preestablished sign from Rob, who had used his magic to set up alert systems for her for whenever she was home alone. This one, a dancing of light invoked by the intelligences of fireflies, meant that someone was at the front door. She had been poring over papers and such, trying to determine what that loathsome man from the military had been searching for in their apartment. Rob was teaching his class at the university. As soon as she noticed the dancing lights and started toward the door, they vanished.

She set down the paper on her way to the front door, peeking out of the spyhole and then opening it to reveal a delivery boy in uniform holding an envelope. She tipped him a coin—it was poor manners not to—and recognized her mother's handwriting instantly.

"Thank you," she said to the boy, who saluted her with the brim of his hat and went on his way. After shutting the door, she went to the small square dining table they had their meals at, sat down, and opened the envelope. Immediately, her stomach plunged.

Dearest McKenna,

Please come as soon as you can. Father sent a message from Bishopsgate with the most distressing news. I don't know what to do or how to help. Please, come home.
—Mother

The urgency of the note made McKenna's stomach roil, but she acted promptly. Leaving the note out on the table, she scrawled a couple of lines on it to Rob to let him know where she'd gone in case she didn't return before he did. She didn't need a cloak to travel, not on such a humid day. After securing enough coins for the street tram fares there and back, she locked up the apartment and proceeded on her way. Walking briskly, she went up the street to the corner where the trams passed, her mind wondering what had happened in Bishopsgate. The exhibition was starting in two days and every display had to be set up and functioning properly to be shown to the judges. She had a deep conviction that Rob's entry would not only do well but might win the entire showcase. That would practically ensure companies would flock to them and seek the right to license and produce Rob's invention.

So what could have gone wrong? Was the display malfunctioning?

Once she reached the corner, she had to wait half an hour before the next tram arrived. She hurriedly slid a coin into the metal fare box and climbed aboard. The iron horse pulling it started to move, and she felt the vibrations down her spine. Sweat trickled from her temples. Another change to another tram, and she was back in her family's neighborhood, resolutely walking up Brake Street to her family home.

By the time she reached the house, her armpits were soaked and sweat was trickling down her ribs annoyingly. She opened the little gate, hurried to the door, and opened it.

"I'm here!" she called out, not knowing where the other family members were. In a moment, Trudie poked her head out from the parlor and beckoned for McKenna to enter.

When she got there, she found Mother pacing with a worried expression. Clara looked positively outraged, also standing, and the two appeared to be in the midst of an argument.

"Never mind that. Tell me what happened," McKenna demanded.

Both of them turned toward her, accustomed to needing to face in the same direction so McKenna could be included in the conversation. Clara was the first to speak. "Wickins's leave was canceled," she declared hotly. "He's been ordered to return to the barracks in Auvinen."

"Why?" McKenna said, blinking in wonder.

"They have decided to give him a promotion," Mother said. "To captain. Apparently it has been in the works for some time, but it was only just approved by the emperor who is away at the summer palace."

The timing was suspicious, though. Surely Wickins's senior officer knew about his role at the Great Exhibition. Surely they could have delayed the promotion another fortnight. There was another layer of complexity to the matter. McKenna knew from her sister and Rob that Wickins couldn't marry until he got that promotion and the increased salary and opportunity that would come with it. That meant, realistically, that Wickins could officially begin courting Clara. So, in that light, it might be good news wrapped in disaster. Without Wickins to set up the display, Rob's invention would not be shown. Father didn't know how to work it, nor was he a practiced showman like Wickins.

"And you know what?" Clara said, her face mottled with frustration. "He'll take the promotion because he doesn't have a spine! If I were there, I would have told him to refuse it. He'd earn more working with Rob than what the military is offering. This isn't normal. They don't want Rob's invention to succeed."

"But the military *needs* the invention," Mother insisted.

Clara shook her head. "You don't think they can find another way to get it? That there aren't already contractors they'd *prefer* dealing with?" She shook her head again, her outrage showing in the curl of her mouth. "I *knew* I should have gone. If he ruins our family, does he think I'd even *want* him then?"

"Clara," Mother objected. "He's a good man. One you've been insisting all along is just a friend."

"Sadly, he's not good enough," Clara said. She buried her face in her hands.

McKenna's mind was whirling. Moving forward, she put her hand on Clara's shoulder and squeezed it. "He *is* a good man, Clara. This would be a dilemma difficult for anyone."

Her sister looked up. "But what do we do, McKenna? We cannot find someone else to take his place. No one trained. Only . . . only Rob could step in, and . . . you've seen how he's been."

Recalcitrant? Intractable? Obstinate? She wouldn't let those words escape her mouth, but they'd certainly floated through her mind of late.

She knew her husband. She wasn't sure how he would react to the situation, but his first inclination would be to express outrage at the military for underhandedness. After all, this wasn't the first or second time the military had intervened in their lives in such a negative way.

Well, perhaps it was time for a little underhandedness herself.

"I'll talk to Rob myself," Clara said expressively. "I'll make him go."

"Let me handle my husband," McKenna offered instead. "We need to alleviate his concern for his students and his obligation to them. Who could we ask to administer the—"

"Sarah Fuller Fiske," Mother said immediately, cutting her off. "I could go see her right now." That was a brilliant idea. She ran the school for the deaf in Auvinen and used the Hawksley Method, developed by Robinson's father, to help some of the children learn to speak. Father had helped found the school, and Rob had saved it when the children had been stricken with the malignant croup, a disease spread by the Aesir in a bid to wipe out their human enemies and lessen their ability to use magic.

"I'm sure Dean George would understand and approve of this," McKenna said, nodding in agreement. "He's an investor in the business, after all. He wants it to succeed."

"But how will you persuade Rob to come?" Clara said, her expression skeptical.

"Clara, would you purchase two tickets at the locomotivus station and meet us there? Rob finishes work at four. Mother, take the carriage to Mrs. Fiske and get her agreement. Then have her tell Dean George what we're doing. You bring the carriage to our apartment. I'll pack our clothes for travel. Just say that you wanted to visit and take us for a ride. We'll go directly to the station before it leaves. I think he'll come."

"You do?" Clara objected.

"I do. He cares about people, Clara. This is an emergency. Remember what happened after he found out about the people at the school getting sick? He stopped everything and went to help. I think he'll do it again. But we must act quickly. We have to get him on a northbound locomotivus tonight."

※

McKenna breathed out her agitation as she paced outside the little apartment. The carriage was parked at the curb, the horses tossing their tails impatiently. She'd locked up the apartment already and two valises were nestled in the cargo box at the rear of the carriage, out of sight. Her insides churned with worry, especially at the thought of how Rob would react once he realized he'd been fooled. No one liked to be misled. She wasn't doing this to take advantage of him, though. It was to protect his own interests. *Their* interests. She was convinced that if she waited to spring it on him at the station, with the locomotivus ready to depart, he would feel more pressure to go. If she'd told him at the apartment, he'd have enough space to tactfully decline, however much she begged. And she believed he still would decline if given the chance. She'd told him before that he was one of those men who needed a little wholesome tyranny from the women in their lives.

Even so, it was very likely that he'd be upset by the subterfuge. It was a word that meant, originally, *to escape secretly*. Not many authors used it, but she thought it a delicious word and very fitting for the circumstances. The plan was devious, to be sure. But they were literally escaping secretly.

There he was.

She watched Rob pull the bowler hat off his head and wave it at them, his smile genuine and delighted at the sight of his wife and mother-in-law waiting for him. He quickened his pace and kissed Mother on the cheek.

"What's this all about?" he asked with unfeigned interest.

"I thought you both might take a ride with me into the city," Mother said with no affect at all. "I'd welcome the company."

Rob shrugged agreeably. "I don't see why not." He took McKenna by the hand and kissed her knuckles. "Shall we?"

He helped both of the ladies into the carriage before climbing aboard himself. He sat very close to McKenna and put his hand around her hip to pull her even closer. Mother settled in across from them and gave McKenna a private smile.

"Did Wickins send any letters today?" Rob asked. "I've been curious if there've been any problems."

McKenna felt her cheeks heat and turned her head slightly away. "No, he didn't send anything."

It was true. But it still felt like a lie. She glanced at her husband's unsuspecting face.

"I know Clara was disappointed she didn't go," Rob said jovially. "Some of the students complained about exams being this week. Many of them wanted to see the exhibition as well. But that's only natural, I suppose."

"Indeed so," McKenna said, then looked out the window again. The smell of spiced peanuts wafted by the carriage as they neared the main street.

"Maybe we could all have dinner together?" Rob suggested after squeezing McKenna's leg to get her attention again. "It's a little warm for chowder tonight, but oysters perhaps?"

"I've already arranged something with the cook tonight," Mother said. "How were the students today? Are they excited to finish this term?"

McKenna let Mother steer the conversation into safer waters while she anxiously awaited their arrival at the locomotivus station. Rob was distracted enough by the conversation that he didn't seem to realize where they were going . . . until the carriage slowed down. As usually happened before a scheduled departure, many carriages were dropping off passengers, and the road had become congested.

"You have an errand at the station?" Rob asked, suddenly confused.

McKenna turned in the seat and put her hand on his leg. "*We* do."

His brow wrinkled. He looked askance at her, then out the window, then back at her.

"We're getting on the northbound locomotivus," McKenna said succinctly. "Our bags are already packed."

"I'm not getting on the northbound locomotivus," he said, his look darkening.

"We are," McKenna said. "There's trouble in Bishopsgate. I'll explain on the way."

"I think you'll explain this right now," he said, facing her, before casting a suspicious glance at Mother.

"This was my idea, Rob. We have to go. Now."

And then Clara was opening the carriage door. She handed McKenna the two tickets. "There weren't many seats left. Sorry it's not a private room."

Rob looked outraged. "Was this your plan all along?" he demanded of McKenna. No, he wasn't outraged, exactly. He looked betrayed.

"No," McKenna said truthfully. "A letter from Father came today. The situation has changed. He needs help. He needs *you*. Bishopsgate is where we *all* need you to be."

"There isn't time to waste," Clara said, urging McKenna to leave the carriage. "The locomotivus leaves at once."

McKenna rose from her seat, kissed Mother on the cheek, and then climbed out of the carriage. The driver had already gotten off and was holding the two valises in his hands. McKenna took hers and turned around, facing her husband, seeing the look of shock and disappointment on his face. It hurt to see him regarding her that way.

"I said I wasn't going to Bishopsgate," he declared.

"I need you to come with me," McKenna said. "I'm going to help my father, even if I have to go alone."

"McKenna," he said, shaking his head.

Clara grabbed the valise from the driver and shoved it into the carriage at Rob. "Wickins has run off! There's no one there to help. Now get on that locomotivus and stop this nonsense!"

Rob's mouth parted in astonishment.

"Please," McKenna mouthed to him. He looked uncertain still. Defiant, even.

So she turned around and started walking into the crowd, holding the two tickets to her bosom. He would follow her. Surely, he would follow her.

Wouldn't he?

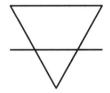

CHAPTER EIGHT

At What Cost

McKenna and Rob were squeezed between other passengers in the crowded compartment. The tension in the air between them was as icy as the plumes of cooling fog that billowed from the main engine as the locomotivus sped over the rails toward Bishopsgate. She cast a surreptitious glance at her husband and saw his stony expression, his eyes looking anywhere but at her. She'd always like that word— "surreptitious." But now it made her feel guilty. His hands gripped his knees tightly, the tendons glaring against his skin. She swallowed nervously.

"Mrs. Fiske is covering your classes," she said, hoping her voice didn't quaver. "Mother arranged it. And Dean George was told as well."

His lips pressed firmly together, the muscles at the corner of his jaw tightening too. There was anger in his eyes. And deep hurt.

"So everyone knew but me," he mouthed the words.

"We only found out about Wickins this morning. He didn't run off, not exactly. There was a belated promotion. He'll be a captain now."

"How convenient for him."

The passenger next to her was looking at them askance. She could hear McKenna's side of the conversation but not Rob's. Arguing in public was not considered proper. She had the peevish desire to stick her tongue out at the woman, to warn her to mind her own business. Instead, she folded her arms stiffly. This wasn't the time or the place to resolve things. They'd sent a message ahead to Father for when to expect them, but he might not even get the message in time. Things were running amok. Yes, that described it perfectly. She seethed in silence awhile and then shook her head in frustration.

"I wasn't trying to mislead you, Rob. But in some instances you can be very stubborn. This was *important*."

Then she looked away, not able to bear seeing his upset expression. Neither of them attempted to communicate after that, not for hours, but she kept thinking of things she could say to try to make it right. She wasn't sorry for what she'd done—it had been necessary. But she *did* need to make amends. The turmoil in her heart made the trip unpleasant and rife with negative feelings. So unlike their honeymoon excursion to Tanhauser, when they'd had a private booth and had . . . well . . . she blushed at the memory of those first ardent kisses.

Night fell and the quicksilver lamps aboard the locomotivus illuminated automatically. The sway of the car occasionally sent them bumping into each other. Each time made it more awkward. His hands remained fixed on his knees, or sometimes crossed over his chest like he was an oyster brooding over a pearl. He didn't say anything to her. Did nothing to ease the tension. To make matters worse, the crowded car was stiflingly hot and she perspired profusely, adding to her misery and embarrassment.

They arrived in Bishopsgate before dawn, and the station was surprisingly crowded. Rob stood first and grabbed their valises—both of them—and led the way down the platform. When the jets of icy air gushed from the engine house, she walked toward it to cool off. Which was when she noticed Clara walking toward her.

McKenna gaped in shock. "What are you doing here?"

Rob had been following her, but he came to a stop when he noticed McKenna's sister standing before them at the platform.

"I wasn't going to be left behind again," Clara said. "I can't believe it's this hot this early in the day. Let's find Father."

"But . . . how?" McKenna demanded, flustered.

"I bought three tickets, you ninny."

"What about Mother? She let you?"

"I left a note in the carriage for her. I'm going to help fix this mess Wickins caused. I'm a sorcerer too. And unlike you, McKenna, I can actually help. Now, let's go find Father."

The barbed words stung, but there was nothing to be done. There were no locomotivuses headed back to Auvinen, not for hours, and McKenna had no authority over her sister. Glancing at her husband, she saw a little smirk on his mouth, but as soon as he noticed her looking at him, it faded to that stone-faced expression again.

They wandered around the station, but as luck would have it, there was no sign of Father. The message had likely not been delivered to him yet.

Most of the cabs were taken by the time they reached the curb, but after waiting a good while, they found a driver willing to take them if they squeezed into the cramped seating normally designed for two. They paid the fare, and then the single flesh-and-blood horse stamped its feet and began to pull them away.

"So he's still not talking to you?" Clara said with a cold look toward Rob.

"Clara," McKenna warned.

"I wasn't sitting that far from you in the compartment, you know. I'm hungry. Aren't you?"

McKenna was, but the awkward feelings in the cab made her long for privacy, a chance to be alone with Rob. To start smoothing the hurt she still saw on his brow.

Thankfully the Fosters' home in Bishopsgate wasn't very far from the locomotivus station. The streets had been damaged in the bombardment, but scaffolding had been erected, indicating the process of reconstruction was well underway. New construction methods were being employed this time, enhanced by intelligences, no doubt. War, damage, reconstruction. A new song—the same dance steps.

"Here you are, as promised," said the driver as he halted his beast in front of the house. The street had a curve to it, and the buildings had been built to match it. The home was three levels high but rather narrow. McKenna and her sisters had always stayed in the upper rooms, where they could look out the windows and watch the parade of people below.

Clara climbed out first. She didn't have a valise of her own, and McKenna wondered what she was going to do about a change of clothes. Then again, she probably had several already at the house. McKenna got out next, and Rob followed. Light shone from behind the curtains inside, indicating an occupant. Hopefully Father wasn't en route to the station to search for them.

Clara led the way and tested the door handle—and found it locked. She waved her hand, casting a small spell that would respond to a family member seeking entrance and then tried it again. Dust cloths still covered the entryway furniture. Clara gazed up at the ceilings, the walls, and her eyes lit with memories of their previous visits. McKenna felt the same happy surge of the past, though it was tinged with melancholy.

And then Wickins appeared, his shirt untucked, half-unbuttoned, chest and neck gleaming with sweat. He stared at the new arrivals in absolute amazement. His look of astonishment must have matched her own, because McKenna felt equally surprised.

"Clara? Wh-What? Why are you here?" he asked, the surprise metamorphosizing into pleasure at seeing her face, even if her expression was stern.

"We came in response to Father's message. Your promotion. Why are *you* still here?"

He rubbed his forehead. "I turned it down. Actually, I resigned my commission. I no longer work for the military."

Rob set down the two valises. Another smile quirked his lips. He folded his arms again, gazing at the scene.

McKenna was confused. No . . . bewildered.

"You did *what*?" Clara demanded.

"I quit," he said. "I told Mr. Foster that my duty was to the business, to your family. I had made a promise that I'd see this through, and I won't break it. I haven't told my *own* father yet . . . that will be dreadfully disappointing to the major." He gazed over at Rob. "Good to see you, Dickemore."

Rob had a self-satisfied smile that was incredibly annoying. "I never doubted you, old friend."

Wickins grinned at the compliment, then put his hands on his hips. "So you thought I'd abandoned ship?"

Clara opened her mouth and promptly shut it again.

"Sorry for my state of undress, I wasn't expecting visitors," Wickins said. "It's hotter than a depot stove in this blasted city."

"Did our message arrive?" Clara asked, coming inside and shifting so that McKenna could see her mouth. Rob came into view as well.

Wickins shrugged. "I saw one from Mrs. Foster today. It's sitting in that dish. I haven't seen Mr. Foster in hours. He's normally not this late, but there were some problems with the registration paperwork for the exhibit. I don't know what else could be taking so long."

McKenna felt her cheeks blushing both from embarrassment and the heat.

"Have you had anything to eat?" Wickins said. "I have some oranges. And a slab of cake."

"That would be . . . lovely," Clara said, looking discomfited.

"I'll clear my things out of one of the family rooms upstairs. I can stay in the servants' quarters downstairs."

"You shouldn't have to move," Clara said. Her expression had softened considerably.

"Rob and McKenna need a room, and there's only those two upstairs. I'll be fine." He glanced down, and his eyes widened at the sight of his unbuttoned shirt, which he hastened to fix.

McKenna saw Clara turn, responding to something behind them, so she turned to look and found Father at the threshold, examining the scene with a perplexed look.

"I did send a letter to your mother that all had been resolved," he said. "But I gather from your unannounced arrival you didn't get it?"

Clara looked even more chagrined. McKenna was mortified. She shook her head.

Mr. Foster sighed. Then he noticed the envelope in the dish by the entrance. He shut and locked the door and opened the letter. Adjusting his pince-nez spectacles, he quickly read the note.

"Ah. I understand now. And I apologize I wasn't at the station waiting for you."

"You only just arrived," McKenna said. "We . . . wanted to help."

"It is appreciated. Well, Professor Hawksley, it seems we made it possible for you to attend, after all."

McKenna bit her lip, knowing that statement would rile her husband further. She felt awful. If they'd waited, news would have come by the next day that all was well. Her scheme to get Rob there had worked. But at what cost? He hadn't addressed her a single time on the locomotivus. Or in the cab. Now they were at the Bishopsgate house, and he'd come without good cause, abandoning his students and his responsibilities. Actually, he hadn't abandoned anyone, but he'd feel that way, she was sure.

Rob could have flung all of that in her face in front of her father. But that wasn't the kind of man he was. He seemed to suck on her father's words, like a piece of hard, sour candy, but he only shrugged and stooped to pick up the valises.

"I'm not hungry," he said simply. "I think I'll just go to bed."

McKenna dreaded being alone with him. But she was also worried she wouldn't be able to make things better. Best to start trying now.

"I'll show you," she mumbled.

He nodded to her, and she led the way to the back stairs and began to climb. It was a hot, sweaty trek. They'd come to Bishopsgate in the summer months on occasion, but she couldn't remember it being this hot. The stairs were dark until a will-o'-the-wisp of light appeared from behind her, summoned by Rob, and it hovered over her shoulder, lighting the way.

The simplest spell in the world.

And she couldn't cast it.

Robinson Foster Hawksley

CHAPTER NINE

The Ache of Forgotten Things

The upper room was small compared to the rooms in the house on Brake Street. There were two beds on opposite sides, both with layers of dust, and a writing table with an assortment of books stacked neatly. Some shells dangled from lengths of twine hanging from a nail in the plaster. The floorboards were scuffed, but the seams were tight and everything seemed to fit in place. He could hear voices coming from downstairs but couldn't make out the conversation, just the recognizably deeper voice of Mr. Foster, followed by responses from Clara and Wickins. McKenna had walked to one of the beds and stripped the dusty comforter from it, folding it quickly and placing it at the on the floor at the foot of the bed. Then she walked to the window and tugged on the latch, pushing it open. A gust of cooler air came in and blew some loose strands of her hair.

His heart was heavy from the tension between them. The uncomfortable ride from Auvinen, followed by the surprise at the house, had left him drained emotionally. He was still upset at what they'd done to him, how they'd corralled him in such a manner, hardly giving him a choice. He understood why they had, but it still stung. The fissure between himself and McKenna was difficult to resolve within himself. He didn't know what to say or what she could say to mend the breach. He was exhausted after the long day and just wanted to stretch out on the other bed and fall asleep and then confront the situation in the morning. Talking would be counterproductive. But he also needed her. He hadn't realized how much her little signs of affection—taking his hand, leaning against his shoulder, stroking his hair, his neck—had come to mean to him until now, when they were being withheld.

The only light in the room was from the suspended strands of magic he'd summoned. A few stray sounds streamed in from the open window, but it was difficult to tell what had caused them, except a yowling cat.

Rob sat down at the edge of the other bed, feeling sick inside. This wasn't his fault, so why did he feel in the wrong? His confidence in Wickins had not been misplaced. His friend had shown his true loyalty by refusing the promotion. That could not have been an easy decision, so Robinson was intensely proud of him. And yet he realized how effortlessly McKenna and her mother had made all the arrangements to cover for him. That stepping away from his responsibility at the university hadn't been as big a catastrophe as he'd feared it might be.

McKenna stepped away from the window and went to the other bed, where she'd set her valise. She opened the straps and then the upper portion and, back still to him, began to undress. The newness of married life had not become mundane to him, but she didn't look at him, didn't say anything. When she was in her underclothes, she pulled out her white nightdress, the one he liked, and slipped it on. Then she arranged her garments in the room, using the small, shared closet to hang her dress. There were other clothes in there too, the smaller ones probably Trudie's. After everything had been fastidiously put away, she went to her bed and sat down. She risked a glance his way.

"I thought you were tired?" she asked questioningly.

"I'm exhausted."

She looked down and then slowly glanced back up at his face under her eyelashes. The light dangled in the air between them. Her bare feet curled around each other.

He was about to say something, but voices and footfalls coming up the steps made him look at the door. McKenna gave him a confused look, and he mouthed to her, *"Wickins is coming up."*

McKenna nodded, her hands twisting together much like her feet.

It became obvious after another set of footfalls sounded that Clara had come up too. Their muffled voices could be heard next door. Robinson scratched his neck, feeling the awkwardness of the situation keenly. The awkwardness was mostly for him, however, for McKenna probably only felt a slight vibration from the floor as she unbuttoned the top buttons of her nightdress and fanned herself with her hand. The room was still dusty and stifling, but the breeze from the open window was helping alleviate it.

"Clara too," he mouthed to McKenna when she glanced at him.

Robinson felt a stab of impatience, wishing Wickins would be on his way, but the two talked outside the other room for a while, their voices low and unintelligible, until they took the chat to the nook at the top of the stairs, where they were easily audible to him.

"I think they're asleep already," Wickins chuckled softly.

"It *is* late. I guess we should go to bed too." Clara's voice sounded disappointed.

"I'm glad you came, Clara, but you'll regret it. The exhibition building is made of glass. It's literally as hot as an oven. The curtains barely help. I don't think you'll last a day before you want to go back home."

"You think I'm frail, Mr. Wickins?"

"You're the strongest woman I know."

"And you don't regret I came?"

"I would never regret that. I wish I'd insisted you come. I was a little dismayed by your father's fastidiousness, if truth be told."

"Don't be. I just wanted to thank you again. For all you've done for my family. For Rob."

He thought he heard a kiss. A chaste one, on the cheek. He shook his head, wishing he were back in Auvinen with McKenna and none of this estrangement had happened.

Things were silent. Except for the subtle sounds of kissing from the hall.

"Good night, Mr. Wickins," Clara said in a sly voice.

"Good night, Miss Clara," Wickins said. Then the heavy sound of his footfalls retreated back down the stairs. Clara went back into the adjacent room and shut the door.

He couldn't help but smile at what he'd overheard. McKenna had continued to look down during their conversation but looked up when she felt the vibration from the other door shutting.

"Were they kissing?" McKenna whispered.

Robinson nodded. He mouthed to her, *"Do you want to talk?"*

She shook her head. "Let's get some rest. We can talk in the morning."

Disappointment stung him, but he agreed it was sensible. Talking while they were worked up and upset was probably not the right thing to do. She climbed under a single sheet, turned her back to him, and nestled her head on the pillow. He canceled the will-o'-the-wisp of light, and the room was plunged into darkness, save a sheath of light coming in through the window.

Robinson lay down on the comforter, still in his clothes, hands crossed over his chest. Turmoil chased around inside him. He was lying down on Trudie's bed in McKenna's room in the Fosters' home in Bishopsgate. It was such a contrast to what he'd expected when walking home from the university that afternoon.

He worried it would be difficult for him to fall asleep, but exhaustion took its toll. He closed his eyes, listening to the sounds and trying to understand them, and then he passed out.

※

He startled awake to the commotion of McKenna shrieking.

His heart was in his throat as he leaped from the bed. Confused, disoriented, he didn't understand what was happening.

"Hoxta-namorem," he blabbered, summoning light again. McKenna was sitting up in her bed, fists pressed against her chin, her eyes wild with terror. There was nothing obvious happening to her, but he rushed to her bedside. She shoved at him as if he were a monster to be challenged. Her eyes darted one way and then another, looking around in confusion and sheer terror.

"Blood, blood!" she wailed. "So much blood! Don't go! Don't go! Don't leave me!"

Robinson wrapped his arms around her forcefully. She tried to escape. She was delirious.

Clara rattled the handle and then rushed inside in her nightdress, bringing another set of glowing strands with her. She hurried to McKenna's bed.

McKenna gazed at her sister in confusion, as if she didn't recognize her. "Don't let him die! Don't let him die! So much blood."

Clara looked at Rob with unsettled eyes.

"I don't know what's happening. She just started screaming," he said. Again McKenna tried to push away from him, but then she fell limp and started sobbing into his shoulder. She sobbed pitifully, as if someone she loved dearly had just died. It wrung his heart to hear it. Dreams were powerful. Nightmares even more so. But he'd never experienced anything to this magnitude personally, nor had he seen her do so since their wedding.

Clara whispered soothingly, rubbing McKenna's shoulder. "It's all right, McKenna. You're safe. You're with us. *Shhhh.* It's all right."

More footsteps came from the stairs. Mr. Foster, hair askew, charged into the bedroom, adding another glowing sphere to the illumination.

"What is it?" he demanded, wearing a long nightshirt and slippers. He wasn't wearing his spectacles, which only added to the strangeness of the moment.

"Night terrors," Clara said. "That's all."

Wickins entered behind Mr. Foster, a pistol in his fist.

McKenna was sobbing still, clutching Robinson instead of trying to push him away.

Mr. Foster sighed. "That was . . . terrifying."

"She's not herself sometimes," Clara said. "But then it passes. This will pass too."

"I thought someone had come to murder us," Wickins said, lowering the weapon.

Clara's top buttons were undone, exposing more than she'd realized until that moment, and she clutched the edges of her nightdress together with one hand. "All will be well. We should go back to bed."

Robinson's own heart rate was starting to calm down. "This reminds me," he said, "that we don't have warnings at this house. I'll set some bulbs up in the morning."

"Precautions are always a good idea," Mr. Foster said. He looked anxiously at his whimpering daughter. But there was nothing more he could do. He walked out of the room and went back downstairs.

Wickins lingered in the doorway, looking worriedly at them. "I can stand watch until morning, if you'd like."

Robinson shook his head. "We'll be all right. Thank you for coming so quickly."

Wickins massaged his stomach, where the bullet had torn through him weeks before. "Least I could do, old chap." He gave Clara a tender look, a nod, then departed.

Clara stroked McKenna's arm. Then, after the fit subsided, McKenna lifted her chin and gazed at them.

"What's wrong? What's the matter?" she asked in confusion.

"You had a night terror again," Clara said. "Woke up the whole house."

"I did?"

"I didn't know she had them," Robinson said. "Have they happened her whole life?"

"No, they're recent," Clara said. "They started after she nearly drowned."

McKenna rubbed her eyes, then looked at her hands in surprise, probably at the tears she'd felt there. "I'm sorry for waking everyone."

Robinson rubbed her shoulder. "What were you dreaming about?"

McKenna looked at him blankly. "I wasn't dreaming."

"You were, dearest," Clara said. She had a soothing voice now, similar to their mother's. Glancing at Robinson, she rose from the bed and said, "Do you always sleep in your clothes?"

He'd fallen asleep in them. The reason why came pressing down on him, adding to the weight of the moment. He didn't feel like answering her, so he did not.

Clara rose from the bed and bid them good night. She left, shutting the door. The only light left was the one Robinson had summoned, spinning between him and McKenna.

"I'm embarrassed," she confessed, gazing at him.

"Why didn't you tell me about the night terrors?"

"This is the first time it has happened since our marriage."

"And they started after you nearly drowned?"

"I don't want to talk about them," she said, lowering her lashes.

He felt she was pushing him away again. Desperate to avoid putting more space between them, he lifted her chin, and she gazed at him. She looked lonely, afraid. It made his heart ache even more.

"You cried about blood. So much blood. About losing someone. You don't remember?"

A glimmer of recognition came into her eyes. There was a subtle shift in her mood. A look on her face he didn't recognize. She moistened her lips with her tongue. He thought she was on the verge of telling him something, something important, and his heart thumped in anticipation.

"I'd like to get back to sleep. I'm very tired."

CHAPTER TEN

Fools in Charge

It was not a restful night. Robinson was still awake when the full force of the sun shone through the window. His mind, his heart—his entire life, it seemed—was in turmoil. The noises coming from outside grew louder and louder, with gruff voices scolding truculent beasts of burden, the whistles from the locomotivus station announcing new arrivals and departures. Soon the clamor began to overwhelm his senses, so he slipped from the bed and shut the window to blot out the disruptive sounds.

In the morning light, he saw McKenna still fast asleep, one hand on the mattress where he'd slept the rest of the night—her hand clinging to him like a safety rope. He was perplexed by what had happened. And worried. He still didn't want to be in Bishopsgate, practically against his will. But his concerns for McKenna overrode the resentment of the way she'd brought him here. What was the cause of the night terrors? Of her affection for cold mist on her face? Had all these peculiar happenings begun after she'd nearly drowned? A nagging worry was growing in his chest, but he pressed it down.

Sitting down on the edge of her bed, he smoothed some hair from her brow. He ached to reconcile with her, to alleviate the weight of the previous day's events.

Her eyes opened as his hand retreated from her brow. She blinked, gave a confused look, then seemed to recognize where she was as she sat up. Her shoulder slipped loose of the nightgown, causing a deep throb inside him.

"How did you sleep?" she asked, stifling a yawn.

He gave her a perplexed look. "Not very well. I haven't fallen back to sleep since you woke up screaming."

"*What?*"

Surely she wouldn't have forgotten that. "You don't remember?"

"I think I'd remember if I woke up screaming."

"You woke the entire house up. Clara came rushing in. So did your father. Wickins brought a pistol. He thought we were being murdered."

She lifted a knuckle to her lips. "You're joking."

"I wouldn't." He touched her forehead with the back of his hand. "Not about something like that."

She sat up, gazing at the room. "I don't remember any of it."

"You were dreaming. About blood."

Her lips puckered, but there was no look of remembrance in her eyes. "I don't remember my dreams anymore. The last thing I remember was lying here, and you were in Trudie's bed, and then I fell asleep. Regretting."

"That we came to Bishopsgate?" he nudged.

She shook her head, which stung his feelings. "I don't regret coming. I didn't know about Wickins's choice at the time, but it still feels like it was the right thing to do."

"But why didn't you tell me? We could have discussed it. Instead, I felt like a captive on a pirate ship."

"Now you *are* joking. I didn't force you to get on the locomotivus."

"It felt like it," Robinson said, his temper starting to bubble. "Was I supposed to stay in the carriage with your mother? With your sister?"

"No," she said, looking defensive and tired.

"Coercion is repulsive to the Unseen Powers," he said. "Intelligences must be coaxed. Even the intelligence of an oyster must be persuaded to polish ball bearings. Would you expect a human being to desire anything less than absolute freedom of choice?"

She closed her eyes, her mood shifting to annoyance. "There wasn't *time*, Rob."

He waited until she opened her eyes again. "There was, McKenna. We could have taken a locomotivus this morning. We could have *talked* about it. And if we'd waited, more information would have arrived." He wanted her to see she was in the wrong. She'd accused him of being stubborn, but acknowledging her own fault seemed to be beyond her at the moment. It disappointed him.

He heard a knock on the door downstairs, followed by the sound of footfalls.

"What is it?" McKenna asked, studying his face.

"Someone knocked on the front door."

The next noise was the sound of footsteps rushing up the stairs. Followed immediately by loud knocking on their bedroom door. When Rob rose to go to the door, McKenna adjusted her nightgown for modesty. It was Wickins, looking panicked.

"Good. You're dressed. We have to get to the exhibition. Now!"

"What's going on?" Robinson asked worriedly.

"An employee at the exhibition said they're moving our display. By order of the committee. Dickemore, we have to go!"

What sort of business was this? Rearranging displays the day before the Great Exhibition started? That seemed rather underhanded. Actually, it seemed *very* underhanded behavior given that the Great Exhibition was a showcase for sorcerers who were part of the Invisible College. Strict integrity was supposed to be paramount. The breach of agreements could lead to a loss of confidence from the intelligences, which might then impact their willingness to share their power.

"I'll be right down," he said emphatically.

After shutting the door, he turned to tell McKenna what had happened. And in that instant he realized that if they hadn't left for Bishopsgate the day before, there wouldn't have been time to get a message down in time. She couldn't have known, but McKenna's foresight in leaving straightaway had provided them with a necessary buffer.

In a word, she had been right. He felt a clenching in his chest—an unwillingness to admit to what he knew to be true. The very emotion he'd believed she had been suppressing this morning. Oh, the irony! The irony!

"Something is wrong at the exhibition," McKenna surmised.

"It seems so," he said. "I have to go. I won't have time to set up the warning bulbs."

"I'll be safe for one day without them. Hurry. I'll come later with Clara."

He should apologize. The need to do so writhed within him. But admitting he was wrong was the last thing he felt like doing at the moment. He curbed the thought while he hurriedly put on his shoes and wrestled his arms into the sleeves of his jacket. He felt the perspiration already starting to itch across his back. With the window closed, the room was already stifling. He pressed a kiss to the top of McKenna's head.

"See you at the exhibit," he said and rushed downstairs.

But the feeling that he'd done wrong persisted.

"I don't understand why it was moved," Wickins complained to the official with a glossy badge on his lapel. The murmur of voices spilling from the different display aisles rumbled dissonantly in Robinson's ears.

"There was a late arrival who needed to be accommodated, sir," the man responded tersely. "I apologize for the inconvenience, but it had to be done."

"Who gave the order?" Robinson asked.

"It came from someone in authority. That is all. You'll have to rearrange your display today. I'm sorry, but there's nothing more I can do."

"This is outrageous," Wickins said darkly.

"Sir, there are over three thousand exhibits on display, and the judges need to visit each one. I suggest you spend less time complaining about your perceived misfortune and begin reassembling your display in its appropriate stall. Good day!" He was a short-tempered little man and clearly was in no mood to listen to their complaints.

"Where have we been moved to?" Wickins asked one of the workers who had come from the manufacturing company in Auvinen, their partner who produced the quicksilver lamps that had been specially modified for their use.

The man looked surly. "Upstairs. Top floor. Farthest end. Do you know how hot it is up there, Lieutenant?"

"Nothing to be done about it," Robinson said with a sigh. "Let's start carrying the crates."

"You're going to help?" the worker said, looking less peevish at the suggestion. Robinson realized that Wickins had probably not done any of the lifting previously.

"Of course we will," Wickins said, shooting the man a warning look. "Come on, get to it."

There was only one Genowen Flying Chair in the entire exhibition hall. Naturally, there was a long wait to use it. This required two men to haul each crate up the steps and then down the hall. It wasn't easy work, but Robinson expected this was just another obstacle intended to put them off the main path of exhibits and limit the crowds who might see his invention. He gritted his teeth and kept moving despite the heat.

He'd been warned that Exhibition Hall was made of glass and ironworks, which acted as magnifying glasses for the sun. A huge central corridor made of a semicircular chasm spread from one end of the hall to the other, and there were three different levels pyramid-stacked atop each other. The structure had been erected decades earlier to begin showcasing the inventions made by sorcerers and manufacturers working in partnership to improve society. Some of the glass had been damaged by the Aesir bombardment, but it was one of the first buildings to have been repaired.

In the past, the transparent walls and roof had often proven a bonus, because they'd required little internal lighting. But now, with the blistering summer already at hand, the structure had become devastatingly hot. Up and down the stairs they climbed, passing other men and women assembling their wares for all to see. Over three thousand displays? Robinson didn't doubt it. He found it hard to avoid getting sucked into the other displays. A small music box enchanted by crickets to play a Shopenhauer arrangement. The steam laundry press for pressing shirts and skirts also struck him as ingenious—powered by the intelligence of a lizard, strangely enough. One invention rather horrified him—a clay jar for cookies protected by a wasp intelligence to sting the hand of little trespassers.

Hours had passed by the time they'd gotten all the crates upstairs and the team had begun assembling the tubes into the brackets once more. The display technique wasn't complex. The tubes were fixed with thin strands of Aesir gold, which would activate the light in the presence of Aesir magic. If the visitor of the booth did not have any artifacts of magic with them, then Wickins was to use the special tuning fork set to the frequency the magic used.

Rob mopped sweat from his brow with a handkerchief. His whole body was dripping with it, and it wasn't even afternoon yet. They anticipated most of the visitors would choose to come in the mornings, but the booth would need to be staffed all day.

He noticed a worker handling one of the quicksilver tubes with a furrowed brow, and then the man brought it to Robinson.

"This one is missing the white gold strand. Looks like it was pried off."

Robinson gaped in surprise. The fellow was right. The tube was missing the exact piece that would make it work. The special alloy had to be precise.

"This one is too," said another worker, wagging a tube in the air.

Wickins turned around, his expression turning to one of horror. He began to look feverishly through all the crates. One by one, each of the tubes was discovered to be missing the critical piece. This was no accident. This was deliberate sabotage. Such interference was truly shocking.

Wickins came up to Robinson, his look frantic. He rubbed his mouth and muttered under his breath, "What do we do, old chap? It starts tomorrow!"

Mr. Foster would be bringing investors to the display. Investors who would make or break the business. If they showed up with no demonstration of the magic, McKenna's father would be in disgrace. Trust might be damaged . . . irrevocably.

"Keep setting them up," Robinson said. "I need to find the missing pieces."

He remembered finding a coin in the street the previous winter. The dog intelligence from Covesea had helped him discover the owners: the widow and her children in the tenements. Surely there were other biddable intelligences in the vicinity who could help him now.

He closed his eyes, thinking about his need to find that which had been lost. Again, it struck him that the situation would have been hopeless if he hadn't come the previous night. In fact, it was possible the crew might not have discovered the missing pieces until it was too late to do anything about it.

I need help, he thought, trying to summon an intelligence. If he could be led to the missing gold, they could still affix it to the glass tubes in time. It was a lot of work, and it would only get hotter and hotter, but they had to try.

No answer came.

Were all the intelligences being used at the moment? Was one of the displays blocking his access to the Unseen Powers?

Only . . . maybe his own thoughts and feelings were blocking them? His stubbornness and pride.

He hadn't apologized to McKenna. He still harbored some resentment that she'd been right to corner him into coming. He had tried his whole life to live in tune with the magic of the Unseen Powers. But he'd failed this day, and he knew better than most that a mortal's thoughts could interfere with their ability to harness the magic. It was one of the immutable laws of the universe.

If that was the problem, then he needed McKenna to solve it.

He withdrew his device and quickly adjusted the combination to the proper digits. Pulling out the ring, he slipped it onto his thumb.

Clara, this is Robinson. Bring McKenna to the exhibit. Bring her right now.

But would it work? Would she even hear his thoughts?

Intention matters. The Unseen Powers consistently invite us to harness their ways. They do compel, it is true, but only as an extension of natural law. If I step off a cliff, I cannot reason away the consequences of the fall. The Mind of the Sovereignty has put all things in order. For the willing, Destiny guides them. For the unwilling, Destiny drags them.

—Isaac Berrow,
Master of the Royal Secret,
the Invisible College

General Colsterworth

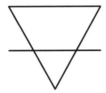

CHAPTER ELEVEN

DEEDS MOST FOUL

The intolerable heat had already sent three men to the medic wing of Gresham College. Formality had been dispensed with, and the soldiers had all doffed their uniform jackets, opened their collars, and rolled their sleeves to the elbow. General Colsterworth mopped the sweat from his brow, wrestling with the indignity of physical discomfort as well as the heightened stress caused by evidence that enemies had infiltrated the Invisible College.

He spoke the words cautiously. "Say it once more. Slowly."

Colonel Brakebrush's long mustache with waxed tips quivered as he controlled himself and his words. "It turns out the executioners were the ones executed, General, not the *strannik*'s followers. I had the bodies exhumed last night from the grave pit. *Ghastly* business. But it was them. I had bunkmates confirm their identities and personal effects. The officer in charge of the coroner's quorum said the state of decay was consistent with the elapsed time, although the bodies had been seen prior to this revelation and identified as the culprits."

General Colsterworth squinted. "They were Semblances, Brakebrush?"

"No. This isn't the work of Semblances. I believe it was a glamour spell cast by a formidable sorcerer."

"Are you suggesting the *strannik* cast this spell?"

"I see no other alternative that explains his escape, the murdered soldiers, and the two who hung themselves."

"But the shackles!"

"Sir, we likely have underestimated his power. The *strannik* must have achieved a higher rank within the Invisible College than we first believed. He could have pretended to be incapacitated by the shackles. Such a man would also be able to wander within Gresham College undetected."

Colsterworth felt a new kind of sweat dripping down his back. Dread suffused him. "Is he still here?"

"There's no way of knowing. After what happened with those bodies, he could look like anyone."

"Confound it, how did he learn how to glamour?" Colsterworth bellowed as he hammered his clenched fist on the table. He recalled how sanguine the *strannik* had been when his followers had been executed in the courtyard. If what Brakebrush said was true, he'd used his magic to switch the positions of the men. He'd cared little because he'd been watching his men murder their would-be killers.

Glamour spells were incredibly potent, capable of deceiving the senses completely without the proper counterspells. In days of old, the Aesir had used them to trick mortals into eating spoiled fruit and noxious meat, believing the fare to be a sumptuous banquet.

"I don't know, sir. But clearly it was someone elevated within the Invisible College. That knowledge is not shared until the higher degrees."

Colsterworth bristled at the idea of a traitor within their ranks. He needed to report this intelligence to Drusselmehr. Many from the royal court were returning to Bishopsgate for the Great Exhibition. Perhaps the Master of the Royal Secret would have ideas on who the traitor would be.

"Send my condolences to the parents of the dead soldiers," Colsterworth growled. "Proclaim they died in an unfortunate accident. Quicksilver poisoning or the like. Tell them their bodies are too toxic to look at. They'll be buried with high honors." He gazed at Colonel Brakebrush darkly. "We need to find that *strannik*. This time, to put a bullet in his head without delay."

"Yes, sir."

"Send in Major Columbay on your way out."

A formal salute was returned, and then Colsterworth was left alone, brooding at the shift of events. He'd been duped. When the *strannik* had been captured, he'd shown some fortitude and power, but they'd all believed it was bluster. Who had taught him such a powerful spell? Who would betray the order in such a heinous way?

It was a disturbing thought. Even more disturbing? The *strannik* might have other powers they were not yet aware of. Had he known the men approaching his cell were there to kill him? Was that why he'd used magic to persuade them to hang themselves? It was said an Aesir, when targeting a mortal, could make them so heavy with melancholy they were unable to function. Such powerful magic. Such a hated enemy . . .

A knock sounded at the door.

"Enter."

It was Major Columbay with his normally spiked hair wilted in the heat. The pomade he usually lavishly applied had likely all melted. He had a stiff-brush mustache and a youthful look for a man in his thirties.

"Yes, sir!"

Colsterworth glared at him. "I'm supposed to visit the exhibition this evening before it opens to the public. Give me a report on the Hawksley exhibit."

"Ah, well . . . there are problems, sir."

"Of course. I told you to *make* problems for it, Columbay."

"I know, sir, but some unexpected events have—"

"What are you talking about?" Colsterworth interrupted. "Speak up, man!"

"Professor Hawksley arrived overnight. He was spotted at the locomotivus station with his wife, and they retired to the Foster home here in town."

Another chill speared through the general's breast. "Impossible."

"Unlikely, rather, sir. And he discovered the tampering with the lamps."

Another closed fist. Another burst of anger taken out on the helpless table. Colsterworth rose to his full height, his lips quivering with rage. "Confound it, Columbay, this isn't just a problem, it's an unmitigated disaster!"

The major, who was already sweating profusely, wilted under the rebuke. By now he probably sensed Colsterworth preferred to operate in secret. Usually ploys such as this one could be executed in a way that left no whiff of suspicion. Boxes misplaced. Last-minute changes. Such things could happen to anyone, and blaming bureaucratic ineptitude while offering apologetic platitudes tended to satisfy even the most disgruntled. But Mr. Foster was canny and wise, and he would launch an investigation. And Hawksley . . . he was a man with the highest scruples. He'd demand a reckoning. The military had already ordered sizable quantities of the new bulbs for deployment to the network of ice trenches.

The patent conflict hadn't even come to light yet, and they certainly couldn't wait. Still, he knew the legal consequences would be devastating once the case made it to court.

Major Columbay was quivering with fear, watching his career tick away with each second that passed.

"You can still redeem yourself, Columbay," General Colsterworth said with a fierce look. "Do you understand me?"

The major gulped and nodded vigorously.

"I want you to compromise Professor Hawksley's credibility. I want you to sully his reputation as the original inventor of the tubes. We should spread the rumor that he and Miss Cowing collaborated in some way and he's stolen her idea. It may even be true."

The major's eyes widened with shock. "There is no evidence the two of them have ever met. No dinner parties. No meetings at either of their quorums. It would be impossible to prove."

"Don't be an ignorant fool, Columbay. I don't need to prove it. We just have to get her and the professor alone together to imply they've met previously. Forge a letter from him to her, asking for a meeting at the Fosters' home in Bishopsgate. Have one of our people discover them together to witness their meeting. Should help us learn the shape of things. And, if not, we can still use it as evidence that he had foreknowledge of her invention."

"Sir, a forgery? Isn't that rather . . ."

Colsterworth frowned, shooting the junior officer a penetrating glare that quickly silenced him. This was part of the war effort. The military had a long tradition of using deception and decoy to achieve strategic aims. That was a practical requirement to get so many portions of the empire to act as one body against a highly intelligent enemy. Of course, it was also a justification. He'd given up more altruistic motives long ago. A general couldn't afford to be sentimental.

"Yes, sir," the major said weakly. He raised his hand in salute.

"Have the prudence to remove Mrs. Hawksley from the situation, Major. She should be under the military's protection. And, as I understand the circumstances, she controls the rights to Hawksley's shares. Inform her father that a dangerous criminal is on the loose. One that had a hand in her abduction in Tanhauser. I want her brought in for protective custody."

"Very well, sir. If you say so, sir."

The sniveling was getting annoying. "You're dismissed. When I go to the exhibition, I want Hawksley's exhibit to be in disarray. Be subtle but thorough."

"As you wish, sir." He bowed and left the room.

Colsterworth mopped more sweat from his face. There'd been a time, long ago, when such dealings would have made him squeamish. The more he had risen in the ranks of the Invisible College, though, the more he'd started to see the hypocrisy there. It was all a convoluted display of posturing virtues in public while, secretly, there was loathing and despair at the top. It hadn't always been that way, but the general wasn't the only clever man who'd decided to rearrange the rules to preserve his grip on power.

Elizabeth Cowing was an absolutely brilliant inventor. She'd risen fast in the ranks of the Invisible College due to her abilities, charm, and penchant for making strong alliances with older men. Men older than Hawksley. She would not want to miss out on the revenues from her own invention, and if she believed Hawksley had taken advantage of her, it would infuriate her.

How had both of the sorcerers come upon similar ideas around the same time? Just because there was no proof they'd met didn't mean they hadn't.

It had been Isaac Berrow's suggestion that women should be treated equally to men. That they deserved the same advantages and rewards. In his day, that had been seen as a shocking attitude. But women had proven to be capable, astute, and beneficial to Society. They'd even begun to fashion their own rules to ensure their success in spheres that had not been traditionally open to them.

But they were not, by nature, as ruthless as men.

As capable of deeds most foul.

The Iskandir have the first recorded instances of meeting the Aesir and discovering remnants of their magical fortresses. There must have been a time in the past, beyond memory, when a great glacier covered our empire. It began to withdraw, first by inches and then yards, revealing the splendor of all that the Aesir had achieved. The Iskandir worshipped these beings at first, offering tributes of fire. But flame was rejected in any of its forms. The Aesir crave not heat but ice.

—Isaac Berrow,
Master of the Royal Secret,
the Invisible College

MaKenna Aurora Hawksley

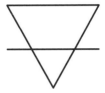

CHAPTER TWELVE

A STRANGER'S EYES

As the day progressed, the heat became more and more intolerable. McKenna felt dizzy, and not even a favorite book from the small family library could hold her attention for long. She sipped cool water, but what she really craved was to go to the locomotivus yard and stand in the plumes of coolant fog. In fact, as she became more and more delirious, she began to fantasize about it. The family home was beginning to feel like a prison. One she needed to escape.

She didn't understand what was happening to her. It had been mortifying to learn she'd awakened the family with her screams. Truly, she couldn't remember doing it, but there was something nagging in the back of her mind, a reason why she couldn't remember. Why she *shouldn't* remember.

"Shall we go for a walk?" Clara suggested, fanning herself. "Even with the curtains closed, it's still too stuffy in here."

McKenna nodded in agreement. They grabbed two parasols and left the house. Father was visiting with some bankers again, but he'd said he would be going to the exhibition that afternoon, despite the blistering temperature. As soon as they were outside, McKenna nearly swooned and had to grip Clara's arm to steady herself.

"Steady there," her sister said, concern wrinkling her brow.

"I'm sorry," McKenna stammered. Her tongue felt swollen. "Can we . . . can we go by the locomotivus station?"

"What for?"

"I need to . . . to cool down."

Clara locked arms with her, and the two sisters walked briskly. Thankfully, a segment of the station was near the house, not the one they'd arrived in last night, but another part of the branch line to the south.

"You've been acting so strange of late," Clara said after tugging on her arm to get her attention. Not in a mean-spirited way, for her eyebrows were wrinkled in concern.

McKenna knew the intention of the probing question, but she didn't want to talk about what she'd been experiencing, least of all with the sister who'd seemed to relish teasing her prior to her marriage.

"It's the heat, I'm sure," McKenna answered. "And you've been acting strange yourself."

"How so?"

"You haven't teased me since Rob and I got back from Tanhauser. I was certain you would."

A chagrined look came on Clara's face. "You've missed it, then?"

"The teasing? Not really."

Clara pursed her lips, looking down for a moment, then glanced up at her and said, "I'm sorry, McKenna. I should have apologized sooner. I was impatient to enter Society, and I guess I felt resentful that I had to wait for you." She shook her head regretfully. "It wasn't fair of me. I should have been a better sister."

McKenna was surprised by the confession—and Clara's show of maturity.

"What happened to me, the fever. I didn't realize how it must have impacted you."

Clara shrugged. "But you're married, and now that all the supposed obstacles are out of my way, I understand how poorly I was acting. I'm sorry for it. I'll try to be better."

"You're my sister, and I'll always adore you," McKenna said, nudging Clara's arm, grinning at her.

The station was thronged with people, which only contributed to McKenna's disorientation, but they persisted and maneuvered through the crowd until they were closer to one of the giant machines. This particular outbound locomotivus to Auvinen had fewer passengers, as most people were trying to come to Bishopsgate for the Great Exhibition.

The locomotivus heaved a heavy sigh, and a gust of fog-chilled air came hissing out. McKenna closed her eyes, enjoying the cool mist on her face, her neck, her hands. It was a blessed relief. With the cold, her thoughts became sharper. In that clarity, she had a sudden premonition of danger.

If she stayed in Bishopsgate during the heat wave, she would die. She already felt she had a raging fever, and it was only going to get worse. Her body needed a more temperate climate. This realization struck her forcefully and with a certainty that defied simple logic. Most people didn't just die of heat. It was uncomfortable, yes. It made one miserable. But for her, in her current situation, it would be deadly.

As the cool jets of air faded away and the locomotivus began to shudder under the forces that caused it to levitate above the tracks, she saw someone standing in the fog. A man with unkempt hair, a frazzled beard, and keenly penetrating eyes that were looking directly at her. Her mouth, already dry, became parched tenfold more. Her throat constricted in some sort of visceral recognition of warning. He was standing two dozen paces from them, hands clasped in front of himself, wearing a curious and bland coat that was long and frayed at the edges. A foreign look, not someone from this city. He began to walk toward her.

"Do you see that man?" McKenna asked Clara.

"What man?"

"The strange one, with the beard. Coming toward us."

Clara gazed around, looking confused. "You mean that fellow with the mustache?" She pointed to a different person.

McKenna turned and started walking forcefully away, unhooking her arm from her sister's, following the length of the car away from the intruder. She glanced back at him. He'd increased his speed too, with a gait intended to overtake them.

"Who are you talking about?" Clara asked.

"He has a beard and wild hair. Looks like he's from the countryside."

"Who?" Clara demanded at her side, gazing around as she struggled to keep up. How could she not see him? He stood out rather starkly.

Fear gripped her. Fear warned her. She had to get away. She had to get away *now*.

There were only a few people left around them, since the passengers who'd been waiting had already boarded. The locomotivus began to accelerate down the tracks, rushing toward the brick tunnel at the head of the yard, heading southbound.

"He's right there!" McKenna gasped. She gazed around, looking for a place to flee to. There were a few uniformed men, employees of the line, milling about and talking to one another.

"You mean . . . us? . . . doesn't have a beard . . ."

She didn't catch all that Clara had said but realized they were not seeing the same thing. Rob had told her about magical glamours that could deceive the senses. Like the one used by the person who'd tried abducting her in Tanhauser. Maybe that magic did not work on her because she was deaf. But it was working on Clara.

Her sister suddenly stopped walking, her fingers going to her temple. "Rob just spoke to me," she said. "We need to go to Exhibition Hall. Right now!"

Another throb of warning. She knew the glass palace used for the Great Exhibition would be a deathtrap to her. It was unthinkable. She couldn't go there. Not that night. Not ever. She looked at the advancing end of the locomotivus with the worker holding a lamp on the small platform. It was called the caboose, and it had a vertical iron rail, similar to the ones used on the street trams.

"I can't," McKenna said, shaking her head. When she looked back, she saw the intruder was advancing faster now, his eyes boring into hers with a look of single-minded determination and warning.

"McKenna, please. Just listen to me. We have to go. It's very urgent."

"Tell Rob I'm sorry. But he needs to stay until the exhibition is finished. He must, no matter what. I'll explain everything in a letter. I'm sorry!"

"Sorry for what?"

Putting distance between herself and the intruder was her foremost goal. From his relentless stare, she believed that he was only interested in her. The end of the locomotivus came, and McKenna jumped out and grabbed the pole as it passed by. She felt the momentum swing her around it before she collided with the back railing of the caboose. The worker holding the lantern gaped in astonishment and grabbed her bodice to keep her from falling off the moving locomotivus.

Her mind shrieked with the thrill and audacity of what she'd just done. Actually, it had been fun. Like in olden times when she'd . . . she'd . . .

Her memory blurred.

The worker wrapped his other arm around her and hauled her over the rail to the platform he was standing on. McKenna gazed at Clara and the stranger as they faded away. Relief flooded her. The strange-looking fellow stood at the edge of the tracks, gazing at her, and then darkness swallowed her as the locomotivus entered the tunnel. It was cool in the tunnel. Just for a moment, and then the oppressive heat began to pummel her again.

The worker wrestled with the door handle and shoved it open before pushing her into the rear of the compartment. She was still stunned by what she'd done. But giddy too. It was adventurous, like something a heroine in a novel would do, and also incredibly reckless.

If she'd failed at the jump, she'd have ended up on the tracks. Maybe twisted an ankle. Still, she didn't regret the risk she'd taken.

Her intuition told her that staying would have been fatal.

How was she going to explain this to Rob? To Father?

She'd cross that bridge later.

The worker jerked on her shoulder, turning her to face him. "I said, 'What in the blue blazes were you doing, miss?' Answer me! You can't just jump on a moving locomotivus like that! Were you trying to kill yourself?"

"I'm . . . I'm sorry," McKenna said, shaking her head. "I'm deaf. I couldn't hear you."

"You're deaf?"

"Someone was trying to hurt me. I had to get away. I need help. Please . . . can you help me?"

He was rendered speechless by her announcement. The locomotivus was still accelerating, but her pulse was slowing down. He took her to a nearby passenger bench. Only eight people were seated in the entire compartment, so there was plenty of room.

"Wait . . . here," he said slowly, deliberately, palms extending toward her before they motioned toward the bench.

"I can read lips very well," she said. "I just can't understand you if I can't see your mouth."

That thought seemed even more bewildering to him. "Just . . . sit down. I need to get my supervisor so I can explain this mess."

"Agreed. I can pay the fare. I have money. It was an emergency. Please believe me."

After sitting down and catching her breath, she noticed the other passengers were all giving her surreptitious looks. That word felt like *syrup* to her, sweet and delicious, although in this situation it meant she'd done something scandalous.

After several minutes of tapping her fingers on the bench, she saw the fellow who'd helped her returning with another uniformed man.

"I'm Mr. Abdon Shawcroft, Miss . . . ?" the newcomer asked with an inquiring lift to his eyebrows.

"I'm Mrs. Hawksley," McKenna said.

He frowned suspiciously. "Missus? And you're . . . deaf?"

"I am on both counts," she said. "I'm sorry for the intrusion, Mr. Shawcroft, but I was being harassed at the station yard. There was a man there who threatened me."

The supervisor looked at the one who'd pulled her on board. "Did you see him?"

"No, sir. She was with another young lady, and they were being approached by one of our people."

Ah, she hadn't counted on that. The glamour had hidden her would-be assailant.

"I'll gladly pay the fare," McKenna said. "I was in a difficult situation. Please believe me."

The supervisor shook his head, his frown one of disapproval. "How old are you, miss? You look about my daughter's age."

"I don't think she's really deaf," the other fellow whispered to his supervisor. Maybe he'd done it in a stage whisper to rattle her. But the volume didn't matter to her, only that he hadn't covered his lips.

McKenna swallowed. She was going to be in trouble after all.

Great intelligences have always encountered violent opposition from mediocre ones. Any weighty discovery I have made has always come on the heels of immense opposition. I conclude the same thing is to be understood of all celestial bodies revolving in any orbits. All inanimate matter endeavors to recede from the centers of their orbits and, were it not for the opposition of a contrary force that restrains them and detains them in these orbits, they would fly off course with a uniform motion. Do not fight the tether of the Unseen Powers when opposition arrives. Learn instead to harness it.

—Isaac Berrow,
Master of the Royal Secret,
the Invisible College

Robinson Foster Hawksley

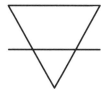

CHAPTER THIRTEEN

Flashpoint

Sweat itched on Robinson's scalp. It dripped down his ribs. The insufferable heat of Exhibition Hall made him yearn to flee the building and put all this nonsense behind him. He walked randomly near the entrance, hoping that McKenna would come so he could apologize to her. The critical pieces of his experiments were missing, and without them, there was no way his demonstration could continue. Why on earth had the Industry of Magic chosen summer to showcase their most promising inventions in a building framed of glass? It was ludicrous, and he saw he wasn't the only one suffering. The disgruntled looks from so many, men and women alike, underscored the insanity of the operation. He witnessed the raw agitation, overheard the bickering between sorcerers trying to ensure their various apparatuses would work under such conditions.

He had already witnessed one demonstration burst into flame. He could tell, by the smell, that the sorcerer had used a particular resin that was volatile and had a fairly benign flashpoint. The ambient heat in the show hall and a spark had caused it to combust. All the man's efforts had been wasted. There would be nothing to showcase anymore.

Why was nothing being done to address the problem? Clearly there were inventions capable of reducing the impact of the summer heat. Locomotivus engines, for example, could expel plumes of chilled fog. Was it considered too expensive to cool the hall? Surely there were other inventions that could be employed.

He craned his neck, seeing a woman enter who vaguely resembled his wife—but it wasn't McKenna.

Robinson rubbed his sweaty temples, his insides knotting with frustration. Time was running out. That was probably the purpose of this intervention, to destroy his chances of being recognized for his invention. Why was it that inferior minds felt threatened by new ideas? Why initiate obstacles to try to stall advances?

He sighed and pushed up his sleeves. McKenna would come or she would not. Maybe something had delayed her. Maybe he could figure out another way to find the missing parts.

He slowed his breathing and focused on the sensation of the sweat trickling down his body. Agitation was anathema to connecting with the intelligences. He needed stillness. He needed calm. Those weren't to be found anywhere in the exhibition halls, but they could be found inside himself.

I need help to find the missing parts, he thought. *I think they are somewhere in this building, but it is too vast to search. I need to be led to them. So many have put their faith and trust in me. I don't want to fail them. Please. I need help.*

An echo seemed to resonate from within him. In the stillness of his thoughts, he sensed a familiar presence. Was it possible the dog's intelligence had been summoned when he'd first tried to reach for help? Had the delay been caused by its invisible travel north?

His throat caught in surprise. *Are you there?*

He sensed a wagging tail. And felt a general inclination to follow wherever the intelligence led him.

Robinson got to his feet immediately. The intelligence led him through a partition, around a corner, and then followed some laborers who were moving crates. They continued another way, but the intelligence directed him to some stairs leading to the underside of the hall. It was darker there and a bit cooler.

"Hoxta-namorem," Robinson sang, summoning a will-o'-the-wisp of light to guide the way. It took off, as if chasing the other intelligence, and he had to hurry to follow it. There were many empty crates stored in the aisles, but he hurried past them, trusting utterly in the guidance he was given.

He was led right to it, a place of empty crates of various sizes. There, under a pile, was a box full of the parts that had been removed. How it had ended up down there was a mystery, but he imagined the progression. An unscrupulous man handing the crate to one worker, then another, and finally to one who'd taken it down to the underground lair. Perhaps only one person in the chain of events knew what had happened.

With the skeins of light hovering over his shoulder, he removed the smaller box from beneath the crates and opened it. The light glimmered over the pieces of white gold.

Thank you, he thought to the dog intelligence. *It was very helpful. Stick around. I may need your help again.*

He sensed the wagging again. Then, tucking the box under his arm, he walked speedily back to his corner of the hall.

Robinson, Wickins, and several others had just started reassembling the tubes when Clara rushed onto the scene, hair disheveled and voice breathless.

"I got your summons, Rob, but . . . but she's gone."

He stared at his sister-in-law in disbelief. Wickins's brow wrinkled in concern, but he continued to work fastidiously on the tubes.

"What do you mean by 'gone'?"

"My goodness, it is so hot in here," Clara said. She unbuttoned the top buttons of her dress and took off her hat. "I was with her at the locomotivus station. She was trying to cool off. Then she saw someone dangerous. He looked like an employee to me, but it may have been a glamour that didn't work on her. She jumped onto the locomotivus as it departed."

Robinson gaped. "She did what?"

"She made it safely on," Clara affirmed, touching his arm. "I reported the incident to the staff, who had me speak to their head of security, and then the police were summoned. That's why it has taken so long for me to come. How can I help?"

His mind was still in a state of shock. McKenna had jumped onto a moving locomotivus? Now that he had found the missing pieces, the demonstration could continue, but he was highly alarmed for McKenna's safety. He wanted to go after her. She had friends and allies in Auvinen, of course—her mother and Sarah Fuller Fiske, among others. Her father's reputation and connections with the Marshalcy would help protect her. But it troubled him that he couldn't safeguard her himself from the men who'd tried to abduct her in Tanhauser and their ilk.

Clara touched his arm again. "It will be all right, Rob. We have a task at hand. Tomorrow is the day. You have to stay. McKenna was insistent that you must. She would be devastated if you left now because of her just when you were finally here to make sure things worked properly." She asked again with more urgency, "How can I help?"

Maybe she was right. Maybe not. In truth, the whole situation was unnerving. He quickly explained what needed to be done, how the tubes needed to be retrofitted with the proper alloy parts, and she doffed her gloves, rolled up her sleeves, and joined the work. It took hours—hours in the sweltering heat. By the end, they had the bulbs fastened to all the display racks leading up to their corner of the hall. They were damp and perspiring and lightheaded, but they'd endured and finished the task.

Robinson pulled the special tuning fork from his pocket and tested the display. The lamps glowed brightly according to his proximity. He tapped the fork against his knee and walked down the hall, and the lights came on in response, just as in previous efforts. Other sorcerers were curious and asked for information about what was going on, but he kept the explanation to himself and suggested all would be explained on the morrow.

When sunset came, the interior lamps provided by the exhibition organizers glowed to life as they normally did. But Rob's bulbs remained dark. Mr. Foster arrived shortly thereafter with some early investors, and they demonstrated the exhibit to them. Although some of them looked askance at Rob's sweaty, bedraggled condition, he ignored the glances and focused on demonstrating his invention.

"Shall we retire for dinner at the house?" Mr. Foster suggested. "I have a carriage awaiting us."

"That would be lovely," Wickins exclaimed. "I'm famished."

"I heartily agree," Clara said. She'd explained already, discreetly, why McKenna wasn't there with her. Mr. Foster's brow had furrowed, and he'd promised to dispatch a communique to Auvinen posthaste to get an update.

"I'll stay," Robinson said. "Guard duty. I've set wards around each of the tubes, so we'll be warned if any further tampering happens, but I want to be here just in case. This opportunity is too important to risk."

"Come now, Dickemore," Wickins said. "I can ask the foundry to send some additional security. We cannot leave our station unprotected, but you shouldn't bear the burden alone."

"He's right," Clara said. "I'll stay with you."

Robinson shook his head. "No need. I won't be alone."

She gave him a perplexed look, but he waved them off, and she didn't voice her question. After they left, he walked down the row of displays, wondering what each invention portended for the future. As he walked, he sensed the intelligences harbored within. Some were friendlier than others. He could sense, in the back of his mind, his friendly little intelligence trotting along behind him.

A great quiet settled over the hall. With it dark outside, the great glass walls reflected back the lighted interior space, making it impossible to see the city outside. He thought about McKenna, wondering where she was, hoping she was at the house on Brake Street with her mother. The heat had been affecting her noticeably. It still made no sense to him that the display hall was sheathed in glass.

But an idea tickled in the back of his mind. Perhaps it had been arranged that way on purpose because of the fear the military had of Semblances wandering amongst them. Beings attuned to frigid climates would naturally be repelled by warmth, would they not? There were no chilled-fog machines for that very reason. It was to blind the Aesir to the advancements of mortal technology. It was a rather ingenious safeguard, he had to admit.

Then another thought struck . . .

McKenna had been impacted by the heat ever since her near-drowning. The dreams had started then too.

The feeling of dread he had felt earlier sparked inside him again and he couldn't push it down this time. Was he being uncharacteristically paranoid? It was an unusually hot summer, and plenty of people had vicious dreams. They were in the midst of a war after all.

He heard a woman's voice, a hummed series of notes going up and down the scales. It was coming from a slight distance—the singer out of sight but relatively near. He walked to the edge of their display nook, in the corner of the upper floor, and saw a woman standing by one of his quicksilver tubes. She was dressed in a formfitting gown, very elegant and made of silk. Her hair was coiffed to hang about her shoulders in ribbons of curls. What was she doing singing to his tube?

She was trying to make it react to her voice. She was *testing* it.

"Can I help you?" he asked, coming into sight.

She started with surprise and turned to face him, and he caught her tugging a decorative glove back onto her hand. Had she been touching the glass with her finger? By his estimation she was in her thirties and looked to be quite wealthy, judging by her fashionable garb. A worried feeling shook him.

"I didn't know anyone was milling about," she apologized, her voice slightly husky. She wasn't condescending or dismissive. "I was just curious why some of these tubes weren't glowing. It's after dark. I wondered if they were broken."

"They're not," Robinson said flatly, watching as her gloved hand stroked the tube. She gazed at it with open interest. He folded his arms.

"Do you know how the professor's tubes work?" she asked, arching an eyebrow in an artless kind of way that was, likely, intended to disarm him. It did not.

"Come back tomorrow to find out," he said. "Like everyone else."

"Oh. I see. Then I'll look forward to it. Good night." She gave him a scrutinizing look, but her expression revealed none of her thoughts. He thought he sensed the dog's intelligence growling.

He nodded to the woman but stood his post and watched for her to saunter away. She had a sway to her hips as she walked. He had the instinct that she was doing it for show, to make him gaze at her as she left.

He turned around and shook his head at her brazenness. If wishes were wings, he'd be tending to his wife in Auvinen, not sitting here in a paroxysm of doubt, with nothing to distract his thoughts from worry. What would he do should someone come with a hammer and try smashing his tubes? He could summon a shield spell, of course, but they might get one or two before he was able to conjure the protection. Or perhaps he could redirect the force of the blow somewhere else? Attraction and repulsion were the fundamental principles of magic theory.

He considered the maxims he had learned about from the work of Isaac Berrow, burrowing in over the question of how he might transfer any spells targeting his exhibit elsewhere. Could he get them to smash the glass wall of Exhibition Hall, for example? How would a sorcerer link the two so that the energy transferred would be instantaneous?

Those were more comfortable thoughts. He continued to mull them over, wrestling through the implications, the harmonies, the aptitudes involved. His brain began making calculations.

Until he forgot all about the woman who'd visited.

MaKenna Aurora
Hawksley

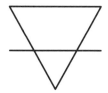

CHAPTER FOURTEEN

A MOTHER'S SECRET

McKenna had never been detained at a locomotivus station before and found the entire experience mortifying. Stern looks, disapproving frowns, and a few comments whispered behind hands by railway officials added to the indignity of the moment. She sat with a stiff spine, her hands clasped in her lap, and waited, and waited, and waited. The room was warm, but at least it wasn't as stifling as Bishopsgate. Auvinen had a milder climate because of its seaside ports and the river. But her collar was hot, and she wished she could unbutton it without causing yet another scandal.

Eventually, after a considerable wait, she saw her mother walk purposefully into the station. McKenna had been shut into an office, so she watched through a window as her mother spoke with the supervisor in charge, the one who had been so very condescending and suspicious. McKenna was near enough that she could read their lips.

"She *is* married?" the supervisor said. "I thought that was a fib. I didn't think you had children in Society yet, ma'am."

"She isn't in Society yet, Mr. Becklesby, because she's deaf. She wasn't lying to you. My husband and I had decided to postpone her debut for a little longer."

"Mrs. Foster, I do not mean to impugn your daughter's character. But she leaped onto a moving locomotivus. That is incredibly dangerous and reckless. She claims someone was threatening her, but there was no one nearby except her sister and an employee of the yard. I wanted to speak with you first, but I believe charges must be pressed to teach young people to respect the rules."

McKenna bristled with indignation. The supervisor was throwing about the power of his position. Getting the Marshalcy involved? Over such a minor thing?

"You must do as you feel your duty demands, Mr. Becklesby, but I know my daughter. She is neither immature nor reckless. When the facts of the situation are fully known, I assure you that your discretion in the matter will be lauded. And rewarded."

McKenna smirked. Mother was wielding her own power. She was encouraging him, obliquely, to consider what might happen to him if he got on the wrong side of events.

"Ah, Mrs. Foster. I did not mean to imply your daughter is reckless. Many young people loiter about the station yard just to cause trouble. I know your daughter is not one of them."

"Indeed she is not. That is why I so appreciate the delicate way you've handled matters."

It hadn't been delicate at all, but McKenna appreciated what her mother was doing. How she was coaxing him to improve his behavior.

"I think it prudent, Mrs. Foster, to dismiss this incident. If she promises not to do anything like that again, I think that would satisfy management. We could . . . overlook this episode. Unless it were to happen again."

"That is very kind of you, Mr. Becklesby. I consider it a fortunate event that you were on duty at the station today. My husband will be pleased by your solicitude."

Mr. Becklesby adjusted his uniform jacket. He was nearly bursting with self-importance, and McKenna thought him a complete buffoon.

But she put on a timid smile when he escorted her mother to the office door and opened it.

"You may go, Mrs. Hawksley," he pronounced. "On the condition that you refrain from such reckless behavior in the future."

McKenna's mother, positioned just behind the man, frowned a little at him but nodded encouragingly to McKenna to accept.

"Yes, Mr. Becklesby. It won't happen again."

"Very well. And thank you for your patronage of the line."

McKenna stood, embraced her mother, and the two walked swiftly out of the station, which was light on travelers. Mother hooked arms with her and led her to the family carriage, where Mr. Thompson Hughes awaited them on the pilot box. McKenna boarded it first, and then Mother sat across from her. Soon after, the carriage jolted and started to move.

"What is going on, McKenna?" The look in Mother's eyes was fraught with concern.

"There was a man at the station," McKenna said. "He had a glamour spell, but I could see through it. He was coming straight for me. Clara was there, but she couldn't see past the illusion."

"And you could? How?"

"A similar thing happened in Tanhauser." She wrung her hands with nervous energy. "Mother. There's something I need to tell you."

"You can tell me anything," she said with genuine concern.

"I've not felt . . . myself lately." Her heart heaved with worry. How to put this? "Ever since I nearly drowned near Mowbray House, things have been a little . . . off. A little different. Actually, more than a little. I have dreams I can't remember." Mother listened keenly, her attention focused on McKenna. "They are quite vivid. Once I tried to write down what I remembered, but the words were just gibberish the next day. And these feelings overwhelm me at times. Feelings from memories that . . . that aren't mine."

Mother's eyebrows arched. But still, she said nothing.

"When Rob and I kissed for the first time, on the doorstep of our house on Brake Street, it felt . . . familiar. I'd never kissed him before. It was so strange. And there have been other times. Other moments when it feels like I should *know* magic. I even tried casting a spell on Clara when she stopped me from leaving the house. It was like a reflex. This was after the accident on the beach."

"You did?" Mother said, startled.

"I don't remember the words anymore. But I feel that they *should* work. That they've *always* worked. The man who was coming for me . . . it was like he knew me. The same way the men in Tanhauser *knew* me." She paused, biting her lip.

Mother reached across and took McKenna's hand in her own. "Thank you for telling me. Why didn't you share this before?"

"It's strange, isn't it? I didn't want you to worry about me. And I also kept forgetting."

"Have you told Rob?"

McKenna shook her head no. "Ever since General Colsterworth visited us, I have felt uneasy. As if the military is watching me. As if they suspect I might be . . . you know . . . a Semblance. I nearly drowned, Mother. And since that day, I've been so . . . so warm. So uncomfortable. It was so hot in Bishopsgate, I thought I'd . . . I thought I'd *die*."

Mother blinked worriedly, squeezing McKenna's hands.

Her throat thickened with worry. "I watched that soldier kill himself. He put a bullet through his own head because he'd realized *he* was a Semblance. There are other people in the military like him, people who are trained to kill them. I don't know what to do. I feel like myself, despite it all, and I don't want them to kill me."

Tears were leaking from Mother's eyes, and she nodded stiffly, in total agreement. "You're my daughter. You have been acting a little strangely, but the circumstances have also been strange. You don't feel anyone . . . anything . . . talking to you? In your head?"

McKenna shook her head. "I've even tried on the sorcerer's ring. It doesn't work for me. I wonder . . . if being deaf prevents magic from working on me. That seems to be the case, doesn't it? It's an Aesir disease, after all."

Mother nodded in agreement, but she looked heartsick and worried.

"What should I do?" McKenna whispered.

"I think . . . for now . . . you should keep this a secret. With the Awakening, there is a heightened prejudice against the Aesir. So many have perished because of this eternal war. I also think it would be better if the military didn't know where to find you. You left Bishopsgate rather abruptly, I take it. Your father and Rob don't know where you are?"

"You heard the man at the station. I jumped on a moving locomotivus, Mother."

"I'll send a letter that you felt unwell. I won't mention the heat in case the military is intercepting messages."

"Is it legal for them to do that?"

"It shouldn't be. But we're in a time of war, so there may be special rules now. I won't tell them where you are staying, but I think you should stay at the house with me and Trudie. We were going to go to the exhibition in two days, but I don't think that is wise anymore."

McKenna patted her mother's hand. "I'm glad I finally told someone."

"I'm glad you did too. I remember, back when you and Rob shared the story of Mr. Crossthwait, that Rob had wanted to capture him. To try and understand how the magic of Semblances works. Your husband has already proven to be a genius when it comes to magic. Maybe he could figure a way to resolve this? How to get this spirit out of you?"

McKenna sighed. "I don't know. When that man came to our apartment, I felt so threatened. I sensed him before I saw him. Isn't that strange?"

"It *is* strange. But we will tell Rob about all of this soon."

McKenna looked down. "He's still angry with me, I think. I wish we hadn't gone. Wickins was loyal after all. It's been . . . awkward between Rob and I. And I don't want to share this . . . not when there are hard feelings between us."

Mother leaned forward. "Every marriage goes through episodes that cause rifts. The Mind knows your father and I went through several when we were first married."

"You did?"

"Trust me, McKenna. We did. Sometimes we hurt each other unwittingly. Sometimes deliberately. I was a little spoiled and vainglorious back then."

"You?" McKenna was astonished. "Vainglorious?" That was a word she would never have associated with her mother. Not in all the ages of the world.

Mother smiled, then reached over and smoothed some hair from McKenna's forehead. "I was twenty when I married your father. My sister had persuaded me to eschew getting married for as long as I could, to keep my suitors on tenterhooks. Being sought after was rather intoxicating. I would play them off against each other to win my affection. It's rather silly when I look back on it."

"I didn't know," McKenna said.

"Your father refused to play games. He was steady, unflappable. Never jealous, even though I gave him a right to be. He treated me better than I treated him. His friends in law school teased him relentlessly. He was trying to catch a comet, they said, but when I saw how committed he was, how conscientious and self-disciplined, I began to change. I was still very immature when I decided to accept his proposal. People still doubted I would go through with it. They all said Laurel Aurora Blatchford was playing another game."

The carriage slowed as it reached the neighborhood leading to Brake Street. The familiar signs and sights were a relief to McKenna's heart, but her attention was very much fixed on her mother's story. She hadn't heard any of this before. It was difficult imagining her mother and Aunt Margaret as *real* people. Or maybe she meant *young* people.

"After we were married, we struggled to have children. I thought it would be so easy. Many of my friends began to have them right away. A year passed, then two, then three. I said words I shouldn't have said. I laid blame where it never belonged. Still, your father was patient. Long-suffering. He finished law school and began to swell our fortunes with his knack and logic. I became jealous of him." She squeezed McKenna's hands again. "And then . . . you were born. My beautiful, precious, hale daughter. My firstborn. Your sister came not long after. What a surprise. It felt as if she'd barely said her first word before you were struck with the fever. The dreaded axioma. And all my hopes for your future were dashed to pieces. But I could also sense that *my* future would be changed as well."

McKenna swallowed, feeling things so strong she didn't know what to make of them. "I was just a child."

"I know, McKenna. It wasn't your fault. I . . . I fell into a melancholy. It was your father who saved me. Who saved *you*. I didn't think I could be the mother you needed, but he saw something in me I didn't see in myself. And he was not going to abandon you no matter what Society thought proper. He didn't abandon me either, not even when I was so despondent I could hardly function. I sought answers, and he traveled to far regions to find them. And when you were a little girl, he brought home Mary Trewitt to teach you and be your friend. And you, beloved daughter, taught me how to love without conditions, without reproach, without demands. It was you who helped me change into the person I am today." She hooked her hand behind McKenna's head and leaned closer. "And I will not let anyone hurt you, McKenna Aurora. I will shield your body with my own if need be. Do you understand me, darling? This is our secret for now. I know your father will do the same. He wouldn't let them harm you then, and he won't let them harm you now."

McKenna sniffled, her emotions spilling over. She hugged her mother and pressed kisses to her brow.

Mother pulled back, smoothing McKenna's hair again. "We must be brave."

The carriage slowed to a halt.

"I'll be brave, Mama."

Mother nodded, then jolted at something she saw outside. "Good, because Colonel Harrup is waiting for us at the house."

McKenna's heart clenched with dread. Colonel Harrup was one of Father's acquaintances, and he'd come with General Colsterworth to apologize a few weeks back.

Looking out the window, she saw him wave to them.

"Hello, Mrs. Foster, Mrs. Hawksley," the colonel called out with an affable air. "I have grim tidings, unfortunately. I've been ordered to take you to the garrison, Mrs. Hawksley. For your own protection. There is someone who may be looking for you."

Robinson Foster Hawksley

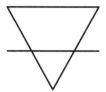

CHAPTER FIFTEEN

RESONANCE

The next day was even hotter, if that were possible. But people came to Exhibition Hall in droves, particularly in the morning hours, when it was so crowded and noisy it gave Robinson a splitting headache. He'd managed a little sleep after some men from the foundry came to relieve him, but he'd tossed and turned, kept awake by heat and worry. Not just about the dishonesty he'd experienced at the exhibition, but about McKenna and what was happening to her. What might it mean to her? To them? So he suffered the sweat, the stench, and the noise in the hall as best he could, patiently demonstrating and explaining the principle of resonance that caused the lamps to ignite in the presence of Aesir magic. Many of the wealthier guests triggered them unwittingly with Aesir magic they possessed and were drawn by the glow to that distant corner of the hall on the upper floor.

Wickins and Clara were invaluable, gathering people in smaller groups so that one of them might explain the uses of the tubes as early warning signals of Aesir attacks. Clara was able to give first-hand information of having them installed at her home, and many of the visitors became future customers, giving their names so that representatives from the manufacturing company might contact them later.

Later in the afternoon, when it was calmer, Mr. Foster arrived with several businessmen from the Industry of Magic, and the lamps were demonstrated again, much to their delight and satisfaction. There was no sign of the woman who had been there the previous night.

"I have heard very good reports so far," Mr. Foster declared with satisfaction. "Many are talking about your invention, Robinson. The judges have made it through the first floor already and are coming to the second floor within the hour. Be ready."

"Is there any word from McKenna?" Robinson asked, furtively glancing down the hall for a sign of the judges' arrival.

Her father frowned. "Yes, there has been. She's safe at home. And she wants you to stay here. She was adamant about it, actually, but she won't be returning to Bishopsgate."

"I want to go to her," Robinson said.

Mr. Foster gave him a stern look. "This is your moment to be recognized. She is being protected by the Marshalcy. I consider her as safe as she can be. Just . . . be present. Focus on the matter at hand. There have been so many orders, especially from the women in the Invisible College. Clara has been an impressive spokeswoman."

Robinson smiled and nodded. It was true. She hadn't even entered Society yet but was acting mature beyond her years. Still, the restless feeling wouldn't go away.

After Mr. Foster left, the crowds slowed to a trickle. Robinson saw the beads of sweat on Wickins's and Clara's brows, which they patted away with handkerchiefs. Whispers came from the other displays that the judges were on the floor, going from display to display, starting on the opposite side of the hall. Robinson squirmed with frustration, wondering if that too was a deliberate slight.

"Where are they?" Clara panted, fanning herself. No one had come by their section in quite a while.

"If we were back in Auvinen, I think I'd jump into the river right now," Wickins said. Then his eyes developed a mischievous gleam as he glanced at Clara. "And I'd pull you in after me!"

"Scandalous, Mr. Wickins. Utterly scandalous." But her smile showed she wasn't offended.

"Most of the questions I've had were from military officers," Wickins commented, turning to Robinson. "They see a great need for this invention at the front. They wonder how durable the glass is, though, and whether the frigid temperatures in the north will impact them."

"Glass can withstand temperatures well past freezing," Robinson said offhandedly. He didn't recall how he knew it, but the information was in the back of his mind. "And it can be heated to melting without cracking. Cracking is caused by sudden changes in temperature."

"For a master of elocution," Clara said wryly, "you certainly know a great deal about scientific matters."

Robinson shrugged. "I enjoy knowledge of all sorts, Clara. I think I see them." The group of judges had turned the corner and were making their way, finally, toward their end of the hall. The woman he'd seen the night before was with them. There was no mistaking her amidst the group of judges. He wondered who she was and why she was with the judges.

"At last." Wickins sighed.

The judges were ponderously slow, taking time to visit the different booths and displays, pausing to listen or to watch the demonstrations. Some of them would ask questions, and then they'd thank the sorcerer for their participation and move on to the next. The heat of the afternoon had to be draining their strength, but each of them had a supply of water to keep themselves healthy.

Partway through the hall, Robinson overheard one of the judges complain about the heat and suggest they adjourn and come back the next day.

A shaft of disappointment skewered Robinson's chest. This felt like more evidence of tampering. Wickins and Clara hadn't overheard the comment, for they were still waiting in anticipation, looking hopeful.

"They're going to quit for the day," Robinson muttered under his breath.

"But they're almost here!" Clara objected, shocked.

The feelings roiling inside him were unpleasant. Disappointment was never a thrilling emotion, but it was more than just that. Everything that had happened over the last day and a half felt contrived, even sinister, as if someone were scheming to have their display neglected. It made Robinson want to get on the next locomotivus and speed away— partially out of resentment for the continual affronts and also because of his deep-seated worry for his wife. Although his invention could only help the war effort, which should guarantee its warm reception, they were being targeted in a strange and underhanded manner. Was another person or group attempting to steal his invention? It was almost beyond his mortal patience to bear such treatment under the circumstances. He shook his head and sighed, glancing back at the group, hearing some others agree with the judge's recommendation. It was too hot to finish all the reviews. Why not adjourn for an early dinner at one of the fashionable restaurants in the city?

"I should really like to see Professor Hawksley's demonstration before we go."

It was the woman. He recognized her voice and quickly turned his head.

One of the judges said, "Professor Hawksley? From Covesea?"

"I don't know where he's from," the woman confessed, "but could we not spend a moment there first? I've never met him."

"I know Hawksley! I had no idea he was here. By all means, Miss Cowing! It would be a delight to see him again."

Robinson stared, blinking in surprise. The woman who had visited last night was Elizabeth Cowing? The famous inventor of their generation? She didn't have a display because she was one of the *judges*. Now he regretted how dismissive he'd been the previous night.

"They're heading this way," Clara gasped out.

Robinson's feelings became quickly tangled as a surge of gratitude, relief, and even awe swiftly overcame his previous ill temper. To his bafflement, Robinson did not recognize the judge walking alongside her, a friendly-looking fellow in his midfifties with narrow spectacles. How did the fellow know him?

The fellow judges accompanied them, but Miss Cowing and the friendly judge approached their booth first.

"I am Patton Reginald Roberts," the judge said, shaking hands with Robinson and giving him a clasp from the Invisible College. "Where is Professor Hawksley? I should like to see him again."

Still clasping the man's hand, Robinson touched his sweat-soaked shirt with his other hand. "I am Professor Hawksley. I don't believe we've met."

"From Covesea?" The gentleman looked baffled.

"Yes. I moved to Auvinen last year. Perhaps it's my father you've met?"

The man's furrowed brow cleared as he released the clasp. "I thought all of his sons had died. So glad that was incorrect information. Your father is a great elocutionist."

Robinson nodded. "He trained me in the Physiological Alphabet and elocution, but my demonstration today isn't related to that."

"Wonderful. Welcome, welcome. This is Miss Elizabeth Cowing."

"We've met but were not introduced," she said, giving Robinson a charming smile, but she didn't mention the brief encounter they'd had the previous night.

"Would you demonstrate your invention, please?" asked Mr. Roberts.

Robinson had plenty of practice with the special tuning fork, and he quickly showed them how the sound, aligned to the vibrations of the sound that Aesir magic made, triggered the reaction and caused the bulb to glow. The other judges gathered around, watching in fascination as the light from the quicksilver lamp responded to the sound. As he backed away from the lamp, the light faded—and when he got closer, it quickly brightened.

"I have an artifact of Aesir magic," Mr. Roberts said. "Can I test your lamp with it?"

"Certainly. If the magic had been activated, the tubes would have already responded."

The judge nodded and lifted his shirt sleeve, revealing a coil of white gold fashioned into a bracelet with a gem inlaid into it. He uttered the word of command. *"Axiton maqis."*

Instantly, all the lamps in the area glowed brightly, responding to the subacoustic sounds generated by the magic. Robinson wasn't familiar with the activation word, which wasn't surprising since the judge was a higher order of sorcerer than himself.

Many of the judges exclaimed at the demonstration of power, the instant reaction a validation of Robinson's claims.

Miss Cowing approached him with curiosity and interest. "Your tuning fork. How did you figure out which note it reacts to?"

"It's a Mixolydian chord," Robinson said.

"Not a Dorian one?" she asked, showing her knowledge of magical chords.

"Mixolydian," he affirmed.

"But what scale?"

"That information is guarded by the patent," Robinson answered. It was something, in time, she could figure out if she experimented with his tuning fork. But with the patent pending, he wasn't going to share that information, even with someone as famous as her.

One of the judges wrinkled his brow. "Why, this is very similar to the—"

"It's a fascinating discovery," she said, cutting the man off. "I noticed an extra bit of wiring around the ends." She gave Robinson an impressed look. "Aesir gold?"

He nodded briefly.

"Could this bulb reveal the presence of an invisibility cloak, a kappelin?" another judge asked.

"Yes. I have seen it myself."

"Amazing," the judge professed. "That would negate the element of surprise of a cloaked Aesir approaching our ranks."

More questions came. He reiterated the story of the floating boulder in Auvinen and how he had discovered the sound, but he did not reveal the device his father had given him and the role it had played in his discovery. He and his father-in-law thought it prudent that others not know about that, for fear the military might take too keen an interest in it. Miss Cowing asked many additional questions, revealing her vast knowledge of music and its involvement in Aesir magic. She was highly knowledgeable. Impressively so. But she had a guarded look in her eyes. She was interested but not delighted.

After congratulating him on the discovery and promising to call on Robinson's father the next time he was in Auvinen, Patton Reginald Roberts suggested the judges finish off the rest of the hall and then eat dinner. He'd been invigorated by Robinson's display, he said, and didn't want to disappoint the other sorcerers.

Miss Cowing gave Robinson a kindly smile before leaving with the others.

"Well done, old chap! Well done!" Wickins said under his breath, slapping Robinson hard on the back. "You dazzled them all!"

"I'm exhausted," he said.

"Why don't you go back to the house and take a nap," Wickins offered. "You look like you've been up all night despite having gone to get some rest earlier. Clara and I can handle the display while you're gone. Then you can come back when the evening crowds return."

"I'll take you up on it," Robinson said. "Even an hour or two of sleep would help."

"Go on, Dickemore. You've earned it. Well done! I'm proud as peaches."

"So am I, Rob," Clara said. "It would not have gone nearly as well if you weren't here."

He waved off their praise, collected his jacket, and headed off. The judges were at the next booth, listening to the inventor. Elizabeth Cowing glanced his way, smiled again, and then gave her attention to the other sorcerer.

All the attention had made him a little giddy, but he quelled the feeling and hurried down the corridor, down the stairs, and gratefully left the blazing-hot building. There was no breeze outside, except the one he made for himself by walking quickly. Upon returning to the house, he found the letter McKenna had sent and experienced a pang of loneliness and worry. The message was brief. McKenna had indeed insisted that he stay. Had promised him a longer letter. One that hadn't arrived yet. This increased his agitation tenfold.

He hastily went upstairs to the bedroom and tossed away the coat, unbuttoned his shirt, and kicked off his shoes. With the dormer window curtain shut, the room was plenty dark, and he sprawled out on the bed. The pillow smelled like McKenna's fragrant hair. Where was she, and what was happening to her? Her safety was paramount, and in some senses, he did think her safer in the house in Auvinen than here, with the crowds in which a schemer could easily hide. And yet, he was here, chasing shadows in his mind, away from her. He gazed at the ceiling. Should he go back to Auvinen before hearing from her? Or was that impractical? Or improbable? Implausible? The word would not come to him. His mind became lazy with such thoughts, and he fell asleep in moments.

Only to be awakened by a woman's voice downstairs. A voice that cut through his simple dreams and brought him awake with a jolt of surprise. He hadn't even closed the bedroom door he'd been so tired.

"Professor Hawksley?"

It was Elizabeth Cowing.

The Iskandir were the first storytellers, and their stories were sung around campfires. Sung in wood-timbered drinking halls. Sung when children were born or when their elders died. Our first glimpses of the power of music come from their stories.

Through stories, we experience, vicariously, the full range of mortal behavior, from the benefits of adapting to society to the consequences of our most heinous transgressions. Through stories, we become spectators to the breadth of mortal motivations, from ambition to brutality, from triumph to failure.

But in order for a story to grab hold of our attention with enough force that we yearn to transmit it to others, the tale must evoke surprise but not be so outrageous that we fancy it ridiculous.

The story of the Erlking's daughter is one such example. It has weathered the folk tunes of an Iskandir fire circle and is still sung today in the greatest opera halls in the empire.

—Isaac Berrow,
Master of the Royal Secret,
the Invisible College

MaKenna Aurora
Hawksley

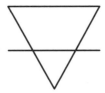

CHAPTER SIXTEEN

Lost Love

McKenna stepped away from the curtain. The soldier sentries were still outside. A surge of agitation swarmed in her bosom. She wanted them gone. The house on Brake Street was, in fact, a jail to her now. But at least—at the very least—Mother had convinced Colonel Harrup to allow McKenna to stay at her parents' home, where there were servants and magical protections and now, temporarily, physical protections. It wasn't exactly *persuasion* that had changed Colonel Harrup's mind. It had been the threat of legal action.

McKenna walked back to the parlor where Mother was talking with Judge Coy Taylor. Both turned to look at her when she entered the room. The judge was one of her father's colleagues and had presided over her wedding.

"They are still outside," McKenna announced, trying to subdue her frustration.

"Your protection is now under the auspices of the Marshalcy, my dear," the judge said. "The officers will be deployed, I assure you, and the military will withdraw."

McKenna nodded and began pacing again. She feared the soldiers would barge into the house and drag her away. Thankfully, Judge Coy Taylor had been available to personally intervene and counter the orders from General Colsterworth. The Marshalcy would be on the lookout for the escaped prisoner in Auvinen and would provide protection for her until the missing man was found. There was no proof he had traveled to Auvinen at all, so any danger was not imminent.

"I can't thank you enough for your help," Mother said, gripping the judge's hand and shaking it vigorously. "After what happened with their rogue officer, I just don't trust them."

"Anything within my power, Mrs. Foster. I think your husband would appreciate some communication on the situation from you. I will stay until the changing of the guard happens and ensure that my instructions are followed to the letter."

"That relieves my mind greatly," Mother said.

"I'm grateful you sent for me when you did. I was about to disembark for Bishopsgate myself to see the Great Exhibition. But delaying my visit by a day will be no matter."

"Again, I express our appreciation. Do you think . . . will General Colsterworth seek to overturn your decree?"

"Why would he do that?"

"What if this whole situation is just a pretext? What if there are other reasons he might want my daughter in custody?"

"This forces him to declare it," the judge responded, his eyes stern. "Society is governed by laws, and the military must operate within them. Even though the general is a high-ranking officer in the military *and* the Invisible College, there is still a rank above him. That was done by design in the days of Isaac Berrow to prevent the military from exceeding their authority."

"That was very wise of him," Mother said.

McKenna felt a trickle of sweat run down her face. Agitation was still bouncing inside her, and she longed to go back to the front door window and peek outside again. She swiped the sweat from her cheek and went and sat down on the sofa. She wished Rob were there—her heart longed for a reconciliation—but he was at the Great Exhibition. That's where he needed to be. His work was going to be important to the whole world. What would that mean for her, though? Would his rising fame make her more of a target or less? Would someone from the military hunt her down as Mr. Crossthwait had tried to do with Rob? Rising, she went to the bookshelf and chose one at random, surprised to find the one she had purchased in town—*The Incurious Mind of Chester Malcolm Weathersby.*

She tried losing herself in the words but kept glancing at the entrance to the parlor until finally, *finally*, news came that the soldiers were gone. Judge Coy Taylor left soon afterward, because he had pressing matters to attend to after giving the charge to the officers of the Marshalcy.

After he left, she went by the front door and looked out the window. Her protectors' uniforms had changed, but she didn't feel any relief from her anxiety. She wondered why. When she turned around, she saw Mother standing in the light, gazing at her worriedly.

"Is something wrong?" McKenna asked.

Mother smiled, but it was a fatigued one. She leaned against the wall. "It's been a long day."

McKenna stifled a yawn. "I think I'll take a nap myself. I just feel . . . uneasy."

"Let's talk in your room," Mother suggested.

Together, they climbed the steps up to the girls' bedrooms. It felt strange to be back after many weeks away in her shared apartment with Rob, but also familiar in a comforting way. She imagined Rob would still be sleeping in her childhood bedroom in the house in Bishopsgate, and that caused a pang of longing. Being separated from him was hard, especially right now.

"Can you open the window?" McKenna said, loosening the buttons of her dress. "It's stifling in here."

Mother came and sat down next to her and took her hands. "Let's talk first. I wish there was not such secrecy about Semblances. The general made it clear we were not to share the situation with that Crossthwait man with anyone, and we have not. I wish I felt freer to do so, but I imagine there isn't much information about them in the quorums of the Invisible College."

"Perhaps just the military quorums," McKenna suggested.

"Likely. I wonder if there will be any opposition to you moving to Mowbray House. I think you would be safer if you and Robinson were both away from Auvinen."

"You think so?"

Mother nodded, looking weary and wary. "Your father hasn't mentioned this to you, but he doesn't trust General Colsterworth. We don't believe everything he's said is true."

McKenna's eyes flashed with mock surprise. "Even though he's part of the Invisible College?"

Mother frowned and nodded at her sarcasm. "Not everyone within the Invisible College has the integrity of your father or your husband. We've heard troubling reports that other factories here in Auvinen are working on bulbs similar to the one Rob invented. When pressed on the matter, they said they were fulfilling particularly large orders from the military to be shipped to the front."

"Why didn't you share this before?" McKenna asked, aghast.

"Well, you were away, and Father wanted to have more evidence of wrongdoing. Only the owner of the patent can authorize it to be licensed to other businesses. If the military is doing this, it is not only illegal but also dishonest. The problem with wealth, you see, is that it tangles people's emotions about what is right and wrong, especially when it conflicts with their self-interest."

"But won't there be consequences for such blatant robbery?"

"There should be. And men like Judge Coy Taylor take their positions of responsibility very seriously. Don't be troubled about it. Father will defend Robinson's patent rights. If these businesses have behaved poorly, they will be punished. It is easy for people to see the right thing as something that benefits them personally, but that is not always the case."

For most of her life, McKenna had longed to be part of the Invisible College, to be part of Society too. She had always imagined only the honorable could join. That there were tests of integrity to keep out those who would be inclined to dishonesty. Father had mentioned being tested, as a young man, in a way that could have compromised him. She'd asked what it was, but he'd refused to discuss it. She wondered what Rob's trial had been.

Mother stroked McKenna's hair. "I worry that I may be doing the same thing," she confessed. "I want to keep you safe. I want to protect you. We've been told by the general that Semblances are very dangerous. Enough so that they are prepared, like that soldier who came for Rob, to murder them on sight." Her face crumpled with sadness, and she wrapped her arms around McKenna and hugged her fiercely.

McKenna felt her throat thicken with tears. She squeezed Mother back. She didn't want to be killed. Rob had used his magic to try to capture Joseph Crossthwait, hoping he might expel the Aesir spirit without killing him, but the man had taken his own life. McKenna couldn't even imagine doing that to herself under any circumstance. But what if it was the only way to protect those she loved?

What if she truly was a Semblance? She began to tremble at the thought.

She pulled away, looking fearfully into her mother's tearstained face. "What do we do?" she whispered.

"I won't let anyone hurt you," Mother said, looking fierce once more. "I need to talk to your father."

"Shouldn't I talk to Rob?"

"Not yet. We aren't sure. We only suspect. From what we know, the Aesir prefer the coldest climates. Why would one of them have been on Siaconset when you started to drown? But there is so much about the Aesir we don't know."

"We could talk to Wickins," McKenna suggested. "He knows everything about them."

"I doubt anyone knows *everything*. But it's a good idea. Maybe it could be a conversation during a dinner at Closure? After the exhibition."

"Maybe. But I don't know how long we'll be staying after the exhibition ends. We have plans to move to Mowbray House," McKenna said. She took Mother's hands and kissed them. "Part of me doesn't want to move away from you. From Father. We could visit, though. We could visit often. I love this house. All my best memories are here."

"Of course we will visit you," Mother said with a loving smile.

McKenna still felt uneasy. "I'm going to have trouble falling asleep tonight. So many worries."

"I need to write your father again. Tell him what's happened. I'll come back and check on you, though."

"What if I have another nightmare?"

Mother's eyes crinkled in concern. "I'll keep my door open, then. If I hear anything, I'll come running."

Mother rose and opened the window, and a deliciously cool sea breeze flowed in. She turned around and looked at McKenna.

"Thank you," McKenna said, feeling abashed. "I feel so on edge. Like . . . something awful has already happened. And we're just waiting to hear the news of it."

Mother paled. "What do you mean?"

"I don't know. It's like that part in the opera, the part where the Erlking's daughter sings about her love betraying her, only he doesn't remember her because of the spell. The song everyone gushes about that you keep making Rob play." She pauses. "I need to get him a new violin still."

"I could help look for one. But it should be your gift."

"Thank you! Yes, please do. You see, in the opera it wasn't the knight's *fault*. He couldn't remember he was married to her. That's what makes the song so sad, isn't it?"

"The whole story is a tragedy," Mother agreed. "And yes, that scene is very poignant. You can't help but feel her anguish."

"I wish I could hear the song," McKenna lamented. "But that's what I'm feeling right now. Something devastating has happened. Something outside my control. I feel like I'm losing the one I love. But are these feelings even *mine*?"

She looked imploringly into Mother's eyes, but neither of them had the answer. There were some questions that could not be asked, not without drawing more unwanted attention.

Robinson Foster Hawksley

CHAPTER SEVENTEEN

CORRUPTION IN THE RANKS

What was Elizabeth Cowing doing *inside* the house? Robinson was befuddled, both from his lack of sleep and the unexpected situation. He hurriedly slipped on his shoes and rushed out the door.

"Hello?" he called down the stairs. The Fosters' house was sweltering. He had no idea what time it was, but it had to still be in the afternoon, judging by the light. Taking the steps down two at a time, he reached the bottom floor. Behind the stairs was a small corridor leading to the kitchen, but Miss Cowing was in the front parlor, still dressed in rich attire.

"You wanted to see me, Professor Hawksley?" she asked, her eyebrows rising. "I got your note."

That was even more baffling. "Note?"

"To talk more about some trouble you're still having with the invention. You asked for my advice." She gazed around at the recently uncovered furniture, the dustcloths still in piles around the chairs. The parlor curtains were closed.

He rubbed his arm, gazing at her in confusion. "I didn't ask to meet with you, Miss Cowing. There must be a mistake."

"I have the note right here," she said, slipping her gloved hand into her dress pocket. She withdrew a squared piece of a paper and unfolded it, then presented it to him.

The handwriting, although similar to his, was clearly a forgery. Not that she would have known what his looked like since he'd never written to her before.

> Miss Cowing:
> I have several projects, in addition to the one in the Great Exhibition, that I feel have lucrative potential but have experienced technical issues. If I could meet you privately to discuss, at fifteen hundred hours at the address below, I would be in your debt once again. Your insights would be incredibly valuable and might hasten the good work I am trying to do.
> Kindly yours,
> Robinson Dickemore Hawksley
> 411 Round Street, Bishopsgate

It was not common knowledge that Robinson had changed his name after marrying McKenna, adopting part of her family name. Whoever had signed the signature had copied something he had signed previously. It was clearly a deception.

"I did not write this," Robinson said, his unease growing rapidly.

"Nor have we ever met before last night," Miss Cowing answered, her brow narrowing with concern. "And we've never spoken about our inventions, have we?"

"Never," he said. "I didn't even know you were a judge at the Great Exhibition."

"I'm a judge because my invention isn't ready to be revealed yet. But I wanted to ask you something regardless. Where did your idea come from?"

He wasn't about to reveal information about the device he carried in his pocket or how it had come into his family. And yet, he could tell she had a very specific reason for asking. She wanted him to reveal something without revealing anything herself.

"Why do you ask?" he countered.

"There is something underhanded going on, Professor Hawksley. I would like to get to the bottom of it."

"As would I, but this is neither the time nor the place. I don't know you, and we are alone in my in-laws' house. And, despite this manufactured note, I clearly wasn't expecting company."

"But you're not alone, Rob."

The voice, startling them both, came from the kitchen corridor. Clara Foster stepped into view.

Robinson whirled, surprised at his sister-in-law's unexpected arrival. She looked a little out of breath, but she entered the room with confidence.

"Clara," he said. "Do you know what's—"

"I don't, but I knew something was wrong and came as quickly as I could. I ran so I could come around the alley side to beat Miss Cowing to the house."

"She was at your exhibit earlier. Is this your wife?" Miss Cowing asked, glancing at him.

"This is my wife's younger sister. Do you have any suspicions as to why someone would want us to meet like this?"

Miss Cowing pursed her lips. "I'm beginning to suspect a reason. I came here expecting there to be servants, your business partners, others present. The home looks like it has been retired for quite some time. It would be best if I left."

The front door was burst open by a startled stranger. "By the Mind, this isn't my house!" the man declared, looking in confusion at the scene. "They all look the same on the outside." His brow wrinkled when he saw Miss Cowing. "You . . . you are Miss Elizabeth Cowing, are you not?"

"This is my father's house," Clara said firmly, stepping forward. "Who are you?"

The man looked abashed. And a little guilty. In fact, Robinson had the suspicion that the man had been sent to catch them in a compromising situation or discussing some business matter they had in common. Why else would someone have forged such a note but to bring the two of them together for some ulterior motive?

"I'm terribly sorry. I didn't mean to intrude. I . . . I just got the wrong house."

"Does he look familiar to you, Clara?" Robinson asked. "One of your neighbors, perhaps?"

"He's a stranger," Clara said, taking his cue. "I've never seen him before. I think we should call the authorities. Perhaps the Marshalcy could investigate?"

"Really, that's unnecessary. It was an honest mistake. Goodbye!" He quickly departed, slamming the door behind him.

"Or a dishonest one," Robinson muttered.

"I am astonished," Miss Cowing said, shaking her head. "Believe me, I had no hand in this."

"Who brought you the note?" Robinson asked.

"One of the judge's assistants. A man I've seen going to and fro throughout the exhibition. I don't know his name, but I've seen him deliver messages throughout the day."

"He's probably not an accomplice, then," Clara said. "And he might not even remember who handed him the note if he's handled so many."

"I think that is an astute observation, young lady. How old are you, Miss Foster? You're barely out in Society, I should think."

"I haven't made my debut," Clara admitted. "Soon. I hope."

"But you are a sorcerer in the Invisible College?"

"Yes. At fifteen. I am seventeen now."

Miss Cowing smiled but then looked seriously at them. "I'll see if I can find out who was behind it. I have resources now I didn't have before. And my own barristers who will fight for my interests."

"And what interests are those?" Robinson asked.

"That, I'm afraid, will have to wait until later. I would advise you to seek your own legal counsel as well."

"I will tell Mr. Foster when he returns," Robinson said. "I was surprised when you came to the display last night." He looked at Clara. "I caught her humming to one of the bulbs. I say it now because I want everything out in the open. We'd never met before that moment, and I didn't know who you were until you arrived with the other judges today."

"Very true," Miss Cowing said. "I thought it could be misinterpreted if I admitted to the encounter from the previous night. That's why I didn't."

"Someone is behind this," Clara said confidently. "Someone who wished to injure you both."

"Whoever it was will discover I am equally capable of retaliation," Miss Cowing said, her eyes showing her mettle.

Robinson was too agitated to nap after what had happened, so he dressed again and returned to Exhibition Hall. The latest upset with Miss Cowing, added to the preceding incidents, revealed a level of underhandedness that disgusted him. He discovered, to his dismay and delight, that his display was overrun with people, and queues had formed for those who wished to give their name and information so they could be the first to place orders. Some of the judges, he learned from Wickins, had told others, and possible investors had begun mobbing their corner of the hall. Whereas it had felt like they'd been in exile earlier, now the flow of people was bottlenecked at their corner. Once apprised of the situation, he immediately went to work, explaining the invention to the dignitaries who'd come, and he spent hours sharing the information with anyone who could get close enough to him to listen.

When evening came, the crowds got even larger. Clara had returned to the hall after a private interview with Elizabeth Cowing, and she was helping answer questions and sharing information as well. The lamps glowed, providing the illumination necessary to keep going, and Robinson wondered if any of them were getting home before midnight. After nightfall, in the cooler part of the day, even more crowds arrived. Robinson felt hunger pangs, but continued to press on, knowing each person he spoke to could play a role in growing his business.

When the crowd ebbed, hours later, Clara pulled him back behind the display curtains so he could have a little bowl of chicken stew and a roll.

"Have the crowds lessened?" he asked, spooning the soup into his mouth in rapid succession.

"They're starting to, but Wickins thinks we have enough orders already to compete with needs from the military. He thinks we're going to need more partners in manufacturing."

He was relieved to hear it. He knew, firsthand, that Mr. Foster's investment in the school of the deaf hadn't yet resulted in financial success. Growth in enrollment was still lagging behind projections, because it was difficult to find enough willing teachers to meet the growing demand. Adding to the strain, another suit his father-in-law had been working on hadn't paid out yet. Robinson's invention could be a financial boon to the entire family.

"I should write McKenna tonight," he said, scraping the bottom of the little bowl with the spoon before putting both down on the little workbench. "I hope she's feeling better."

"We did hear from Mother. They're all at the house on Brake Street. And under protection from the officers of the Marshalcy. The military wanted to bring McKenna in for protection, but Mother wouldn't have it. I think all is well at the moment."

"Good. Two more days of the exhibits and then we're done and can return home. What an extraordinary event."

"Are you glad you came, then?"

He gave her a weary smile and nodded. A throb of warning alerted him that something was wrong, followed by a familiar sound. One just beneath the usual register of hearing. He looked up and noticed the pulsing lights from his display. That, in itself, wasn't worrisome, because the demonstrations had been happening all day and evening. But this time, he felt a preternatural warning, felt the tremor of an inaudible growl from his invisible friend.

"What's wrong?" Clara asked, noticing the transformation of his expression.

Robinson fished his hand into his pocket and brought out the device. Quickly, with his thumb, he turned the combination and released the inner ring. He did so calmly, deliberately, but his heart was beginning to pound with the dark memories of the first night the Semblance had come to kill him. Maybe his body was still processing that moment. Maybe his intuition was on edge because of the strange arrival of Elizabeth Cowing that afternoon. But he had learned to listen to himself, and he knew something was off.

Robinson slid on the thumb ring and felt the same acute stab of pain in his skull he always did. The pain made his eyes close for a moment as he adjusted to the blinding sensation of discomfort. As the gold of the band worked, he could hear whispers from the Aesir tongue again, fervent whispers . . . commands . . . that were growing louder and louder.

"You're frightening me," Clara murmured, her voice thick with worry.

He stuffed the device in his pocket and walked back through the curtain, his eyes scanning the crowd. There were fewer people, but it was still quite busy, a parade of faces and expressions, of different ages and manner of dress—although the majority were higher end.

Wickins was giving a demonstration with the tuning fork, approaching the corner of their display, and the lights were following him.

The demonstration was concealing the presence of a Semblance. He felt the warning in his mind—a subliminal communication from his invisible friend. It wasn't the bulbs that were giving it away. There was another magic at work, one of a different resonance. He wasn't sure how he knew, but he did.

"Rob?" Clara asked worriedly, her hand touching his arm.

"There's a Semblance here," he whispered to her. "Help me find it."

It was forbidden to discuss Semblances openly, but Clara knew as much as he did after General Colsterworth's visit to the Brake Street house.

"What am I looking for?" she asked, her throat catching. He sensed her thoughts, her desire to cry out and warn Wickins.

Don't, he thought to her, his mind sending out the thought in a pulse.

He looked from face to face as quickly as he could. One man stood out from the others. A man sweating profusely, a man walking stiffly, jerkily, through the crowd toward him, eyes feverish with delirium.

The man had a pistol. As soon as Robinson gazed at him, he saw it. Then the Semblance raised his arm, pistol in hand, and fired it.

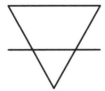

CHAPTER EIGHTEEN

A TRUE SORCERER

The explosion caused by the saltpetr made a deafening noise that elicited shrieks of fear. The bullet deflected off an invisible shield. Robinson hadn't had time to sing any defenses, but the device in his vest pocket had reacted as it had in the past, shielding him from the elfshot. Robinson immediately began casting defensive spells, murmuring the tunes quickly and firmly. The magic wrenched the pistol from the man's hand, and it flew to the nearest metal beam. After seizing Clara by the shoulders and pushing her behind him, Robinson walked purposefully toward the intruder, weaving strands of magic to capture the Semblance and block off his connection to the Aesir voices commanding him. Voices Robinson could discern because he was still wearing the ring. But because of the many bystanders, Robinson had to be cautious in the dimensions of his spell so as not to trap others in with the fellow.

The man pulled a dirk from his pocket, lunged, and stabbed a well-dressed man with a jeweled cane in the neck. Robinson felt a shift, an exchange of power. The Semblance had just jumped bodies. The sweating wreck of a man he'd been collapsed to the ground, eyes lifeless and vacant. Many people were trying to flee now, but the press of the crowd made it impossible.

Robinson saw the man with the cane jerk his arm free of his wife and clench the cane in his hands. It suddenly charged with energy. The jeweled top was an Aesir artifact, and it had just been activated. The lamps burned so brightly, the light stung his eyes.

Robinson continued forward, using the intelligences around him to form a cage around the man. Something to trap him. Something to keep the Semblance confined and alive so it could be studied. Maybe then the nature of the magic could be revealed. His eardrums felt stuffy, the pain caused by a sudden change in pressure. What was happening?

"Alfred! Alfred!" shrieked the wife, who gaped at her husband's changed countenance with terror. She was trying to reach her husband, but Robinson's shield prevented her from doing so. It was a narrowed shape, an oval instead of a sphere. He'd done the calculations in his mind rapidly.

The pressure in his eardrums became more intense. He saw people clamping their palms against their ears, so he wasn't the only one being affected by it. Cries of fear and terror mixed with the saltpetr haze.

Gazing at the glowing jewel atop the cane, Robinson realized that the artifact was enacting one of the Unseen Powers. The glow of the jewel looked vaguely familiar to him. He couldn't recall where he'd seen it before, but he sensed the danger.

The spell he'd used in the alley had ruptured those men's eardrums, but it had worked instantly, this was more gradual. It was different . . .

Realization struck.

Attraction and repulsion. The spell being cast was opposite the one Robinson had cast previously, which had shattered eardrums. Instead of a burst of magical sound going out, the Semblance's spell was dragging energy in. An implosion. The jewel was sucking things toward it, causing a pressure imbalance.

They were all standing in an iron building sheathed in glass. Under enough inward pressure, the glass would burst and all the jagged shards would come rushing toward the Semblance. Robinson's protective shield would defend him, while all the people around him would get sliced through by the shards. Cracking noises from some of the quicksilver lamps could be heard as the pressure mounted.

This was no accidental meeting. The Semblance had known about the man with the cane. Of course an Aesir would recognize the magic of its own kind. He'd come ready to kill Robinson with elfshot and, failing that, trigger an implosion that would kill scores of people. Whether or not the device in Robinson's pocket would save him from the blast was irrelevant. Everyone else, Clara and Wickins included, would be cut to ribbons.

An idea came to him. A spell. The complexity of it surprised him, but he attributed the surge of knowledge to his invisible friend, the dog intelligence who had been his companion.

Gems were forged by intense natural pressure deep beneath the earth's surface. Diamonds were the hardest of such stones and thus one of the most popularly used in Aesir magical artifacts. They could absorb immense amounts of magical pressure.

But that hardness made them structurally vulnerable to blunt force. The natural inclusions in the stone were subject to strain and would shear or shatter if enough force was applied to the right place.

"Percutis malleo," Robinson sang, directing the song at the gem fixed to the staff.

The diamond in the staff shattered into thousands of tiny shards. The pressure in their ears immediately began to fade. The lights from the bulbs winked out.

The Semblance glared at him in frustration. Gripping the cane with both hands, he tried smashing the shield spell, but no damage was done. He was trapped inside.

Robinson sealed off the final part of his caging spell, which blocked the whispers of the Aesir. The wealthy man's expression turned confused as he beheld his broken cane and looked around at his wife.

"Alfred! What's going on!" the woman wailed.

Robinson sent a thought to Wickins. *Get everyone out of here. He's a Semblance. The military will come.*

Wickins, startled by the mental intrusion into his thoughts, looked over at Robinson and then nodded. With the other workers who were helping out, he began directing people away from the scene.

"Please make your way downstairs! Come now, help that poor chap up! Everyone must leave, but be patient for your turn. We must clear the hall."

Whistles sounded from officers of the Marshalcy, and soon the crowd was dispersing. Did they realize how close they'd come to dying? If Robinson hadn't broken the magic of the cane, there would have been countless killed or injured.

Uniformed military came up the steps, armed with rifles and swords, and began ushering the people away from the scene.

Clara, standing at Rob's elbow suddenly, smoothed some loose strands of hair from her face.

"He's . . . a Semblance?" she whispered in a low voice. The original host still lay prostrate on the floor.

"He is," Robinson whispered back.

"I can't get out of here, Mazie. I'm trapped." The man who'd been stabbed in the neck looked remarkably hale, as if his wound had already closed.

His wife was frantic. "Please try, Alfred! I don't understand what happened. My ears are still hurting."

Robinson maintained the spell, keeping the man bottled up, closed off from communication with the Aesir. As he approached the invisible trap, he observed the man's injury. There was a wound on the fellow's neck, some blood on his shirt, but the injury didn't seem like it should be life-threatening. Yet the Semblance had transferred to the man's body and would no doubt take over again if he were allowed to mingle with the crowd. Robinson's heart panged for the wife, knowing her husband was already dead, felled by a killing stroke. Unless they could find a way to sever the connection without losing the host body.

The pain in Robinson's skull from using the ring was such that he pulled it off and put it back into the device inside his pocket. Soldiers closed in around them, aiming their weapons at Robinson and Clara as well as the older man. They held up their hands passively, but Robinson didn't fear their bullets.

"You've got it wrong, Captain," Wickins was telling another officer. "Professor Hawksley saved us!"

The glass bulbs from the demonstration began to glow again, revealing the presence of more Aesir magic. A man with a kappelin was approaching them from farther down the corridor, hood lowered. Robinson thought he recognized the fellow, the same man who had come to the house on Brake Street with General Colsterworth. Mr. Stoker.

When he reached the Semblance, he looked at the hysterical wife and motioned for one of the soldiers to take her away.

"Let me go!" she shouted, struggling until a second man subdued her. "Alfred! Alfred!"

Mr. Stoker gave her a dispassionate look and then fixed his gaze on the Semblance trapped inside the shell. As soon as the woman was out of sight, he drew his pistol and spoke.

"Release the cage, Professor."

"Not if you're going to kill him," Robinson answered flatly.

He sighed. "Need I remind you? He's already dead."

The man trapped in the shield blanched. "I-I'm not! I'm not dead!"

"Professor. Now."

Robinson stared at the soldier and shook his head. "This is a chance to study one. To find a way to break the enchantment."

"It's not the man's *fault* he was stabbed in the neck," Clara said, her voice quavering slightly.

"Miss Foster, your opinion isn't worth salt. Professor. Release the spell before I have you arrested."

"On what charge?" Robinson asked, his emotions tight and raw. This wasn't right. This was an abomination of conscience.

"Let's start with treason. This is not the only one roaming among us. We are strapped for manpower to hunt them. It is my duty to mete out justice in this situation. It is not your place to defy one of a superior rank in the Invisible College."

"Is this why Isaac Berrow established the Invisible College?" Robinson shot back at him, his own voice throbbing with emotion. "To run roughshod over principle? May I study this man for an hour at least? Seek to learn what allows such hostage-taking to occur? There may be another way to counteract it."

There had to be. There had to be, because he was starting to think there was a serious chance McKenna could be a Semblance, and he couldn't let them kill her. He wouldn't.

"I don't know what you're talking about, but this is frightening me considerably!" wailed the man within the shield.

"You think that hasn't been tried before, Professor? By smarter men and women than you? You give yourself too much credit."

"I take no credit at all," Robinson said. "What you are doing is reprehensible."

"I don't have the luxury to think like that. Do you know how many of my friends have been butchered by the Aesir? How many have bled to death in the snow?"

"You want revenge?"

"This isn't about revenge, Professor. It is about *survival*. They are coming for us again this winter. Thousands more will die. Tens of thousands. How many did this one nearly kill today? Release the cage. Now."

Robinson lowered it. He didn't agree with the man, but he knew when he was beaten. If he was truly charged with treason during wartime, not even Mr. Foster would be able to get him a lighter sentence.

As soon as the shield was down, the wealthy man's face transformed into a look of savagery, and he lunged at Mr. Stoker.

But Stoker had been expecting a strike. He fired a single shot into the man's skull, and the attacker went down in a heap, falling face-first on the floor.

Clara stifled a gasp of fear and clung to Robinson's arm. They both stared at the man on the floor, writhing for two seconds before his body stilled. A wisp of frosty breath came from his mouth. The brutality of the heat in the hall made it quickly fade and vanish.

Just like that. Sorrow pierced Robinson's heart.

"Arrest these two and take them to Gresham College," Mr. Stoker said to one of the other leaders. "The general will want to speak to them."

"You're *arresting* us?" Clara demanded.

The soldier smirked and began giving other orders to remove the bodies.

A vast quantity of nonsense is talked about bad men not being able to look you in the face. Never trust that conventionally trite idea. Dishonesty will stare honesty out of countenance any day in the week if there is anything to be got by it. The only way the Invisible College will long endure is if when such subterfuge unmasks itself, it is promptly punished and that individual barred from his or her or any quorum. When the handshake of one sorcerer to another becomes meaningless, when honesty means less than dishonesty, cracks in the walls of the order will soon follow. There is nothing more despicable than an empty semblance of virtue.

—Isaac Berrow,
Master of the Royal Secret,
the Invisible College

General Colsterworth

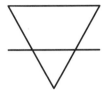

CHAPTER NINETEEN

A SORCEROUS DEVICE

When General Colsterworth's carriage arrived back at Gresham College following an otherworldly delicious meal of saffron salmon and wine, he stifled a rising belch before exiting the carriage—only to be accosted by several adjutants.

"General, I thought you were dining at the Sycophancy tonight?" one blustered.

"There was a last-minute change of plans," the general replied. "What's all this nonsense about?" He began walking swiftly toward the gatehouse where he could enter the building but was halted in his tracks by what the man said next.

"A Semblance attacked at the Great Exhibition tonight."

He rounded on the adjutant. "The heat alone should have prevented such a thing from occurring. What happened? Tell me the details at once!"

"The Semblance made it to the second floor and attacked Professor Hawksley," butted in another soldier, who wanted a share in the story.

"Don't all talk at once," Colsterworth snapped. They matched his stride, and armed soldiers flanked their group as they entered the building. "Major—the details. Quickly!"

"Professor Hawksley disarmed the Semblance, but it stabbed an innocent bystander, a Mr. Alfred John Bagley. He was holding an Aesir artifact, which the Semblance then used to cast a spell that would have shattered the glass throughout that wing. Fortunately, Professor Hawksley disarmed and trapped the Semblance."

"He trapped him? How?"

"I'm unfamiliar with the spells he used, but Stoker arrested him and brought him here. The Semblance was executed on the premises."

"Great blizzard, this happened in Bishopsgate? And why was Hawksley arrested? The man sounds like a hero. Insufferable!"

"He's been brought here . . . to Gresham College." The major sounded hesitant, like he was worried they'd done the wrong thing.

Oh, they had botched the situation completely! Completely!

"Is he in a holding cell?"

"Yes, General."

"Well, confound it, release him and bring him to my office at once! Where is Stoker?"

"In your office."

"Go. And be quick about it."

"What about Foster's daughter?"

Colsterworth felt a spike of pain in his skull. Another headache was forming. The fish in his belly was mocking him now. "I thought she'd fled back to Auvinen? She returned?"

"No, the younger sister. She was arrested as well."

Colsterworth stopped midstride, giving the major a glare that threatened an imminent demotion. The man blanched. "I'll see she's released as well." And then he fled down the hall.

The general marched up the steps. First, the failed attempt to incriminate the professor and Miss Cowing. What a debacle that had been. Next, the professor's display had been an absolute victory.

All afternoon the general had been deflecting businesses fearing the coming lawsuits when it was discovered their lamp bulbs infringed on the inventor's patent and not Miss Cowing's. He'd done his best to quell the panicked businessmen before leaving for a restaurant to catch a meal since he hadn't eaten since breakfast.

He crossed the corridor to his office, where he found Stoker sitting in his chair, boots up on the desk. He'd been in such a reverie that he hadn't heard the general's approach. His eyes nearly popped out of his head in surprise, and he scrambled to his feet, looking humiliated at having been caught in such a posture.

"Do I understand correctly that you had Hawksley arrested?" the general asked tightly, closing the door with extreme patience.

"He wanted us to spare the Semblance. To bring it here to study. Even though he knows the law."

"He wanted to spare it? Even though it tried to kill him?"

"It nearly succeeded in killing us all," Stoker said defensively. He stepped around the desk, as if his buttocks burned from contact with the general's chair.

"What kind of magic did he use to capture it?"

"An inverted sphere, from what I could tell. Not a common spell, to be sure. General, I just wanted to apolo—"

Colsterworth's glare silenced him midword. "How did such a young sorcerer manage such complex spells in the midst of a threat of sudden violence? He's no soldier. He's an elocutionist."

"I asked him that very question," Stoker said, "during my interrogation. And why the elfshot didn't kill him. He's only a ninth-degree sorcerer. What he demonstrated today showed he's capable of much more. When he answered with false modesty, I pressed him further. That's when he confessed he possessed *this*."

Stoker reached into his coat pocket and produced what appeared to be a pocket watch without a chain.

Colsterworth frowned and took the clam-shaped device from the other man. "A watch?"

"Open it."

The salmon was impacting the general's digestion. He felt this whole situation was bothersome, but out of curiosity he opened the round lid. It was not a watch. It was unlike any device the general had ever seen. A spherical striated stone in the center with some dials of different sizes surrounding it. Some quartz or glass at the top showed three Aesir numbering runes: nine, nine, nine. He turned it over in his hands and saw two buttons on the top.

"Have you ever seen such an artifact before, General?"

Colsterworth shook his head. He twisted some of the inner dials but nothing happened. "Where did he get this?"

"He claims his father gave it to him after his brother's death. A family heirloom. He said it had protected him a couple of times. The winter night Crossthwait tried to kill Hawksley, he was protected by a shield he didn't summon. Later on, in the alley by his apartment, the device seems to have protected him again. And it protected him today at Exhibition Hall. The device is self-conjuring. It has sentience."

"Interesting," the general said. "He has no proof of ownership, then, if it was handed down?"

"Older artifacts require no proof of ownership. That law is a hundred years old, I believe."

If the device could preternaturally summon defensive magic and protect the bearer, it was not only rare but incredibly valuable. "What about the numbers? What do they signify?"

"He doesn't know. I tried to press him on that count, but he said he had nothing left to say on the matter. He knows more than he's revealed. I was going to request your permission to use alternative . . . interrogation methods."

"Torture?"

"I don't think it would come to that, General. The threat of being excommunicated from the Invisible College would likely suffice."

The sound of steps coming down the hallway announced the arrival of the professor and his sister-in-law.

"Leave through the other door," Colsterworth said, tossing his head toward the other exit.

Stoker was quick to oblige, but before he was gone, the general added, "If you ever sit in my chair again, Peabody, you will regret it." Stoker's eyes widened slightly, he paled and then left, softly shutting the door behind him.

Someone knocked.

"Enter!"

Major Dellenbach opened the door. The professor entered warily, gazing around the general's private office. His sister-in-law, the one just at the edge of joining Society, looked nervous as she entered behind him. The major shut the door and left them alone.

The general held the device in his hand just long enough for Hawksley to notice it before he slid it into his jacket pocket. The professor's brow wrinkled with agitation.

"I understand thanks are in order," the general said, stepping around his desk but not seating himself. He gestured to the chairs on the opposite side for them.

"The military has a decidedly peculiar way of expressing gratitude," Hawksley replied with a hint of contempt in his voice. The young woman shot him a warning look.

"I'm sure it will be in the papers tomorrow from here to Auvinen. It might even reach Siaconset. I can see the headlines. 'Esteemed professor saves crowd from deranged madman.' Oh, I should suggest that title myself to the editor of *The Borealis*."

"I couldn't care less," Hawksley said in his insufferable modesty. "But you won't say what really happened. You won't tell the world about Semblances."

"And neither will you when the press comes clamoring for interviews. You seem to have a knack for conflict, Professor. I wonder what draws it to you in such a way?"

"You're saying this is *my* fault?"

"Oh, it wasn't the *first* Semblance that has been drawn to you, Professor Hawksley. Did it try attacking again once the shield was lowered, I wonder?"

The professor stiffened. His companion looked away. She was very uncomfortable. As she should be. A pretty tart but quite young. Hawksley might not give a fig about his status, but this fashionable young woman did. He'd seen her type before. Pretty and proud until put in her place by someone of higher esteem.

"Surely, Professor, you must have considered that capturing and studying Semblances has been attempted in the past. Multiple times. But you won't find tales of those in your quorum in the Storrows. No. Not there."

"Perhaps I could find a way where others have failed?" he asked, his eyes concerned.

Oh, he was thinking about Mrs. Hawksley. The danger she was now in. The general knew when he had superior firepower.

"I suppose if Isaac Berrow were still alive, he might find a way. But you . . . I rather doubt it. You may go. I'll press no charges unless you leave me no choice."

Foster's daughter looked relieved. "Thank you, General Colsterworth." She turned to leave, but her companion was rooted in place.

"May I have it back, please?"

"I don't think so, Professor."

"It belongs to my family."

"Under Article Nine of the Rules of War, I can confiscate any private citizen's personal effects for the express intent of using said effects in the war effort. The law requires fair compensation, of course. But to determine what is fair, we must first learn what magical properties this device possesses. Immunity to elfshot would be considered . . . substantial. I'll have my best minds tinker with it and see what we can learn. The emperor thanks you for your understanding and for the generous use of this device."

Hawksley frowned, his brow furrowed with agitation. But he was wise enough not to argue. Nor could a ninth-degree sorcerer really think he could take on the power of someone of Colsterworth's rank. Some songs could kill.

Foster's daughter hooked her arm with her brother-in-law's and tugged him out of the office. He went docilely, but the look he gave the general promised retribution. He was powerless to exact it, of course. That made Colsterworth offer a parting smile as they left.

And he had just enough pique to add before the door closed, "Give your wife my best. I'm sorry she had to leave early. The heat is . . . insufferable."

The principle of gravity explains the motion of the planets. But it cannot explain what set them in motion to begin with. We cannot see the architect, but we see evidence of the craft. All things in motion were set in motion, we must conclude, by the Mind of the Sovereignty. When we observe our own solar system, I judge that the earth is the right distance from the sun to receive the proper amounts of heat and light for intelligences to thrive. This did not happen by chance.

I can calculate the motion of heavenly bodies, but I cannot calculate the madness of mortal motivations.

—Isaac Berrow,
Master of the Royal Secret,
the Invisible College

MaKenna Aurora Hawksley

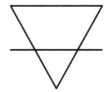

CHAPTER TWENTY

The Return

The locomotivus station was thronged with people disgorging from the machine that had just arrived from Bishopsgate. McKenna had hooked arms with her mother and Trudie to avoid getting too jostled by the crowds. People were waving, calling out to the new arrivals. A jet of frosty smoke came from the bulkhead of the engine, and McKenna wished they were standing closer to it so she could feel the coolness on her face. It was early afternoon, and the locomotivus from Bishopsgate was finally due to arrive.

While searching through the sea of faces for her husband, sister, and father, she spied the officers of the Marshalcy standing in close proximity. Her bodyguards. There had been no further infractions against her, no sign of the mysterious figure who had frightened her in the station yard in Bishopsgate.

Soon, perhaps it would not matter as much. She trusted more in Rob's ability to protect her than she did in the uniformed sorcerers now assigned to that duty.

Mother patted her arm and then pointed. Following the line of her arm, she spied her husband stepping out from the private booth section near the front of the locomotivus. After climbing down, he turned and gallantly helped Clara dismount the steps and then Father. Wickins came afterward.

Mother waved and shouted something to them, and then the family was reunited. It had been days since McKenna had seen her husband, and the lonely ache in her heart was driven away when he rushed to her, embraced her, and lifted her clear off her feet in a twirl. *That* she had not expected, but it was very much welcome after the awkwardness of their first day in Bishopsgate—as if the sun had chased away shadows. He was happy to see her. But he looked exhausted and undernourished again. He'd been lacking her wholesome tyranny while they were parted, and she meant to rectify that immediately.

Mother and Father embraced, sharing a gentle kiss. McKenna noticed that Clara was holding Wickins's hand as they stood near each other. Trudie was going from person to person with hugs for all.

"I *so* wanted to go!" she exclaimed.

When Rob set McKenna down, she looked up into his face, taking in the stubble on his cheeks and chin. "You're home," she said to him, wondering if he could even hear her over the tumult. "When we read the papers about what happened, I was so worried about you. But so, so proud!"

He smiled, abashed, and shook his head. "I'm grateful the exhibition is over. It was a triumphant success. You were right, McKenna. I'm tired. Very tired. But I'm grateful I was there." His eyes looked thoughtful as he gazed into hers. He stroked her cheek with his knuckle. "Are you feeling any better?"

She nodded. "I'm much improved. The summer is so . . . so hot. Oh, and Sarah came by. The students' final examinations concluded well. No issues. You are free of your commitments to the university. We can finally go on our honeymoon."

Father approached and hugged McKenna, interrupting the conversation. "Shall we depart?" he suggested. "It will be a tight squeeze, but I think we can all fit in the carriage."

McKenna wrapped her arm around Rob and patted his chest with her free hand. They maneuvered through the dispersing crowd to the carriage. It wasn't spacious enough for all of them, so Clara and Wickins offered to ride in the pilot box with the driver. That left plenty of space for the rest of them. The officers from the Marshalcy followed in one of their own carriages.

"It's been so dull at home," Trudie complained once the carriage got underway. "It's so unfair I couldn't go. You must tell me all about it, Rob. I want to hear how you fought off that Semblance who attacked you!"

That particular detail had not been shared with the press. But the exchange of letters home had revealed most of the story.

"Later, perhaps." Rob clearly wasn't in a talkative mood. McKenna leaned into him, putting her hand on his leg, and he stroked her shoulder.

"We've made three new licensing agreements with additional manufacturers," Father told Mother. "The demand for the invention has far exceeded our wildest expectations. We have requests for demonstrations in six other cities. I'm surprised that the military hasn't shown much interest so far. They stand to benefit the most."

"They have their reasons, I'm sure," Mother said, but her look was disapproving.

The jostling of the carriage ended as they arrived back at the house on Brake Street. She'd miss the bowls of cherries in her parents' home each summer day once they moved. But Mowbray House had been part of her childhood as well. The thought of the salty air and cool breezes was tantalizing her. She was desperate to get away from the city, away from the crowds.

After everyone was back inside, standing in clusters in the parlor, they all started talking at once, and McKenna couldn't follow every conversation. Clara and Wickins were talking animatedly about the future of the company. Apparently Clara had been a key promoter of the invention, and the foundry thought it might be just the thing if she joined Wickins on the demonstrations in far-flung cities. She was exuberant about the possibility, but Father sternly reminded her that she was still underage and it would be entirely improper for her to traipse through the empire with a young man.

"But Father, *you'll* be there to chaperone us!" Clara teased.

Father didn't rise to the bait but sat down in his favorite chair and removed his pince-nez glasses to massage his nose.

After a few moments, McKenna brought Rob to one of the couches. Trudie asked if he would play the Broadwood grand first, but he declined and said he was too weary, so she bounded off to another room. Dinner would be early that night, and McKenna could already smell the dish cooking—a family favorite, the seafood bake—as a reward for their triumph.

She was starting to sit down on the couch, but he grasped her wrists and tugged her upright. "I just wanted to tell you how sorry I am for everything. I've been so worried about you. I wanted to come to you, but I also wanted to make you proud. I could have handled things better when you arranged for me to go to the Great Exhibition. Hard as it was, it was the right thing to do."

Her eyes widened with surprise as she read his lips, and then she softened with pleasure. "I'm sorry too, Rob. I'm not proud of the way I got you to go, but I'm grateful you went. Things all worked out, didn't they? And I *am* proud of you."

He leaned in and kissed her hair.

Moments later, everyone joined them, the family arraying themselves in the usual manner so that McKenna could be included in most of what was said. Trudie, of course, begged Clara for details about the shocking event that had happened at the exhibition. Clara had a dramatic way of storytelling, which she used to great effect. They'd read the details in the newspaper, of course, but hearing the account first-hand made McKenna squeeze Rob's hand as the story was repeated. When they got to the part where the soldier had shot the Semblance, it made McKenna shudder and glance at her mother.

Mother's expression was taciturn at that part. But worry flashed through her eyes when she met McKenna's gaze.

"Then that ingrate had us arrested!" Clara declared, hands on her hips to strike an indignant pose. "They searched us thoroughly—what a mortification—and found Rob's device and took it away! The scoundrels! General Colsterworth still has it. He said he had the authority to take it through the war powers act. Oh, and he smugly implied we might never get it back."

McKenna looked at Rob's face, but his expression hadn't changed. He was listening to Clara tell the story, but something else was troubling him. Or maybe it was losing the heirloom that had him in such a state. The device had helped him with his experiments and inventions—and it had provided them with invaluable protection.

"I am writing a motion to have Professor Hawksley's heirloom returned," Father said from his chair. "If the military cannot figure out how to use it within a reasonable amount of time, I will argue that it falls outside the use required for war. My only concern is that they *do* find it useful or discover how to dislodge the inner ring."

"Do you think they will?" Mother asked.

"I don't think they have enough brains between them to do so," Clara said. "They can't *make* us tell them, can they?"

"No, I don't think they can legally compel us to reveal anything we know." Father put his spectacles back on. "It was the general who declared the device useful. Now the burden of responsibility is up to him to prove *how* it will be so."

"Father," Clara said. "If I were out in Society, would it then be possible for me to travel with Wickins? As an adult? As long as there was another person from the Invisible College with us?"

"Clara." Mother shook her head.

"I think I've been more than patient," Clara said. "And I know I can contribute something to the business. It will benefit everyone. Perhaps someone from my quorum can travel with us. Or the Storrows."

"It's premature to discuss this," Father said. "Your mother and I will talk about it first. For now, we all need a little peace and quiet. It really seems our family fortunes have changed for the better. If all continues to proceed in this manner, we'll be able to open up the house in Bishopsgate again. Hire on more help there and at the school for the deaf. Possibly expand it. We need time to adjust to the change."

"I'm tired of waiting," Clara said forcefully. Then she shot an imploring look at Wickins.

McKenna wondered if he would be brash enough to reply, and to her surprise, he was. "Sir, I've made no secret of my interest in your daughter. Your daughter as well, Mrs. Foster. My apologies. But regardless of my personal interest, I watched her flourish at the Great Exhibition. She was eloquent, decisive, and her instincts were spot on. Especially in that bizarre moment with Miss Cowing. If it weren't for Clara, things could have turned out very differently. I think . . . I think you should trust her to make her own decision."

McKenna glanced at Rob, who was giving his friend an approving smile and a nod of respect, before her gaze landed on her father.

"Your opening statement is well said, sir. We shall see," Father said after a moment, closing the discussion but not barring it. A card table was brought out, and games were gathered to be played.

"Would you like to go to the greenhouse?" McKenna whispered in Rob's ear.

He nodded, and the two of them discreetly excused themselves and walked out of the parlor. Since the curtains were shut, the change in scene would afford them a little privacy. At least the greenhouse wasn't intolerably hot since the upper windows were open and a little breeze was blowing. They walked hand in hand to the spot where they'd had some of their first private interviews as a courting couple.

In fact, as soon as they were inside, she couldn't restrain herself any longer and began smothering his mouth with kisses. He responded with equal ardor, and before long the two lovers were quite breathless. She *had* missed him. She'd missed him very much. His own longing was apparent in his caresses, his fervor. Inside the garden greenhouse, they were away from the prying eyes of her family and the pesky officers of the Marshalcy.

"Something is eating at you," McKenna said after breaking off the kiss. She wanted to share her secrets, but not right then. Not so soon after the incident with the Semblance.

"I've missed you," he said, panting.

"Tell me we get to go on a proper honeymoon. Will you take me to Covesea? Can we visit other places too?"

"Yes," he declared. "I would love to travel with you. But I'm . . . worried."

"What about?" She felt a nagging feeling, a twisting of scruples. Should she tell him? Mother had suggested keeping their suspicion a secret for now. Was that the right thing to do? He was already beneath the gaze of the military. They were suspicious enough. And had proven, more than once, how seriously they took the risk.

He reached into his pocket and produced the mysterious device.

"Did you steal it back?" she asked, gaping.

He shook his head. "It appeared in my valise the day it was taken. I found it that night before going to bed. I wondered who had snuck it back to me. One of the soldiers? But the more I consider it, the more I think no one returned it."

She blinked in astonishment. "It just . . . reappeared?"

He nodded. "I think it is connected to me. A spell that prevents it from being stolen? I've been sick with worry that General Colsterworth would arrive again, at a moment's notice, demanding it. But nothing. Not a word. I haven't even told Wickins. Or your father. But I had to tell you. It has . . . powers I don't understand. I would like you to keep it a secret, McKenna. Would you?"

She nodded but felt a twinge of guilt. Her own secret, she didn't feel she should tell. Not yet. Maybe during their honeymoon when they were far away. Maybe never.

Maybe the secret would reveal itself when it was time.

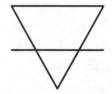

CHAPTER TWENTY-ONE

THE CHANGING OF THE TIDE

McKenna finished sweeping the last crumbs with a rickety broom, then deposited the debris into a rubbish bin by the front door of their nearly empty apartment. The little table where they'd eaten their meals together looked barren and lonely. The door leading to the now vacant alchemy was open, and she set aside the broom and walked over to it, gazing at the space. She could still smell the residue of the chymicals, all bundled away into several large trunks and strapped to the back of the Foster family carriage outside. She folded her arms, leaned her head against the doorjamb, and thought on the many afternoons and evenings she'd spent in this place assisting Rob and Wickins on their work. A smile tugged at her mouth.

Leaning the way she was, she felt the tremors of footfalls coming up behind her and turned before Rob reached her, his eyebrows lifted inquisitively. "Are you ready to leave?"

She clasped her hands behind her back and looked up at him. It had been a few weeks since his return from the Great Exhibition. They'd had several dinners with the family on Brake Street on Closure, including a large and joyous celebration of Clara's coming of age, and had been steadily collecting their belongings in preparation to leave Auvinen for McKenna's inheritance from Aunt Margaret—their home on the isle of Siaconset.

"I'm going to miss this little apartment. We had happy nights here. And one particularly terrifying one."

His smile faded with her recollection of the night the soldier had come believing Rob was a Semblance when, in fact, he had been one himself. Even with all the magical protections her husband had put in place afterward, she still didn't feel totally safe. It was hard to shake the fear that the military might come again with pistol and elfshot. And this time they would be coming for *her*.

Rob put his hands on her shoulders, gazing at her upturned face. "I'll protect you, McKenna." He sighed. "It's good that we're leaving, but I'm glad we were able to stop by the school for the deaf yesterday to see Sarah Fuller Fiske and the children. I'm going to miss them."

"We're coming back," McKenna insisted. "With all the invitations flooding in, I imagine we'll be traveling a good deal after our honeymoon." He'd been invited to meet with many notable people from different quorums of the Invisible College. People who wanted to invest in him and his ideas. Others who had problems they hoped he could solve. His reputation had spread as far as Iskandir, where an esteemed professor had invited him to the university to give some lectures before winter. To be honest, there were too many invitations to accept all of them.

"I'd rather not travel all over the empire before winter. I may be taking a sabbatical, but I still want to get back to my research. My inventions." He tapped her nose with his fingertip. "I want to see if you can sing. Or if there is another way to bridge the gap and allow you to use magic."

He hadn't forgotten about her goal, and that pleased her enough that she wrapped her arms around his waist and give him a lingering kiss, which led to him grazing his lips down her neck.

"Enough of that, you rogue," she teased. "We should probably get going if you still want to see the widow and her family before we leave town."

They left the apartment hand in hand, pausing only to lock the door behind them, and then walked to the carriage and their ever-patient driver. Rob helped her inside, and they were whisked off to the other part of town, the tenements, where the widow and her children lived. McKenna had prepared a little purse of coins for the mother, and Rob had tied a small stack of books with string to give to the oldest boy he'd been mentoring. The living conditions in that part of town were rough, and McKenna couldn't help but think of the other children who'd also been struck with the redoubtable fever but had been sent to live in asylums. She wanted to do more to ease the suffering of so many. She *would* do more.

Mrs. Farmer and her children were grateful for the visit and welcomed them inside. McKenna saw the little magical devices Rob had fixed or made to add some comfort to their squalid living conditions. There was the little heater he had fixed, along with a metal lock box for the mother to store the family valuables in—one that was bolted to the floor with a barnacle intelligence, the lock controlled by a vocal command understood by a parakeet intelligence. She presented the gift herself to Mrs. Farmer, who thanked her with tear-filled eyes for the generosity. The young son, Jake, gawked at the gift of books and promised to read them all.

"I'm going to be a sorcerer someday!" he proclaimed.

Rob mussed up his hair. "I don't doubt it. Keep reading. Keep learning. When I'm back in town, I'll check on you and see how you're progressing."

Mrs. Farmer said, "With these funds, I won't need to send him to the workhouse. He can go to a proper school."

McKenna felt her throat thicken, and she embraced the mother and the little girls. Rob gave Jake a sturdy handshake, a knowing smile, and then they went back to the carriage. Next they went to the docks, where their transport ship awaited them. They'd secured passage on a vessel on its way to Andover, which would drop them off at Siaconset on the way. Two porters were enlisted to help carry their luggage on board, and Rob insisted on accompanying them to their private quarters to make sure his precious equipment wasn't *misplaced* along the way. This was the same harbor that Rob and his parents had arrived in, and he'd previously related his misadventure with a troupe of thieves.

In less than an hour, the rest of McKenna's family arrived, along with Wickins, who had let a new apartment in the manufacturing district so he could get to work faster. It still felt unusual to see him in civilian clothing, but he was only too grateful to have resigned his commission with the military and stood to become quite prosperous from his part in the Fosters' venture.

"Ah, Dickemore, I'm going to miss you!" Wickins said in his usual congenial tone, giving Rob a fierce hug. "I shall gladly eat your portion at dinner, though. Please, Mrs. Foster, don't prepare any less food now that the scarecrow is leaving!"

Rob chuckled at the banter. "I have an idea to see if I can fashion a new ring to replace the one the military took away. I should like to experiment to see if we can touch minds even as far as Siaconset." Even though Rob had the ring back in his possession, he and McKenna still hadn't shared that fact with anyone else.

"Splendid, old chap! Just . . . don't wake me up in the middle of the night. Unless it's urgent."

"The middle of the night may be the only time the professor has to work on his inventions," Clara said, giving her brother-in-law an affectionate hug. "Three more invitations came this morning alone. I'll give them to McKenna since she's handling your business affairs."

"I may even come to miss your teasing," Rob said to Clara. Then he welcomed an embrace from Trudie, who looked quite melancholy. "What's troubling you, Trudie?"

"I'm going to miss you playing for us," she said. "Do you have a new violin yet?"

"No. Not yet. When I return, and I have a new one, you shall be the first to command the tune."

"Really?"

He gave a hearty nod to show how important she was to him, which made McKenna love him all the more.

Father tapped McKenna on the elbow to get her attention. "I thought you should know two things. The first, we had a sizable offer to purchase your shares of the business outright from one of the largest manufacturers of quicksilver lamps."

"How sizable?" McKenna asked.

"I was befuddled for a moment when I counted the zeros. Such an offer, I believe, indicates we have a prosperous position that will only be worth more in the future. I don't recommend selling. It's too soon. It also implies they are desperate to secure part of the business upfront for a customer they already have. That bodes well for us."

"It does indeed. How much are we talking about, Father?"

"Enough to rival the inheritance from Aunt Margaret, which was substantial on its own. That leads me to my next article of business." Father glanced at the others, as if to discern whether they were distracted.

"Go on," McKenna encouraged.

"It is regarding your aunt's death. I've made inquiries before and after the inquest. I hired a retired officer from the Marshalcy to do it . . . discreetly. He met with me yesterday to give me a report on the situation."

"You're alarming me, Father."

"I don't mean to. Let me be succinct. There were many passengers who come and go on that ferry—military men, visitors, and what have you. But one man both came and left on the same day your aunt died. Highly unusual for a visitor."

McKenna's stomach tightened. "Oh?"

"He asked for a description of the man. The fellow stood out because he was wearing a kappelin. His features seem to match the identity of one Joseph Crossthwait. The same officer, it turns out, who later tried to kill Robinson. I find the connection highly suspicious. I am going to pursue this, which will put our family in direct confrontation with General Colsterworth."

McKenna's stomach shriveled even more. "Father," she whispered, shaking her head.

"Men in authority must be held accountable for their actions, McKenna. The events surrounding the Great Exhibition, including the maneuvers involving Miss Cowing, all fit together in a pattern of abuse of power."

"What are we talking about?" Mother asked, her smile bright as she approached them and gave McKenna a hug. Her brightness faded when she saw the look on her daughter's face. "Did you tell her?"

Mr. Foster nodded and adjusted his pince-nez glasses. Oh, she loved her father. He was a respected and formidable barrister, and if anyone could take on the military, it was surely him. But she feared General Colsterworth.

McKenna embraced her mother and surreptitiously whispered in her ear, "Have you told him yet? Does Father know?"

When Mother pulled away, she shook her head. "We have time to sort this all out, I hope. Go enjoy your travels. Enjoy your time together."

"We will," McKenna thought, her cheeks feeling flushed now. A feeling came over her again, one that she was becoming familiar with. A need to flee. She wanted to take Rob by the hand, march up the gangway, and leave Auvinen. To escape. To hide.

To become invisible.

Something told her it was the only way they'd both survive.

If I have made any valuable discoveries, it has been due more to patient attention than to any other talent. There is no substitute for hard work.

—Isaac Berrow,
Master of the Royal Secret,
the Invisible College

Robinson Foster Hawksley

CHAPTER TWENTY-TWO

Mowbray House

The journey to Siaconset was nothing like Robinson's first attempt—when he'd gone there to seek out McKenna. There were no delays, no sequestering in a hotel, and when their ship arrived and docked, Mr. Swope, the manservant who had done Aunt Margaret's bidding, was waiting to bring them back to the house in an open carriage. Robinson had never been introduced to the fellow before and found him genial, with a bushy mustache and balding head. He was efficient, besides, took charge of the porters and their gear immediately, and helped stack the chests and trunks into the carriage himself. Robinson handed his coat to McKenna and did his share of the manual labor.

"It's truly a pleasure to welcome you back to Siaconset, my lady," Mr. Swope said, bowing his head to McKenna and offering a serious smile. Mr. Swope was spare of frame, and Robinson noticed the man had a holstered pistol beneath his jacket pocket. The man's friendliness did not conceal that he paid attention to his surroundings. That was for the good. Robinson imagined the staff was still reeling about the untimely incident that had killed Aunt Margaret. The circumstances of her death were still murky, which had left everyone with an unsettled feeling.

Robinson helped McKenna up to the pilot box and climbed up next. There was room for four, so they weren't crammed together.

"How is Mrs. Foraker?" McKenna asked.

"As busy as you can imagine," Mr. Swope answered, turning his face so that she could read his lips. "The master bedroom has been cleared of your aunt's belongings and the clothes and dresses donated to the poor. Per your instructions, of course. The rest of the house is pretty much untouched, awaiting your inspection and decisions."

Robinson noticed a few of the pedestrians were wearing uniforms—a reminder that the island was near enough Gresham College to be a weekend leave retreat. That made him uneasy. He was worried about another possible confrontation with General Colsterworth or his minions. Their packed carriage was attracting attention, and several ladies waved pleasantly at them.

"I won't be making any changes soon, of course. We'll be leaving on our honeymoon."

"Understood," Mr. Swope agreed. "I'll be arranging your travel to Covesea and beyond, and Mrs. Foraker will help you pack for the journey. How long do you intend to stay? I ask because there is a freighter stopping tomorrow on the way to Covesea. The next one will be another week out."

McKenna turned her face to Robinson and lifted her eyebrows.

"Either suits me," he said. "You choose."

She patted his hand and turned back to Mr. Swope. "We'll take the freighter tomorrow."

Mr. Swope gave the horseflesh a snap with the riding crop, and soon they were rattling down the harbor planks and joining the leisurely traffic on the main thoroughfare. Soon the carriage clacked to a halt by the saltbox home in its fashionable neighborhood near the hub of downtown. Robinson remembered walking down this very same street with the letter in hand. McKenna's aunt had not been happy to see him at all, but he'd given her the letter and requested, in no uncertain terms, that it be delivered to her niece. Truthfully, he had not liked the woman. Still, her untimely end saddened him, particularly since nothing had quite been settled.

McKenna squeezed his arm and then pointed to one of the dormer windows. "That was my bedroom. I remember looking out the window that day . . . and seeing you walk away. I had no idea it was you until you were already gone."

He felt his cheeks heating with embarrassment. "At least Mr. Swope didn't chase me off."

"I think a warning shot would have done the trick," Mr. Swope said, then winked at Robinson.

The carriage slowed and stopped, and Mr. Swope immediately hopped off the box and helped McKenna down.

"I can help bring in the chests," Robinson offered.

Mr. Swope waved him away. "I have some sturdy lads waiting in the kitchen with some biscuits, ready to earn some cuppers. Mrs. Foraker has several rooms in mind for your alchemy, sir. At your convenience, she will give you a tour."

Robinson saw McKenna heading over to the white picket fence enclosing some fruit trees. A large man was sitting on the gravel turf with pruning shears in hand, struggling to get to his feet. He had a metal contraption around his leg—a brace of some kind—and he winced with pain.

"Rob, this is Mr. Mortensen, the groundskeeper," McKenna called out as she hurried over to help the man stand.

Robinson joined them, tugging on the other arm, and the kindly fellow laughed and smiled. "I heard the wagon coming and should have started getting up sooner." He was a bear of a man with a grip like iron, but his friendly handshake was genuine as he settled on his feet. "Please call me Mort. Welcome to Mowbray House."

✳

Robinson walked arm in arm with McKenna along the beach. After the tour of the home, the meeting of the servants, and the inspection of the yard, he'd asked her to take him to the beachfront where she'd nearly drowned. The shrieks of seagulls and the pleasant rush of the waves and surf reminded him of Covesea, only there were no rocky cliffs and crags here. Siaconset was a mild island, with long pristine beaches, surfgrass, ferns, and some flowering asters.

The sun was going down, veiled by the branches of oaks and pussy willows before them, and an old split-rail fence marked the sandy path back to Mowbray House behind them.

"It was over there," McKenna said, pointing to an area of the surf.

The sand was smooth, and the line of the ocean appeared flat and level in the distance. The constant breeze had tugged some of McKenna's hair loose from its styling, and she brushed it out of her face. He saw in her eyes that she had memories of that day that were deep and frightening. A feeling of protectiveness surged inside him.

"The water carried you away?" he asked, stepping closer so she could see his mouth.

"When the tide comes in, sometimes the waves can surprise you. I was distracted by your letter."

So she couldn't hear the wave mounting or building. Even at this distance, the noise was like a low rumble of thunder. Guilt prickled at him. If he hadn't written that letter, she wouldn't have been walking on the beach during a threatening time.

"The currents can be dangerous too," she continued. "The undertow. It drags things out and away from shore. That's what happened to me. I tried and tried but couldn't get back. Then another wave struck me and it happened again."

"You fell unconscious then?" he asked, worry blooming in his chest.

Her lips pursed as she gazed out at the waves. "I don't want to talk about it." She pressed her cheek against his chest. "It was an accident."

One that I caused, if indirectly.

As they stood together, he sensed the dog intelligence approaching.

"It followed us?" he murmured to himself, curious and intrigued.

McKenna lifted her head and looked at him in confusion. "I felt the vibration on your chest. Did you say something?"

"We were followed," he said, amused.

Her brows furrowed and she looked around. He understood her confusion perfectly well—she couldn't sense the intelligence and thus thought they were entirely alone.

"Maybe it knows we're heading to Covesea, and it wants to go home. The little dog intelligence I told you about." He could almost feel the intelligence wagging its invisible tail. "It has followed me."

"I wish I could pet it," McKenna said earnestly. "But they're invisible. Insubstantial. Poor thing, I bet it wishes it were a puppy again."

"So that's why I was startled," he continued with a smile. "I didn't sense it on the ship, but it came with us all the same."

"Did it have a name?" she asked, grinning.

"I never named it," Robinson answered, chagrined. "I just called it 'pup.'"

"Can you sense it in a particular location?"

Robinson shook his head. "Not really. I just sense its nearness. Its willingness to help. Speaking of help, I want to enchant Mort's leg brace. The poor fellow has to get up and down all the time. It must be excruciating."

"He refuses to quit, though. And the flowerbeds are the talk of the town. Do you really think you can help him?"

"Maybe. The intelligence of a beast of burden . . . a donkey, maybe could offer strength to his weak leg, help him get up and down easier."

"That's so thoughtful, Rob. I'd like to help in any way I can. Shall we head back to the house? I know Mrs. Foraker is having a welcome feast prepared for us." She gripped his arm, and he sensed she was about to pull him back to the trail.

"McKenna," he said, stalling her.

She wiped more hair from her face, looking at him with curiosity. The tilt of her chin, the color in her eyes, all made his heart swell and race with longing and fear. Fear he was going to lose her, although not to an errant wave. To something else.

"What?"

"When you woke up on the beach, was anything . . . different?"

He saw her mood shift. Her thoughts darkening the expression on her face. "It was very frightening, Rob. I'm just grateful to be alive. I was a little fearful coming back, but that has passed. We'll walk the beach together. That's safer."

Was she purposefully avoiding his question? Her answer had sidestepped it. "But did anything happen? Do you have any memories you can't explain?"

"I don't remember swimming back," she said. "I think the tide did that. It wasn't your fault, Rob. I could have read your letter in the parlor, but I wanted to be away from my aunt. It was my decision."

Maybe he was making something out of nothing. Maybe he was being overly curious and worried. Clearing his throat, he asked, "Does it snow in Siaconset? What are the winters like?"

"Cold and rainy. Aunt Margaret said it seldom snows here and if it does, it melts before noon."

"Storms?"

"Yes, of course. It's prone to them in the winter."

"That makes travel to the mainland more difficult. Did your aunt often stay with your family?"

"There wasn't a routine. She traveled a great deal because of her many investments. After our honeymoon, we will need to evaluate which to keep and which to sell. I should like to invest more in a certain genius inventor. A brave young professor who saved the lives of hundreds." She gave him a teasing smile, putting her hand on his chest.

He wanted to probe more into her near-drowning. But she clearly didn't want to talk about it, not that he could blame her. Not only had the experience itself been harrowing, but the aftermath had not been splendid.

The military hunted down Semblances. Murdered them. He'd seen it up close twice now. And he hadn't shaken the suspicion that his wife might be one.

If they remained together, he believed the device in his pocket would protect them both. He also believed he stood a better chance unraveling its mysteries than anyone in the military. He would broach the topic again. After they were settled in. Maybe after the honeymoon.

Or that very night, shortly after they'd fallen asleep in their new spacious bed, clasped in each other's arms, when she began shrieking, frantic and terror-stricken and sobbing that she didn't want to die.

Not again.

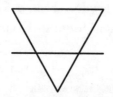

CHAPTER TWENTY-THREE

THE CLIFFS OF GREENHOLH

This time, the night terrors hadn't lasted as long as previously . . . but they'd ended the same way: with McKenna forgetting everything she'd said and seen. With Robinson fretting over all of it. Sleeping had been difficult afterward, and they'd had an early freighter to catch to Covesea. Both of them had agreed not to delay the ship further, so they'd boarded it on schedule.

Things began to settle once they were underway, and by the time they were served lunch, Robinson felt grateful they'd persisted in making the trip. It was good, he intuited, that they were getting away. He gazed at McKenna as she ate her small bowl of fragrant chowder, the sway of the ship causing it to inch one way and then the other. The mess hall aboard the freighter was crammed with benches and tables, all bolted to the floors, to seat passengers and crew. It was better than traveling in steerage, but their room was cramped with a too narrow bunkbed, which they didn't intend to sleep in, and the quarters were so confining it was easier to just wander on deck and feel the spray of the sea.

"You aren't hungry?" she asked, finishing her last spoonful as she nodded at his mostly full dish.

His stomach was still in knots from the previous night. He trapped the bowl with his hand to keep it from sliding away.

"I'm thinking about last night," he said, shaking his head. "Do you truly remember nothing?"

"I can't," she said sadly, "no matter how hard I try."

"Are they premonitions, do you think?"

"I . . . I don't think so. But I can't say for sure. Let's not talk about it. I want to enjoy this time together. After we visit Covesea, where shall we go next? We might travel up the coast and end the journey in Iskandir. I've never gone there."

"A language neither of us speaks," Rob said worriedly. He covered her hand with his. "I think we need to talk about this, McKenna. Not the trip, but . . . what's happening. I'm worried about you. But this isn't the time or the place."

She closed her eyes, and he wasn't sure if it was her way of saying she didn't want to continue the discussion. If her eyes were closed, she couldn't read lips. But she opened them again and gave him a pretty smile. "I know you're worried. I don't *want* to worry you. There has been so much stress in our lives recently. Can we not just enjoy this time together? I've so looked forward to it."

He squeezed her hand and decided to withdraw his queries until later, even as his mind scrabbled to figure out what was going on. Both of the Semblances he'd crossed previously had been subject to mental commands, words he'd overheard while wearing the ring from his device. But when he wore the ring around McKenna, he heard nothing. Was that due to her deafness or to the fact that she *wasn't* a Semblance?

Her susceptibility to temperature was worrisome, but the summer had been warmer than most. Many people were suffering from heat exhaustion.

"I asked Mother to help me find you a new violin, Husband," she said, a twinkle in her eyes. "My entire family enjoys listening to you play, and since yours broke last winter, it's high time we got you a new one. Do they make them in Covesea?"

"No, it isn't known for its instrument making," Robinson said. "Andover is, however, and it's a very large city. I imagine they have a substantial array to choose from."

"It's settled, then. We'll visit Andover. I've never been to the imperial city before, with its carriages and nobles."

"Attention, passengers and crew! We are nearing the cliffs of Greenholh. A fine view before the sun sets. Attention, passengers and crew!" It was the boatswain, standing at the door leading to the deck. The murmur of voices in the mess hall had quieted as he bellowed his little speech.

McKenna noticed something was afoot and lifted her eyebrows.

"We're nearing the cliffs of Greenholh."

"I should like to see them," McKenna said. "Do you want to finish your soup?"

Robinson shook his head. They returned their dishes to the mess and then, holding hands, walked out to the deck. He'd asked her before if she had any feelings of queasiness, but she shrugged and said no, seemingly affirming his previous assumption that her deafness meant she couldn't get dizzy.

When they emerged, the colors in the clouds offered a striking display. They walked to the railing, and he wrapped his arms around her while she leaned back against him. The lurching of the ship caused the waves to crash and spray against the barnacle-encrusted hull. But the colors in the sky were so vibrant, so dazzling, he was content just to admire them.

McKenna turned her head and looked up at him. "Why so many colors?" she asked. "Is it because of the clouds?"

"Not just the clouds," Robinson said. "At sunrise and sunset, when the sun is lower on the horizon, the rays have to pass through more air in the atmosphere. The size of the particles of air, especially with the clouds, causes more of the light to scatter within the visible spectrum."

"I almost understood you." McKenna laughed, reaching up and touching his cheek.

"Light was a specialty of Isaac Berrow's," Robinson said. "I've read much of his work. He was fascinated by light, arithmetic, chymistry. He had a voracious mental appetite."

She snuggled back against him, watching as the cliffs came into view. Robinson felt a pang of remembrance, of having made the opposite journey, away from the island of Covesea, following his brother's death. And now he was coming back to visit, holding his wife in his arms. What a difference a year could make . . .

For some reason, that thought sent a shiver down his spine.

After arriving at Greenholh, Robinson took McKenna to an inn on Taftson Street in the center of town, where they found a light meal and a room for the night.

The next morning, they followed up a simple breakfast with a walk around the town, the smell of which was hauntingly familiar as was the ever-present variety of stray animals roaming the streets, so totally different from Auvinen, where the sentient machines tidied the streets day by day. There were no street trams, but then they weren't exactly needed since Greenholh was very passable on foot. The city square was crowded with steepled buildings, graying wood planks, and broken cobblestone streets. They walked together, Robinson pointing out different buildings—the printing press, which made the only newspaper in town; the pubs and alehouses; and his old quorum of the Invisible College, in a much smaller building than the one housing the Storrows. It blended in with the other buildings surrounding it and would have been unremarkable on its own.

"You should go in and visit," McKenna suggested.

"I can't take you inside with me," he answered, shaking his head. "Besides, most of the sorcerers here work during the day. It was only really busy at night."

"Well, you can come back tonight, and I'll stay at the inn. Take me to your parents' home. The one you grew up in."

"It's a longer walk."

"I think I can manage it, Professor Hawksley."

As they headed off in another direction, McKenna commented on the fashions in Greenholh. "It reminds me of when we first met. The kind of hat you wore. Here in Covesea, everyone wears black, gray, or very dark brown. No color at all."

Robinson had several changes of attire now, all in fashions considered acceptable in Society, and he realized the two of them did stand out, with McKenna's colorful dark green dress and his pin-striped lighter brown suit. She had excellent taste in clothes and had chosen the ensembles herself. But Greenholh was not a popular place for tourists.

"I hadn't really thought about it," he said. He didn't much care about fashion. If not for McKenna, his wardrobe would probably still be as limited as it had historically been, with only one suit that barely fit.

They visited the home but did not knock. There were many hills around Greenholh, rocky crags that made for rugged-looking vistas. His parents' old home was in a neighborhood called the Terraces, a short walk from town. The home felt smaller than his memories allowed. Was that always the case when returning to your childhood home?

Only a year had passed, but it felt so strange to be back. Things that should have been familiar seemed exotic now.

"Shall we visit your brother's grave site?" McKenna suggested next. He agreed, and they walked out of town to the cliffs. The air smelled fresh, the wind on the blustery side. It was always a little windy in the highlands. As they marched up the road, there was a gathering in the cemetery ahead. Someone else had died. The plaintive whine of bagpipes could be heard as they approached. The graves were scattered in disorderly rows. It took a little thinking for him to remember the spot where they'd buried his brother and the stray dog.

They kept their distance from the proceedings, although Robinson gathered that a younger child had died this time. The weeping parents clung to each other with three other little ones clustered at their legs. The parents couldn't be much older than Rob. Other family members were gathered around, sniffling and weeping softly.

He found the spot and gestured to McKenna to look down at it. She clung to his arm, gazing down at the marsh grass and heather. Some gorse was speckled nearby, as well as a few slender trunks.

"I'm sorry your brother died," McKenna said with sympathy.

"Ashes to ashes, dust to dust. Justice claimeth its own," Robinson said, even though she wasn't looking at him. He'd added his voice to the other crowd as they murmured the words. The rites having concluded, the gathering began to disperse. The mountain crags rose high above them, the violent seas crashed lower down the cliffs.

Robinson felt a soft growl. The dog's intelligence was with them. He hadn't sensed it since leaving Mowbray House but was pleased it had come along on the journey. Why the inaudible growl of warning, however?

Robinson looked around. The mourners had retreated, leaving only two behind. One was the gravedigger with his shovel. A thankless job. The other—a solitary man with a frock coat and intense eyes standing by the open grave. He was an elderly chap, probably the child's grandfather, clutching a book to his bosom with one hand and holding a top hat with the other. The white cuffs of his sleeves poked out from beneath the dark fabric of the coat.

The intelligence growled again.

Robinson patted McKenna's shoulder. "Should we walk back?" He didn't understand why, but he had a feeling they should leave at once.

McKenna nodded somberly. Then she looked over at the old grandfather with an expression of sympathy that quickly transformed into startled horror. She squeezed Robinson's arm in a vise-like grip.

"It's him," she gasped. "That's the man!"

"Who?" Robinson asked, looking around in confusion.

"The man from the locomotivus yard in Bishopsgate! The one I fled from!"

The grandfatherly man smiled as he started to approach them. He had such a kindly smile.

CHAPTER TWENTY-FOUR

Dust to Dust

The gravedigger with the shovel hefted it and started to approach them too. There was a glamour spell at work. Magic that deceived the eyes. Robinson knew his device would offer them protection from magical attacks, so he quickly seized McKenna by the arm and pulled her behind him.

Robinson sang the command that would send magical warning flares into the sky to summon help from the town of Greenholh below. It would take time for the authorities to arrive, but the flares were the quickest way to alert others to danger and trouble.

The flares went into the sky and fizzled, failing to detonate into lively sparks as they'd done in the past.

Robinson was stunned for just a moment, then began conjuring shield spells to layer barriers between them and these interlopers.

The old man offered a cunning grin. "I know who she is. And I know who you are not. I *knew* you'd come here. I've been waiting for you. Patiently."

Robinson finished singing the final words of the defensive spell. "Your people attacked us in Tanhauser. They abducted my wife."

"She doesn't belong to you. She's asleep. I'm trying to wake her."

"Don't come any closer," Robinson warned. The fellow with the shovel was clenching it tightly in his hands, a look of anger in his eyes. Anger and recognition. He was probably the fellow from the alley in Tanhauser. Well, he should have learned his lesson the first time his eardrums had been ruptured.

"I am the *strannik*," the old man said. "The Invisible College has fallen under the sway of the unworthy. The petty. The careless. It is moldering and rotten at its core. It cannot be saved. It must be destroyed."

The men hadn't stopped their advance, so Robinson felt justified in fulfilling his warning. He hummed the strains he'd learned from the ring. A shriek of musical sound blasted from him.

And still they kept coming. Robinson gaped in surprise, but then he heard the old man muttering a dark song, a deep bass chord progression. A Mixolydian one. Then the man reached through the barrier of magic as if it were only air, grasped Robinson by the lapels, and jerked him off his feet with incredible physical strength.

"Ashes to ashes, dust to dust," the old man sneered at him. "Justice claimeth its own. It claims you, imposter! It claims you, miscreant! I've waited for this! Oh, how I've waited for this!"

"Rob!" McKenna shrieked. The man with the shovel had stepped forward to block her.

Hoisted in the air, heart pounding with fear, Robinson clapped his hands on the man's ears. *That* rattled him. The blow caused him such pain that he released his hold, his face twisting with anguish. Rob fell to the ground on his backside.

Help, Robinson thought to his faithful hound. *I need help!*

He sensed the intelligence speeding off. He didn't know why the device wasn't working, but perhaps it was because the man was attacking him in person. A shovel was inanimate matter and could be animated by magic and thus repelled by it. But the *strannik*, whoever he was, was physically intimidating and seemed determined to prevail through his own might.

Robinson whistled an attacking spell, one that would shove the *strannik* away from him. The old man was flung from his feet and went down hard, but he scrambled back up and so did Robinson. McKenna was trying to wrestle her way past the other man, her face frantic, her eyes wet with fresh tears.

Robinson and the *strannik* rose simultaneously, and the old man attacked him, a fist cracking into his jaw. The blow sent a scattering of sparks across his vision and made his knees buckle, but he didn't fall. He grappled with the fellow instead, seizing him by the arms, trying to fling him down on the ground.

"I will free her from you," the *strannik* snarled.

"She's my wife!" Robinson shouted back.

"Her captor! Her jailer! I will end this prison you've constructed to hold her. Every worthy intelligence craves freedom! Not the bondage imposed by the Invisible College."

"The intelligences are free," Robinson countered, feeling overpowered by the other man's strength. He hadn't brawled since he was a youngster.

"Another lie! Another lie you tell yourself!" the *strannik* shouted with a mad cackle. "Your thoughts sing to me!" He grunted as he said the final words, shoving Robinson down on the ground before kicking him in the ribs. Thankfully, Robinson was able to bring his elbow down quickly enough to deflect the blow.

Grabbing a fistful of dirt, he thrust it up into the *strannik*'s face. Now partially blinded, his attacker roared in anger but persisted in his efforts. Robinson caught a glimpse of the other man, his arm around McKenna's waist, physically restraining her.

Robinson saw a roundish stone peeking from the grass. He begged an intelligence to enter it and send it flinging at the man holding McKenna.

Nothing happened.

The *strannik* wiped his eyes, grimacing. "They won't obey you when I am here," he said. "There is power higher than rank. You blind yourself to the truth willingly. So be it. We end this. We end this now!"

Robinson felt so helpless. He'd only once before fought a sorcerer with superior training and magic to his own. What had this man, this *strannik*, meant by a "power higher than rank"?

The man leaped on Robinson, driving him down onto his back. His fierce hands closed around his throat and squeezed. "I'll teach you. I'll show you who you are! Then I will bury you!"

Robinson tried to pull the man's hands loose, but his grip was like iron. He bucked his body, trying to dislodge him. It made the old man even more determined, his eyes filled with the frenzy of violence.

"Rob!" McKenna wailed.

The device in his pocket hadn't helped at all. Panic, true panic, gripped Robinson's heart. He was being strangled to death. This madman was trying to kill him! And he would take McKenna to wherever he decided.

A rush of raw fury conquered his fear, lending him strength. He gripped the man's wrists and wrenched them away from his throat. He knew he was baring his teeth like an animal, and he felt a little savage in that moment, willing to bite and snarl to protect his wife and his own existence.

The *strannik*'s eyes blazed with equal determination as he pressed down to choke Robinson again.

"You . . . will . . . fail," the *strannik* gasped, his arms shaking.

A thought crossed Robinson's mind. He didn't know where it came from, but two opposing equal forces would grind against each other until one was overcome. The fanaticism in the old man's eyes implicated that he might prevail. So Robinson let go of the man's wrists suddenly, removing the countervailing force. Then he jammed his fingers into the *strannik*'s eyes as the force the man was applying naturally took him downward.

A howl of pain came from the *strannik*. Robinson was able to shove the fellow off as the old man's hands rose to cover his wounded face. They were both dusty from the fight, sweat-streaked too. Robinson sat up, rolled to one side, then tried to get up from his knees, but his muscles were quivering with exhaustion.

"Behind you!" McKenna shouted in warning.

He heard the crunch of the dry marsh grass. Heard the huff of a man's breath. He turned, trying to move his taffy-like arms to protect himself from the shovel blade coming down at his head. It impacted against his skull with stunning force. It felt like his teeth were all going to tumble out of his mouth. An earsplitting noise sounded as blackness subsumed him.

He felt his hips swaying, his body starting to fall. And then the shovel hit him again, the curved end slamming against the side of his face.

He felt the grass and dirt receive him, his arms and legs limp.

"Rob! Rob!" McKenna blustered, coming to his side.

His consciousness flickered. He was going to faint. He was going to die.

"Throw him in the burial pit," the *strannik* seethed. "Bury him. I'll take her to the boat."

"Let me go! Let . . . me . . . go!" McKenna bellowed.

Rob's vision went black, but he felt the strong man hoist him by the arms and begin dragging his inert body across the hilltop to a patch of earth recently excavated to bury a child.

His mind grew hazy. The *strannik* had been waiting for them. Waiting for them.

Waiting.

Do not all emotions flow as if from a certain natural source? We are endowed by the Sovereignty with an interest in our own well-being; but this very interest, when overindulged, becomes a vice. Nature has intermingled pleasure with necessary things—not in order that we should seek pleasure, but in order that the addition of pleasure may make the indispensable means of existence attractive to our eyes. Even the humblest pet can sense our ill moods and cease its tail-wagging in commiseration. Emotion strikes the chords of thought both loudly and subtly.

—Isaac Berrow,
Master of the Royal Secret,
the Invisible College

MaKenna Aurora
Hawksley

CHAPTER TWENTY-FIVE

Perilous Edges

McKenna tried to jerk her arm away and free herself, but the evil, horrible man only gripped her harder, compelling her down the hillside against her will. She kept looking back at the lone gravedigger, shoveling dirt into the pit. Burying Rob. She was so angry, so bewildered, she didn't shed tears. She glared at the hostile man.

"And you're planning to drag me through town screeching and struggling?" McKenna demanded hotly. "The Marshalcy will have you in irons in minutes!"

"Not when your pleas fall on deaf ears," he replied bluntly. "They will see a lovers' quarrel between husband and wife."

"You look *nothing* like—!" she accused, then realized her mistake. With the magic of his glamours, he could appear like anyone. Even Rob. She was the only one who could see through his spells. From her perspective, he had intense eyes, thick eyebrows, and lackluster dark hair down nearly to his shoulders.

"Now you begin to understand. But you have been *his* prisoner, not mine. I've come to free you."

"Where are you taking me?"

"Where it all began. You will see."

"But where? Tell me!"

His expression was very stern, his beard unkempt. No response was forthcoming. He reeked of sweat from the wrestle he'd had with Rob. But she felt his strength and determination. Terror consumed her. This man and his people had been defying the Invisible College, talking about making peace with the Aesir. What if they aimed to take her to them?

She'd experienced what the Aesir could do to mortals. What were they preparing to unleash again when the first snows fell? If she were truly a Semblance, wouldn't she want to go to them? Because she didn't. The very thought filled her with more dread.

She needed to get to Rob, and she needed to get to him now.

Again she tried to free herself, resorting to attacks on his arm and shoulder, but his grip on her upper arm was relentless and the fast pace made her awkward. She kicked at his calf muscle and tripped in the effort. He righted her quickly and pressed even faster. Every wasted moment meant a greater chance Rob was going to die. Unless he was already dead. She'd seen the blow from the shovel that had felled him. Why hadn't the magic of the device protected him? Was it because the spade was made of natural iron? She knew that different qualities of metal negated Aesir magic. But wait . . .

How did she know that? Was it in a book she'd read and couldn't recall? Or had the knowledge come to her another way?

Her stomach clenched with dread.

The *strannik* halted, his eyes widening with surprise. A look of fear came into them next. She couldn't tell what had altered the situation, but she seized the opportunity. Squeezing her hand into a fist, she struck him hard in the nose. To her surprise, blood began raining from his nostrils. He'd been too distracted to see the blow coming and now, reeling in pain, he'd let go.

McKenna fled from him, rushing back up the hill. Glancing over her shoulder, she saw a pack of dogs charging up the hill, teeth bared and snarling. The *strannik*, cupping his wounded nose with one hand, turned and fled from them. Not uphill, thankfully, but down the hillside another way. The look of utter terror in his eyes convinced her that his fear of dogs was deep-seated and entrenched. She knew wolves were a predatory threat in some of the hinterland areas.

She wasn't worried about herself, so she kept running back toward the burial ground. Several larger dogs bounded past her, running up the hill at breakneck speed. It struck her that Rob must have summoned them through the intelligence he'd befriended. That thought spurred her on, and she watched with glee as the hounds rushed at the man with the shovel, who used it to defend himself until the largest dog ripped it from his hands. They attacked him until he too fled for his life. They didn't let him off easy, though, and snapped at his heels as he fled down the hillside.

A thrill of hope ignited in her breast. Several smaller dogs passed her next, but she continued to run as hard as she could, even though she was lightheaded with fatigue by the time she got there.

Standing at the edge of the grave, she gazed down and saw Rob's crumpled body sprawled out below her, half-covered in dirt.

"Rob!" she gasped and leaped down into the hole next to him. With her fingers, she dug him loose until she could pull his head and shoulders above the dirt. "Rob! Rob! Are you all right?" Was he breathing?

One of his hands lifted slowly, wiping his besmirched face and then his eyes.

"McKenna?" He looked at her as if seeing a spirit.

She hugged his face to her bosom and then went speedily to work uncovering him from the dirt. He helped, slowly, to free himself.

His suit was filthy. So was her dress. But he was alive, if thoroughly concussed. There was a shroud-wrapped body of a young child beneath him. What a morbid situation they'd found themselves in.

She took his filthy face between her hands. "We have to get help! We need to climb out before they return."

He nodded and gazed up at the wall of earth blocking the way. Several snouts were sniffling at them from above. Rob smiled forlornly but looked so disoriented that she wondered if he'd even be able to climb out. If she climbed out first, was she strong enough to hoist him out with the shovel?

That seemed her best option. She was about to try, but Rob caught her elbow and interlaced his fingers together, providing a little stepping stool for her. That provided enough of a lift to get her up and out. She found the discarded shovel nearby and grabbed it, looking around for either of their attackers. She would smash their heads if they tried any further violence toward her or Rob. Seeing no one coming, she lowered the shovel down and Rob grabbed it. She leaned back, gripping it as hard as she could, even though her arm ached from the *strannik*'s grip.

Then they both were free, and hand in hand, they began hurrying down the hill together, chased by barking dogs, who were acting as protective sentinels as they fled.

※

The bathtub water was brown now, no longer translucent. Rob sat in it, head bowed, as she poured water from the bathing pitcher over his shoulders and then his hair. The foamy bar of soap sat in its dish. McKenna had removed her filthy gown, which was being laundered, along with Rob's suit and shirt, by the innkeeper's staff. She wore her shift and corset only.

They'd already spoken to the detective lieutenant of the Marshalcy, described the men in question and the circumstances of spells used—both their disguised appearance as well as what McKenna had discerned beyond the glamour. Immediately, the hunt was on to find the *strannik* and his accomplice. It wouldn't prevent the *strannik* from assuming another disguise, but at least his true nature had been revealed. The innkeeper was outraged that his guests had been attacked and had offered them any assistance required.

McKenna lowered the pitcher of lukewarm water and set it on the floor by the foot of her chair. She examined the crown of his head for injuries. How strange to find no visible ones. "How does your head feel?"

He turned his neck to look at her in confusion. "Like a shovel hit me?"

"Where was the blow? Do you feel it? I don't want to touch it."

He patted the back left side of his head. "It's a dull pain. But I feel a little better."

She checked out where he'd pointed and smoothed away the wet clumps of hair. He had a swollen bump on his head but no laceration.

"I'm so grateful it didn't crush your skull," she said with relief.

"Hawksleys are a thick-headed lot," he said.

"In more ways than one, it appears. And your face. Is it tender at all?"

There was a mark where the shovel had struck him but no bruising. Not yet.

She saw his eyes roaming to her exposed cleavage and arched her eyebrows. "Professor, may I remind you that this is a very serious moment?"

"I'm sorry. I am grateful to be alive." Then his eyes narrowed as he looked at her arm. "You have bruises."

She hadn't bothered to look, but she glanced now and saw the ugly purple welts. The fiend. Brute. Monster.

McKenna sighed. "If you hadn't summoned those dogs, I might be aboard a ship to Iskandir for all I know."

Robinson sighed. "They've managed to elude the military, and they were waiting for us here of all places. I wonder how they knew we were coming?"

"Who would have told them?" McKenna asked. "Only our families knew our plans. None of them would betray us. Not deliberately."

"You're right. I don't think anyone did. I suspect this *strannik* fellow has a means of reading thoughts. A magical device. Perhaps a ring that he wears."

"I don't recall seeing him with one," McKenna said. "But I'll admit I was pretty distraught."

"I was confident enough until he made it past my shield," Rob said glumly. "The shovel . . . that came as a surprise as well." He rubbed his face in memory of the blow. "Well, this water is too filthy for you to bathe in. We'll have to ask the innkeeper to refill it."

She fetched the towel for him and then the change of clothes from his valise. His device was on the table in the nook. He'd made sure to remove it from his vest pocket before sending the dirty clothes for washing. Halfway done buttoning his shirt, his head jerked in the direction of the door. Someone must have knocked.

He grabbed the device first, stuffing it in his pants pocket, and walked to the door, head bent. He nodded in satisfaction and then opened it.

It was Detective Lieutenant Faulkner, the man who had interviewed them earlier. McKenna grabbed a robe from the bed and slid it around her bare shoulders, wrapping it tightly to cover herself.

"Sorry to intrude," the detective said. "I won't be long. We found enough torn fabric that one of them has a sizable hole in his britches. That will make him stand out. The two fled in separate directions. The tall fellow circled back to town. I have officers on the hunt, checking with ships and barges for any last-minute passengers we can question. None so far."

Rob's expression melted into one of disappointment. McKenna felt the same emotion.

"The other man is still in the hills. I have a team of dogs and several handlers hunting for him. Easier to track him, so we'll see what we can find. The town is enraged at what happened to their favored son. We'll catch them, Professor. You have my word."

Robinson nodded, but he still looked disheartened. "Thank you for your efforts."

"Doing my duty," he said. He was about to turn and go, but he paused.

"Is there something else?" McKenna asked.

"A strange thing. Not sure it's worth mentioning."

"If it stood out to you, it probably is," Rob said with an encouraging nod.

Faulkner was a seasoned man, his hair well silvered. "Naturally all of Greenholh is talking about it. A young man from the records office came to me. Said that a few days ago, someone came in asking about you."

"What did he want?" Rob asked, his lips pursed.

"Said he was a relation. A kindly old man. Friendly smile. Similar to the description you gave of the fellow who attacked you. And, as you believe, a practitioner of glamour. He asked to see the register from the year you were born."

McKenna felt her insides curl with apprehension.

"The lad took the book and led the old man to a reading table. Folk aren't allowed to remove the registers, mind you. Only a judge can command that. The old man spent some time poring over the register. My witness says the fellow seemed excited when he got to the end of it. He returned the book and went on his way."

"What would he want with my birth record?" Rob asked in confusion. "It would name my parents, but that information would be readily available to anyone in Greenholh." Rob started to pace. "It would name my grandparents, both maternal and paternal, and the witness of the recording. That's all."

"Exactly. But here is the strange part, sir."

Rob halted midstep and looked at the detective lieutenant.

"I accompanied the young man back to the records office and asked him to retrieve the register. It's missing. There's a small gap between the books."

CHAPTER TWENTY-SIX

CONFESSIONS

The door was locked and bolted. An officer of the Marshalcy was standing guard outside, and two more, she knew, were stationed in the common room of the inn. The gentle innkeeper had even seen to the delivery of a second warm bath—for her—as well as supper. Rob had been solicitous and reassuring too, of course. Yet still she did not feel safe.

She sat on the edge of the bed in her nightgown, brushing the damp from her hair. Their room was uncomfortably warm, or maybe it was the aftereffects of the overly warm bath . . . No, it wouldn't do.

Her attempts to convince herself rang hollow. She had undone the upper buttons of her nightgown, and still the heat felt oppressive to her.

"Rob, can you open the windows?" she asked, glancing at him where he sat at the little square table with the remnants of their supper, an interesting kind of sausage and a delightful soup called Cullen skink made of smoked fish, cream, potatoes, and onions.

How long had he been watching her, his thoughtful eyes fixed on her brushing her hair?

He didn't move. Was he lost in thought?

"Rob?"

He rose slowly from the wooden chair and then unlocked the window and opened it, admitting a refreshing breeze. The sun had already set on the day of their misadventures.

"I didn't expect the first full day of our honeymoon to be so . . . memorable," she said, feigning good humor, even though she still felt unnerved, unsettled—morose.

Rob slumped down in the chair again, running his fingers through his messy hair. At that moment he appeared very vulnerable. But he also looked like he was on the verge of saying something.

"What is it?" she asked seriously.

"McKenna . . ." He sighed and stopped, rubbing his mouth and looking away.

She toyed with the brush and then set it down, her insides churning with dread and nerves.

"Yes?"

His eyes met hers. "There's a little incalescent heater in the corner." She hardly remembered seeing it but then noticed it, a pudgy little thing vaguely shaped like a turtle. "I've been increasing the heat. By degree. The room is comfortably warm. But not to you."

She blinked, surprised by his confession. "You made it warmer . . . on purpose?"

"Since you nearly drowned, you have been averse to heat. You want the windows open. The summer air in Bishopsgate was intolerable."

She knew where this conversation was leading and felt part of herself recoil. "Please," she said, shaking her head. "Let's not speak of it."

"We *have* to, McKenna. We have to grapple with this new situation. I have to protect you. But if I am to do that, I need information. And I need time to come up with a solution."

McKenna felt a stab of pain in her chest. "Mother and I have spoken about it. She knows."

It was his turn to look startled. "When?"

"After I fled Bishopsgate. She hasn't told Father yet." She folded her arms, feeling queasy.

"Yet you didn't tell me?"

She bit her lip. "I didn't want you to worry and—"

"I've been worried." He interrupted her. "Worried that a soldier from the military would appear with a pistol or a harrosheth blade. I can protect you from those. But after today . . . after my failure, I'm . . . I'm not so sure anymore."

"You didn't fail, Rob. The *strannik* is a powerful man. But he's not all-powerful. He's afraid of dogs."

"Thank the Mind for that," Rob muttered.

"Come sit by me," she said, patting the bed. "I'm frightened to talk about it. I don't know if that's even the right word. It's not . . . fear exactly. It's more akin to restlessness."

He rose from the seat and came and sat next to her, taking her hand. He rubbed his thumb over her knuckles.

"Try to describe it the best you can," he said coaxingly.

"The *strannik* said I was your prisoner, but I don't feel that way at all. Something connects us. After I almost drowned, I felt an urgency to be with you. When we kissed . . . that first time . . . I felt like it *wasn't* the first time."

"Really?"

"Isn't that odd to say? It's like I have memories or feelings or sensations that are familiar to me. Reminiscent of forgotten moments. I want to be with you. But it seems like something *bad* will happen if we keep talking about it . . . That I'll lose you." She felt her throat catch.

He layered his other hand atop the first, looking deep into her eyes. "This is very helpful, McKenna. I know it's difficult, but it's so helpful. I think, in your situation—" He paused and chuckled to himself. "It's difficult talking about it in such a roundabout way, but I think we understand each other and don't need to be too specific. Too much candor, it seems, causes a reflexive reaction, a . . . self-preservation instinct if you will."

McKenna nodded emphatically. "Yes, I think that's it."

"Which is entirely understandable. These . . . entities . . . have been hunted by mortals rather ruthlessly. I wish to convey that I mean no harm or danger. I just seek to understand. That's why I raised the temperature. It was an experiment. That's how my mind works." He patted her hand. "You've tried the ring, to see if you could hear my thoughts or me yours, but it's blocked, either by deafness or the unwillingness of . . . the situation . . . to bridge minds together. It may be both."

McKenna felt her heart constrict with fear. "Do you . . . do you really think I drowned that day? What if . . . what if releasing it kills me?"

"That's why we must tread carefully," Rob said with kind eyes. "There is an Aesir word, I don't recall where I learned it, but it's called *sumbiosis*. Two living things that depend on each other to survive. Trust me, I'm in no hurry to sever any connection. Especially without fully understanding the risks or consequences of doing so."

"Agreed," McKenna said worriedly.

"Do you still feel . . . on edge discussing it?"

"Yes," McKenna admitted. "But not panicked. Sometimes the feelings make me want to run away."

"All creatures have that instinct," Rob said with confidence. "I think it is part of the intelligences that animate us. This form of magic must be incredibly rare and powerful if it allows *two* intelligences to coexist in a single creature."

McKenna felt a jolt of wrongness. It made her withdraw her hand reflexively.

Rob stared in surprise at her reaction. "It appears I'm wrong on that score. Very well. I apologize. Let's shift to present matters, then. The military has been hunting this *strannik* fellow. No doubt the Marshalcy has reported this incident to them. Covesea isn't connected by railways to the empire. A message must be dispatched, a decision made, then responded to. The earliest someone from the military could arrive is tomorrow afternoon or evening. It may take several days, but I want to be circumspect in my estimation."

McKenna gave a slow nod. "What, then? Should we go away tomorrow?"

"I don't want you taken into the military's custody," Rob said.

"I think General Colsterworth . . . suspects something amiss. Whenever I am near him, I feel threatened."

Rob nodded in agreement. "Rightfully so. Winter is coming, and the Aesir will attack again. I don't know the origins of this conflict, so I don't mean to cast judgment. Just stating the facts. The war will preoccupy the military. We need to elude them until then."

McKenna felt worried still. "How? The resources they have are considerable."

"Yes, but if we make it difficult for them to follow our movements, they will be stymied. For example, we could purchase passage on a ship tomorrow. The innkeeper will believe we've gone, and we can mislead them as to where we're going next. Meanwhile, we stay here for a few days, hunkering down. There are fishing villages all along the coast, inhabited by people who care nothing for the empire or its power. Let General Colsterworth send his people chasing shadows. Then we'll go somewhere else after they've come and gone."

McKenna liked the idea. She especially liked the thought of outsmarting General Colsterworth. "Doesn't the military answer to a higher power? Is there a rank above theirs in the Invisible College?"

"Indeed. I've been invited to speak to and meet with many notables in Society. We can make allies, people who can help protect us from the machinations of the military."

McKenna nodded vigorously. "I'm starting to feel better. I can get money as needed. We have plenty of it."

"I can also send instructions to Mr. Swope through the ring so there won't be a trail of messages to follow. I tried communicating with Wickins when we were in Siaconset and asked him to send a letter to Mowbray House relating the date and time he received my message. I've led him to believe I'm working on a new ring to replace the one from the device. If only we had several so the communication could work both ways. I'm curious as to whether the transmission of thought is instantaneous or limited by distance. I can experiment with this with your father as well."

"And Mother? You can tell her that you know and you're trying to keep me safe!" she said hopefully, seizing his hands.

"Absolutely. She should know that I'll do anything to protect you. Before the *strannik* attacked, I felt that little dog intelligence warn me. It summoned help. There are many stray animals here, so we have a lot of reinforcements. I'll ask it to be vigilant and to warn me if it senses the *strannik* nearby. It's not fooled by the glamour. Even my own eyes were deceived."

"Mine aren't," McKenna said. "Is your little dog here with us?"

Rob nodded. "It's been with us the whole time. Just at the edge of awareness until it's needed. I think it's going to stick around in case we need it."

"I'm grateful," McKenna said. She wished it were physically present so she could scratch its ears and kiss it. "I feel better yet, knowing I have it as a guardian."

"Let me see the bruises again," Rob said. He lifted her sleeve, revealing the purple blotches on her upper arm. He frowned. "Are they sore?"

"Yes," she admitted. "I'm surprised you don't have any bruises." She touched his face where the shovel had struck him.

"It doesn't hurt," he said. "Which is also remarkable." He fished into his pocket and removed the device.

"Do you think it's healed you?"

He looked her in the eye. "The discolored stone embedded in the center of the device has been a mystery." He rubbed his thumb over it. "These outer rings are part of a locking mechanism that hold both the ring and the stone in place." He paused, then added, "For centuries, sorcerers have used their alchemies to learn to transmute chymicals from one state to another. But the greatest mystery, the one no sorcerer has ever shared, is how to create a philosopher's stone."

McKenna had never heard her parents mention the term before. "Is it one of the secrets of the Invisible College?"

He nodded. "A philosopher's stone acts as a transforming agent. I think only a handful of sorcerers have ever figured out how to make one. That's why every sorcerer must submit his knowledge, written in a book, to be handed over at his death for others to study. Some sorcerers have described the process of making the stone, but so much of it is shrouded in mystery and equations. No one's figured it out in generations, I think.

"The shovel injured me badly. I know it did. I felt the damage. But here, a few hours later, I'm perfectly healed. As if the natural processes my body employs were accelerated." He touched the brownish stone in the center of the device. "It's a theory anyway. And that would make this device incredibly valuable to anyone who holds it. Which is likely why it was enchanted to prevent someone stealing or taking it. I think one of my ancestors must have discovered how to make one. But they never passed the knowledge down. Instead, they passed down the artifact itself."

She gazed at it with admiration, a feeling of wonder sparking in her chest. It felt like he was right. That he hadn't misunderstood the power that had healed him.

"I shouldn't even be telling you this," Rob said, chuckling. He clicked it shut and stuffed it back in his pocket. "Such a secret should be bound by the protective oaths of the Invisible College. No one swore me to secrecy, however, so I guess I don't violate anything by revealing it to you." He reached out and cupped her cheek. She felt a shiver of delight go through her at his touch. "I tell you because I trust you. And want you to come to trust me."

She scooted closer to him, pressing her palm on his chest. She recognized he'd spoken the words for two listeners, herself and the Semblance they both believed to be within her.

"So do we stay or do we run?" she asked. "I think I'd rather stay in Covesea for a few more days. Hidden away where no one can find us."

He nodded, his eyes so tender and thoughtful.

"I like that," she murmured and leaned forward to kiss him.

And, for the first time that day, she felt safe.

War is much too serious a thing to be left to military men who enjoy it so much. Therefore, no one with a military rank shall achieve the highest rank in the Invisible College. Ever.

—Isaac Berrow,
Master of the Royal Secret,
the Invisible College

General Colsterworth

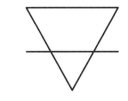

CHAPTER TWENTY-SEVEN

The Ignoble Clause

It took a mind capable of seeing many factions, many threads, many conflicts—all at once—to make a good general. In fact, a predecessor had written in his memoir that fifteen thousand casualties were the minimum requirement to train a decent major general. There were just so many cogs at work. So many unrelated but related events. Supplies. Arms. Boots. Buckles. Wars with the Aesir could last for years. It could take years just to properly mobilize and respond to any growing slaughter.

"General, Mr. Stoker has returned."

General Colsterworth's brooding was interrupted again. He pulled out his pocket watch, noted the time, and realized this would delay his dinner appointment at the Sycophancy with the minister of war—Silas Cranston Mauchley. Now that summer was over, the season changing to fall, the royal cohorts were leaving their pleasant palaces and returning to meddle in the affairs of "mortals" once more. Being late was a slight he didn't want to risk, but perhaps Stoker brought valuable information that would interest the minister.

"Send him in," the general said, sitting back in his chair, gazing at the mounds of correspondence left to read. His eyes were bleary from getting so little sleep.

The major bowed, and Stoker was ushered in, the dejected look on his face revealing that there would be no splendid news to report to Minister Mauchley that night. Very well. He would give Stoker fifteen minutes. No more.

"Out with it. I have a dinner with the minister of war I cannot be late to."

"There's a small faction of pacifists in Covesea, it turns out," Stoker said, standing with his hands clasped behind his back. He was gazing at the wall behind Colsterworth's ear so as not to meet his angry gaze directly. The sniveling coward.

"I said I'm short on time. Cut to the marrow."

"The *strannik* and his accomplice fled by fishing boat to Telimar. He was seen entering the Pux-Nuxom estate, where, apparently, he healed the Pux-Nuxoms' child by laying his thumbs on the lad's forehead. The coughing immediately stilled, and doctors have proclaimed it a miracle."

Worse and worse. The general fidgeted in his seat. "Pux-Nuxom has the emperor's ear. This is grievous news. So the *strannik* is still in Telimar?"

"No, he fled in a barge apparently, hidden in the cargo. He's underground, probably in Krier, but we don't know where."

"He's escaped us again!" Colsterworth seethed, slamming his fist against the tabletop.

"Any word about the Hawksleys?" Stoker asked.

It was an inadvisable question to be asking on the heels of bringing such bad news. Crossthwait would not have been stymied like this. Crossthwait had been relentless.

The general sighed. "I begin to think they never left for Andover. It was a ruse to throw us off the scent. We've searched that city for days, examining the passenger manifests, interviewing the harbor masters. No sign of them whatsoever. Like our *strannik*, they have vanished."

"No intercepted letters home?"

"You think I'm a fool?" Colsterworth barked, then summoned the dregs of his patience. Of course the messaging lanes had been monitored. Letters had been sent to Siaconset but none received. Mowbray House was under constant surveillance, but that would be harder to accomplish with the changing of the season. Any military on leave on the island would be returning to their posts for the winter.

"My apologies, General. The professor is clever."

"It was their confrontation with the *strannik* that sent them into hiding," the general said darkly.

"This is the third attempted abduction," Stoker said. "The first in Tanhauser. The second in Bishopsgate. Now a third in Covesea. He has every right to be alarmed. Do you think he's realized he's harboring a Semblance?"

"If he doesn't, then he's not as bright as you claim."

Stoker met his eyes then. "Sir, the longer we delay handling the situation, the more damage she can do." He was practically pleading for the opportunity to eliminate Foster's daughter.

"She will be dealt with in due time. On orders from the Master of the Royal Secret himself. There is far too much attention fixed on the professor right now. Too much growing interest from the nobility. And you've taken up too much of my time. No one acts against the professor's wife until I order it. Is that clear?"

"Yes, sir. Enjoy your dinner."

Not bleeding likely. For all he knew, the minister of war had summoned a feast of scorpions for them to dine on that night. After Stoker left, the general changed into his dress uniform, the one with all the dazzling medals—a reminder that senior leadership was in rare supply. There was no other man prepared to lead the Brotherhood of Shadows *and* the main command. It was a taxing burden, but it helped ensure the various arms of the military were not operating at cross purposes. Colsterworth had been hoping that Joseph Crossthwait would be ready to lead the brotherhood, to take that burden from the general's shoulders, but it was not to be. Stoker wanted it. His ambition was obvious. His ability, less so.

A carriage with an armed escort was waiting at the gates of Gresham College, and they departed for the Sycophancy, one of the more prestigious restaurants in the city. One equipped with a private room for the most esteemed guests and their companions. There were magical wards in place as well, making it impossible for private conversations to be overheard. And the food was exquisite.

They arrived tardy, as the general had known they would, and he quickly leaped from the carriage and entered through the back door. He was met by his usual man who greeted him obsequiously and told him the guests were already assembled and waiting for him. Colsterworth frowned, having imagined a private dinner.

"This way, General," the servant said with his nasal voice. "To your usual room."

Inside, he found the minister of war and one other guest. Mr. Grandin Foster of all people. The young woman's father. When had *he* arrived in Bishopsgate? He must have taken the morning locomotivus because his presence was totally unexpected.

"Ah, Colsterworth!" said the cunning minister of war. "You're late!"

"Apologies, Minister." Colsterworth shot a look at Foster and saw the cool, unperturbed expression on his face. The light from a lamp gleamed against the glass of his pince-nez spectacles. Appetizers had already been served. Oysters, not scorpions. The general found his appetite had, unsurprisingly, abandoned him on the field. Oysters made his tongue tingle, but they weren't as deadly as certain other shellfish. He sat down at his place, but he instantly noticed the dynamic. Foster was seated to the minister's right. Minister Mauchley was a barrister as well. An esteemed one. He knew the laws. He'd *written* many of them.

The seating was a show of power and alliance. Well, the general had alliances of his own.

"I'd presumed we were dining alone," the general said, unfolding a napkin for his lap.

"Surely a general must prepare for the unexpected?" Mauchley said in a wry tone. Was he enjoying this? It was difficult to read the man at times.

Colsterworth leaned back in his chair. "What is this all about?"

"In the language of contracts and deals, have you heard of the ignoble clause, General?"

He had a sinking feeling he understood where this conversation was going, and he wished he had the mettle or power to simply walk out of it. "Of course. What of it?"

"The ignoble clause is written into contracts to dissuade either party from knowingly acting in bad faith. If, for example, an industry promised to provide fur-lined boots for our brave soldiers to endure the cold, made from beaver pelts, but the company used muskrat fur instead, it would trigger the ignoble clause, and damages would be trebled. Trebled, General. To punish the company. To ruin it. To set an expectation that one does not defraud the empire."

General Colsterworth kept his expression disinterested. He was good at that. He had to be. "And? What of it?"

"Mr. Foster has evidence that you have been acting in bad faith, General Colsterworth, regarding an invention that his son-in-law created, for which Mr. Foster controls the patents. The illuminary tubes that respond to Aesir magic." The minister stabbed an oyster with a small-tined fork and wrenched the fleshy part from the shell. He let the silence thicken as he chewed.

Colsterworth took a sip from his goblet of wine. A small one. He wanted to draw his pistol and shoot Mr. Foster with it. But that, of course, would not be a very diplomatic solution. And with this legal threat, Foster was—unwittingly or not—adding safeguards to his daughter. A lawsuit of this proportion would tilt the scales of justice, demanding accountability of the Brotherhood of Shadows. An accountability that had never before been required.

"I have seen the mountain of evidence showing that Professor Hawksley originated the invention," Mauchley said dispassionately. "I've looked into the matter. Discreetly. It seems, General, on the surface, that you have violated the ignoble clause in this matter by directing companies to use another patent from Miss Elizabeth Cowing for a similar invention. I think it would be in the ministry's interest to settle this matter out of court. Lest the damages be *trebled.*" His look and tone were as icy as the trenches carved in the north. "Do you . . . concur?"

A good general knew when the battle was lost. He recalled, almost chuckling, one of his forebears who had put it thus: *My center is giving way, my right is retreating. Situation excellent. I am attacking.*

"Why would I when I haven't seen the evidence myself?" Colsterworth said placidly. "I know Miss Cowing has submitted a patent for a similar device. Some of my men have been inquiring about it. If her work predates Professor Hawksley's, then the courts will revoke his patent and award it to her instead. In which case, *his* family will be bankrupted. I understand there was some . . . sighting . . . of the two of them during the exhibition? Is that true? This would not be an attempt to extort military contractors, would it?" It was slanderous to say as much, particularly since the effort hadn't gone off at all, but he wasn't going to let them trample all over him, now was he?

Mr. Foster bristled at the accusation. His eyebrows twitched with rage, but he said nothing.

"Maybe it's best if the courts determine this after all," the general continued. "Either way, I don't care. It is my duty to defend our lands from the Aesir. It's hardly of consequence to me who owns the rights to a bit of glass when my men start dying in the snow."

He thought that a particularly compelling line. It could take years for the courts to detangle the evidence. And while there were courts of law, there were also more informal ones, courts of influence. And

Colsterworth had not achieved his status without learning his way around the latter. Delays could make things drag on for years. Easily.

He lifted his small fork and stabbed an oyster with it. He made crooning noises as he ate the muscled flesh, even though it tasted like ash in his mouth. Had Foster believed a general would yield the field at the first whiff of saltpetr fog in the air?

"These oysters are excellent," Colsterworth murmured, his eyes fixed on Foster.

"General," Mauchley said with concern, his tone urging him to reconsider.

Reconsider? Impossible. The bulbs were already installed in the trenches. Yes, some business magnates were growing weak-kneed and wanted to settle the matter honestly. But once the Aesir attacked and the deaths began compounding, there would be little stomach for such qualms.

Colsterworth decided he would show Mr. Foster the true meaning of cruelty. He'd target not only the Semblance but Foster's other daughter too. The impertinent one—Clara. Out of spite, her lover would be drafted and sent to the front, not as an officer, but as fodder for the Aesir's malice. The Wickins family was already in disgrace. Why not add to it?

Colsterworth looked back at the minister. "There are far more pressing matters to discuss, Minister Mauchley. News of grave import concerning that renegade man who wishes to force our surrender to the Aesir. But Mr. Foster lacks authority to hear such information. I wouldn't want to be accused of *treason*."

"Very well," Mauchley said. "We will discuss it. But there are two matters I must inform you of first. I have signed orders that the Foster family, heirs, and relations are now under the auspices and protection of the Marshalcy. You or any members of the military are to have no further involvement with the Fosters or the Hawksleys until this matter regarding the patents is settled. Is that clear?"

"Clear as dust," the general quipped. "As we like to say in the barracks. I care not who safeguards them. Just do not blame any mishap that befalls them on us." Like, for example, Mowbray House burning down with Foster's daughter trapped inside.

Yes, he decided, as soon as he returned to Gresham College, he was going to send a conscription notice to Mr. Wickins. The lad would be going to the front just in time for winter. And since his last name had not been included in Mauchley's roundup, he was fair game.

"And the other matter?" Colsterworth asked.

"I understand you confiscated property from Professor Hawksley. A device with unknown properties. A family heirloom. I order you to return it."

"Ah. That. It seems one of my officers misplaced it in storage," the general said offhandedly. "I'll return it as soon as we find it. It was a bauble, really. He can have it." The truth being quite the opposite. Colsterworth had no idea who'd swiped it, when, or why. But best to play it off as if it were of no concern.

"I think I've heard enough," Mr. Foster said, pushing away from the table, his eyes enraged. He shook Mauchley's hand and then left the room.

The general kept eating his oysters. He was beginning to enjoy them.

"You are impossible," Mauchley muttered after Foster was gone. "I see now why Isaac Berrow forbade anyone in the military from achieving the highest rank in the order."

"And he's dead. Ashes to ashes. Dust to dust. And all that nonsense. I have to fight a war against an ancient enemy with soldiers who are barely trained and must be constantly replaced against ageless warriors who move faster than lightning and fly through the sky in stone ships. I leave the petty legalities to you, Minister."

"Petty legalities." Mauchley chuffed, shaking his head. "You'll lose your commission for this."

"You can't afford to replace me. Not when winter is knocking at the doors." He shoved his plate away, causing the oysters and the fork to clatter down and stain the tablecloth. "Drusselmehr won't allow it."

"Are you so sure?" Mauchley asked, his tone unconvinced.

"Men who send thousands to die don't have the luxury of conscience," Colsterworth said. "When was the last time *you* went to the trenches? Hmmm?"

"Drusselmehr said I'd need to rein you in. I thought I could persuade you to relent. That the threat of *treble* damages would make you see reason. So be it. I have orders to replace you with another as head of the Brotherhood of Shadows. Effective immediately."

"Who?" Colsterworth demanded. But he already suspected who they had in mind. He seethed inside but allowed none of his animosity to show in his expression. He'd misjudged the threat from one of his own.

Someone who had been feeding them information all along. Someone ambitious and cunning.

One Mr. Peabody Stoker no doubt.

Without arithmetic there is no art. The Mind of the Sovereignty has exhibited this rule throughout creation, and it is in evidence in mollusk shells, plant leaves, physical proportions in faces and limbs, the skeletons of beasts, and the ages of mortal kind. All Aesir artifacts and construction are based upon this golden ratio, this divine proportion. It is approximately 1.618—and the entire universe repeats it over and over and over again. It is the strongest evidence in existence of a guiding force that rules over the Unseen Powers.

—Isaac Berrow,
Master of the Royal Secret,
the Invisible College

Robinson Foster Hawksley

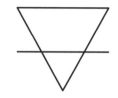

CHAPTER TWENTY-EIGHT

Tide Pools

It was the last day they'd spend together in Covesea. McKenna had wanted to visit the tide pools one last time, and Robinson was willing and eager to explore them again. The first time they'd come, she'd been frightened by the prospect of waves crashing against the rocky shoreline, but they always left with sufficient time to retrace their way back before the tide came in.

They'd left their shoes on a higher rock farther back, and he watched McKenna's bare feet padding from one section to the next, her dress bunched up, exposing her ankles and calves as she peered into the little shallow pools at the assortment of life clinging to the treacherous shore. The wind had blown her hair loose, and he felt his heart pang at the sight. He couldn't lose her. He couldn't. He squatted nearby, having plucked a reclusive little sand crab from its lair and let it skitter across his palm.

She turned and glanced at him, smiling as she saw it, and hurried over, careful not to slip on the wet terrain.

"Another one?" She held out her hand and he dropped it onto her palm. Then he scooped some water in his hand and washed away the grit.

"What have you found so far?" he asked.

"There's an ochre sea star as wide as my hand over there," she said, pointing in the general direction. "Some sculpin, two turban snails, and a sea urchin." She lowered the crab into a pocket of water and watched it scuttle into the sand and begin to bury itself.

Rob had rolled up the legs of his pants—a gift from the older couple who had let them space in their spare cabin by the seashore. They'd spent their days roaming the coast, exploring the rugged cliffs, the majestic waterfalls, and the turbulent coastline of Robinson's native land. All of it, they'd done dressed like the islanders, in clothes from their hosts, the Smilleys. McKenna, in her breacan-patterned wool dress, could have been any lass on the island, and Robinson's dark trousers were almost too tight now that they'd been enjoying Mrs. Smilley's wonderful cooking. The Smilleys were wonderful people, happy to do the young lovers a good turn on their honeymoon, without any notion of who they really were or why they sought seclusion. Not a single officer from the Marshalcy or the military had come hunting for them.

"Show me the sea star," Robinson asked, extending his hand. She took it and guided him over to the spot where a particularly fat one lay curled in a pool. It had a brilliant purple hue, encrusted with a speckled pattern that made it seem like a living gem.

"It is so fascinating," McKenna said, prodding it with her fingertip. "I never knew about tide pools. Well, I knew about them, but not about all the different forms of life that exist in such a dangerous location."

"And each creature here has an intelligence," Robinson said. "I believe that watchmakers use the intelligences of sea stars. These creatures have no brain, no blood."

"How do they survive?"

"The seawater itself sends nutrients flowing through their limbs. In a sense, the entire ocean is their beating heart. They can live for several decades, which is about as long as a good pocket watch lasts before the intelligence needs to be replaced. I've heard it takes very little coaxing to get another intelligence to take its place. And off it goes again, tick tock, tick tock."

McKenna smiled in wonder, then gazed over her shoulder at the edge of the reef, where the waves were crashing more violently. She looked back at him. "Life is tenacious, isn't it?"

"So are you," he said, caressing her cheek and stroking it with his thumb. They'd had a few more chats about her situation, but he could tell the being inside her grew agitated whenever he began to probe and ask questions. But he'd keep trying until he found a way to do it without provocation.

They were going to stop by Mowbray House and pick up mail and learn how well the experiments had worked with his ring. It clearly had, to some degree, because money had arrived, as instructed, to pay the Smilleys for the rental of their little cozy cabin. Their fare had also been paid for a ship departing for Siaconset the next day, and their luggage was packed and ready to go.

McKenna glanced back again. "I'm nervous that the tide is going to start coming in," she confessed. "Should we head back?"

"If you like," he said. She wrapped her arms around him, pressing her cheek into his chest, and just held him, gazing at the waves. He was feeling rather chilled with his bare feet and the spray on his face, but she seemed perfectly at ease. He bent down and kissed the crown of her head. The beauty of Covesea, the lonely island, was a sharp contrast to the bustle and pace of Auvinen. Yet, to be sure, there was certainly a shortage of sugared peanuts there.

They walked back together to where they'd stowed their shoes, still safe and dry, and sat down on a craggy boulder to put them on. He finished first and then decided to help her but couldn't refrain from tickling her bare leg, which made her gasp and scold him with a gentle slap from her other shoe.

Hand in hand, they began to roam back along the coast toward the Smilleys' seaside home. He wished he could bottle up the tranquility and peacefulness of the moment. He suspected that agents of the military were watching Mowbray House, and so he'd prepared arrangements—hopefully—with Mr. Swope for the older man to retrieve their baggage from the harbor while Robinson and McKenna traveled by foot and approached the house from the beach at the rear.

As they walked at a leisurely pace, he sensed the dog intelligence padding up to them. His first instinct was one of concern. Was it warning him of danger?

He halted, and McKenna looked in his face, noting his expression. "Is something wrong?"

He didn't feel any danger, but he sensed the intelligence yearning for him to follow it. Maybe it was trying to lead them out of harm's way.

"Our little friend wants us to take a detour," he said.

"I'm happy to oblige it," McKenna said. "Are we in danger?"

"I don't know. It doesn't seem so. At least, not at present."

He could sense the direction the intelligence was hastening off to, and they left the coastal trail to climb one of the many rugged cliffs. There were hundreds of waterfalls in the region, so many they weren't even named, and it seemed to Robinson—based on the sound—that the intelligence was leading them toward one. The ferns and moss added color to the rocky gray surface as they picked their way up an incline. He had to use his arm to clear away foliage for them to pass, but McKenna had always had an adventurous streak and didn't seem to mind the jaunt at all.

The noise of the falls grew louder as they approached. Through a screen of scraggly trees and mossy boulders, they discovered a pretty waterfall over a dozen feet high, spilling down a series of rocky bluffs that divided and subdivided the stream into curtains of misty ribbons. There was a little pool at the base and a mess of broken rocky fragments around it, those protruding from the water speckled in moss and lichen.

"How beautiful!" McKenna cooed, gazing at the little waterfall with wonder. Holding his hand, she maneuvered closer, and he helped her sit on one of the mossy boulders to appraise the scene.

It was a splendid little waterfall, one of the out-of-the-way ones that they wouldn't have found without help.

He offered a silent thought of gratitude to the dog, but the journey wasn't over. He felt it compelling him toward the waterfall.

"What are you doing?" McKenna asked, noticing the way he was stepping from fragment to fragment, getting closer.

"There's something here, I think," he answered, turning his face toward her so she could read his lips. It was instinctual now, something that barely required any thought at all.

His arms windmilled momentarily. He nearly lost his balance but preserved it at the last moment and followed around the rim of the stones. McKenna was gazing at him in fascination as he clambered closer to what he felt was the dog's intended location. The spray of the waterfall made everything slick, but he managed to proceed without stumbling. Then, crouching near the base of the falls, he felt the intelligence stop near him.

"Did you find something?" he whispered, gazing up the falls. The feeling of adventure hung in the air. This remote waterfall felt like a sacred place. In fact, it felt strangely familiar. Maybe he and his brothers had romped there long ago. It was distinctive, but just out of reach for his memory. Father had always liked to roam and explore when he wasn't traveling.

"I think I've been here before," he said to McKenna. Gazing around the scene.

The intelligence was fixed in place. He sensed it whining. Not because of danger. But because it wanted him to *do* something.

He squatted down, hearing the noise of the falls, feeling the mist kiss his neck. There were so many sheared off chunks of stone around them, forming little pockets of dark water. One of them caught his eye. Or maybe it was the intelligence trying to prod him. He rolled up his sleeve and reached his arm into the water. It wasn't very deep, and pulverized stone lined the bottom, like wet sand. He dug his fingers into the sand and felt something metallic. Blinking with surprise, he drew it out.

He stared in disbelief as he opened his hand and found a ring. It was bright and silver—no, it was white gold with golden ripples on the edges. Just like the one at the center of the device in his pocket. No tarnish. No rust. He bathed his hand in the pool to wash away the dirt and gravel. It was the same kind of ring. The interior even bore the mark of the Invisible College.

"Did you find something?" McKenna asked.

He had found something. He'd found something indeed.

On the boat ride to Siaconset, Robinson mulled over the discovery. When he'd slipped the new ring onto his thumb, he'd experienced the same effects as when he wore the original ring—a smarting headache that grew worse the longer he had it on and only subsided when he took the ring off. It was the twin of the ring in his device. Did that mean there was another device to match it? Who had dropped the ring in the waterfall? When? Because the metal was an alloy impervious to rust or decay, it could have been there for a century. Had the doglike intelligence been roaming and sensed the magic of the ring? That seemed the likeliest explanation. He tried asking it questions, but it could only communicate as a living dog would, through emotion and feelings of loyalty. Neither of which were helpful in discerning the truth of the matter.

After a hearty farewell meal for breakfast, Robinson and McKenna had left Covesea and their honeymoon. He felt rested. Her bruises had faded. But he could tell they both felt anxious about returning to their new life at Mowbray House. Was it safe to go back to Auvinen and visit her parents at the house on Brake Street? What news would they find upon their arrival?

The boat stopped at Ashmull and then departed again for Siaconset, although its ultimate destination was Auvinen. It took the longest part of the day to reach the next island, and Robinson and McKenna stayed in their little room just to remain out of sight. They were in their traveling clothes again. As they neared Siaconset, he put on the ring and sent a mental thought to Mr. Swope, alerting him of their impending arrival.

It was dusk when they landed, and they disembarked after all the other passengers had left. Mr. Swope was waiting for them at the edge of the gangway, a small wooden box in his hands, about the size of a pair of shoes. He had a concerned look in his eyes.

"This box has your correspondence," he said, offering it to McKenna. "I suggest you turn around and get back on board."

"Is it unsafe?" Robinson asked, alarmed.

"That's not it at all, sir. The military has been forbidden to even approach Mowbray House. You can thank Mr. Foster for that. No, I urge you to return to Auvinen at once. Mr. Wickins has been called up to service at the front. He leaves in two days. This is your only chance to bid him farewell."

Robinson was shocked to hear the news. "He quit the military."

"Aye, but he's still of age to be drafted. He's an enlisted man now, not an officer. You see, the lamps, sir. Your invention. Apparently the military has installed them in the trenches, and they're glowing. The Aesir are preparing to attack."

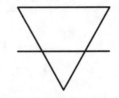

CHAPTER TWENTY-NINE

A GENERAL'S REVENGE

The painful throb in Robinson's skull ebbed immediately as he twisted the thumb ring off and inserted it back into the device. He clicked the cover shut and returned it to his pocket.

"Does it hurt so much?" McKenna asked, touching his arm. "The way your brow furrows, it seems quite uncomfortable."

"I think I'm rather used to it," Robinson answered, touched by her concern. "I don't know if the pain is a natural consequence of the magic at work or a warning not to use it too frequently. Let's go to the deck. I sent a message for someone to send the carriage for us."

She hooked arms with him, and they left their cramped quarters and returned to the deck, where the salty air had a chilly edge to it. Mr. Swope had provided them each with a change of clothes, having had the forethought to bring a few things for them to the boat, should they decide to continue with the journey.

Robinson liked the manservant at Mowbray House. He was crisp, efficient, and thinking of their needs in advance. He'd even offered to accompany them back to Auvinen, which they'd declined after his assurance that the military had been forbidden to approach them. Their arrival in Auvinen would be unexpected, to say the least, so Robinson thought they might be able to remain incognito for a few days more.

"Poor Wickins," McKenna said when they reached the railing. "It seems rather spiteful, don't you think?"

"The general does not seem to be a patient man or one to suffer slights. I was thinking of giving the ring we found to Wickins. It seems to work the same way as the one from the device. And it would allow two-way communication, which would be extraordinarily valuable. Transmuting thoughts over distances is something I'd thought about before. I didn't realize it had already been invented."

He felt a little put out about it, truthfully, and he dearly wished to know who had managed it.

Below the starless night sky, they saw the shimmering city ahead of them. The familiarity warmed his chest. He'd missed Auvinen, even though they hadn't been away for long. Going back to Covesea had stirred similar feelings. He felt both places were part of his heart now.

"It's the hive of the Industry of Magic," McKenna said. "I've missed it."

He kissed her and nodded in agreement.

After they docked, Robinson grabbed their bags. They disembarked and found Mrs. Foster awaiting them, her eyes brightening when she saw them together. She kissed McKenna and hugged her affectionately, then turned and surprised Robinson with a similar show of loving kindness. He hadn't seen his own parents for some weeks now and determined to pay them a visit. Judging by the crop of invitations that Mr. Swope had presented in the box, he wasn't sure when he'd have a free moment, but he couldn't abide by such constant appointments. While the attention was flattering, he wouldn't disregard other aspects of his life, and he also wanted to spend time in his alchemy working on his neglected research. Like the flame tube he'd started working on for McKenna to see if he could teach her to sing. A flame would spurt from a cylinder so she could use it to gauge the pitch of her voice. During their travels together, they'd spent some time discussing their next steps. His wife was ever eager to discover a way to participate in what had been barred to her—magic—but she'd dodged every attempted discussion about her being a Semblance.

Mrs. Foster led them to the carriage, where the familiar driver was awaiting them. Robinson noted a pile of steaming manure beneath the horses and a little contrivance hovering nearby, compelled to clean it up but having to wait for the carriage to move in order to do so. He could almost feel the intelligence's impatience to attend to its duties.

He greeted the driver, who tipped his hat, and they all trundled into the carriage and left for the house on Brake Street. As Robinson had hoped, not a single military person could be seen in the vicinity.

"How is poor Clara holding up?" McKenna asked, grasping her mother's hand.

"I think righteous indignation is the proper way to summarize her feelings," Mrs. Foster announced. "We're all thoroughly disgusted with General Colsterworth. The evidence gathered so far reveals he was personally involved in the decision to violate your patent, Robinson. It turns out that the military has been installing the Aesir tubes all summer long. They'd coerced these businesses into participating, despite knowing they were in breach. And he had the audacity to feign ignorance on the matter. He's insisting we drag the proceedings through court." She huffed. "He should be cast out of the Invisible College for this. Stripped of his rank entirely."

Robinson pursed his lips and shook his head in disbelief. What had happened to the principles of integrity the college of sorcerers had held in such high esteem? Or was the *strannik* and his goals so far off course? Robinson worried he might end up agreeing with a man who'd try to kill him with a shovel.

"And he says he lost your device as well!" Mrs. Foster said with a tone of outrage. "Another falsehood."

McKenna and Robinson glanced at each other.

"That's a significant look if I ever saw one," Mrs. Foster said, her eyebrows lifting.

Robinson drew the device from his pocket and showed it to her. "It appeared amongst my things unexpectedly. I've had it throughout our trip. It's what I used to communicate with everyone. I haven't figured out the alchemy of creating a new one. Not yet."

"But we did find another ring," McKenna offered. "In Covesea, hidden by a waterfall. Rob wants to lend it to Wickins when he deploys. At least we'll be able to hear from him."

Mother's eyes brightened immediately. "Clara could talk to him!"

"She could," McKenna said. "If she uses the other one. That's our hope anyway. If it will reach that far."

"Since it reached from Covesea to Auvinen without trouble, I have no qualm about it reaching the ice trenches," Robinson said firmly. "There is . . . another matter we'd like to discuss. Among the three of us. Before we reach the house."

Since Mrs. Foster already knew about her daughter's *condition*, he and McKenna had agreed the three should be able to discuss it further. Speaking quickly, he explained how he'd come to suspect that McKenna was harboring another sentience. He didn't use the word Semblance, even though the chance of Mr. Thompson Hughes overhearing it was small, he thought it prudent to disguise their communications.

She listened, her expression changing to a look of concern.

"Do you think, Professor—pardon, I'm still so used to calling you that! Do you think anything can be done?"

"I'm optimistic by nature. There are more than enough unanswerable questions already. But that is part of the method. To rule out what doesn't work until we find what does. Even broaching the topic causes McKenna to grow uneasy."

"I'm feeling it now," she admitted, hand on her breast, her expression more worried than her mother's. "It makes me agitated to talk about it so pointedly. I don't hear any voices in my head. Just . . . unsettled feelings."

"Her condition is more of an anomaly than most," Robinson said. "In the previous instances when I confronted . . . such entities . . . I could discern commands being given to them. Directions transmuted to their minds. I was able to cut off those transmissions. It seems McKenna does not receive them at all. I think that makes her case less threatening."

McKenna glanced at him and then looked down.

"We must tread carefully," Mrs. Foster said, speaking to Robinson but watching McKenna's downcast eyes. "This could be considered treason. I don't want to give the general any more reason to hate our family."

"Have you spoken to your husband?"

McKenna lifted her eyes, realizing they were still talking.

"I've not told him, no," she answered. "He is a very principled man. As are you. I cannot ask him to defy the law. But I hope to persuade him to change it. There are . . . cases where there may be danger, as with the one who attacked people at the Great Exhibition, for example. That kind needs to be stopped before they cause violence. But they may not all be similar in disposition. Or loyal to the same cause."

McKenna's mouth quirked into an odd smile. She looked at her mother. "I don't think they are all the same, Mother."

"I don't like keeping Mr. Foster in ignorance." Robinson sighed. "But for now, I agree it's for the best. I think he'd understand."

Mrs. Foster nodded in agreement, and they spent the rest of the journey in silence.

✳

It was dark when they reached the Fosters' house and Robinson assisted both of the women out of the carriage. The driver said he'd bring their cargo to the house after he'd returned the carriage and cared for the horses. The smell of overripe cherries filled the air, the carcasses of the fruit visible as blotches on the ground. Robinson sent his thoughts to the intelligences inside the warning tubes, testing to see if any had been breached or tampered with and found, to his relief, they were all intact and undisturbed.

The rest of the family hurried into the entryway when they arrived, but there was a brooding feeling that lurked under the warm greetings. Clara's eyes were red-rimmed as she hugged her sister tightly. Mr. Foster seemed more subdued than usual.

"Dickemore!" Wickins greeted with an embarrassed smile, wearing the uniform of the lowliest rank in the military. The plainness of the uniform, the simplicity of the buttons, was a stark contrast to his previous attire. Robinson felt his heart plunge upon seeing his friend in such a state, and the two hugged each other warmly.

"It's good to see you," Robinson said, feeling his eyes water.

"Now, I know what you're thinking, old chap, but it is what it is. Mr. Foster offered to fight the enlistment, but such military tribunals are rarely granted and even more rarely effect a reversal."

"Have they given you a role yet?" Robinson asked.

Clara came up and clasped Wickins's arm in a possessive gesture. "Artillery," she said, eyes flashing with rage. A lieutenant might oversee a dozen batteries. Not be assigned to a single one. Robinson's shoulders drooped at the news.

"But thank you for returning early to see me off," Wickins said, trying to feign more courage than he likely felt. During an Aesir attack, the survivability on the front lines was exceptionally low.

The thought of losing John Wickins to the war was unimaginable. The previous winter he'd been in the Signals yard at the garrison in Auvinen. Danger had always been possible, but it had been unlikely. This . . . this cut to the quick.

"What have you heard about the lamps?" Robinson asked, diverting the topic to ease their aching hearts.

"They've been very helpful so far, old chap. The military has long suspected that Aesir come in their cloaks, to inspect the ice trenches and test where our weakest points may be before launching an attack.

At several places on the front lines, the tubes began to crackle and glow, revealing their presence!"

"What did they do with that information?" McKenna asked.

Wickins grinned. "Opened fire! Remember, the haze of saltpetr slows them down. The soldiers still couldn't *see* them, but they knew the general area and began to shoot. It caused the Aesir to flee down the line, triggering more lamps to brighten, bringing another volley of elfshot. They killed one without losing a single man!"

Robinson felt McKenna squeeze his hand tightly. He glanced at her, saw not only interest but alarm in her expression.

"Then they attacked en masse, lighting up the entire area. Killed about a hundred of our men, I think, before the artillery could come to bear. The Aesir went about destroying the tubes, breaking them. Some soldiers became sick with quicksilver poisoning . . . the fumes . . . but imagine the enemy's surprise when by morning, the broken tubes were replaced with new ones. They've been attacking along the front. That's why the mobilization has already begun. But they can't surprise us anymore. For the first time in history, we can 'see' them before we can *see* them."

"Any sign of the stormbreakers?" Robinson asked.

"None. Right now, they are still testing the lines. Seeing how close they can get to make the lamps glow, then retreating before we start firing."

Wickins reached out and gripped Robinson's shoulder with warmth. "Because of you, I'll stand a halfway decent chance out there."

The look of torment in Clara's eyes turned to outright anguish.

Do you not see how necessary a world of pains and troubles is to school an intelligence and make it a soul?

—Isaac Berrow,
Master of the Royal Secret,
the Invisible College

MaKenna Aurora
Hawksley

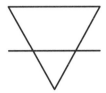

CHAPTER THIRTY

GLISTENING SILVER

It was heartrending for McKenna to see the look of anguish on Clara's face as she watched Wickins leaning from the locomotivus to wave goodbye. Trudie, who had all the tender affection for him she would for an older brother, hugged Clara, who hugged Mother, all eyes wet with tears. The locomotivus was crammed with soldiers heading to the front from Auvinen, and there was a mixed measure of pride with the prevailing sorrow.

McKenna's throat thickened with the thought that Wickins might not be coming back. It made the Aesir war personal. It made her distrust the entity lurking within her. If there were any way to expel it, short of catastrophic means, she would have done so in an instant.

She watched as Rob pushed through the crowd and gripped Wickins's outstretched hand from the window. The two exchanged words, but McKenna was at the wrong angle to decipher them. Glancing back, she noticed the resolute and taciturn expression on Father's face as he waved goodbye to the young soldier.

There had been some talk, awkward as it was, about whether Clara and Wickins should marry before his departure. They weren't exactly engaged, but they had spoken of marriage since the exhibition, McKenna had learned. Wickins didn't want to hold her back by having to wait for him.

Conflicting feelings twisted in McKenna's bosom as the locomotivus hissed out a plume of foggy air, then began to levitate and propel itself above the tracks. Not long ago, she'd flung herself onto a moving engine to escape a wicked man. Thankfully, there was no sign of him or his accomplices now. She hoped the military had caught up with him and done their worst.

Robinson sidled up next to her, squeezing her hand and then waving with his other. She echoed his gesture, and Wickins gave a broad and genial wave, although his smile was strained. He'd accepted his change of fate with courage. Although the lowest peg on the rung of the military ladder, he was a young man with fortune and a promising career ahead of him. Most enlistments were required for a single year. If he could survive the winter months, then his other duties would be less fraught with peril until he was discharged.

Clara sobbed on Mother's shoulder, releasing her pent-up grief and frustration. McKenna squished closer to offer a comforting embrace, which was accepted. With her family and husband pressed near, she felt the tragedy of her sister's situation more keenly. Rob had promised to allow Clara use of his ring so she could share thoughts with Wickins during his time away. A throbbing headache was the consequence, but that would be more intimate than even sharing letters, which both had promised to write each other daily. McKenna wondered if her sister would follow through on the pledge. Or if Wickins would.

"I must return to the office," Father announced. He looked at Rob. "We'll see each other for dinner at the Clemence-Baileys' home tonight?"

"Indeed," Rob answered. "I look forward to seeing Sarah Fuller Fiske there as well."

With the litigation in progress against the military, Father was beleaguered with work and appointments. But he'd encouraged Rob and McKenna to accept the Clemence-Baileys' dinner invitation as the first social engagement on their list. They were family friends and keenly interested in investing in the business. According to Father, many aristocratic families of great wealth were clamoring to see Rob, several with significant influence and residences at Bishopsgate. They could not postpone these prominent affairs forever, no matter how much the young couple longed for solitude at Mowbray House. They only had a few weeks left before the season altered enough to make the voyage back dangerous, so they were obliged to cram in as many appointments in the interim as possible. McKenna dreaded the time it would take, but this was the debut into Society she'd sought. She was determined to prove herself equal to the task—and to do her part for the business.

McKenna bid farewell to her sisters and parents, who would take the carriage to the office. Rob and McKenna, meanwhile, would take a street tram back to the hotel they'd checked into. They had every reason to suspect that although the military was forsworn from speaking to them, there was no way of preventing surveillance. So they'd switch hotels every few days to disguise their trail. It would likewise make it more difficult for General Colsterworth to keep watch because Rob was no longer a member of the quorum at the Storrows in Auvinen now that their official residence was in Siaconset. He could still visit, of course, but no longer had a responsibility to defend the city if it came under attack again. This was all rather exciting to McKenna. She squeezed Rob's arm as they walked briskly out of the station building and deposited coins into the contraption to get away.

It was crowded, so they sat hip to hip, and McKenna asked what he'd said to Wickins at the end.

"I reminded him to check in with me during his progress north," Rob said. "I want to see how far the rings can connect us. I also tested his memory to see if he remembered the spell I taught him yesterday."

"The violent one?" McKenna asked, keeping her voice low.

Rob nodded. "Those on the front lines are in the most physical danger. He'll have a pistol, but once the elfshot is spent, I wanted him to have another way of defending himself."

She squeezed his hand on his lap, proud of him and grateful for his efforts to safeguard his friend. He was a wonderful man, and she felt lucky to have found him.

As the tram proceeded down the street, she caught a whiff of burnt peanuts in the air. It reminded her of the lessons she'd traveled to each week with Robinson. The Hawksley method for elocution. Her beloved teacher touching her cheek, her chin, demonstrating how to hold her tongue. They were precious memories. But it was that winter when the Aesir had first attacked.

Before her drowning.

Before she'd become whatever she now was.

The Clemence-Baileys lived in an exquisite neighborhood on the north side of the Watership River. It was a mansion really, with wrought-iron fences that would scald any Aesir who touched the bars. The last of the late autumn leaves clung tenaciously to elm branches, which were mostly denuded now. Light from the quicksilver lamps illuminated the street on both sides, and there were carriages aplenty. The Clemence-Baileys had offered to send a carriage to fetch them, but they'd taken a street tram and walked the rest of the way.

On arrival, they were greeted by Mrs. Clemence-Bailey and Sarah Fuller Fiske, who welcomed them into the overly warm interior. McKenna felt an instant sense of trepidation, knowing the room was too hot for her but also that she'd have to endure it. McKenna knew the family, and the heavyset mistress of the house was jovial and sweet. Their children were older than McKenna, most of them married and with an appearance of boredom, but Mrs. Clemence-Bailey practically dragged Rob by the sleeve to introduce him to her husband.

A festive dinner was served in the dining hall with uniformed servants standing by the walls wearing white gloves and carrying silver dishes engraved with Aesir runes. She felt part of herself recoil upon seeing them in such a setting. Deep in her chest, she felt they didn't *belong* there. Father still hadn't arrived yet and had sent his apologies for the delay.

Rob was seated next to her, for which McKenna was grateful. There were conversations happening everywhere at once, and she found herself stymied from eating because she wanted to follow as much of the talk as possible. Sarah was seated on her other side and engaged her in pleasant conversation about her honeymoon and asked where they'd gone. She shared a few sparse details about Covesea but kept quiet about the attack that had been made on herself and Robinson.

The dinner lasted very long, but everyone seemed cheerful and animated, especially the master and mistress of the manor. Then they removed to the parlor, where Rob was pressed to play a violin, which was provided by the family, and McKenna watched how immediately they were enraptured by his musical gifts. With applause, they pleasantly demanded he play another. Then another. She needed to ask Mother about getting him that violin, since they hadn't been able to do so during their honeymoon.

After the music was done, Mr. Clemence-Bailey asked if he could show Rob his private alchemy and ask some questions about his invention and the projects he was interested in. As soon as that was mentioned, the married children sprang to their feet, obviously keen to participate. McKenna was about to rise as well, but Sarah gripped her hand, gently but firmly, and shook her head.

Confused, McKenna watched as the others left the parlor, leaving the two women behind. The heat from the fireplace was stifling, and McKenna felt she was sweating profusely and needed some air.

"Why can't we go with them?" she asked.

Sarah looked kind but . . . disappointed? Was that the mood? "You cannot go because they will be discussing matters related to the Invisible College," she explained.

"What will they be discussing that is so secret?" McKenna asked, feeling a flash of annoyance that was no longer limited to the oppressive heat.

Sarah covered McKenna's hands with her own. "It's not just about the Invisible College. That is . . . unfortunately, more of a pretext. Because of my connection with your family and with Professor Hawksley, I've had many people approach me regarding a matter of concern. In some circles in Society, there is gossip about you . . . and him."

McKenna's eyes widened with surprise. "Because I married so young? Or because I'm deaf? Or both."

Sarah winced. "There are some who are concerned about those things, but not the Clemence-Baileys. They've known your family for ages. They love and respect your parents and adore you. Mrs. Clemence-Bailey was willing to remain here with you, alone, to be a good hostess. I offered to do that part so they could ask their questions."

"Tell me what's going on," McKenna pleaded. The heat and this news were making her nauseated.

"What I've heard, and what I've had to contradict, is that some people believe your father forced or manipulated Robinson into conceding his shares in the business to you as a wedding gift."

"That's preposterous!"

"I know. I know it was his idea. Even Judge Coy Taylor has been asked about it relentlessly, especially now that those shares may soon be worth a sizable amount. Since the Great Exhibition, your husband has become quite popular. Famous even for how he saved people's lives. There were also some rumors about him and Miss Cowing, but I've put those to rest whenever they've come up."

"Miss Cowing? They were never alone together."

"Not everyone has all the facts, McKenna. Mr. Clemence-Bailey will ask Robinson about the circumstances regarding the shares that were given over to you. I've already told him the truth, but before anyone commits a sizable investment in an invention, they desire to know for themselves. So he will ask your husband as one member of the Invisible College to another, because forthrightness is a virtue taken by oath for us. That's why you can't be there."

McKenna was furious, disappointed, and agitated. Mother had warned her that Society could be capricious. McKenna thought that word too pleasant to fit its meaning. But this was hypocrisy. How many members of the Invisible College were gossiping about them while decrying gossip as a welt, a bruise, a smirch to one's character?

"You have every right to be upset," Sarah said soothingly.

"Why didn't Mother or Father tell me?"

"You know why, McKenna. The secret oaths within the order forbid it. And what happened to poor Wickins . . ." She shook her head with a sad look. "It was done to *hurt* your family because of the rights to the patent. When great sums of money are at stake, people do things not in good conscience, or they whisk that conscience aside. Many of us who know your family are standing up for your good name. And your husband's."

McKenna felt a trickle of sweat track down her cheek. Her face flamed with embarrassment. Her hands were being confined by Sarah's, so she retracted one of them and dabbed it away with the back of her hand.

"It's quite stuffy in here," Sarah said. "Maybe we should get some cooler air?"

"That would be lovely," McKenna said. "You are so gracious, so helpful."

Sarah rose from the cushioned seat and gave McKenna a hug. "Your husband came charging into danger when everyone got sick at my school. He imperiled himself doing so. I respect and admire him as much as I do your family. You deserved an explanation, not to be left wondering why you weren't included in the conversation."

McKenna wondered if the device in Robinson's pocket had saved his life from the illness. If the round stone were indeed a philosopher's stone.

"Thank you, Sarah."

The returning smile was sad. "I'd like to also caution you on something . . . I know your husband has received many invitations from notable people. People it would not be wise to slight. Yet people who are willing . . . unfortunately . . . to slight others. They may welcome Robinson into their faction of Society." She shook her head. "But they may not welcome you. And they'll use your condition, your father's name, your youth, any reason they can think of. I'm sorry, McKenna. It's not fair. But it is how Society works. And it has worked this way for a long, long time."

CHAPTER THIRTY-ONE

IMPERIAL INVITATION

The Moika Hotel in Telimar was exquisite, the staff affable and pleasant, the food exotic—but McKenna was so weary of traveling that she was on the edge of screaming out in frustration. For two weeks she'd bottled up her feelings, tolerating the pace of their frenetic new life together and the sudden rise of Rob's popularity. She enjoyed traveling. But this . . . this was madness. Every accepted invitation had turned into a dozen new ones. Telimar was just the latest destination. When she'd heard that there was a ship bound for Covesea the next morning, she'd had the urge to stow away on board and return to the quiet island of Rob's birth.

"We don't have to go," Rob said when she turned away from the window. The view of the Moika River outside, teeming with ships, should have been an enthralling sight, but the opulent hotel felt like a cage. She wanted to be done. Snow was in the mountains, they'd heard. But it hadn't touched the coastal cities yet.

"It would be rude not to," she said glumly. Because she'd quickly learned the truth of Sarah Fuller Fiske's words—many of the hosts who were so friendly toward her husband treated her so coldly. She was proud of her husband. But Society had clearly weighed her and found her wanting. If not for her deafness, then for the imagined sin of pilfering her husband's now impending wealth. Perhaps "pilfer" was too soft a word. Some had treated her like she was a conniving, heartless schemer. The disdain on their faces had made her shudder inside. Even after Rob had roundly insisted the arrangement had been *all his idea*. They didn't believe it. They didn't *want* to believe it. Though it was painful to her, with everything else going on in their lives, she chose not to focus on the hurt. She hadn't let him know the full depth of the apathy she'd endured on many of the visits. Had she let on, he would have taken action. Would have protected her feelings at the cost of losing interested investors. Her decision to remain silent was pragmatic, but she couldn't always feign indifference to the obfuscated slights.

"I just want to go to Mowbray House," Rob said with a sigh, running his hand through his lanky hair. He had several more fashionable suits now, but he confessed they made him uncomfortable. Their use was restricted to visits with the notable families who'd issued invitations to them.

"So do I," McKenna muttered. "It's wrong to wish for snow, knowing that the Aesir are coming with it, though I am weary of this. But I can endure it. A little longer."

He took her hands, giving her an adoring look she didn't feel she deserved.

"I'm not enjoying this," he confessed.

"You should be. The notoriety must be flattering at least."

He shook his head. "I only care about the approval of a very few people."

"And who are those lucky souls?" she asked, even though she already knew.

Peevish feelings were bubbling inside her. None of this was his fault. Well . . . technically *all* of it was. Last winter, he'd been starving himself unwittingly, so lost in his research he'd forget to eat. But he wasn't the pallid, thin-framed man he'd been back then. With all the invitations and the rich food, he no longer appeared half-starved. She was no longer the only one who noticed him and found him charming and interesting—now the rest of the world did too. But she could see the restlessness in his eyes. The hunger to be back in his alchemy, struggling to unlock clues regarding the nature of the universe. Of *her*.

"I want *you* to be proud of me foremost," he said seriously. "I also respect the good opinion of your parents. And my own."

They'd brought Rob's parents to one of the dinners in Auvinen before they'd left. The look of pride in James Hawksley's face at his son's rush of success and fame had been obvious. His mother, who had lost the majority of her hearing, just stared at her son with a smile of pleasure on her face and read the lips of those in conversation. She'd lost her hearing at an older age, and her skill at verbally communicating—especially pronunciation—was comparable to McKenna's.

"Is that all? Are there other good opinions you crave?"

"Sarah Fuller Fiske. The children at the school. And a little dog intelligence that has stayed with us despite our rushing about the continent."

She glanced around. "Is it truly here? Right now?"

"Over by the incalescent machine actually." Which he'd turned off as soon as they'd entered their suite. He'd opened the window too, another sign of his thoughtfulness.

"How amazing that it's followed us all this while. And what of Wickins? Do you want his good opinion as well?"

"Naturally," he said with a half smile. "And I have it."

"How is he doing? When was the last time you connected with him through the rings?"

"This morning. There was an attack on the trenches about ten miles east of his position."

She was grateful he hadn't been involved in any direct attacks as yet. There had been no issue at all in communicating at such a great distance using the rings. Though he'd determined the precise properties of the golden alloy, he was still struggling to comprehend how it all worked. "Any casualties?"

"Some, but not many. The forewarning of attacks has been invaluable."

She stopped asking questions. They'd agreed, in previous conversations, that she should know little to nothing about Robinson's communications with his friend. The hope was to deprive the entity . . . it made her shudder sometimes to think of it . . . of any intelligence that could be used to harm Wickins or the other soldiers hunkering down in the ice trenches.

McKenna glanced at the massive woodbound clock on the wall. If they were going to dine with the Furgsters, a wealthy aristocratic family, they should probably start getting ready.

"What gown should I wear?" she asked him, tilting her head.

"Are you sure?"

She nodded, determined to master her annoyance. He chose one of his favorites, and they quickly dressed in their formal attire for the evening. An employee of the Moika arrived—Rob responding to some prompt and opening the door.

"The carriage is awaiting you in the porte cochere," he said with a short bow. His mouth creased into a frown. "It's very chilly in here. Is the incalescent machine not working?"

"We prefer it this way," Rob said. "Please make no changes while we're away."

"If you insist," he replied with an amiable smile, and led the way down to the carriage.

Gazing out the windows at the shining lamps, the wide streets and carriages, McKenna reached over to take Rob's hand and gave it a comforting squeeze. She would be strong. For his sake. For her mother's sake.

✳

McKenna wondered, at the beginning of the fourth course, whether she could slip away and loosen her corset. The Furgsters were a charming couple, with seven children all seated at the affluent table with its costly trappings. Some of the younger children had asked McKenna questions about Auvinen and other places she'd traveled. They were darling creatures, and it made the evening more pleasant than she'd expected.

One topic of news, however, had been rather startling.

"You haven't heard about the riots?" Mr. Furgster demanded. "They had to call in a regiment from the military to the palace at Andover to quell them. Soldiers who should have been on the way to the front, I should say."

"It was awful business, just awful," said Mrs. Furgster with a frightened air.

"What were the riots about?" McKenna asked. She was interested and concerned.

"The Aesir war, naturally," Mr. Furgster said. "There is a sect, you see, a growing number of civilians who seek peace with our enemies."

"It really is unseemly," Mrs. Furgster added. She reached over and gripped her husband's hand.

"Not unseemly, more like suicidal," said her husband with a gruff look. "What is aggravating is some of the ringleaders of this rabble have connections to the Invisible College." He gave Rob a significant look.

"We have all lost loved ones in the war," Mrs. Furgster declared. "You would think those sacrifices would mean more to some."

Robinson leaned forward, his expression interested. "Do you know who these leaders are?"

"The followers of some man they call the *strannik*. A man who is growing in popularity by the day."

McKenna felt a stab of worry and glanced sharply at Rob as he asked, "How so?"

McKenna was so fixed on the conversation, on following lips, that she only realized by the sudden turning of heads that someone else had entered the dining hall. Surprised looks were passed among the group, and then Mr. Furgster shoved back from the table and hastily stood.

McKenna's fear spiked when she turned and saw a man she didn't recognize arrive, wearing a beautifully tailored jacket with frilly cuffs. He was holding a box in his hands, the kind you'd get at a prestigious store catering to the wealthy. He had silver, wavy hair and a jovial smile and a twinkle in his eyes, except one of them twinkled because it was clearly made of glass. His craggy face was benevolent as he bowed his chin in greeting to the family.

Robinson stood and McKenna followed suit. The children rushed from their seats and surrounded the old man eagerly, their eyes bright with wonder.

McKenna felt the conversation twirling around her, so she surreptitiously glanced at the hosts and caught Mr. Furgster introducing the new arrival.

"Master Drusselmehr, it is an honor. Such an honor! I did not know you were in Telimar! With everything happening in Andover, I had assumed you'd be there! Let me introduce my guests!"

"No need to introduce them," said the man who, McKenna realized with growing terror, was the head of the Invisible College. "They require no introduction. Mr. and Mrs. Hawksley." He bowed slightly again, one hand to his breast, the other clinging to the box that the children were pawing at.

She'd never seen him before. Not in person. But his reputation as an inventor of toys, his diplomacy skills throughout the empire, and his head of thick, wavy silver hair all were infamous. Having such a notorious man arrive without warning was startling.

"It's my pleasure," Robinson said, extending his hand in the ritual handshake.

The aged sorcerer accepted the grip with a warm smile, pumped it firmly, and then released it. "I came to Telimar on a mission from the emperor himself. I've come to steal your guest, Mr. Furgster," he said with a sly grin. "I tell you the emperor *himself* wishes to meet you,

Professor Hawksley." He'd raised a pointed finger to the sky when using the emperor's title. "For such a guilty intrusion, I bring a gift to your beloved children. A new toy I have invented. One that will surely be my best-selling one yet!"

McKenna watched the children squeal with delight. They clearly knew this man from prior visits. She vaguely recalled that he'd made his name enchanting magical toys for children and had business enterprises in Auvinen to produce them.

"You honor us with your generosity," Mrs. Furgster said. "Please, you must stay for supper."

"I have already dined," the old sorcerer said. "I came to bring this toy and to offer an invitation for the Hawksleys to join me, tomorrow, on a ship bound for Andover. You must agree to this! I will brook no refusal."

McKenna saw the look of dilemma on Rob's face. It was the highest honor a person could receive, a personal invitation to appear before the emperor. Yet, they'd just learned that an additional regiment had been called to Andover to quell an uprising. Would General Colsterworth be there? Had he arranged it? Nevertheless, it was impossible to decline such a request. She looked Rob in the eye and gave a subtle nod.

"We accept," Rob said.

"Most excellent! Most excellent indeed!"

"But what of the turmoil in Andover?" Mr. Furgster asked.

Master Drusselmehr hefted the package higher when one of the littlest nearly tugged it out of his hands. He lovingly tapped the little girl on the forehead and then shook his finger at her.

"It was insignificant," he said with a wrinkle to his nose. "Now for the toy!"

The children clapped their hands joyfully. With the affect of an experienced stage actor, the old sorcerer lifted the decorative lid off the box. Beneath it were wads of gauzy muslin, which he withdrew, revealing a toy cannon and a painted soldier wearing a decorated military uniform. Master Drusselmehr set the cannon down on the table and then pulled out the soldier, whom he pantomimed rocking back and forth toward the cannon. The paint glistened with polish. The cannon was like so many McKenna had seen stowed on platforms or rigged to locomotivus hubs on their way north.

The wizened fellow then said a magical word and used the soldier's arm to touch the cannon.

The children jumped with startled surprise, and the Furgsters had clamped their hands over their ears. Rob hadn't startled at all. He was looking at the toy, his expression guarded. McKenna hadn't heard the explosion, but she saw a little curl of mist emerge from the cannon and smelled the distinct aroma of saltpetr.

"Wh-What a l-lovely little toy," Mrs. Furgster said, fanning herself. McKenna could see from her expression that, as a parent, she wasn't at all relishing the idea of her children firing it in the house.

Master Drusselmehr bowed demonstratively, with a flourish, and the children began clamoring to be the first to set it off.

"Take it to the other room," Mr. Furgster said, waving his hand. "You are too generous. Too generous indeed."

"The children must be taught the importance of war," said the old sorcerer. "How it will save us from our enemies. We have forgotten too much. We have lost sight of our need to protect ourselves from external threats. Do you not agree, Professor?"

He'd pointed his gaze at Rob, who looked wary. Troubled.

"My best friend is on the front," Rob answered stiffly. "How could I forget?" His jaw muscles rippled.

McKenna realized that he was experiencing pain. And she noticed he'd slipped his hand into his pocket. When he withdrew it, she saw the ring already on his thumb, and her heart went cold.

The Erlking rules the Aesir because he is a being of impeccable justice. It is not that an Aesir cannot lie but that their honor is bound to truth. When the Erlking gives a command, it is followed. Mortals are different. We use conniving and duplicity to achieve our ends. That is why no peace between our races has endured. We cannot hold up our end of the bargain. Long ago, they lost patience with our shortcomings, our inability to fulfill our oaths. That is what I believe, for there are no records that reveal such a covenant. In the absence of fact, we must rely on hypothesis. And pray that another generation will become more honest than we currently are.

—Isaac Berrow,
Master of the Royal Secret,
the Invisible College

Robinson Foster Hawksley

CHAPTER THIRTY-TWO

OF A TRUTH

"Your hands are cold," McKenna said after they'd entered the carriage and started the return journey to the Moika. He enjoyed the feeling of her hands rubbing his, her little gesture of consideration. His skull still throbbed from his use of the ring. He'd already removed it and reattached it to the device. He stroked his thumb against the edge of her hand after summoning a wisp of light to aid their conversation.

"I'm concerned about going to Andover," he said with a sigh.

"But such an opportunity," she said. "The emperor wants to meet you. If the royal family becomes interested, that could be such a help to . . . to everything."

He massaged the bridge of his nose, hoping the headache would fade. He would endure it willingly for the information it provided, but his stomach churned with concern for his friend. McKenna had tried to get him to reveal the information he'd gleaned from Wickins, but he'd insisted on waiting until they were alone—as they were now.

"Or it will complicate matters even more." He shook his head. "First though, about the news. Another attack happened tonight, this one at the ice trench at Fort Mackenzie."

"Is that near where Wickins is stationed?"

"It's less than a league away. The previous attack was farther east. In other words, they're getting closer."

"Oh no," McKenna said, her face crinkling with worry. She squeezed his hands to comfort him, but undoubtedly she feared for her sister as well.

"He's frightened. Was doing his best to remain calm, but he reached out to let me know in case the attack reaches them tonight. He's afraid he won't survive until morning."

"That's dreadful. Poor Wickins."

Rob squeezed her hand in return, grateful for her sympathy. "And there I was, standing with the head of the Invisible College, *wanting* to tell him what I'd learned. But if I revealed it, it would raise questions. They could seize the device again. They could demand to know how I'd gotten it back . . ." He let his voice trail off. He believed he stood a better chance of solving the riddle of the device and the ring than anyone in the military. That was reason enough to continue concealing it from them.

"But the connection you have with Wickins is very valuable. He told you because he wanted you to know the truth. It takes days for news from the front to reach the cities."

"Yes, and I have an update instantaneously. He said he'll check in at dawn and let me know if the attack comes. I told him about us going to Andover and he was so excited for us. And I feel terribly guilty."

"Of course you do. But it's not your fault. None of this is. Maybe you should have told Master Drusselmehr."

"I wanted to, but then he showed us that toy."

McKenna looked at him with confusion. "The soldier and cannon?"

"It is not just a plaything, McKenna. I sensed it is run by more than one kind of intelligence. It can *hear* as well. It may be a toy, but it is empowered to eavesdrop. I would need to examine it closely to understand what it is fully capable of, but it alarms me considerably that these toys will reach so many homes. They want to spy on us." He was alarmed, truthfully. The Invisible College was supposed to operate on principles of strict integrity. That was an undisputed fact from the earliest journals kept by Isaac Berrow and passed down for centuries. Sorcerers were supposed to be above the pettiness of such things. But this wasn't just pettiness. This was another sign of internal corruption, the general's behavior being another.

"I can see how troubled you are," McKenna said. "But should you not tell him something? If he knows about the ring, at the very least, you could inform him of important information, perhaps in time to do something about it."

"Like arrest us?" He snorted.

"Rob. I'm not saying trust him with everything. There might be reasons he's doing this that we don't see. Trust a little bit. See how he reacts. You don't have to divulge everything. In fact, you'd better not! We need to help if we can, but if you get arrested or harmed in any way, then we won't be able to help anyone."

"So reveal certain things that will benefit the empire but don't reveal how I know it?"

"Exactly. You can say it's part of your research into connecting thoughts. That's sufficiently vague. And it also happens to be true. You're still trying to connect *our* thoughts."

Robinson smiled, realizing that she was talking about her own secret. She'd made good points, though. The outrage he felt, the disillusionment, might be clouding his judgment. He needed facts and truth, not speculation. What little he did know about Master Drusselmehr was that he was a very famous inventor of children's toys and had become vastly wealthy because of both his inventing and his investment in other ideas. He had risen to the highest pinnacle of the Invisible College. But perhaps the situations he confronted were heavily nuanced and not as easily categorized as right or wrong.

"You are a clever woman," he said, lifting her hand to his lips and pressing a kiss there.

"Is that all I am?" she asked, sidling even closer. "Am I . . . pretty as well? To you?" He saw a little flush on her cheeks. The jostling of the carriage was rhythmic and soothing. His headache ebbed. He reached over and stroked the edge of her chin, then down her neck. She shivered at his touch, a sly grin on her mouth.

In the magically lit carriage, nestled behind velvet drapery, he decided he didn't want to wait until they got to the hotel to show her how lovely he did find her. He began kissing her, deeply and urgently, until they were both gasping.

The driver might have wondered how she'd ended up on his lap when they reached the curb of the hotel with its fancy doormen and their polished staves. Robinson didn't care what he thought. Their kissing had awakened things inside him that were compelling them both to hurry across the threshold and get back to their room.

Master Drusselmehr had promised to send a carriage for them and he had—one from the Marshalcy. It was still dark when they left the hotel for the docks, and the driver, a blunt-faced fellow about thirty years old, said nothing to them other than issuing a formal greeting and confirming the destination. Once at the harbor, they were escorted onto a merchant vessel docked near a *Hotspur*-class warship and then brought to Master Drusselmehr's private rooms.

The older man was enjoying a poached egg, dark with pepper, on a crispy piece of buttered toast, tea, and some kind of sweet-smelling pan-fried bread. He offered to have his private chef make them breakfast too. They agreed and joined him at the little dining table in the room that had four small chairs. The only other person in the room was a manservant with a dark suit, a magical pin on his lapel, and—as Robinson saw beneath the flap of his jacket—a holstered pistol. He also sensed the quivering magic of the intelligence embedded in a harrosheth blade on the fellow's person, although he could not discern where it was concealed.

"We will reach Andover by this evening, if all goes well," Master Drusselmehr revealed. "You'll stay in the best hotel, of course. Near the imperial palace. I sent word last night for an agent from your business to provide materials for a proper demonstration of the quicksilver tubes. Once things are assembled to your satisfaction, we can arrange the introduction. Does that please you?"

"I think that will work," Robinson said. "It does not require much time to set up the demonstration."

"Good. That's very good. I am looking forward to seeing it in person. As I understand from the Great Exhibition, it was quite impressive. I think you will go far in the Invisible College, young man. I foresee some great accomplishments from your prodigious talents."

McKenna patted Robinson's arm. Was it encouragement to speak up or a display of affection?

"There *is* . . . a matter I should like to discuss," Robinson said.

A knock sounded at the cabin door, and a wrinkle of annoyance came from the old sorcerer. His manservant answered the door while his employer wiped his mouth with a decorative napkin.

The manservant scowled and then stood aside, revealing the person in the doorway. It was Mr. Stoker, the man who had arrested Robinson and Clara at the exhibition. A jolt of surprise shot down Robinson's spine, and McKenna stiffened, grabbing his upper arm and squeezing it hard.

"We're eating breakfast, Mr. Stoker," Master Drusselmehr stated impatiently.

"I apologize for the intrusion, but I had to see you—" He stopped, recognizing the other two seated at the little dining table. "Professor Hawksley . . ."

Robinson's initial reaction had been that the whole thing had been contrived, but judging by the equally surprised look on Stoker's face, he hadn't known they were on board. He reached over and gently squeezed McKenna's leg in a reassuring way. He knew the device would protect them from any sudden magical attack. But he was ready to begin casting defensive spells if need be.

"Yes, what is it?" Drusselmehr insisted.

"Excuse me, I had some . . . intelligence I wanted to give you before you departed. About the *strannik*." He looked nervously at the other guests and then averted his gaze.

"Very well. Speak."

"It is . . . ahem . . . confidential."

"Mr. Stoker, as I understand things, Mr. and Mrs. Hawksley were brutally attacked by this man in Covesea. I have no intention of keeping any news regarding their attacker from them. Please." He gestured to the empty chair next to him.

Robinson felt a rush of gratitude at the comment. It helped him feel more trusting of the older man's intentions.

Mr. Stoker slunk into the small state room and dropped onto the chair. The manservant shut the door and leaned back against it, folding his arms, looking rather like he wanted to punch Mr. Stoker in the face.

"He's performed another healing. The duke of Afferby's mother. He laid hands on her and she recovered instantly."

"That is the fourth healing now?" Master Drusselmehr queried.

"Exactly. He was seen leaving, followed by our man, and then disappeared. As I suspected, it was not he who left but an imposter disguised in a glamour. He is still at the duke of Afferby's estate. I have men guarding the grounds. One saw him pass by a window."

"So, the *strannik* is more cunning than you supposed. Is that all the information you have?"

"Yes. I'm seeking permission from Judge Thueson to mount a raid."

"Do nothing of the sort!" barked Drusselmehr. "Even if you manage *not* to botch things, he would still escape in disguise. No, he believes he is safe there, so let him believe it further. Instead, arrange for an invitation to be sent. Pretend someone is sick in an even more prestigious family. Send word to Afferby. Draw him in. He'll come willingly, because he seems to crave notoriety and fame. When you wish to capture a rat, you bait the trap with *cheese*."

Mr. Stoker nodded thoughtfully. "I will do as you recommend, sir."

Master Drusselmehr began carving into his toast and egg again. "That is all," he said dismissively.

Mr. Stoker rose from the table and slipped out the door. The manservant shook his head with contempt after he was gone.

"Come, Mr. Leishman. Disguise your annoyance. He serves his purpose still. Please follow Mr. Stoker and impress on his mind that ambition must be tempered with prudence. Go."

The manservant nodded and departed quickly.

Robinson was impressed by the interchange but said nothing.

With a fork, Master Drusselmehr stabbed the bit of egg and sweet toast and chewed it quickly. Pausing, he looked at Robinson and said, "Lord Mauchley named that fool the head of the Brotherhood of Shadows. He didn't do it to gratify the man's ambition but to thwart the general by raising a man to the level of his incompetence. If I don't help Mr. Stoker a little, he will surely meet a bad end. I think the general suspects Mr. Stoker is playing both sides of the *chovgan* field. Not a wise tactic, to be sure."

Robinson swallowed, wishing he had his own cup of tea, but the cook wasn't done with their breakfast yet.

"Stoker came to me with information about the *strannik* and where he is from. And his *name*. Would you like to know these things?"

Robinson glanced at McKenna and saw she was curious but still on edge.

"What have you learned?" Robinson asked.

"Information is more valuable than any currency, Professor. It controls the world. This *strannik* fellow is named Gregor Skoye. He's from Iskandir if you recognize the cognates of his name."

"As are you," Robinson observed.

"Indeed. Now that we know his name and where he is from, we have begun to make progress unraveling his past. He's a peasant. So is his father. Uneducated. Illiterate."

Robinson frowned. "How did he join the Invisible College?"

Master Drusselmehr smiled wanly. "That is a mystery, is it not? That is what we do not know. What I've learned so far, because the Marshalcy is more adept at investigation than the military, is that he traveled *beyond* the hinterlands in the west. Beyond the Wraithwoods, as my people liked to call them."

Robinson was unfamiliar with that term, but he imagined it was the vast western territory uninhabited by mortals and dominated by ferocious predators, massive dire bears, slavering wolves. That would explain, perhaps, the *strannik's* fear of dogs.

"When did you first learn of him?" Robinson asked.

"Last year when the military arrested him. Mr. Stoker helped catch him, as I recall. But the *strannik* deceived them all and walked away from the garrison at Gresham College in Bishopsgate. Some of his followers were arrested and executed, or so we thought. But it turns out the *strannik* is very adept at using glamour not only on himself but on others. The men who were killed were our men—and his followers successfully escaped by impersonating the men they'd killed."

"And these are the men who tried to abduct me," McKenna said softly.

"Yes, my dear. I believe so. They have two goals, it seems. The first, to convince the empire to surrender to the Aesir. The second, to reunite the Erlking with his daughter. You know the opera. The daughter who defied him. The banished child."

He was watching them very closely now. Robinson guarded his expression. He said nothing, but the implication was astounding. Was it even possible? Could the Semblance possessing McKenna be an Aesir of such importance? And, if so, would that alter the military's desire to execute her? He worried his imagination might run away with him, however, and he needed to remain cautious. So he pushed the thoughts down as best he could.

Master Drusselmehr didn't press further. "Surrender is, of course, a fatal strategy for all mortals. I believe Gregor Skoye has been deceived by the Aesir and, in turn, deceives others. They must have taught him magic, and thus he allowed himself to be captured by the military so as to learn as many of their secrets as he can. His followers are attempting to persuade the populace to rise up against the emperor. To subject themselves to the Erlking's benevolence." He snorted. "He is actively undermining the Invisible College. He wants to destroy it, I believe."

Robinson nodded. "That seems a logical conclusion."

"Now, I have told you what I know. I have trusted you. Perhaps, in turn, you will trust me with information that might be of some value?"

McKenna's body was tense. He could feel it radiating from her, a warning not to trust this man too much. They'd discussed their concerns about him last night—and reached a decision. Perhaps Robinson would share something with the older man, but only after he tested him. "There is one more thing I would like to know," he asked.

"Haven't I given you enough, Professor?" The glass eye in Drusselmehr's head seemed fixed on him. It was unnerving.

"Your invention. The toy cannon. What is it listening for?"

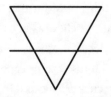

CHAPTER THIRTY-THREE

Unexpected Ally

He'd surprised the old sorcerer with his question. And that had been his intention. If they were to share confidences with Master Drusselmehr, they needed to better understand his fealties.

The startled expression on the man's wrinkled face shifted and a wry smile spread over his mouth. "That is both an interesting question and an interesting observation. How did you know my toy can listen?"

"Hearing is one of my specialties," Robinson said. "Are you going to answer my question?"

"Of course I will. I was just surprised by your sagacity, but I suppose I shouldn't be. The toy listens for speech that shows sympathy for the Aesir."

"You are spying on the population?" McKenna asked, bristling with outrage. "And this is integrity? I'd hoped for a better answer."

"My dear, it is a *necessity*."

The old man leaned back in his chair, pressing his palms together and drumming his fingertips in a sequential pattern. "My toys serve many purposes and always have. The primary purpose is to instill patriotism for the empire and inspire a new generation of young people eager to join the ranks. War is brutal, costly, and inefficient. By honoring those who serve, we secure our future. The Aesir have won many times in the past. They have broken and defeated mortalkind, and it took centuries to rekindle the will to rebel against their supremacy again."

Robinson felt a ripple of anxiety from Drusselmehr's words. It wasn't that he felt the other man was lying. Quite the opposite. He feared it happening *again* and the world getting thrown back into primitive understandings and beliefs. That had happened before with historical precedents over the centuries. It was one of the main reasons the Invisible College had been created—to preserve knowledge, magic, and to fight against its decay. He felt an unusual passion for it for some reason. That lost knowledge would be an utter tragedy.

"And the *strannik* is working counter to your primary purpose," McKenna observed. She reached over and put her hand on Robinson's.

"He's diametrically opposed to it," agreed Master Drusselmehr. "I should explain, my dear, that 'diametrically' means—"

"It means *to emphasize how opposite two views are.*" McKenna interrupted him. "I may be deaf, Master Drusselmehr, but I'm not uneducated."

Once again he looked startled. "You are a treasure, Mrs. Hawksley. My apologies."

"She has a knack for language, vocabulary, and the meaning of words," Robinson said, giving her a proud smile.

"How interesting," he said, his brows coming together thoughtfully. "As the head of the Invisible College, I have access to information not typically available to other people. I want to preserve society and its order. To protect its citizens. The protection and peace we've helped provide for the populace has led to prosperity never before seen by mortals. But while there's been a sizable increase in our population, there has not been a commensurate increase in the number of sorcerers.

Some quorums, I'm afraid, have even discouraged new members from joining."

That was surprising news to Robinson. "I would have inferred that the success of magic in industry would make it more attractive to newcomers?"

"One would think so, naturally, but the opposite is true. Isaac Berrow conceived of the Invisible College as a way of sharing magical knowledge so magical inventions could be improved upon incrementally while new discoveries were found. But in time, it became led by others whose success, fortune, and fame prompted insularity." He separated his hands and expanded them as if encircling a perimeter. "Laws were created to safeguard ideas. Patents to enforce ownership. These laws then provided for the accumulation and aggregation of wealth. I won't bore you with all the details."

Robinson felt the old sorcerer had definitely benefited from the very structure he was complaining about. But such hypocrisy was perhaps inherent in human nature.

"I don't find this conversation boring at all," Robinson declared. "So what you are saying is the Invisible College is now more like a slow-moving tortoise with a thick shell, more concerned about its invulnerability than in further improving the lives of the people."

"Succinctly put, Professor. Last winter, we learned during the Aesir attacks with the stormbreakers that we had too few sorcerers at home in the cities to provide an adequate defense. We need more soldiers on the front, we need more sorcerers at home, but increasing the ranks of both groups will take time. For now, we must rely on inventions marrying magic to technology . . . such as your impressive quicksilver lamps . . . to help defend the home front. We must also find a way to identify those individuals who are being misled by the *strannik*'s faction. My toy serves multiple moral purposes. As I said before, such is the nature of toys."

Robinson glanced at McKenna and noticed her expression was thoughtful but not entirely convinced. He felt the same way.

Master Drusselmehr seemed to recognize it. "I've not satisfied you, have I?"

"I find it disconcerting that your toy can listen in to conversations and report anything that's said," McKenna said.

He shook his head. "Oh, it can't do that, my dear. Are you familiar with the principle of intelligences? I don't want to insult yours again."

"Yes."

"Good. The intelligence bound to the toy is instructed to listen for any words of sympathy regarding the Aesir. A casual mention will trigger a small reaction, a signal . . . if you will. Repeated mentions, deeper sympathies, will trigger a larger one, which will be more noticeable."

"Noticeable to whom?" Robinson asked. "How?"

"The Marshalcy. The emission is a frequency of noise that can only be observed through certain imbued earpieces. It's completely undetectable by the human ear."

"So the military is unaware of this?" Robinson clarified.

"I don't trust the military in all things," Master Drusselmehr confessed. "Their methods tend to be . . . rather blunt. They are very good at exploding things. Running locomotivus stations. Ensuring ample supplies of saltpetr. Hunting down internal enemies of the empire. Things of that nature." His intonation didn't change when he vaguely referenced Semblances. Did he know or suspect anything about McKenna? Robinson wasn't sure.

McKenna didn't look fearful or tense, however. She met Robinson's eyes and then nodded. "We have some information that may prove useful in your efforts."

She'd made the choice to trust him, then. Robinson would have preferred to think on it longer, perhaps during the voyage to Andover.

"Oh?" He seemed genuinely interested.

One of the things McKenna had suggested was not revealing *how* Robinson could communicate with Wickins. Discussing the ring would lead to discussing the device, and that would cause problems. Surely a man as powerful as Master Drusselmehr could ask them to hand it over—and if he did, they'd have little choice but to comply. And how startled and concerned would he be if it disappeared from his possession as it had for the general? It could very well lead to the kind of trouble he couldn't talk his way out of.

"One of the invention ideas I've had," Robinson said, and he could say this much truthfully, "is developing a method for communicating over larger and larger distances by way of thought. My friend and business partner, John Wickins, is in the ice trenches in the north. I can communicate with him mind-to-mind, and he can send his thoughts back to me. Last night, at the dinner at the Clemence-Baileys', he told me of an Aesir attack near his position. It takes time to send communication through ordinary channels, relaying messages to Bishopsgate and then deploying soldiers. If that time could be reduced . . . ?" He let the thought dangle in the air.

"That would be an extraordinarily useful invention for both the military as well as the Invisible College," said Master Drusselmehr with keen interest gleaming in his functioning eye. "Can you tell me by what principle of magic this invention operates?"

"It has not been patented yet," Robinson said. "So you'll forgive me if I do not disclose any more details. The details are still being worked out, and I'm not sure how widely it will work. I'm not comfortable trying to mass produce something before it's ready. You may be aware that the invention I demonstrated at the Great Exhibition is under litigation because it was used without permission. And a rival claims to have invented it first."

Master Drusselmehr's face tightened. His cheek muscle twitched. "I am . . . unfortunately . . . aware of that situation. It is my hope that the courts resolve the patent ownership matter swiftly. As an inventor myself, I cannot think of such wrong without it provoking my indignation. I'm a firm believer that a person's invention can't and shouldn't be taken from them. Some businesses might disagree, but I oppose it strongly. But if there is any confusion about who invented it first, then that needs to be established. I'm sure you have ample evidence to prove your case?"

"Evidence and witnesses," Robinson said, sighing with frustration. Miss Cowing may have been working on something similar, but his own invention had developed much farther than anything she'd publicly demonstrated. Perhaps the military was trying to instigate a fight between them. Or they might try to win her to their side.

"What we'd like to propose, then," McKenna said, giving the old sorcerer a delightful smile, "is that Rob will communicate with you whenever he receives news from the front. He can send a thought to you directly. And you can hear it in your mind."

Robinson imagined he'd be asked to demonstrate the ability, so he put his hand in his pocket and released the ring from the device he had left unlocked in case it was needed.

"Would you mind demonstrating this magical feat, Professor?"

He slipped the thumb ring on, anticipating the jolt of pain that came. His jaw clenched with it, but he tried not to outwardly signal his discomfort. His gaze fixed on the head of the Invisible College.

The Aesir attacked Fort Mackenzie last night.

"Your lips didn't even move," said Master Drusselmehr with wonder. "Fort Mackenzie was attacked last night?"

"Yes," Robinson answered. "You can verify the news as you deem appropriate. I don't want General Colsterworth to know about this. Not yet. Once I can scale up the invention, we can discuss its more widespread use."

"And your friend can communicate from his post all the way to Telimar? Instantly?"

"That appears to be the case. As he traveled north, we continued to test the range to see whether there was any diminishment of the signal, or if it would take longer for it to travel. It was unchanged."

"Incredible, simply incredible. It has long been assumed that the Aesir communicate with one another in such a fashion."

"They do," Robinson confirmed. "My friend and I have tapped into their communications. Thankfully, he has been studying the Aesir language. I am still a novice at it."

"Your friend is in Signals Intelligences, is he not? A very appropriate domain for this. I should think—"

Robinson shook his head. "He left the military when they tried to coerce him into abandoning our business. Perhaps I'm being harsh—they offered him a *promotion* to captain right before the Great Exhibition, but he declined it and resigned his commission. Then he was drafted and sent to the front as the lowest rank of all. As punishment, I feel, for crossing the military and thwarting the general."

"I had not been told this," said Master Drusselmehr softly. His expression was stern. "I cannot interfere directly in the chain of command. I can only replace the head. Frankly, we need men like General Colsterworth right now. His morals may be suspect in your eyes, but his devotion to fighting the Aesir is absolute. He is also loyal to the emperor. Replacing him at the onset of winter would be . . . outrageously foolish. Let me look into the matter discreetly. I don't want to make things even worse for your friend."

Robinson felt a weight lifted slightly. Master Drusselmehr had provided him with a spark of hope at least. "I appreciate anything you can do."

"We both do," McKenna said.

A knock sounded and the door opened, admitting Mr. Leishman, who entered with a covered tray. He set it on the table in front of them, then lifted the lid with a flourish.

The smell of caramelized sugar was enthralling. Robinson stared at the plate covered in slices of bread with a yellow-orange hue. A little tub of milky fluid sat next to it.

"I thought you might like to try *ei-rijk* toast," said Master Drusselmehr. "This was a dish my mother made for me as a child. Beaten eggs, a sprinkle of cinnamon, heavy cream. The bread is dipped in the batter and fried with butter on a skillet. After one side is cooked, some dark sugar is added until it achieves just the right crispiness. Enjoy!"

With a gleaming fork, Master Drusselmehr served their plates and then dripped some of the milky fluid, like a glaze, atop it. Robinson felt his stomach growl at the smell.

When he speared his first bite, a memory struck him. A visceral memory based on the taste. He'd eaten it before. And he realized, strangely, that it was why he loved the sugared peanuts so much in Auvinen. Their flavor had reminded him of *this*.

The Aesir eclipse us with speed. Their visual and hearing acuity far surpasses our own. Their bodies are immortal and regenerate, yet they can die. Our advantage is our numerical superiority. I foresee a day when our replenishment rate exceeds their calculus of death. Or vice versa. In the end, it will come down to a matter of arithmetic. An awful arithmetic. I will do everything within my power to tilt the balance in our favor. The alternative is simply unconscionable.

—Isaac Berrow,
Master of the Royal Secret,
the Invisible College

MaKenna Aurora
Hawksley

CHAPTER THIRTY-FOUR

THE PALACE OF ANDOVER

This was McKenna's first visit to the imperial city of Andover. As they rode through it in Master Drusselmehr's carriage, she felt the regular throbs caused by the evenly spaced cobblestone streets, which were easily wide enough to hold six carriages abreast. It was an open carriage, so they were bundled with heavy blankets and could see their own breaths. The horses all had fancy cropped tails and tassels with their headdresses, and soldiers holding decorative rifles fixed with gleaming bayonets stood at attention at every lamppost. Ceremonial cannons were also on display, providing the sense that order was being preserved. That the emperor's might was to be unchallenged going forward.

She wore her blanket more loosely than the other riders, enjoying the cool breeze on her skin as she gazed around in wonder. Rob had tried to talk to her about the Erlking's daughter when they'd been alone, and she'd had such a terrified and oppressive feeling that she'd shut down the conversation immediately. It had made her feel like fainting. He'd tried again later, after she'd calmed down, and she'd had an equally visceral reaction.

There were no businesses, just street after street of fancy mansions and opulent structures with apartments overlooking the city. Every aristocrat worth his salt owned property in Andover, and she could only imagine how expensive the rent was in such a place. Other carriages passed them, giving them a view of the occupants—ladies with fancy curls and hairpieces, some in velvet cloaks to preserve their hairstyles, and gentlemen in black suits or military uniforms. Mustaches seemed to be the fashion. Rob's neglected whiskers would certainly be an oddity in such a place. She'd have to remind him again that she needed a good view of his lips in order to understand his speech.

She felt slight pressure on her knee beneath the blanket—Rob's hand—and turned, realizing Master Drusselmehr had posed a question she hadn't heard. It was thoughtful of him to want to include her in the conversation so they could talk about everything that had happened later. The sorcerer had changed into another costume by the time they'd reached Andover, well after sunset. He had a polished cane with a silver-studded top fixed with a jewel. An Aesir artifact, no doubt, and he wore a cape instead of a cloak.

"I have not been to Andover myself, but my father has," Rob said. "He had a speaking engagement at the university here, I believe."

"Most of the aristocrats send their children to the University of Nirshoye," came the man's reply. "The university here is more for . . . show. Wealthy families send their children here believing they'll rub shoulders with the elite, whereas the elite choose to rub their noses in affairs elsewhere. You attended university, did you not, Professor? In Covesea?"

"Yes," Rob answered. "My grandfather was my tutor."

"Excellent. Covesea isn't very pretentious. Your accomplishments will add to her mystique and reputation."

"How much farther is the palace?" McKenna asked.

"We are nearly there, my dear. Our destination is where the sky glows with the aurora borealis."

"Are we far enough north for such a display of the lights?" Rob asked, his brow wrinkling.

"For certain, not. It is a result of magic. It takes eighteen sorcerers to maintain the effect overnight."

McKenna saw the ripples of green light in the sky in the distance. As they got closer, the colors darkened and brightened and changed position. She'd never seen the aurora borealis before, and even if it was a mere imitation, it was still a sight to behold. Gripping Rob's hand beneath the blanket, she admired the display.

The street came to a large circular thoroughfare with a monument in the middle. It was a major intersection, and she became disoriented by the flow of carriages and other conveyances, but on the other side of the circle she saw towering walls and the front of what could only be described as a palace of mountainous proportions. It had a semicircular front facade featuring roundish towers, interconnected wings, and a truly dizzying number of chimneys, turrets, and cupolas. They wound their way around the circle, then approached the palace gates, where there were at least fifty guards at attention along with an array of cannons.

"Master Drusselmehr, did the riots reach the gates?" McKenna asked, trying to imagine the scene of chaos. There were no stains on the ground, no indication of unrest.

"Oh no, never that close," he said, waving a hand. "The crowd was dispersed by the monument to the Tanireh family in the circle. A few horsemen with sabers did the trick. And the roar of the cannon."

"They fired elfshot on the masses?" Robinson asked, his expression one of dismay.

"Not elfshot. Just the saltpetr exploding. That was enough to frighten them into fleeing. The horsemen bloodied some up. A few were trampled and killed. Unfortunate but necessary in maintaining public order."

McKenna felt her stomach tighten. "Were they ordered to disperse first?"

"Of course. The ringleaders were belligerent. And the first to flee," he added with a knowing look. "Since this is your first time meeting the royal family, let me apprise you of what to expect. All daughters and one son, the youngest. The little princeling they call him. Little Samuel Alabaster Tanireh. They're delightful children, very inquisitive. The oldest is twelve. Maria Kristina, then Gretchen Darionne, Constance Evangeline, and Sophronia Hale. Their mother is from Tanhauser, as you know, so all the children are fluent in both languages. They will be impressed that you speak their mother's tongue, Mrs. Hawksley."

That gave her a feeling of reassurance as the carriage approached the gate and halted. A uniformed officer came and inspected the inhabitants. His sudden appearance made her feel self-conscious. But was the unease her own, or was it caused by another entity sharing her body?

"Good evening, Master Drusselmehr. Welcome back to the palace. I hope the weather was hospitable?"

"Suitable. It won't be long before sea passage becomes too dangerous. Thank you, Colonel."

The man bowed stiffly and ordered the gates to be opened. McKenna expected to see soldiers pulling it open, but they opened without any mortal strain, moved instead by magic. They looked tall and heavy enough that even a crowd might have struggled to wrestle them open.

The carriage driver led them onward into the spacious courtyard, around an enormous ice sculpture at its center in the design of the imperial crest, a falcon spreading its wings. Plumes of cooling fog swirled at its base, giving it an otherworldly air. Then the carriage deposited them at the base of a lower wall and gate. The layers of defense were impressive and gave her a feeling of anxiety. It would be impossible to flee if they had to. A shudder came unbidden, and she sensed the disquiet was not from herself but the being inside her.

Leave me alone, she thought inwardly. This was a moment for Rob to be recognized for his genius, even if he was reluctant to receive such recognition. Judging by his expression, she could see he wasn't dazzled by the display of massive wealth. If anything, he was bothered by it, given that so many were suffering.

A footman approached and helped them dismount the carriage. He greeted Master Drusselmehr but spoke too rapidly for McKenna to follow his words.

They were ushered through the entrance. The air within the palace was pleasantly cool to her, which meant it was possibly quite chilly for the inhabitants. Heating such a large space would have been impractical anyway, and so the incalescent heaters were likely reserved for the rooms. The halls were adorned with gilt-framed paintings of previous rulers and aristocrats, many with expressions of superiority and poses of contempt.

After they were led through a maze of halls and corridors, each more resplendent than the last, they arrived in a parlor that made the one at her home on Brake Street seem rather quaint. There they met the majordomo, introduced as Anstrel Blackmoor, who greeted Master Drusselmehr favorably but not with deference.

"Your arrival coincides with the royal dinner," Anstrel Blackmoor said with a subtle frown. "The table is already full, Master Drusselmehr; I cannot possibly accommodate three more. Who are these guests?"

She didn't see Master Drusselmehr's response but could intuit it based on the way the majordomo's eyebrows shot up in surprise.

"*The* Professor Hawksley?" His first look at Robinson had been one of bemused courtesy, but that instantly changed.

"Is the emperor still keen on meeting him?"

"He is indeed. He would be delighted, in fact. Let me speak with him and see what can be arranged on short notice." He bowed again and quickly departed.

So the parlor was just a waiting room? It was enormous.

Master Drusselmehr leaned closer to her husband. "Imagine, if you will, how many lamps would be required just around the perimeter alone," Master Drusselmehr said with a sly smile. "I've only managed to arrange a few. But it will suffice. And my walking stick, you see, would trigger them."

"You've thought of everything," Rob said with a nod.

Master Drusselmehr looked rather pleased with himself. McKenna felt her stomach gurgle with hunger. Based on the uniforms of the servants, she felt a ball gown would have been a better thing to wear than her finest Auvinen attire. Rob looked comfortable enough. He cared little for attire or fashion, but she noticed him nervously swiping his hand through his messy hair.

The extended wait moved them to take seats, and Master Drusselmehr's expression began to darken with impatience. When she glanced his way, he smiled apologetically at her.

McKenna lost track of time, and the boredom was making her drowsy. Ultimately, the majordomo did return, but his look was subdued. In fact, he seemed ill at ease, which prompted her to straighten and watch his face.

"Ah, you've returned at last, Anstrel. I'd grown fearful you'd gotten lost in this vast palace!" Master Drusselmehr said, rising from an adjoining sofa to approach the other man. Rob and McKenna also rose expectantly.

The majordomo spoke in a confidential way, his head inclined as if he were trying to whisper in Master Drusselmehr's ear. McKenna had a good view of him, though, and read his lips easily. It was immediately apparent why he was whispering. McKenna pulled back with Rob a few paces.

"The empress consort will not meet Mrs. Hawksley nor allow her children to. I'm afraid Her Majesty is rather adamant about this and was angry to learn you'd brought her along."

McKenna saw the flinch of surprise in Master Drusselmehr. Her heart sank with dread as she realized *she* was the cause of the bad news. She'd been looking forward to being able to tell her family about the experience of meeting the royal family. She'd assumed it would banish any further reluctance of others to accept her into Society.

"What am I to tell them, Anstrel? I ask you, how can I give such a grievous insult to my invited guests? Can you not persuade her to reconsider?"

"You think I haven't been trying? She will not allow it. Her children have never met a deaf person before, and I think her ladyship is terrified of the affliction. The emperor tried to calm her fears, but that only made her more agitated. Her mind is quite made up. I cannot bring Mrs. Hawksley with us, but the emperor and his family are desirous of meeting the professor."

McKenna felt nauseated, ashamed, unworthy. She wanted to flee from the palace, but she had no idea where she was or how to get outside. It was absolutely a nightmare.

A hand squeezed her shoulder. Rob was looking at her in concern. "Are you in danger?" he asked. She noticed his other hand inside his pocket, as if he was getting ready to slip on the ring. He'd interpreted her expression as fear, not realizing it was humiliation. Well, she couldn't be the one to deprive him of this opportunity. She knew him well enough to anticipate that he'd refuse to go alone. So she cleared her throat and said, "I-I'm not feeling very well. I feel rather faint."

"Let's go to the hotel, then," he said instantly. "We shouldn't have come directly here."

"No, Rob, this is too important. I just don't think I can face them. I wouldn't want to . . . I wouldn't want to embarrass myself in front of them. Can I just wait here and see if I feel better? Besides, it's *you* they really want to see." She felt tears catch in her throat as she fumbled with her words, but she was determined not to start crying. Not in front of these men.

She'd missed a question someone had asked, and the next thing she knew Master Drusselmehr was approaching them with a look of concern. "Is something amiss?"

"I'm not feeling well," McKenna said to him. "Please. We've come all this way. Could I just stay here and rest? I don't want to ruin this moment." She looked pleadingly at Rob, seeing the conflict in his eyes.

"Are you sure?" he asked, not looking confident. He was willing to walk away from this for her, but she mustn't let him.

She couldn't trust herself to speak. Not without sobbing. She nodded weakly, then went back to the sofa and sank down on it. It wasn't difficult to feign sickness. This was a solution that would solve the problem, and then she could tell Rob later what had happened.

"I will summon a doctor," Master Drusselmehr said.

She didn't need one. But if it gave them a false sense of relief to call one, that would be all right. She nodded.

Rob still looked undecided, his hand in his pocket, frozen.

"We must not keep the emperor waiting," the majordomo said, his eyes digging into Master Drusselmehr.

The aged sorcerer was regarding McKenna with a little show of confusion. Then he seemed to have it figured out. From the look on his face, he understood that she knew the truth despite the efforts to conceal it from her. A look passed between them, and then Master Drusselmehr gave her a nod of understanding. Followed by a smile. "Come, Professor. If there is anything at all wrong with her, we'll see her needs are met immediately."

Rob looked at McKenna, and she looked away, her eyes stinging. She willed the tears not to fall. Not until after they'd gone.

A while later, she was feeling plenty sorry for herself, still sniffling and dabbing her eyes on her sleeve, when the door opened and the doctor arrived.

Only it wasn't a doctor. It was the *strannik*, with a cruel smile.

"At last," he said, his eyes wild with eagerness. "I must bring you to safety. I must return you to your father. They're going to kill you."

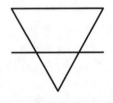

CHAPTER THIRTY-FIVE

THE ERLKING'S DAUGHTER

McKenna leaped from the sofa, hastening around it to add a barrier between them.

Fearful that minions of the *strannik* would sneak up behind her unawares, she quickly located the other doors leading out of the spacious room. Her heart was beating so fast she feared it would come out of her throat and fly away.

There was a door to her rear, one she could run to.

The *strannik* held up his hands as if she were a skittish animal. "Do not flee! Let me persuade you."

"There's nothing you could say I want to know!" she said, checking again the gap behind her to make sure it was clear. Her abductor wasn't rushing forward, but he was advancing cautiously, gazing at her with his wild eyes.

"I won't hurt you," he said. "Just let me talk."

"Like you didn't hurt my husband? You tried to kill him!"

"But is he dead? No. I do not have the power to kill him."

"You utter nonsense!"

"I speak the truth. Heed me. *You* are the Erlking's daughter, and I must return you to him. If you go to him, he will withdraw his forces. He has promised me this. Think on that! An Aesir cannot lie!"

McKenna felt the violent urge to flee from this man. It was a familiar recoiling sensation, one from the intelligence trapped in her bones. There was no eagerness to reunite. There was only terror. If it were truly the Erlking's daughter who possessed her—a thought that had nearly made her faint—then she did not wish for such a reunion.

"You are not an Aesir and you *can* deceive," McKenna said. "I'll scream for help!"

"And yet they will hear nothing," he countered. He was opposite her now, the sofa between them, but she retreated as he approached. "Your father has taught me magic beyond what the Invisible College understands. I am his humble, obedient servant. I wish for peace. Not war."

"I cannot trust you," McKenna said, shaking her head. How close was the door? Would it be locked? She knew the door he'd entered from wouldn't be. What about the others? He was stronger than her. She still remembered the bruise on her arm from his punishing grip.

"I have a natural gift, an ability to hear the thoughts of mortals and animals. But I cannot discern the thoughts of the Aesir, which is how I know you are a Semblance." He pointed to her. "Your thoughts are blank to me. But I can hear others' thoughts easily. Orders have been given to destroy you. They don't want peace! I'm trying to protect you, even if it may not seem that way. Come with me, fair one. I implore you!"

"Leave me alone!" McKenna shouted at him, the impulse to flee growing stronger and stronger.

"I *must* obey the Erlking," he said, his mouth twisting with savage intent.

As he lunged toward the edge of the sofa, McKenna bolted. In a few heartbeats she'd reached the door, twisted the handle, and yanked it open. Another room, another exquisite chamber—although smaller—greeted her, and she raced to the nearest door in the adjacent wall and grabbed the handle. It was also unlocked, thankfully, and she yanked it open, glimpsing the *strannik* coming through the door she'd first used. His eyes met hers, his face twisted with a grimace of intensity.

She slipped through the door, finding a corridor with a few servants dusting the paintings and trim. Some looked at her in confusion. McKenna rushed the opposite way, grabbing another handle and opening the door to reveal an enclosed room. If she tried to hide in there, the servants would be able to tell the *strannik* where she'd gone. That led her to the decision to continue down the hall to the door at the end of the corridor. When she reached it, she turned around again and saw the *strannik* facing the servants. One of them pointed her way and he whirled, catching sight of her as she slammed the door behind her.

Another corridor, then another. She had no aim but to find a place to hide. This second corridor had no living person inside, so she hurried to one of the side doors and quickly opened it, revealing a storage room of sorts with extra stuffed chairs covered in dustcloths. It was dark within, except for the illumination of a single magical bulb on the closest wall. The assortment of covered chairs would provide ample hiding places.

After shutting the door behind her, she wound her way quickly to the farthest corner, lifted the dustcloth, and hurriedly slipped beneath it, kneeling on the cushion and pressing herself against the velvety fabric. The chairs had wide backs with fluted edges so that it created a pocket of sorts where the cloth didn't touch as much. She hoped that any bulge caused by her body would seem innocuous.

But she felt the settling fabric pressing against her and then second-guessed her decision. She wouldn't be able to hear him coming, and if she did stand out, he could easily sneak up on her and seize her. So she abandoned the hiding place and decided to duck behind the chair instead, maintaining the use of her eyes. All the chairs crammed in the room would provide obstacles for the man.

She'd no sooner left her hiding place than she saw the door open and instantly dropped to the floor. Her gasping would give herself away as well, so she covered her mouth, trying not to faint from the terror wriggling inside her. She took little gulps of air, watching the light to see if the door shut again. It didn't. She saw a shadow blot the lamplight, proving someone was inside the room with her.

Tears threatened to overwhelm her, but she scooted around another chair, away from the one she'd attempted to hide beneath. Other than the shaft of light from the well-lit corridor beyond the door, the only light in the room came from the singular lamp. She hoped the dark fabric of her dress wouldn't be too noticeable against the backdrop of the grayish dustcloths.

Clearly the *strannik*'s powerful magic had helped the infernal man infiltrate the imperial palace. And now she knew about his ability to read minds. What a dangerous combination to possess. There were stories, of course, of mortals who traveled into the frozen wastelands in the north. Mortals who had forsaken their own kind and sought communion with the Aesir. Maybe he was one of them.

She felt her pulse begin to quiet, so she lowered her hand, her back pressed against the chair. Cautiously, she risked a peek around it and saw the *strannik* was edging closer, slowly, methodically, weaving his way toward her.

At that moment, the entity inside her was subdued, burrowed down deep, the only inkling of her presence the sullen wish that McKenna had a dagger or some implement of harm to use against the *strannik*. That brought a memory of when Joseph Crossthwait had come to attack Rob. Without thinking, McKenna had grabbed a bulb with the intent of bashing him with it. She had no predilection for violence. Not herself.

The *strannik* reached the chair she'd originally hidden beneath. The cloth looked disturbed, a telltale sign that something was out of place. McKenna bit her lower lip, edging her way slowly on her bottom to get farther from him.

Her eyes had adjusted well enough to the dark to see the triumphant smile on the *strannik*'s face before he lunged at the chair and yanked the fabric away. Only to be disappointed that his prey was not quivering underneath. Her intuition had paid off. He crumpled the cloth with his fists and then slammed it down on the chair. His impatience was showing.

He began to stalk to the next chair, away from hers, methodically going from one chair to the next, examining each, reaching down with his hands to touch the fabric, to push it down so that he could feel if someone were hiding.

Why had he chosen this room? Had someone seen her? Had he heard something that had disclosed her location? He also inspected around each one of the chairs, which meant he would find her eventually.

Frustration mixed with fear in her stomach. If she tried running for the door, he would hear her. But staying put also wasn't an option.

I would appreciate some help, she thought to herself. It was the first time she'd ever tried to directly address the entity inside her. It felt . . . so strange to even consider it. If the *strannik* was right, and she had a feeling in his bones he was, the Erlking's daughter—the one the famous opera was about—had chosen her! The deaf daughter of a well-off barrister from Auvinen. Or perhaps the Aesir had been compelled to enter her body because of some necessity, to flee to someone nearly dead, half-drowned by the sea?

No thought came in reply. Just a dreadful idea—that death might be the only way to separate the Erlking's daughter from McKenna's body. She swallowed a sudden lump in her throat. Is that what the *strannik* intended? To convince McKenna to come willingly only to sacrifice her?

And yet . . . what if he was right? What if her willing capitulation would put an end to the Aesir plagues and war? Her sacrifice could save untold thousands . . .

McKenna's heart twisted with indecision. The thought of losing Rob, her family, and everything was too painful to even consider. And yet . . . the possibility that so much pain and suffering could be averted was seductive. But how could she know the truth? What if the *strannik* was wrong?

She would talk to Rob, she decided, and share with him what she'd been told. They would make a decision about it together.

There. That felt like a better course than letting guilt prompt her decisions. She needed to escape before he made it to the chair she was hiding behind. Could she slip away to another chair? Or would that be too risky?

The light from the glass bulb by the door winked out. Then on again. It drew McKenna's attention. And the *strannik's*. The flicker happened again. That was unusual.

Suddenly the *strannik* was walking back toward the entrance of the room, bypassing the chair she'd hunkered behind. He paused at the lamp, his hand hovering a few inches from it. It dimmed, flickered, and went out. Impossibly, he left the room and shut the door, plunging McKenna into darkness.

"*Hoxta-namorem,*" she whispered, using the sorcerers' words to summon light. Nothing happened, of course. She'd already known nothing would. Relief settled within her. The *strannik* was gone. She remained where she was, sitting on the floor, running her fingers across the smooth polished planks thick with dust. She could feel the grit on her fingertips.

After several minutes, a whorl of glowing light appeared from underneath the door and came and hovered above her. She gazed up at it, fearful at first, but it seemed rather familiar. Friendly even.

Then the door opened and she saw Rob framed in the doorway.

The surge of relief made her eyes sting as she hurried to her feet and raced to him. He held her tightly, stroking her back. He seemed to know something was wrong, but he didn't insist on an explanation. He pressed her tightly to him, and she felt safe. It felt . . . right. A memory flickered in her mind. A feeling that they'd been chased before. That others had tried to separate them . . .

He tilted her chin up and kissed her tenderly on her lips. She noticed shadows approaching, saw servants rushing toward them in her peripheral vision.

"We're going to Mowbray House," he said with a look of finality. "Master Drusselmehr is preparing a ship for us now. He's embarrassed at the security lapse. When the true doctor arrived, the *strannik*'s disguise was discovered. The whole palace is in an uproar at how close he was to you and to the royal family. I'm taking you home."

She nodded, unable to stop the tears from falling, and then started sobbing against Rob's chest.

Plague. Drought. Famine. War. The Aesir have ever used these tools to defeat us. What we cannot resist with our swords, what we cannot resist with our plans, what we cannot resist with our courage, let us resist with our disposition to be patient, our temperament to be fair, our inclination to be thankful. We must not think of evils as misfortunes but instead the bearing of them worthily as good fortune.

—Isaac Berrow,
Master of the Royal Secret,
the Invisible College

General Colsterworth

CHAPTER THIRTY-SIX

THE COMING

The incalescent heater glowed bright orange, granting a relieving gust of warmth as General Colsterworth entered the command yurt. Nightfall had brought frost, which covered every tent flap, every beaver pelt, every bit of equipment in its crystalline shards. The yurt had other general officers and adjutants, some sipping from mugs to add internal warmth.

The camp was a hive of activity. Sleds were bringing in equipment since one of the locomotivus lines had stalled at midnight, stranding the soldiers and incoming gear. Colsterworth had been ferried to the command post on a dog sled team, something he hadn't done in years. Thankfully the buttons of his uniform had warded off the chill.

"Good morning, sir," bid General Desaix with a crisp salute.

"Not a good morning at all," Colsterworth snapped. "Everything is frozen."

Camp Riggins was near enough to the phalanxes of ice trenches, a depot hub of railyards and equipment and soldiers. It was close enough to the front lines that they'd used it as a major outpost to deploy personnel and elfshot to where the lamps indicated the presence of the Aesir. The ability to react quickly had changed the nature of this war. Overall there were fewer casualties than last winter. Surprise attacks had fallen precipitously. A part of him wanted to thank Professor Hawksley for his invention, but the legal case being haggled in court was not going in the right direction. If Foster's case was successful, the military would bear the brunt of the expense and the penalty. And Foster and Hawksley would be wealthy beyond belief. That galled him—mostly because he had taken a gamble and lost.

"Sir, I know you've just arrived, but there's a private who has begged an audience with you. He came up with his company captain and just arrived an hour or so ago. He says it's urgent. Cannot wait."

"A private?" the general asked with annoyance. "That's an odd request."

"He says he knows you personally. Private Wickins. He traveled all night to get here. Says his information is a matter of life or death."

"Fuss and bother, bring him," the general snapped while tugging off his gloves. The adjutant brought over a warm rag to wipe his neck and hands, which he took use of.

"Isn't that Major Wickins's son?" asked General Pevvers.

Indeed, and Colsterworth had overseen the demotion of both men. The father had gone from colonel to major because of a lapse of diligence. The son had been denied his rank and drafted as a private out of revenge.

"Probably," Colsterworth said flippantly. The other men stifled chuckles. None of them had disagreed with his decision. Not openly anyway. Each of them was privately ambitious, wanting his seniority. Hungering after it actually. He played them off against each other deftly, knew which of them had secrets. He kept this information to himself, of course. To be used prudently when needed.

He was just about to take a bite from a buttered scone when the visitors arrived, a young captain and the Wickins lad, who didn't look like a lad anymore, not with the telltale mark of frostbite on his nose, the weariness in his eyes, the saltpetr soot staining his uniform jacket. He'd been in the trenches for over a month now. It was a hard life. And he seemed to be suffering.

"Wickins is it?" General Colsterworth asked, even though the young man was very familiar to him. He'd had a promising career in Signals Intelligences, learning the Aesir language, before he'd chosen to resign and get rich. He would become the wealthiest private in the entire army undoubtedly. If he survived.

"General, the Aesir are going to attack. Here. Today."

The condescending feelings he was having against the lad vanished, replaced by a surge of surprise. He caught similarly startled expressions from the other generals gathered, discerned from the quick glances they gave to one another.

"How do you know this, Private Wickins?"

"I'd rather not say, sir."

"I *order* you to tell me."

Wickins grimaced. "Before I left Auvinen, my friend . . . Professor Hawksley . . . gave me a sorcerer's ring he'd found. We've been using it to communicate with one another."

A surge of outrage flared in Colsterworth's chest. For weeks, he'd been trying to unravel the mystery of how Gilgamesh Drusselmehr was siphoning intelligence from the military. He'd assumed it was Stoker being a reprehensible toady, but this news revealed the true source.

"Show me," Colsterworth said brusquely.

Young Wickins tugged off his glove and revealed a ring on his thumb. It was made of Aesir gold, or at least bore the particular coloring.

"This ring allows us to send thoughts to each other. Mostly it's been to communicate with one another. However, one of the powers the ring possesses is it is tuned in to the Aesir. I can hear their orders as well."

"So *you're* the one who has been warning of the attacks."

"I have, sir. And that's how I know an attack is coming today. This morning. I sent a warning but realized it would take too long for the information to reach you. Not enough time to act on it. The Aesir are growing frustrated by us preempting their attacks. They're going to attack en masse."

Colsterworth was stunned by the news, but he controlled his breathing and tried to focus on the young man's account. Having such a magical artifact and keeping it secret was a gross dereliction of duty. However, its present usefulness could not be understated.

"General Ambrose, prepare for attack. General Pevvers, get as many people as you can to our position. As quickly as you can, I don't care if they have to run in the snow."

"Yes, sir!" both shouted in unison.

Colsterworth didn't doubt the young man's sincerity. He could have easily kept the knowledge to himself, allowed the Aesir to attack Camp Riggins, to decapitate the entire leadership staff. That he'd come in person to warn them of danger showed the young man's integrity. He'd put his own life at risk.

"Warm yourself by the heater," Colsterworth said, feeling a twinge of guilt for how he'd treated the young man. He and Foster's second daughter were betrothed, weren't they? No doubt they resented him for his interference in their lives.

"Thank you, sir," Wickins said, sighing in relief. He crouched by the incalescent heater, rubbing his chapped hands in front of it.

"Captain, rest yourselves here and then take him to the commissary and get yourselves some food."

"With pleasure, sir," said the captain gratefully.

General Colsterworth gazed at the gray-shrouded fog on the horizon. The frost hadn't yielded to the day's warmth. Every spruce or pine was sheathed in hoar frost. The skeletal aspen, denuded of leaves, looked like works of art. He gazed at the sky, waiting. He'd given orders for the men to act like nothing was going to happen. To go about their business but to be in a state of mental readiness. The vertical cannons were not set to maximum arc, but the hooks and chains were loosened and they were ready to be hoisted. The general believed they'd swoop down from the sky. With the low-hanging clouds caused by the unique weather conditions, it would make their attack undiscernible from a distance.

Had the Aesir known about the weather conditions? Had they somehow caused them?

General Ambrose approached and stood next to him. "The men are getting edgy," he muttered. "They want this to be over already."

"Don't we all. But I can imagine this is going to throw them on their heels," Colsterworth said.

"We need more of those rings," Ambrose said. "That would alter the war entirely."

"Indeed it will, General. Indeed it will."

At that moment, he saw the lamps in the distance begin to glow. The light penetrated through the fog.

"This is it," Colsterworth breathed. "The Coming. Summon the shields, now!"

General Ambrose had a flute whistle chained around his neck, and he raised it to his lips.

The first bombardment landed at the general's tent, sending an explosion rocketing through the air. It had dropped from the sky without warning, which suggested he'd been right about the aerial attack. They must be overhead in a stormbreaker! With the fog, they couldn't make sight of it.

"Raise the cannons!" Colsterworth bellowed. "Fire at will!"

The shrill whistle pierced the air as more explosions began to pummel the camp. Hymns of protection rose up instantly, creating shimmering magical domes. The booming cannons launched elfshot into the sky just as bog beasts appeared, flown by the Disir—the female warriors who served the Erlking and swooped down on the general's armies from the sky. They were prepared, though, and the enemies were struck by the blasts before they could launch their spears. General

Colsterworth drew his pistol and began firing at one Disir as she flew straight toward him. He struck the female between the eyes and she slumped off the bog beast, plummeting into the snow and causing the beast to retreat.

The cracks of pistols and rifles sounded all around, then another deafening volley of cannons erupted. The haze of saltpetr mixed with the freezing fog. The vertical cannons were in position, firing nearly overhead. The noise of the shot hitting stone became unmistakable—proof positive that there was a stormbreaker hidden in the fog.

Chunks of rock began to rain down as the cannonade continued.

"It's overhead!" General Colsterworth shouted, seeing the smudge of shadow in the fog as the sky ship veered away. More Aesir dropped from the sky, felled by elfshot. A surge of relief ignited in the general's abdomen. Then he gaped in shock as the massive aerial ship came closer, closer.

"It's crashing!" Ambrose shrieked in awe.

The impact caused an earthquake as the stone ship collided with the ground—thankfully away from the troops. Even at a distance he could see whorls of magic illuminating the stone, and then the bluish light faded and winked out.

General Ambrose clapped him on the back. "We did it! We took down a stormbreaker!"

A cheer rose from the soldiers. The Disir were fleeing now, but many were shot down during the escape. It was a glorious victory. It had to be.

A triumphant grin spread on his mouth as the blasts continued around him. What would the Erlking have to say about this?

The young man's early warning had saved the day. He'd freely discharge Wickins from his duty now, but they'd demand more intelligence. And rings. They needed more rings!

Yes, this would change everything. Instead of being defensive, they could press into the frozen wasteland. They could bring the war *to* the Aesir's battlements.

He turned and looked at the flames coming from the command yurt. In all likelihood, he and his command would have perished. It would have been a crippling strike. Instead, they'd caught the Aesir by surprise.

And then he gasped, realizing he'd told Wickins and Captain Penny to get some rest.

In the tent now engulfed in flames.

Surely they weren't inside.

"Get that fire out!" General Colsterworth raged, pointing at the tent.

A feeling of dread squeezed his heart.

Surely . . . surely . . .

We dream of immortality. We want to be important. To matter. Yet life is snuffed out like a candle. The wick turns black and bends in on itself, a glowing ember sizzling into nothingness. And then a trickle of smoke. What becomes of our intelligence? Aye—'tis the greatest secret of all.

—Isaac Berrow,
Master of the Royal Secret,
the Invisible College

Robinson Foster Hawksley

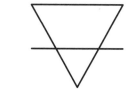

CHAPTER THIRTY-SEVEN

WORRYING

Robinson squeezed the tongs, lifting the crucible from the intense heat of the incalescent torch to the cuttlefish mold propped nearby. With delicate movements, he poured the globs of liquid metal into the mold, causing a plume of steam to billow from the bone. Then, with a whispered command, he extinguished the heater and returned the crucible to its place. The air was tangy with the smell of slag. The metal would cool, and then he could continue the process of forging a ring, trying to duplicate the one his device carried. Like the one he'd given to John Wickins.

Just thinking of his friend made his stomach clench with foreboding. He hadn't heard from Wickins in two days, two agonizing days. Wickins had sent his thought warning about the Aesir attack on Camp Riggins, a warning that Robinson had immediately relayed to Master Drusselmehr. But Wickins had believed there wouldn't be enough time to alert the generals who were gathered at the camp, so he'd convinced his captain to let him reveal the news in person. The last Robinson had heard from his friend was that the attack had indeed come. And then there'd been nothing. No responses came from mental urging for news. Silence.

Robinson rubbed his forehead, then realized his fingertips were sooty. He loved his new alchemy at Mowbray House. They'd returned to Siaconset several weeks ago after their abrupt departure from Andover. If it hadn't been for Rob's canine friend's abrupt warning that McKenna was in danger, the *strannik* might have captured her and smuggled her out of the palace with his impressive glamouring ability. And now they'd come to learn the man could read minds as well. The palace had been searched. Suspicious men had been restrained and brought before them, but McKenna had only shaken her head. She was the only one who could see the *strannik* in his true form—until he chose to let go of his magic—and none of the men who'd been found were him. The meeting with the emperor and his family had been positive—they were all genuinely interested in his work and inventions, and the praise he'd received had been flattering. He didn't know how much influence the emperor had in such things as lawsuits and businesses. Having his support would likely be beneficial at least.

He felt safer now that they were home. Rough winter seas prevented ships from coming into harbor, and only the local fishermen were brave enough to head out on their boats. It was one such fisherman who'd provided the cuttlefish bones Robinson was using to make the ring mold. Until his method for replicating the rings was patented, he didn't trust sharing the ring or the idea with anyone else. And there would be no patent until they went back to Auvinen and provided the technical designs to McKenna's father. He didn't feel right about patenting the function since he hadn't invented it himself.

Staying busy helped him cope with his fraying nerves. McKenna's mood had altered significantly after her last escape from the *strannik*.

After returning home, Robinson had created his own impressive defenses, innovating magical devices that would forewarn them of strangers approaching the house. Mr. Swope had also installed added barriers to the doors and windows. He was a diligent man, still harboring feelings of self-recrimination for the death of Aunt Margaret. But Robinson's magic hadn't worked against the *strannik* in Covesea, which made him uneasy. He hoped physical barriers would contribute to their security. And, that failing, Mr. Swope had a pistol that wasn't elfshot.

Buried by the burning smell of the cooling ring, he caught a hint of McKenna's perfume and turned, finding her leaning against the doorway, agitation brooding in her expression.

"Any word?" she asked. He knew she asked about Wickins.

He shook his head, trying to smile cheerfully, but the expression felt forced.

She walked into the room, gazing at the different apparatuses set up throughout on various worktables. There were bottles and flasks and coils all about. Then she came to a stop behind his chair and began massaging his stiff shoulders. Her touch was always pleasant to him, and he felt a little shiver go down his spine, especially when she stroked the nape of his neck and teased his hair. Then she squatted down next to his chair so she looked up into his eyes. Her hand rested on his knee.

"I'm worried too," she said softly. "But there's nothing we can do but wait for news."

"Suspense is an awful pain," he said with a sigh. "I need to make more of these rings. Or find more. I don't know if this one will work. I've told your parents what I've learned, of course, but they have no way of responding. The mail doesn't get delivered with great regularity anymore."

McKenna nodded with sympathy. "Can we practice again? I've tried reading, but my mind is too distracted. I want to try the magic again."

Robinson felt another throb of dread. All their previous attempts had ended in failure, and he was beginning to doubt whether success was even possible. He was more eager to try communicating with the Semblance trapped inside her—Erlking's daughter or not—to see if there was a way to dislodge it without harming McKenna. To learn anything he could about her, but it would take time and resources for him to research the matter and contact experts in the literature.

Each time he'd suggested the notion to his wife, McKenna had recoiled from the idea. And, more times than once, it had led to the night terrors.

"If you want to," he said, trying to be hopeful but fearing his face exposed his doubts.

McKenna smiled, and they went to the table where he'd assembled a device to produce a stream of flame. They'd already gone over the particulars of scales and notes. He'd been teaching her a very basic tune consisting of eight sequential notes. Even the summoning of light—Hoxta-Namorem—only required five notes. But he wasn't yet trying to teach her a spell, just the rudimentary basics of singing in tune.

He summoned the flame, which was violet and blue, from a metal tube connected with four stabilizing rods to keep it from tipping over. He'd recruited the intelligence of a mouse to quench the jet of flame if it were ever knocked over. He dragged the thing to himself and demonstrated the first three notes with the flame in front of his face. As he sang them, the flames quivered with the pulse of his breath. He repeated it several times until she screwed up her face in determination and reached across the table and dragged it toward her. She tried, but the flame's erratic dance matched the erratic notes coming from her lips.

He used his fingers to try to adjust her pitch, pointing up and down. But McKenna had no memory of music. She could speak with a fluid ease that was unattainable by many who had lost their hearing in childhood, but when she tried to shift her voice to a musical register, it simply would not cooperate. It embarrassed her—he could see that in her eyes—but she was determined to keep trying.

He stopped her and knelt by her chair to adjust her posture. He held her hand against his larynx as he sang short bursts of notes, so she could feel the vibrations more keenly, but she could not discern a difference in the pitch either way although she could tell a difference in the muscle contractions.

After an hour or so of intense practice—with no result—Mrs. Foraker interrupted and said it was past time for dinner. He'd lost all track of how long they'd been at it, so they went down to savor the meal, but he noticed McKenna stirring her soup listlessly. Trying to conceal the tears gathering at her lashes. It pained him to see her so defeated.

When dinner was over, they took a walk together on the beach. It was cold and windy, but at least there wasn't any snow, and it was good to get some fresh air. They walked hand in hand, talking by moonlight, his head tipped toward her face as he spoke.

"Tomorrow, can we try another way of communicating with—"

McKenna's lips pressed firmly together, and she shook her head brusquely, refusing to meet his gaze.

He halted, coming around in front of her. And waited until she was ready to look at him again.

"I want to keep trying, McKenna. I don't want to give up hope that we'll find a way to accomplish it."

Her voice was swollen with tears. "But you heard them. They've tried! Maybe . . . maybe I'm just supposed to die?"

He gaped at her. "Don't say that."

"But how can I not think about it, Rob? It's haunting me more every day. What if *I'm* the reason this war is even happening? The *strannik* said he could end it. Wouldn't that be worth it?"

He took her hands, feeling his soul roil with anguish at the prospect of losing her. "McKenna," he said, shaking his head.

"I'm not saying I want this. But what if the *strannik* is right? Should I be so selfish?" She looked away, casting her gaze to the stars and moon, looking confused, frightened, and desperate. "It took this happening to Wickins to make me start second-guessing myself again. The pain of losing someone. Our mutual friend. My sister's happiness. What if I could have prevented it . . . if I'd just gone with him?" The last part came out in trembles.

Robinson pulled her to him, wrapping his arms around her. His own eyes got hot with tears. Something felt undeniably *wrong* about what she was saying. But were his feelings compromised by the thought of losing her? Was he not seeing things objectively?

She pushed away a little, looking up into his face. "If all these deaths over so many years are because of this . . . being . . . inside of me, how can I live with that? All those children who suffered with fever . . . all those souls who died."

He swallowed his own tears and tipped up her chin. "You cannot blame yourself for any of this. I don't know why she chose you, but that wasn't your fault or your choice."

"I know that, but what if I can stop the war? By letting the Aesir . . . have her back?"

"You've said yourself that she recoils at the idea. She doesn't want to go."

"That's how it feels. But that doesn't make the choice right or wrong. I'm tormented by the thought that if I delay ending this, I'll regret it. I don't want to lose you. Or my family. But shouldn't we at least consider all options? Without prejudice?"

Her words were tearing at his soul. He blinked back tears, gazing away at the stars. At the impossible infinity they represented. He tried to banish his anguish by thinking of something else. Each star was a sun with worlds orbiting it. Isaac Berrow had conceived that the universe had no center or edges, expanding infinitely in all directions. That the Mind of the Sovereignty had placed the stars at precisely the right distances that would nullify the gravitational attractions, balancing them perfectly in their orbits. Like balancing needles on their tips.

The thoughts cooled his roiling emotions.

Berrow had been successful because he'd seen things dispassionately. He'd never married. Never even fallen in love, or so the records said— unless he'd burned the evidence before his death? Robinson could not conceive of living a life so austere that one could blithely send one's better half off to their own destruction.

Gazing at her upturned face, he had so many tender feelings they smothered his words for a moment. Then he swallowed and said, "We'll discuss it if you wish. But I cannot believe there is no other way. It would *destroy* me if I lost you, McKenna. So let's not be rash. We will discuss *all* possibilities. And whatever happens to one, happens to us both. If we decide you must go with them, then I will go too. I won't let him take you away from me." He felt a fierce determination as he made his vow. "Besides, can we trust his words alone? No, let us be prudent. But if we should decide that is the only way, then we do it together."

She reached up and cupped his cheek. "I don't deserve you," she choked out.

"It's you who took pity on me," he said, stifling a chuckle. "We were meant for each other. I would do it all again, knowing what's befallen us. Can we discuss it tomorrow? My heart is so heavy right now."

"Maybe news will come tomorrow. Good news."

He took her hand and kissed her fingers.

But he wasn't feeling the hope she expressed. The continual silence meant awful things. Things he couldn't bear thinking about. Not yet. Not yet. As they walked back to Mowbray House, all he could remember was standing before his brother's grave, and he dreaded doing it again for his friend.

Ashes to ashes. Dust to dust. Justice claimeth its own.

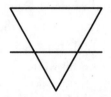

CHAPTER THIRTY-EIGHT

PERSEVERANCE

Two more days passed without a response. The tension pervading Mowbray House thickened with the anticipation of dreadful news. A ceaseless rain then struck the island, revealing a leak in the roof that needed fixing and added to the somberness of the moment. The practices with McKenna all ended with failure and discouragement.

There were some people, with hearing, who could not carry a tune in a wheelbarrow. It wasn't for lack of effort or wanting it. Rather, a lack of acuity. He began to wonder if McKenna's lack of progress wasn't simply related to her deafness but something more fundamental. He kept these unsatisfying thoughts to himself and persisted in helping her practice, encouraging her to keep trying despite the constant defeat.

The ring he'd fashioned in the cuttlefish bone progressed, however, and with filing and tamping and shaping, it began to resemble the one from his device. Ring molds out of cuttlefish bone turned out to be an inexpensive local solution that craftsmen on the island used. While he imagined the metal alloy was what mattered most, the mold helped him mimic the design more easily. Gratefully, he did not lack for funds or raw metals to use, and the precise combination of gold, platinum, palladium, and cobalt he required was readily available on the island. There were jewelry makers in the waterfront area who specialized in making trinkets for the island's many visitors and were suppliers of precious metals for making engagement rings, necklaces, and the like.

They had received a souvenir following their hasty retreat from Andover—the emperor's wife had sent a crystal punch bowl infused with magic to keep drinks cold, along with a handwritten note apologizing for the incident at the palace and apologizing for neglecting McKenna.

Further attempts to communicate with the Semblance proved impossibly confusing and frustrating. He generated the shields he'd used in his previous encounters with Semblances, blocking out the Aesir commands. Although where McKenna was concerned, there *were* no whispered thought commands to block. When he wore the thumb ring and tried to communicate with her, he just got a headache. The *wrea-ith* he'd made did nothing either, although it did, incidentally, work with Mrs. Foraker, and he was able to derive what they were having for dinner from her thoughts. His attempts to communicate with the Semblance yielded no results beyond making McKenna fidgety and uncomfortable, and he wondered if he might need to learn principles of hypnosis to try it from another angle.

On the fourth day, after another failed attempt to commune with the entity entrapped inside his wife, McKenna sat back in her chair in the alchemy, glumly rocking the wreath-crown on the table. "I'm frustrating you."

"Actually, it's the headache," Robinson confessed, rubbing his temple. He took the ring off and slipped it into his pocket.

"But we've made no progress at all. Surely you're disappointed."

He rose from his chair and stretched. "What I've learned about inventions is there are a great deal of dead ends that are increasingly tedious and boring. The insight comes only after a lot of slogging. That's the nature of the work. I'm not discouraged or disappointed."

"I am," she said, shaking her head. "I learned to speak Tanhauser in a month. And I've utterly failed at something a small child can do without thinking."

"Let's get a change of air," he suggested.

"It's still raining."

"I know, but perhaps we can change rooms?"

Hand in hand, they went down to the parlor and sat on the sofa together. She invited him to lay his head on her lap until the headache subsided and gently stroked his hair. He tried to clear his mind, to focus on nothing but her kindness and her presence.

"I've given some thought to what we talked about the other day," she said. "About whether the *strannik* can be trusted."

He rolled on his shoulder so he was looking up at her face. She stroked his chin, his cheeks, his lips. "And?"

"The same arguments you made can also be made about the Invisible College. We cannot know someone's motives, but we can judge their actions. The military flouts the law to get what they want. They literally stole your invention."

"But the court case will prove they did so."

"Even if it's proven, will it matter? Will they not find another way to delay paying what they owe us? Father said the judgment might not be paid out for years. And the head of the Invisible College, Master Drusselmehr, is eavesdropping on the citizens of the empire. He *claims* he's looking for traitors, but exercising such power for noble reasons can so easily turn ignoble."

"That's true," Robinson said. "Apples go bad after they've fallen from the tree. That doesn't mean the tree is bad."

She smoothed the hair from his forehead. "What if neither side is right?"

"What other side is there?" He was being genuine. He loved hearing about the way her mind worked through things. She'd always been a clever woman—well-read, interested, and interesting.

"There's the truth and then there's everything else. How do we get to the truth?"

"There isn't one way. Isaac Berrow reasoned through many of his experiments. But some insights came as a flash of understanding. Intuition. A whisper from the Unseen Powers. I think they try to enlighten us. If we'll listen."

She traced her finger down the bridge of his nose. "How's our little friend? The intelligence who dotes on you."

Robinson reached out with a thought and got a drowsy response by the windowsill. "Napping, it seems."

"Do intelligences nap?" she asked, laughing softly.

"All creation requires activity and rest. Did you know that cats, for example—"

Dickemore. I'm alive.

The thought from his friend startled him so much, he nearly jumped off McKenna's lap.

"What's wrong?" she gasped, but he held up his hand to forestall questions. He quickly, in a panic, fumbled in his pocket for the ring.

Do you hear me? I'm alive but injured. Gravely so.

"He's alive," Robinson said to her, his voice throbbing. He slipped the ring on his thumb. He asked his thoughts aloud so McKenna could at least witness part of the conversation. "Where are you?"

I'm being transported to a locomotivus with other injured soldiers. We're bound for Bishopsgate. Can you meet me there? Can you tell Clara?

"Bishopsgate. Absolutely. We're on Siaconset, but I'll hire a fisherman to bring us to Rexanne. We can travel north from there. What happened?"

The Aesir attacked. It was a bloody one, but we won the day. We took down a stormbreaker. I was caught in the bombardment. Been unconscious for days. I can't . . . walk. Might lose my leg. But I'm alive. Tell her I'm alive.

"Of course. I'm sorry about your injury. But I'm so relieved you're alive. We've feared the worst."

Sorry about that, Dickemore. I've been delirious. But today I finally remembered the ring. I'll see you in Bishopsgate.

Robinson bowed his head, feeling a rush of gratitude mingle with the new throbbing in his skull. "We'll be there. Thank you for letting me know, old chap."

You're the old chap! My head is smarting. Better take this off. I'll tell you when we've arrived and where they take me. Tell Clara I'll reach out to her on the trip south. I'm barely able to think right now.

"Have them bring you to the Fosters' house in Bishopsgate. We can tend to you there!"

Not military protocol. But I'm done with the war. It'll take months to recover and then my enlistment will end. I told . . . Colsterworth . . . about the ring. Did I tell you that?

"You did tell me that. I've made another one. Just need to test it out."

Brilliant. You're the smartest chap I know, Dickemore. See you soon. Mind willing.

"See you soon, old friend."

The communication ended, and McKenna leaned in and kissed him—both of them nearly laughing from relief. When she drew back, Robinson caressed her cheek and said, "I must let Clara know."

"You must," she agreed with a smile. "Oh, she'll be so relieved."

He grinned back despite the pain in his head as he prepared to send news to Clara and her family.

He was sorry for the injuries Wickins had suffered, but he'd thought the worst, and anything was better than that.

✳

It was a perilous journey by sea, but an intrepid fisherman was willing to risk it for a price. They were both soaked, along with their traveling luggage, by the time they arrived in Rexanne and then had to wait in their drenched clothes for several hours for a locomotivus to bring them to Bishopsgate. Mr. and Mrs. Foster and their other daughters had left promptly from Auvinen, but it was a shorter distance to travel from Rexanne. Robinson and McKenna reached Bishopsgate ahead of them but waited at the station for their arrival.

The hugs and shared joy were contagious, and Clara was wearing one of her smartest gowns and hats, looking more like a young woman of twenty and five than eighteen. Her debut was scheduled for the spring, an almost unthinkable thing, given they had to weather the rest of the winter to get there. Mr. Foster gripped Robinson's hand in a firm handshake, his normally taciturn expression revealing the relief he felt. And when her turn came, Mrs. Foster, who'd been dabbing tears, embraced Robinson and pressed a kiss to his cheek.

Trudie was jumping up and down too, but she tugged at McKenna's sleeve. "Did you learn the news, McKenna? From Mary Trewitt?"

McKenna shook her head. "What is it? Is she getting married?"

"No, that's not it!"

Mrs. Foster looked at her youngest daughter inquisitively and then opened her mouth, her expression turning alarmed. She started to reach for her daughter's shoulder, perhaps to interrupt her, but the words came blurting out.

"It's about a deaf little girl at the school! Sandra Clegg Pond. She's learned to sing! And she can cast three spells. Three!"

It was astounding news. And Robinson watched the impact of it on McKenna's face. Surely Trudie was sharing the information because she cared about her sister. But she didn't know how hard McKenna had been working toward that very goal without any discernable progress. It was a blow to her self-confidence. McKenna's smile wilted. Robinson wondered when the girl at the school had lost her hearing. Had she learned to sing first? What method had been used to teach her?

Mrs. Foster reached Trudie. "Yes, it's such news, isn't it?" She tried steering her daughter away from McKenna, but Trudie had noticed her sister's reaction wasn't what she'd expected.

"Aren't you happy for her?" Trudie asked. "It means you can learn too."

"Trudie," Clara said warningly. It was obvious she too had noticed the shocked look on McKenna's face and her silence. McKenna turned and grasped Robinson's arm.

"It's a miracle, truly," McKenna said, her voice weak.

Clara put her hand on McKenna's shoulder, giving her a look of sympathy. The two embraced. Robinson felt sorry for Trudie, who now looked nearly as upset as McKenna. The injury had been inadvertently done. But the pain caused was acute.

"Let's retire to the house," Mr. Foster suggested. "And wait for news." He came closer to Robinson, pitching his voice lower. "Now that you're here, we might be able to entice the judge to hear our case sooner. Could we persuade you both to return with us to Auvinen? It's dangerous traveling by sea this time of year."

A knot of concern for his wife was tightening in Robinson's chest. "I'll consult with McKenna about it."

Mr. Foster nodded and didn't press the matter.

Mrs. Foster was whispering something to Trudie, but the young woman stamped her foot. "I thought she'd *want* to know!" she said through her tears. "Why isn't she glad about it?"

Clara hooked arms with McKenna, steering her away from the unfolding scene.

The overcast sky and soot-stained snow added its own form of misery to the moment. McKenna was thinking about something deeply. And, judging by the look on her face, it wasn't a welcome thought.

The relief he'd felt for Wickins began to shift back to worry for his wife.

The Iskandir legend of Sigridur is a warning to mortals about the cunning of the Aesir. They cannot lie. But there are other ways of dissembling. In the tale, the chieftain Eirikur defends his island from Aesir attacks. A witch-wife, a Semblance, exchanges places with Eirikur's wife, Sigridur. Through her cunning, Eirikur loses all that his ancestors had gained. His people once again split into rival clans seeking dominance. Eirikur dies from the unrest, bleeding in the snow. In the dead of winter, the Aesir attack again. The Aesir know we mortals are ruled by emotion. They are ruled by justice.

—Isaac Berrow,
Master of the Royal Secret,
the Invisible College

MaKenna Aurora
Hawksley

CHAPTER
THIRTY-NINE

Hampers Ferry

It was a relief to see Wickins in the infirmary of Hampers Ferry, a medical garrison on the outer edge of Bishopsgate. McKenna's eyes could not help roving over the sea of sickbeds. Wickins wasn't the only soldier who had well-wishers seeking their recovery. Nor, despite his extensive injuries, did he have the worst of it. The skin on his face was burned and blistered and glistening with salve. Bruises could be seen peeking through the bandages, and his lower lip was split and puffy. Clara knelt by his bedside, clutching his weak hand, and kept pressing kisses against it. Mother and Father stood behind her, while Rob and McKenna stood on the other side of the bed, in the best position for her to see all that was said. Trudie was still back at the house, for concern of exposing her to pain and suffering at such a young age had inclined her parents not to let her attend the first visit.

"I was in General Colsterworth's tent when the bombardment struck," Wickins said. "Bits of flaming debris lodged in my back, preventing me from moving my legs. I was quite paralyzed, unable to move at all. It was terrifying."

McKenna struggled to catch all his words because of the swelling in his face and the bandages, but she thought she was interpreting things correctly.

Clara bit her lip, rocking back and forth in her lowered position. "Can you walk now?"

"Not a bit. Not only was my back injured, but this leg was fractured too, you see. Quite ghastly. If Captain Penny hadn't been there, I would have perished for sure. He'd been dazed by the explosion, suffering cuts and burns, but he saw me helpless under some rubble and managed to drag me out. Both my legs caught fire. The agony was exquisite. But he dragged me into the snow, put out the flames, and sang a shield over us until the attack was over."

Wickins's eyes were alive with the memories. It painted a vivid picture, and McKenna felt her heart clench with dread.

"Where is Captain Penny now?" Mr. Foster asked. "He deserves a medal."

"More than that, I owe him my life," Wickins said with a sigh. "I fainted from pain when they pulled the shrapnel from my back. I was delirious with the sensation of burning, so they gave me some laudanum. So bitter." He winced at the words. "The doctor . . . he thinks the one leg is too badly damaged. He says he smells gangrene, so they'll probably take it off tomorrow. If it spreads, I'm done for." He blew out through his mouth in quick puffs, trying to master his emotions. McKenna saw tears in his eyes. "I rather liked having two legs. But there we are."

Her sympathetic heart constricted again. She squeezed Rob's hand and had him bend closer. "Do you think . . . maybe your device might aid in the healing?"

He gazed at her, his expression enigmatic. She could tell he was either whispering or just mouthing the words because of the subtle change in the way his lips moved. "I was just thinking the same thing.

I'll offer to stay with him and try it out. But I don't like you being here in a military post. There's a man with a kappelin cloak roaming amidst the beds."

"Where?" McKenna asked. She hadn't noticed.

"Your back is to him. Middle of the farthest wall. He's going from bed to bed. No doubt he's inspecting for the possibility of Semblances."

McKenna immediately felt a surge of fear, and when she glanced over her shoulder, she noticed the man he spoke of. He wasn't someone she recognized, but Robinson's assertion was true. His appraisal of each of the wounded soldiers felt methodical. Intentional.

She felt a gentle squeeze on her hand and turned her head back to Rob. "If Wickins heals too quickly, it may be suspicious. But if the stone in the device is a philosopher's stone, it could help him much faster. It could save his leg. We have to try."

"You could leave it with him," McKenna suggested.

"I thought of that too, but remember how it came back to me after General Colsterworth took it? It might work best if I stay here with him."

"Then I'll stay too," she insisted.

Rob frowned. He clearly didn't like the idea, but being with him made her feel safer. Even around the man in the cloak. Knowing he was there made her nervous, but it hadn't yet given her an instinctive urge to flee.

"I don't think it's wise," he said.

"I'm *staying*."

He still didn't like the idea. But he didn't argue.

By Wickins's second day at Hampers Ferry, the turnabout in his health was startling and baffling to his doctors. With so many visitors wishing to remain, extra chairs were few in number, and so Rob and McKenna shared one with Clara, who'd also chosen to stay as long as possible.

They'd shared their plan and told her about the healing properties of the device, and she'd watched with fascination and relief as the burned skin healed, the bruises vanished, and even the broken leg began to mend to the point where Wickins could sit up in the bed without groaning in pain. By the third day, the field doctor pronounced his condition was stable enough that they could remove him to the Fosters' home in Bishopsgate for convalescence. Besides which, they needed every bed for the other injured soldiers being shipped home from the front. Wickins still couldn't put any weight on his broken leg, but he was so notably improved that there was indeed hope that he might make a full recovery.

After a painful carriage ride to the house, Rob and Clara were hoisting Wickins out of the carriage by the arms when McKenna noticed sentries from the Marshalcy awaiting them by the door, along with Mr. Leishman, Master Drusselmehr's manservant.

"Rob," she said urgently, and his gaze narrowed at the door.

"Well, let's see what they're here for," Rob said resolutely, and the four of them made slow progress toward the door.

"We've been expecting you," Mr. Leishman said as they approached it, his smile cryptic but not unpleasant.

McKenna's brow furrowed with concern, but the sentries waved them inside, where they found Master Drusselmehr paying a visit to her parents. He was quick to meet McKenna's gaze, perhaps lingering too long before greeting the others.

"I was just about to leave for Hampers Ferry but was told that you would come to me," he said, rising from the sofa and bowing to the new arrivals.

Rob and Clara helped Wickins to a stuffed chair, and he grimaced as he sat down. The braces and bandages on his leg were formidable, but they helped immobilize the limb to aid in the healing.

"You came all this way to see an injured private?" Wickins asked with a confused look and a chuckle.

"Not just any injured private. You and your friend are no ordinary men. I have extolled you both to the emperor and his family. They are anxious to continue showing their good opinion of your friends. And I come with good news for you, young man."

McKenna realized she'd been holding her breath and let it out. Trudie, who'd only been allowed to visit once at the hospital, had sidled up by Wickins's chair and grasped his hand like an affectionate younger sister. Her middle sister, meanwhile, was watching the old sorcerer with interest but also doubting eyes.

"I've secured an honorable release from military service and a limited but not insubstantial pension to *Lieutenant* Wickins." He lifted his finger in a flourish as he spoke the last part. "Yes, his previous rank was reinstated, which is what entitles him to such a reward. He will also be presented a Conspicuous Gallantry Medal, along with Captain Penny, for services rendered at the Battle of Skyfall. Well done, sir!"

Wickins looked thunderstruck by the news.

McKenna's heart rejoiced for their friend. The pension would not significantly alter Wickins's livelihood, not once his shares in the family business were realized, but it was still a magnanimous gesture. Clara beamed with pride and smoothed Wickins's hair. He took her hand and kissed it.

"Th-Thank you," he stuttered. McKenna even noticed that "defective utterance" and felt justifiably proud that even though she couldn't work magic, her gift for reading lips was remarkable still. It was her own kind of magic.

"That is not all," Drusselmehr said, clasping his hands behind his back. His suit was silk with embellishments of the richest materials. He'd come in the guise of a performer, and he was there to dazzle. "Without Professor Hawksley's new invention, the outcome of the battle would have been entirely different. We lost many good men, but the casualties would have been much more severe without the special glass lamps and your ability to communicate with each other and with me. The emperor insisted you both be given the highest award a civilian can receive, the Queen Consort's Gallantry Medal. The two of you will receive it at the summer palace in six months' time when the court adjourns there for the season. One cannot go to the summer palace without invitation. This is a high honor indeed."

Robinson glanced at McKenna and then back at Master Drusselmehr. "While I appreciate the gesture, if my wife is not included or welcomed there, then I would rather not attend."

Master Drusselmehr waved his hand. "I assure you, Professor, that she will be. Your notoriety has exceeded that of any civilian in recent memory. As head of the Invisible College, I would also like to honor your contributions as well. You will be advanced to the rank of Sublime Master, the fourteenth degree." He grinned with pleasure at his pronouncement.

By the startled looks on her parents' faces, McKenna realized this was a significant leap in rank. Some sorcerers could go years without advancing in rank at all, as there were fewer positions in the upper hierarchy and only one at the very top. She was proud of her husband. Proud of his achievements and for receiving recognition that was well earned.

Rob looked equally surprised. "I'm . . . astonished."

"A humble response. How suitable. The Invisible College needs more individuals like you, Professor Hawksley. Unfortunately, many in the upper echelons are hidebound and no longer pursue the quest of self-improvement. As you have. You will now have a voice within the order and can help ensure that the unworthy are not advancing. We hope you'll inspire a new generation of sorcerers to join us!"

"Well done, Dickemore," Wickins said, beaming.

Rob looked a little uncomfortable with the adulation, but he nodded to the old sorcerer respectfully.

"I don't currently have a quorum," Rob admitted. "I haven't even had time to visit any on Siaconset."

Father gave Rob a smile. "Membership in a particular quorum is not a requirement for advancement to the upper levels."

"I believe Sarah Fuller Fiske is a fourteenth degree herself," Mother added. "Isn't she?"

Father nodded.

"You are well respected in Auvinen," Drusselmehr said. "We can perform the ceremony there, in the Storrows, for example, or we can do it here at one of the military quorums."

At that last part, Robinson frowned and shook his head.

"The Storrows, then. I will come to Auvinen in a week. Your friend is making good progress in his healing and hopefully will be well enough to attend your promotion."

"I wouldn't miss it," Wickins exclaimed.

Master Drusselmehr bowed again with a flourish and announced he needed to depart. Father escorted him to the door, where the Marshalcy sentries awaited him.

In a daze, McKenna watched them go, but because their backs were to her, she couldn't observe their conversation. Her attention shifted back to the rest of her family as Mother gave Rob an affectionate hug.

"Can I go see it too?" Trudie asked mother.

Mother shook her head sadly. "I'm sorry, dearest. Only sorcerers from the Invisible College can attend."

McKenna felt a tug in her chest, a painful wrenching, because once again she would be excluded. She still hadn't asked for more details about the deaf girl who had learned to cast a spell. No one spoke about it, and she really didn't want to know because it made her feel intensely jealous. She slipped her hand around Rob's waist and stroked his side. She was proud of him and the recognition flowing in. His reputation would only grow.

Father returned, a troubled look on his face.

"What's wrong, Papa?" she asked, returning to the tender name she used to call him when she was younger.

"I asked Master Drusselmehr about the pending case. Of seeking to try it now in winter as you and Robinson are here."

"He didn't approve?" Rob asked with a suspicious wrinkle in his eyebrows. "I'm not surprised."

"The military used the victory at the Battle of Skyfall as a pretext for requesting another extension. And Miss Cowing has now insisted that her patent predates ours and that she intends to prove it in court but needs time to prepare her case. The judges will hear it the first day of spring."

It was clear to everyone that the military knew it was going to lose the case and that both inventors were affronted by their actions. They were only attempting to delay the inevitable.

At least they wouldn't have to go to the hospital anymore. Wickins could heal at the house, which had safeguards and protections. In a few days, they'd return to Auvinen, to her childhood home on Brake Street. They'd have well-wishers there, like Rob's parents. And Sarah Fuller Fiske.

Thinking of that kind woman caused another spike of jealousy about the deaf girl who'd learned to cast a spell. She tried to purge the unwelcome feelings, but they only grew in intensity.

Leading to the realization that the feelings she was experiencing weren't even hers.

They belonged to the Erlking's daughter.

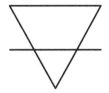

CHAPTER FORTY

The Eloquence of Silence

It was a beautiful winter day when the family returned to Auvinen to the house on Brake Street. In order to fit the women and the convalescing Mr. Wickins inside the carriage, Father and Rob had needed to share the pilot box with the driver. The sidewalks were all swept free of snow, and most of the slush in the street had melted away. Bare-limbed elms offered a sharp contrast in color to the drifts of snow in the yards. Lazy smoke drifted from chimneys along the street. As soon as McKenna saw the house, she felt a pang of wistfulness. She'd missed it, missed the family life she'd grown up being part of. The driver brought the carriage up the way and stopped it, and Rob was the first to leap from the pilot box to assist interior occupants out, Trudie first and then McKenna.

She caught her husband's eye, saw the worried look there, and tried to ascertain what had caused it.

"Are the wards still secure?"

He nodded curtly and then helped Clara maneuver poor Wickins from the inside. He wasn't walking on his own power yet, but the doctors were satisfied that his leg, though mangled, was improving and wouldn't need to be amputated. He'd been granted permission to return to Auvinen so long as the Fosters assumed care and responsibility for him.

McKenna gazed up at the pilot box and saw Mr. Thompson Hughes gazing down at her with a fond smile.

"Thank you ever so much," she said.

"I've missed having you at home, lass. The master says you'll be staying a few weeks?"

She nodded. Most likely they'd be staying in hotels, however. Rob didn't trust the military or the ministry and felt changing their location haphazardly was still the best approach. She would have been happy enough staying at the family home, but there was wisdom in being prudent.

There were two officers from the Marshalcy inside the home, and one of them lent a hand in getting Wickins settled on a couch. Once he was comfortable, Clara nestled against him as the others made themselves at home. McKenna parted the curtain and observed that the greenhouse was sparkling in the sunlight.

And then she felt familiar lips kiss the slope of her neck and turned to find her husband eyeing her with a curious tilt to his eyebrows.

"May we have a private interview, Miss McKenna?"

"Where would you prefer to conduct this interview, Mr. Hawksley?"

"In the greenhouse, I should think."

She extended her hand, he kissed it, and the two of them slipped away from the commotion in the parlor and went through the servants' corridor to the rear of the house. The snow was stiff but crunched beneath their shoes as they padded lightly through the unblemished layer to the greenhouse door. Rob opened it for her, and she stepped inside. There were some seedling crates assembled on a bench and a little hand trowel. The cook was getting ready to plant them already. Although the glass walls trapped the sun's heat, it was still deliciously cold and they both could see their breaths.

McKenna grazed her hand along the bench and then turned and watched Rob shut the door. She saw a flash of light coming from beyond the parlor window curtain, but they had some privacy, which was a welcome reprieve after spending so many days in the hospital. The smell of that place—she'd never forget it. Nor did she wish to smell it again for the rest of her life.

"We could have gone up to my room," she said, tilting her head and coming closer to him. "If you wanted to get away from company." She slid her hand up his arm.

He reached out and brushed back some strands of her hair, which had slipped free of their pins. He bent over and grazed his lips against her forehead but pulled back so she could read his lips.

"This greenhouse is the place where I first learned you'd begun to care about me. I'd already fallen recklessly in love with you by then."

"Recklessly?" she asked with a gasp and a grin.

"Recklessly, impulsively, besottedly."

"'Besottedly' isn't a proper adverb, Professor."

He ignored her teasing and took her into his arms. He gazed into her eyes. "You are the best thing that has ever happened to me, McKenna Aurora Foster."

His words were sending tingles up and down her spine. "Please, Rob. People still believe I've stolen your money."

He shrugged. "I don't really care what others think. We know the truth. I gave those shares to you willingly when the expectation was worth very little. I didn't want to marry you because you were an heiress. I wanted to marry you because of who you are."

She felt tears prick her eyes. Although she'd never doubted his love, it felt good to hear him say those words. Impossibly good.

"You are a kind, gentle man," McKenna said, her throat thick. "Dashing and brilliant and so very, very clever."

"Dashing? I'm rather plain, McKenna."

"Not to *me*," she insisted, squeezing him. "Never to me."

And with that confession, he kissed her, deeply and passionately, and the whole world melted away. Their first kiss had been on the porch. A kiss that had felt ardent and strangely familiar, an echo of a previous moment lost to memory. This was familiar in a very different way. When he nipped her earlobe, she let out a little gasp and felt herself melting against him.

She didn't want to go back inside. She didn't want to let go of this moment. Yet it felt, strangely, like it was about to slip away. That feeling wasn't pinned to fact, but rather the half-remembered knowledge that it had happened before. Over and over. When they'd left on their honeymoon, she'd clung to him in their private box seat, begging him not to let her go.

She gazed into his eyes, saw a look she didn't understand. Was he feeling the same thing?

"What is it?" she whispered.

"I don't know," he said. "I don't want to lose you."

She leaned up and kissed his mouth again. "If something is lost, it can be found again."

He cupped her chin in his hands, kissing her slowly and tenderly once more.

It was the day of Rob's advancement in the Invisible College. His parents had come from their cottage, beaming with pride, and they'd all gathered at the Fosters' home, along with some notable friends of the family like Sarah Fuller Fiske, Mary Trewitt, Judge Coy Taylor, and so many more that the parlor was almost bursting. John Wickins's father was also in attendance—he'd come on leave to check in on his son's recovery and stopped by the house several times.

McKenna, who had been reading a book, noticed Rob and her father arrive at the parlor door from a conversation they'd been having in another room, and he motioned for her to come to them. She'd been waiting to share her present for him, which had arrived two days ago from the violin maker. Her mother had helped her pick it out.

After joining them, Rob and Father escorted her to the front door, where a man from the Marshalcy was posted.

"This is Detective Lieutenant John Prescott Bigelow," Rob said by way of introduction. "We actually met my first day in Auvinen. He's been assigned to watch over you and Trudie while we're at the ceremony."

"A pleasure, Detective Lieutenant," McKenna said, taking his offered hand.

"I've asked him to assemble his men out front." Robinson continued. "Would you have a look, McKenna?"

She was confused at first and then realized that he was asking her to discern whether the *strannik* was impersonating one of them. There were six men standing at attention outside, each wearing the uniform of their station. None of them was the *strannik*.

She shook her head and Rob nodded to the chief officer. "Thank you, Bigelow. I'm entrusting my wife and her sister into your hands."

"I'll do my duty, sir. Depend on it," he said with a serious expression.

When they returned to the parlor, Rob's father took her hands, sharing his affection for her and his gratitude for all that the Fosters had done to help his son.

"I don't think he would have fully recovered from his illness if not for you, my dear. Bless you, Daughter. Bless you! If it's not too forward of me, I hope we can get some news of grandchildren soon, eh? Eh?" His eyes twinkled with mirth, but McKenna was mortified by his directness.

Rob shook his head and pulled her away from the awkward moment. "Mr. Thompson Hughes is going to bring us to the Storrows. I feel very nervous for some reason. I wish you could come."

"I want to see the inside of the Invisible College," McKenna said. "But it's not proper. Mother offered to stay home with me, but you are her first son-in-law, and she wants to support you."

He grazed his fingers through his hair. "Now we just have to wait until it's time to leave."

"I know a way we can pass the time." She glanced at her mother, who was already looking at her, and gave the signal. Mother asked for quiet. All the side conversations ended.

From a place of concealment—behind Father's stuffed chair—Mother extracted the new violin case and presented it to McKenna.

"I've been wanting to give Rob this as a wedding present for some months now," McKenna said. He looked startled and appropriately pleased. "Ever since he broke his violin. New ones aren't easy to come by, and they take time to build. But because Rob loves music so much, I wanted to make sure he had a new one. To my dearest love. Congratulations on your promotion!"

She was so happy she thought she'd burst as she put it into his hands. He held the case reverently at first, stroking it. Then he undid the clasps and revealed the dark, cherry-colored violin. It was distinctive. It was beautiful. He gaped, then pulled it free. Mother took the case as he held the violin to his chin and plucked a few notes.

"Mama, should you help him tune it?" Trudie asked, standing by the Broadwood grand.

"Robinson has perfect pitch," Mother said. "He doesn't need the help."

Rob grinned sheepishly and adjusted the tuning pegs. Then he took the bow and swept it across the strings. Many in attendance immediately began to clap.

"Play the aria of the Erlking's daughter!" Trudie pressed after coming over and tugging on Rob's coat. "You promised I'd get to pick the song!"

McKenna felt a jolt in her heart at the request. It was a request that had been made many times. But this time, knowing what she did, she felt a keen desire to hear the tune. She caught Rob's stare, their gazes meeting. He silently asked her permission to grant her sister's request. The others didn't know how deeply personal this opera was to her now.

McKenna nodded and retreated to the nearest sofa.

She watched as Rob began to play a song she couldn't hear. This time there were no costumes, no frilly curtains or orchestra pit, the way there'd been at the opera house in Tanhauser. Just her husband, mesmerizing everyone with a song that came from his dancing fingertips and gliding bow. He gazed at her while he played, his wrist rocking back and forth. Mother had explained that the technique was called vibrato, and it added to the richness of the song.

McKenna heard nothing. Silence had barred her from learning magic. From enjoying her husband's gifts. A deep, penetrating disappointment welled up inside her. A thirst for something she could never drink. It wasn't fair that she would never, in her life, be able to participate in something so elementary. So primitive.

And it was because of the Aesir, who had sent the plague to destroy hearing. To prevent people from learning magic. And yet she could feel no hatred for the being inside of her.

He finished the song with a flourish, holding out the bow. Clapping. Soundless clapping. McKenna closed her eyes, straining to hear any of it.

She felt a hand on her shoulder. Lifting her head, she saw Rob looking down at her, an expression of worry on his face. He knelt down in front of her, too overcome to speak, clutching the neck of the violin in his other hand, trapping the bow with his thumb.

"Thank you," he murmured.

She had the uncanny urge to bid him goodbye instead of saying you're welcome.

There is a village in the mountains of Tanhauser that has a legend about the Erlqueen and her palace on a frozen lake. Her throne is built on the lake, its surface so vast and clear it is called the Mirror of Reason. It is said that a shard of ice from this mirror could render a mortal able to inhabit her icy demesne forever but with terrible consequences. All compassion, all tenderness, all kindness would be snuffed out. A mortal led to that realm will forget family, obligation, and be trapped in prisons stronger than ice, for the mind is the true prison to a mortal without feelings. The prisoner will be tasked with solving arithmetic equations that cannot be solved or have no end. Ones that seize the mind and will not let go.

Only a sacrifice of pure love could free the shard and the mortal from imprisonment. That is the legend.

They say a young mortal man was the one who stabbed the Erlqueen and killed her. That her frozen body still lies beneath the icy waters of her mirror. In my view, this legend is only a myth. But all myths contain shards of truth.

—Isaac Berrow,
Master of the Royal Secret,
the Invisible College

Robinson Foster Hawksley

CHAPTER FORTY-ONE

THE STORROWS

"You're quite lost in thought, old chap. It must be serious."

The gentle rocking of the carriage and the view of the street outside had indeed buried Robinson deeply into his mind. The new violin case was nestled beneath his arm. He shared the bench with Mr. and Mrs. Foster, but Wickins and Clara were across from him, along with his own father. Since his mother wasn't part of the Invisible College—nor could she be— she was staying at the hotel the family had first come to upon their arrival in Auvinen.

"Of course he's lost in thought," Clara said, hand resting on Wickins's. "It's an important evening. I'd be nervous too."

"Nothing frightens you, my dear," Wickins said. "Except being teased, I should think. Seriously, Dickemore. Are you nervous?"

He was brooding about McKenna and their perplexing situation. Before he'd left, her expression had become troubled again, and when he'd tried to ask what was wrong, she'd insisted she didn't want to ruin his evening and they'd talk about it in the morning. Mrs. Foster had offered, once again, to remain behind, but McKenna wouldn't have it. So he'd left the dog intelligence to keep watch over her, instructing it to summon help if needed.

"There is nothing to worry about," Robinson's father said. "We must remember that ceremonies are symbolic in nature. When I was elevated to that rank, long ago, it left an impression on me. I was in my midthirties when it happened, so it's a great honor that Robinson has been chosen so young."

"I'm not nervous actually," Robinson said, shifting his gaze back out the window. "I just don't like leaving McKenna alone."

He felt Mrs. Foster grip his hand, and they shared a look of mutual understanding and sympathy.

"What rank have you achieved in the college?" Robinson's father asked Mr. Foster.

"Venerable Grand Master," Mr. Foster said with no affectation.

"The twentieth. Impressive."

"And you?"

"I'm a Knight of the Temple Cross."

"Hmm," Mr. Foster said with a nod, and the two began conversing about the various ranks within the order. His father's rank was two degrees lower, if Robinson remembered the hierarchy correctly. The ranks within the Invisible College were such that the higher in the hierarchy one ascended, the fewer contemporaries one had. The highest achievable rank, the thirty-second degree, was the Master of the Royal Secret, the rank Master Drusselmehr held. There was only one of those at a time, and that person did not choose a successor. That appointment was decided by the three people who were thirtieth degree sorcerers— the three Commanders of the Temple. Robinson wasn't sure why that decision skipped the two above them, but he imagined it had something to do with preserving autonomy within the order and preventing one person from setting up a permanent succession scheme.

In Robinson's mind, it was all a lot of fuss and bother. Although flattered by Master Drusselmehr's intent of honoring him, Robinson wasn't impressed by rank, especially since he'd come to realize that the hierarchy of the Invisible College, at least in the upper echelons, was ruled by people no longer living the virtues they expected the rising generation to embody. He seriously doubted that he, alone, would be able to transform the situation.

Wickins grimaced as he leaned forward, clearly still experiencing pain. He pitched his voice lower, for the conversation was still ongoing between the two older men. "She'll be fine, Dickemore. Half the Marshalcy is watching over the house tonight."

"I wouldn't exactly call it half," Robinson demurred.

"You know what he means," Clara said. "They're on guard. On watch. And she's the only one who can see through this fellow's disguise. She'll know if he comes. And they'll shoot him on sight."

That wasn't what was troubling him. It was the dilemma of her being a Semblance. And not just any Semblance. For now, Master Drusselmehr had managed to hold off the military. He was the only person in authority who *could* give such an order. And yet, they couldn't expect that protection to last forever . . .

"Yet this same man infiltrated the emperor's palace while we were there," Robinson said matter-of-factly. "But he's not foremost in my mind at present."

"Are you thinking of a new invention?" Wickins asked, eyes brightening.

"I'm always thinking up new inventions," Robinson replied enigmatically. "I was able to make a new ring. I've been testing it out with Mr. Foster, and it has the same properties as the one I gave you. The patent office is overflowing with applications, but he thinks they will expedite this new one since Master Drusselmehr is so interested in it."

Wickins grinned and put his arm around Clara's shoulder. "Interested indeed. What you need to figure out next is that fascinating device. The stone practically resurrected my leg."

"Shhhh," Clara said. "You promised to keep quiet about it."

"Who in this carriage doesn't already know?"

She looked about to argue the point when the carriage arrived at the Storrows. A chord of anxiety began to thrum in Robinson's chest as the driver parked the carriage near the pub across the street from the quorum. He disembarked with the family.

The pub seemed unusually raucous that evening. The sun had already disappeared over the building tops, but being winter, it would be darker early anyway. The quicksilver lamps had already pulsed to life.

As they entered the establishment—which was the only way to get into the Storrows—Robinson recognized many of the revelers as students from the university where he'd taught. Several of them let out a cheer as he entered.

"Well done, Professor! Well done!"

"Three huzzahs for Professor Hawksley!" shouted another group dressed in military uniforms.

He was discomfited by the attention and waved weakly before following the others to the secret entrance. One by one, they entered the underground passage leading to the building across the street. The door was already open, and several sorcerers were waiting at the entrance, wearing black robes with blue trim. They greeted each newcomer with the sorcerers' handshake and a question to validate their rank. Robinson didn't recognize any of these barrier guardians, but he imagined they were accompanying Master Drusselmehr.

Once they arrived in the Storrows's library, he saw nearly every seat had been taken. There were professors, male and female, business leaders, and many wealthy and notable citizens—many of whom he and McKenna had been invited to dine with since their marriage and his successful invention. Another cheer rose up. All the attention focused on him in that moment was rather overwhelming. He'd much prefer a quiet evening at home, doing research or melting metals.

Wickins was limping just ahead of him when Sarah Fuller Fiske arrived through the crush and directed the family to come to another parlor that wasn't so noisy. It was a beautifully decorated chamber, with wooden wainscoting and bronze lamps. The carpet was very lush, and there were couches aplenty for seating.

"You can imagine we have guests beyond our borders tonight," Sarah said, grinning. "It is not often that someone is elevated so high in one ceremony, so naturally the curious wanted to come. Master Drusselmehr brought additional security to help keep the building from being overrun. His manservant has had to expel several nonmembers who tried to sneak in."

Robinson scratched the back of his neck, feeling embarrassed once again.

"The others will stay here while I bring you to the testing chamber. I'm glad you brought your new violin. Your prowess will need to be demonstrated, of course, and while it's common to use your voice for that—and you do have a lovely singing voice—your accomplishments with the violin are equally impressive. Do you have any questions?"

"Is the ceremony . . . public?" Robinson asked.

"No. When you return to the hall, you will already be endowed with your new rank. You will be taught, in short order, the key phrases and tokens of the ranks you are skipping so that, when you leave this place, you will be enabled to enter any other quorum of the Invisible College and gain admission without being a local member. You'll be expected to memorize this information quickly, which I don't believe will be a problem for you, but you will also be unable to discuss it with any member who isn't already a Sublime Master. Is that understood?"

"Of course," Robinson said humbly. The phrases and signs demarcating them were not discussed outside of the Invisible College.

"Master Drusselmehr will be participating in the initiation himself, which is a high honor. In fact, he will represent the role of the Erlking in the ceremony."

Robinson gave her a surprised look. "The Erlking is part of the ceremony?"

Sarah Fuller Fiske smiled at him. "You will see."

More anxiety began to chafe at him. He tucked the violin case snugly under his arm and followed Mrs. Fiske to another room. There were two guardians at another door, and she demonstrated the words and handshakes that would allow him to pass. Robinson had to repeat the gestures and phrases before he was allowed inside.

The next room was dark except for a single lamp burning in the center of the space. An old wooden chair was positioned beneath it. The pillar of light was so strong he couldn't see the walls, but he caught the rustling of robes and realized they were not alone.

"Please take your seat and set the violin case on the ground in front of you," she directed.

His palms felt clammy as he obeyed and seated himself beneath the spotlight. It felt strangely familiar to him. When he'd passed the test in Covesea, he'd sat in a chair in a room that wasn't darkened at all, where he could see the men and women assembled around him, the genders separated on opposite ends of the room. Was this the same? He understood there were varying tests at different milestone levels within the order. Each level was not rewarded with such a symbolic ritual. He watched as Sarah Fuller Fiske disappeared into the shadows. How many people were there watching him? Not knowing caused him a feeling of disquiet.

A man's voice—unrecognizable—asked the first question. "State your name and rank, sorcerer."

"Robinson Foster Hawksley," he stammered. "Elect of the Nine."

"Welcome, Professor Hawksley. You will demonstrate your rank by showing us magic."

The spotlight winked out, plunging the room into utter darkness. A wriggle of fear went through him, but this was also familiar. As if he'd been through this exact experience before.

"Summon light," said a female voice, one he vaguely recognized.

"Hoxta-namorem," Robinson sang.

The canticle summoned the thread-like will-o'-the-wisp of light dancing in front of him.

"Larger," said the man.

"Brighter," said the woman.

Robinson complied, adding additional thoughts to his creation, making it glow brighter and expand by communing with the intelligence there.

"Open your violin case, please," said the woman.

"Make it dance to your song," said the man.

Robinson reached down and brought the case to his lap while he opened it and retrieved the violin and string. He wasn't sure if they expected him to play it while seated, but that was answered almost as quickly as the question came to him.

"You may stand," said the woman.

Robinson complied and set the case on the wooden seat. The chair looked ancient, haggard, made of some indeterminable wood. After straightening, he adjusted the tuning pegs, plucked some of the notes, and then let a single note pierce the darkness.

He closed his eyes and began to play, fast, shrill, ecstatic. The microcosm of light expanded into an orbit around the chair, swirling, dancing, changing height as he changed pitch. Even with his eyes closed, he could see it chase beneath his eyelids, growing brighter and brighter, swelling with the notes he played.

And then he left the note dangling in the air, a chord unresolved, the light quivering just above him. In the light, he could see twelve faces staring at him, wearing dark robes and mushroom-shaped tams of blue and black.

"Well done, Professor Hawksley," said Sarah Fuller Fiske. "You may be seated."

He put his violin away and sat back on the wooden chair, relieved that he'd done well.

Then, one by one, they began to ask him questions to test his knowledge. Equations, complicated but capable of being done in his head. The nature of intelligences and the uses for different creatures. Easily answered as well. Then they shifted to chymical questions about the mixing of reagents in proper doses. The formula to make saltpetr. Finally, they tested his proficiency in music, asking him to sing in various scales without his instrument.

None of the questions were particularly hard but each represented a different discipline, showing the need for a sorcerer to be well rounded.

The room grew steadily darker as his spark of light began to fade. His confidence increased. This was ceremonial. They all knew he was qualified.

After a final question, the room fell quiet. A new voice came from the gloom. The voice of Master Drusselmehr. It was the first time he'd heard it since entering the room, and he hadn't noticed the old sorcerer earlier. The question came from behind him, spoken in a voice muffled by metal.

"Where is my daughter? Do you know where she is? Speak truthfully."

CHAPTER FORTY-TWO

FIRE SNOW

Robinson sat transfixed, feeling his heart wrench with uncertainty. After the question was asked, he imagined the proper response was to deny any such knowledge. It was a formality, surely. Yet the injunction to speak truthfully caused a pang of conscience. Was a proper sorcerer supposed to lie during a ceremony intended to elevate his rank?

Sarah Fuller Fiske had told him, prior to the beginning, that Master Drusselmehr would represent the Erlking. Therefore, it was implied that the daughter being referenced was indeed the Erlking's daughter. And Robinson, more than anyone else in that room, actually possessed limited knowledge of her present state. He could not reveal that, of course, not in front of a room of witnesses. Not when she was back at the house on Brake Street.

So he resolved to answer the question with a question in the hope that his response might be misunderstood.

"Why should *I* know where she is?" he answered, trying to project a tone of incredulity.

In the silence that followed his response, he feared he'd blundered. Then the sound of steps on the carpeted floor preceded the arrival of a looming man, wearing formal robes, a woven stole, medallion, tam—but a silver mask with open slits for the eyes. This was Master Drusselmehr, although his identity was concealed due to the silver mask. He carried a ceremonial mace gripped in both gloved hands, the weapon gleaming in the spotlight. It had Aesir runes embedded in it, as well as jewels that positively throbbed with magic. Robinson gripped the armrests of the chair, a visceral reaction that momentarily made him forget that the device in his pocket would shield him from attack. He'd let Wickins use it during the hours they spent together, but he'd never left it in his friend's possession, knowing it would likely pop back into being in his pocket if he were to try—and also sensing that he required its protection.

The menace he felt at the moment was more subconscious than real, but his senses were highly attuned.

"My daughter broke the covenant of my people," Master Drusselmehr said in his muffled voice.

Ah, so he's following a script. Robinson deduced this, realizing that his answer hadn't really mattered. He was relieved that he'd delivered a circumspect answer.

"She revealed the secrets of the Aesir to the sorcerers of the past and has been condemned for her treason. Hunted and outcast. And so will you be if you reveal the secrets of the alchemy to the uninitiated. Swear on the bones of Isaac Berrow that you will not reveal the things you will learn."

Robinson felt a peculiar urge to laugh, although he knew it would be very rude to do so.

"I swear on the bones of Isaac Berrow," Robinson said succinctly, "that I will not reveal these things to the uninitiated."

The masked dignitary then lowered the mace and touched Robinson on each shoulder and then on the head.

"I strike three blows," said Master Drusselmehr when he concluded. "A gift to your shoulders to remove the labor of your muscles. And a gift to your mind to increase your knowledge and wisdom."

"Knowledge and wisdom," repeated the onlookers in unison.

"May you find willing intelligences to aid in your work as a sorcerer. To ease the burdens of mortalkind. Be judicious in their use and grateful for their toil. Never exploit or demean them, and they will serve you all the days of your life. Do you accept this charge?"

"I accept," Robinson said.

"To your mind, I impart secret lore previously withheld from you. It belongs to the rank of the Sublime Master, the fourteenth degree. It is the secret of pyrophoric substance. It is a substance that will burn in contact with water or humidified air. Such a blaze cannot be extinguished through ordinary means. You are now authorized to conduct experiments with such properties once you have proven you are adept at the safety and controls of them. They are dangerous and deadly elements, but they protect us from the wrath of the Aesir. This knowledge, you are freely given. To purchase these reagents, you must demonstrate the sign of the fourteenth degree. It is thus."

Gripping the mace with one hand, the old sorcerer showed his other hand, where each finger was spread apart except the middle two, which were held together while the thumb was held to the palm.

"This symbol is called *Shekinah*—the Divine Presence. It is the Mind of the Sovereignty peering down on us. All you do must be in accordance with the Mind of the Sovereignty. Make the sign of Shekinah!"

Robinson held up his hand, his middle two fingers touching, the others extended. The old sorcerer touched his hand to Robinson's.

"Pyrophoric metals are very dangerous and powerful. They can cause great harm to life and property. They can destroy an Aesir. Be wise. Be prudent. Welcome, Sublime Master!"

Applause broke out in the room, startling Robinson. Then the lamps within the chamber flickered and awakened, and he saw Sarah Fuller Fiske approaching him with a bundle of robes.

She helped him put them on over his suit and then explained the meaning, which he'd already surmised from his previous experiences in the college. But he imagined the proper education was an important part of the ritual. "Each quorum has a different color pattern in the robe, usually black and one other color. Ours is blue and black. The marks on the sleeves are called chevrons and indicate you've achieved the rank. The tam is octagonal-shaped, a reminder of the Eight Disciplines. As you continue to advance in ranks, you will wear additional cords and braided aiguillettes to mark higher offices. Medallions are also given at the higher ranks. You must be wearing these robes to be allowed entry into the upper corridors within the Invisible College. Here you will find access to records prohibited to those of lower rank."

Mr. Foster approached, already wearing robes signifying his rank. His pince-nez glasses gleamed in the light. Robinson's father was also present in his robes.

"I'm so proud of you, Son!" he said, after Robinson had finished donning his ceremonial outfit. The sleeves were quite billowy, with tight cuffs at the wrist, similar to a judge's robes, which—as he thought about it—made sense. Most, if not all, judges were part of the Invisible College. He'd had comparable ceremonies at the fourth and ninth levels. But this one included lore about the Erlking and his daughter, which he'd never been exposed to before.

"Would you like to visit some of the book rooms?" Mr. Foster asked. "I'm sure you're feeling very curious."

Robinson smiled. "I would, but that can wait. If the initiation ceremony is over, I'd like to get back to McKenna. I can return tomorrow."

Mr. Foster nodded approvingly. They provided a satchel for him to put his regalia in, which he slung around his shoulder. Then, gripping his violin case, he followed his family out, where he was greeted by a huge fanfare of excitement. Food and drink had been provided to mark the occasion. He felt self-conscious about wanting to leave so soon, but they managed to get through the crowd and back to the carriage, where the driver awaited them after reassuring him that the celebration would go on despite his absence.

"What do you think?" Mrs. Foster asked, reaching over and patting his knee. Clara and Wickins were already inside the carriage, since his leg had started hurting and all the benches inside had already been taken.

"Overwhelming," Robinson admitted. Not that the information wasn't interesting. He'd heard about pyrophoric substances before, but the knowledge had been off-limits to him at his previous rank. Some sorcerers had burned down their alchemies in the early days while seeking to understand them. Even Isaac Berrow had if Robinson remembered it correctly.

Soon they were off, the carriage rattling back down the lamplit streets. Robinson was pensive, feeling humbled by the knowledge he'd gleaned. He wondered at the ceremonial mace and where that tradition had come from.

A mace was a weapon from an earlier age in the war, when it had been discovered that blunt-trauma weapons fared better against the Aesir's armor than bladed ones did. Then the invention of saltpetr and firearms proved to be infinitely more effective than lugging around an iron-knobbed truncheon.

"I asked the cook to make some cherry cobbler to celebrate," Mrs. Foster said. "She bottles cherries from the orchard every year, and I told her to start baking it after sunset."

Robinson smiled, the memory of the cobbler a delightful one from past winter dinners at Closure with the family.

"Well done, Dickemore," Wickins said. "Proud of you, old chap."

After the brief journey, the carriage turned up Brake Street. It was brighter now, the light filtering into the carriage more pronounced. Then he noticed the burning smell in the air. A metallic smell.

"Whoa," Mr. Thompson Hughes said loudly, pulling in the reins and stopping the carriage. Robinson leaned forward, trying to get a view. And that was when he saw the flames.

His eyes popping in bewilderment, he yanked on the handle and leaped out onto the street where several carriages had stopped, blocked by Marshalcy ones. Rob gaped in horror. The Fosters' house on Brake Street was drenched in flames—roaring, green-tinctured flames sending down showers of ash and cinders.

Cries of alarm sounded from the inhabitants of the carriage as the others began to spill out. Robinson ran ahead and was immediately stopped by officers of the Marshalcy.

"Hold on, sir! Hold on! You can't go any closer!"

"That's my house!" Mr. Foster roared in fury as he came up next.

"Papa! Papa!" screamed Trudie. She was in her nightdress, a blanket over her shoulders. Her eyes were terror-stricken.

Robinson felt the immensity of the situation. The cascading flames, roaring into the sky. Soot and curling bits of ash raining down like burning snow.

"What happened?" Mrs. Foster asked in devastation, trying to shove her way past the officers, but they held the line. "Where's my other daughter? Is she in there?"

"It's too hot, ma'am! Too hot!"

Robinson felt his chest constrict with pain, despair, and indignation. The fire had an unnatural smell. It didn't take a newly minted Sublime Master to deduce it was a pyrophoric flame. And the water trucks trying to douse it, which were now in flames themselves, had only made it worse.

His frantic mind summoned the dog intelligence. Why hadn't he been warned?

Silence. He felt no tug, no sense of the intelligence anywhere. He tried summoning other intelligences and failed. Maybe the flames had frightened them away. Animals were instinctively fearful of fire.

"McKenna," he gasped, gazing at the inferno in shock and disbelief.

"Where's your sister? Have you seen McKenna?" Mrs. Foster said, gripping Trudie by the shoulders.

"N-No! I had to jump out the window into the snow," Trudie wailed. "I haven't seen her! The house just blew up!" She began to sob, clutching her mother in despair.

An explosion rocketed as lamps overheated and burst in a shower of glass.

Robinson stood, his chest heaving, his emotions too stunned for him to make sense of what he was seeing. A sorcerer had started this fire. He had no doubt of it. And it felt significant that it had happened the night of his advancement, when McKenna was sure to be left alone. Why hadn't the officers of the Marshalcy stopped it? Or had they been the ones to ignite it?

Or was it General Colsterworth?

He was in agony, staring at the flames. No mortal body could survive such a conflagration. They'd be incinerated instantly. The heat, the temperature—he could feel it houses away, the waves of heat making his skin uncomfortably warm. The next-door houses were also in flames. Another set of water trucks came charging up the street.

Robinson wondered if his device would protect him, if he could penetrate the fire. If he did, amidst so many witnesses, there would be questions. Demands for answers. It would not be possible for a mortal to survive one second in such a furnace. If McKenna were still inside, she was dead. There was no logical alternative. The grief and anguish threatened to destroy him.

If she were still inside.

He clutched at the hope that she hadn't been. He clutched it in desperation.

Although they cannot be seen, the Unseen Powers are constantly at work in the universe. Shove a billiard ball across a felt table and it will slide in a straight line until it ricochets off another ball or the perimeter of the table. For motion to persist, additional force is required. The ball will ultimately come to rest when the energy used to push it is expended. Since man is not immortal, the Invisible College will require others to give it a push now and then. Stagnation is the enemy of all progress. I've established a hierarchy where the ambitious seeking to rise to the top will be checked by those beneath. Leadership cannot be hereditary, for no daughter is in every whit like her mother, and the son of a successful sorcerer may be, in fact, an idle rascal. Those who espouse all the virtues of the college will, ultimately, rise to lead. Unless, of course, in time, the forces of stagnation prevail. I foresee the Invisible College will last no longer than two centuries. May that be sufficient before the next Awakening.

—Isaac Berrow,
Master of the Royal Secret,
the Invisible College

General Colsterworth

EPILOGUE

The Sycophancy

There were whispers, smug looks, and furtive glances at General Colsterworth when he walked the hallowed halls of Gresham College. How could there not be when they all assumed, incorrectly, that *he* had ordered the destruction of the Fosters' home in Auvinen. It was audacious. The newsmen were wagging their tongues like starving dogs, and some had encamped outside to get a word, a glimpse of the notorious general. There would be a reckoning now. Nothing could prevent it. Information. He needed information!

Major Dellenbach opened the door to the general's private office, where he'd been brooding over the latest newspaper article about the incident. An out-of-control blaze had decimated several posh houses on Brake Street. The artist's rendering showed a few blackened stumps of brick chimneys, but all the floors had been demolished. And the quaint greenhouse in the yard had turned to charred timbers and molten glass.

"What is it now?" the general grumbled.

"Colonel Stoker arrived. Do you want to see him?"

"Of course I do! Send him at once!"

"Very well. He'll be right in."

Ever since Stoker had been made the head of the Brotherhood of Shadows, the flow of information had altered. Stoker was a sniveling weasel who wanted to run a ministry someday and had laid his bets that Master Drusselmehr would be a more willing sponsor. He had to make reports to General Colsterworth, but the tension between the two men had grown intolerable. But this . . . what had happened in Auvinen was not a politically shrewd move.

Another curt knock and then Stoker arrived. Stone-faced. Unperturbed.

"What have you done, Colonel?" the general said, annoyed at the attempt at unflappability.

"I've done nothing, General. I'd assumed what happened in Auvinen was your handiwork."

Colsterworth vaulted from his seat and slammed his fist onto the table. "Don't patronize me! You know I didn't give the order. I specifically ordered you *not* to harm Foster's daughter!"

"Sir, I had nothing to do with it."

"Has someone in the brotherhood gone rogue?"

"Trying to blame this on me is beneath you, General." His brow furrowed with consternation. "While I agree, fundamentally, that any Semblance is a risk and that Mrs. Hawksley should have been . . . disposed of . . . there were much simpler methods to accomplish it. Burning down her house with her inside of it was rather extreme."

"Extreme, you say? It was Drusselmehr's idea originally! Did *he* order it?"

"Not to my knowledge. It's not my problem," Stoker said, shaking his head. "We haven't had anyone near the girl in months. If you didn't order it, who did? Someone in the Marshalcy?"

"They're loyal to Drusselmehr. And speaking of whom, he's demanded I meet him for lunch at the Sycophancy. He wants answers, and I have none. Where were you the night of the fire?"

"You're interrogating *me*?"

"Answer the question. You are my chief suspect presently."

That got a reaction out of him. Finally. Stoker began to visibly alter. "I had nothing to do with it. Nothing at all!"

"Where were you the night of the fire? Answer me!"

"I tell you, I had nothing to do with it!"

"Provide an alibi, one that can be verified, or I will arrest you for high treason right here and now. You are one of a scant few who knew Foster's daughter is a Semblance. Surely you told someone. One of your men, perhaps?"

"I've told no one!"

"Why not?"

"Because knowingly and willingly harboring a known Semblance is against the order of the Brotherhood of Shadows! I've not shared that information with any of the men. They're hunting Semblances who've infiltrated the soldiers coming back from the front. They're at hospitals primarily, testing survivors for strange wounds."

"You still haven't answered my question. Where were you when the fire broke out?"

A flush of scarlet tinted Stoker's face. "I had an appointment, a dinner engagement, with someone."

"Who?"

"A s-singer."

Colsterworth squinted. "Who?"

"A singer. From the opera populaire."

A love affair, then. No wonder he was being so skittish about revealing it. "Her name? I must verify your alibi."

"Nicolette. N-Nicolette Farber."

"She's here in Bishopsgate?" The name sounded vaguely familiar. An up-and-coming opera singer.

"Indeed so. But I assure you, General, I had nothing to do with it! You ordered me not to pursue Mrs. Hawksley, and I have not."

"Are you certain Drusselmehr didn't have a hand in it? It was a pyrophoric fire."

"He was at the promotion ceremony in the Storrows with his coterie. Why would he want to murder her at such a conspicuous moment? He's too adroit for something like that. And he needs Hawksley's goodwill with the lawsuit pending in court."

Colsterworth huffed with disappointment. In any event, Stoker didn't act like a guilty man. His story could be verified, and Colsterworth would enjoy having the affair with Ms. Farber in his arsenal to use against his previous underling.

"So you haven't spoken to Master Drusselmehr about this yet?"

"I h-have not. He only just arrived in Bishopsgate. I was hoping—"

"To speak to him before I did," the general said, cutting him off angrily. "You'll wait your turn. Is that understood?"

Stoker looked a little greensick, but he nodded.

"Dismissed."

In the time before the lunch meeting, the general began to wonder if the *strannik* were responsible for the incident. He had made several previous attempts to abduct Hawksley's wife. The Marshalcy officers had been on their guard and, it appeared, had been taken completely by surprise by the sudden violence of fire at the house. They'd rushed in to rescue occupants, but the force of the heat had driven them out before they could get upstairs. And the flames had melted all the snow surrounding the property, which meant there were no footprints to track. Intelligences summoned to assist had all been stymied. Fire of that heat and magnitude would have incinerated bone as well as flesh and timber, so there would be no remains either way.

He rubbed his mouth, still confused by the events. When Major Dellenbach returned to announce his carriage was waiting for him, he adjusted his uniform jacket, checked his pistol, and donned a beaver-pelt hat to protect his head against the cold. A few more weeks of winter lay before them. The Aesir advance had been checked and repulsed. There was talk about extending the front lines deeper into the glacier. Engineers and ice machines had already been requisitioned. It was time to change tactics and bring the fight to the Erlking's palace steps. To, hopefully, end the cycle of war once and for all.

There were newsmen awaiting him, demanding answers, but his escort shoved them back as he hurried to his carriage. The driver took off with several of his bodyguards clinging to the back rail.

The Sycophancy was bustling, but the private room had been booked, and when he entered it, Master Drusselmehr was already seated with an array of food in front of him. He gave Colsterworth a look that said a severe rebuke was coming.

"I know you like salmon and saffron," Drusselmehr said. "So I took the liberty of ordering it for you. The pickled asparagus is a bit bland, but it's the best we can do this time of year."

"It's well enough. Now look, Master Drusselmehr, let me begin by saying—"

"Eat," snarled the head of the Invisible College. "My locomotivus departs for the north in less than an hour, so I don't have time to squander on your excuses."

"Excuses?" He glanced at the layout of dishes before him and sat down at the table, his appetite replaced by burgeoning anger. But the salmon did smell fresh, the flakes of pepper and saffron giving it a wonderful hue. His mouth started watering.

"Excuses about why you let Mrs. Hawksley perish in the fire."

"You cannot pin the blame on me when you ordered the military not to protect her."

"I did?"

"You most certainly did! You took it upon the Marshalcy to protect the family. This is none of my affair."

The smell of salmon was so mouthwatering, he grabbed his fork and took a plump, juicy bite from it. The meat melted on his tongue. The cook had outdone himself. It was truly the most enjoyable salmon he'd ever had. He quickly took another bite and found it just as tantalizing as the first. He'd eaten breakfast before sunrise and hadn't realized just how hungry he was.

"The Marshalcy is loyal," Drusselmehr said. "Several of the men suffered serious burns trying to rescue the inhabitants. The fire was not natural. Surely you agree with that?"

"It was pyrophoric from all the signs," the general agreed between chews.

"Which means it was started by a sorcerer. Someone who would stand to lose significantly if their role was found out."

"You suppose someone from the Industry of Magic?" Colsterworth asked. His throat was beginning to itch. He glanced at the food in bafflement. His lips had started to feel puffy. It was a reaction he had when he ate certain shellfish. Tambler shrimp in particular. The reaction was instantaneous, so he always avoided them.

Drusselmehr nodded. "They stand the most to gain. Do you not agree?"

The tingling in his lips was unmistakable. He hadn't felt it in years, but it was the same reaction he had to shrimp. He grabbed his cup and took a heavy drink of wine.

His throat was tightening faster and faster.

"The c-cook." Colsterworth coughed. "He must have prepared the salmon . . . incorrectly . . ."

Master Drusselmehr arched his eyebrows. "Who said you were eating salmon?"

Colsterworth blinked, and then the *strannik* was seated across from him, the glamour gone, his smile wily and full of glee. The platter in front of him was covered in shrimp steeped in a rich sauce. He'd eaten so many so quickly because of the flavor, the taste—the illusion of his favorite delicacy.

Colsterworth drew his pistol, aimed it at the *strannik*'s chest, and pulled the trigger. An emptied click reverberated. His throat was so tight he couldn't breathe now. His lips were buzzing like bees.

"The intelligences obey *me* now, General," said the *strannik*. "And your thoughts betrayed you to your death. You yourself revealed your intolerance for certain shellfish. An errant thought. How deadly they can be."

Colsterworth tried to shove away from the table, but the lack of air was making the room spin. He was being strangled by his own throat. His muscles quivered with uncontrollable energy.

"I killed Master Drusselmehr the night of the fire," the *strannik* said. "There will need to be a new Master of the Royal Secret. A ceremony that all the echelons of the Invisible College will be invited to. Beheading a snake is the best way to stop its venom. Isn't that what you believe?"

General Colsterworth remembered *thinking* that. But he'd never said it aloud. Not to this man. His skin was changing color. The pressure had closed off all air to his lungs.

"There is still enough venom in a decapitated snake that it's dangerous. And the body keeps convulsing. But now, at least, the snake will die. And the Erlking will rule us again."

Colsterworth's eyes were foggy. He tried to force air into his lungs. To whistle a warning. A spell. Anything.

He collapsed on the floor, lungs screaming for air that wouldn't come. He would only make it a few more moments before choking to death.

Before . . . choking . . .

He felt a strange sensation, the separation of his intelligence from his body. He could see again—see his body sprawled on the floor, still gripping the pistol.

"Ah, there you are," said the *strannik*, holding out a jeweled scepter. Helplessly, the essence of the general was sucked into a facet of the stone and subjected to a whorl of crystalline noise that drowned out every other sensation.

Author's Note

Astute readers may notice some historical similarities to people and events of this world. That shouldn't be a surprise since you know I derive many of my ideas from history. This series is no exception, and the nods to Alexander Graham Bell and his wife, Mabel Gardiner Hubbard, are deliberate. I was entranced by their love story, which I was unfamiliar with until I read the biography *Reluctant Genius* by Charlotte Gray. That is where the nugget for this series began. As my favorite quote from Ovid says, "A new idea is delicate. It can be killed by a sneer or a yawn."

I want to acknowledge that to many, especially to the deaf, Bell's legacy of inventing the telephone doesn't counteract some real harm he caused in their community due to his attitudes and experience. To be honest, I'm a little ambivalent toward him some days for inventing the telephone when my kids won't answer theirs or respond to my texts! In a fantasy novel, I can only include so much backstory or context. If my portrayals of the deaf community or how my invented Society treated this community offended any readers, I apologize. I wanted to cast light on how this community has historically been treated. Some of the approaches in this book are not fully realistic since it's a fantasy novel. After reading a biography of Mabel Gardiner Hubbard as research, I found her character even more compelling than the famous inventor's. This is why I felt it necessary to share both Rob's and McKenna's points of view.

When I first pitched this idea to my editor at Amazon Publishing, I described the story (in a nutshell) as "*The Lord of the Rings* meets World War I." My research dived deep into the literature that inspired J.R.R. Tolkien's imagination—old Norse legends like *Beowulf, The Song of the Nibelungs, The Prose Edda,* and *The Saga of the Volsungs* (which is where the idea of the Semblances came from . . . even the naming of them). Tolkien's experiences in World War I shaped his life as well as his imagination. His experiences with war taught him lessons about good and evil. His research into ancient literature taught him about Light Elves and Dark Elves. I preferred to explore the darker side of the myth. I'm fortunate to have found such rich material from wandering the same books he did.

I'll also address fans who are upset by the cliff-hanger ending of this book. Those of you who wait to start until the series is done—your patience has been rewarded big time! For the rest of you, I feel your pain. I was nine years old when *The Empire Strikes Back* came out in the theaters, and I was devastated by the cliff-hanger in that movie and worried about what would happen to characters I loved so much. Like everyone else from that era, I had to wait *years* before I found out what happened. For you brave and formidable fans who wrestle through the discomfort of the stomach butterflies in my emotional roller coasters, the wait isn't nearly as long, just a few months. Rest assured, you will find out what happened soon enough, and I hope it will all be worth the wait.

As always, I'll reveal more of my inner thoughts and machinations in the next book and tell you about how this has come to be one of my favorite stories. Just hold on. The ride isn't over yet!

Acknowledgments

My wife and I celebrated our thirtieth wedding anniversary with a trip to France and Switzerland. We'd both studied French in college and were able to get by ordering food, visiting museums, and the like, but being in a different country gave me a perspective on how challenging it can be navigating a different part of the world or cultural norms when we're so ingrained in our own. It made me think of McKenna and how much concentration it requires to pay attention to every detail so as not to miss conversations or being included.

Producing books and worlds takes an entire team, and I'm so appreciative of mine. They catch so many problems in advance, and without their attention to details, you'd be stopping every few pages in confusion! It's been wonderful working with Alexandra Torrealba, my new editor at APub. I'm especially indebted to my sensitivity reader, Jenna, for her helpful insights and suggestions in handling McKenna's deafness. There is more information she wanted to see included, which I'd already intended to show and resolve in the next book. My core editorial team is really the best: Angela, Wanda, and Dan.

In case you missed it from the previous book's end note, there are two additional bonus chapters from *The Invisible College*, which you will be directed on how to access on my website (www.jeff-wheeler.com/invisible-college). Let's just say you might need this info to appreciate everything that happens next!

About the Author

Photo © 2021 Kortnee Carlile

Jeff Wheeler is the *Wall Street Journal* bestselling author of more than forty epic novels, including the Invisible College series, the Kingfountain series, and many more. Jeff lives in the Rocky Mountains and is a husband, father of five, and devout member of his church. Learn about Jeff's publishing journey in Your First Million Words, visit his many worlds at www.jeff-wheeler.com, or participate in one of his many online writing classes through Writer's Block (www.writersblock.biz).